MAD HATTER

ESSENTIAL PROSE SERIES 164

Canada Council   Conseil des Arts
for the Arts   du Canada

ONTARIO ARTS COUNCIL
CONSEIL DES ARTS DE L'ONTARIO

an Ontario government agency
un organisme du gouvernement de l'Ontario

Canada

Guernica Editions Inc. acknowledges the support of the Canada Council for the Arts and the Ontario Arts Council. The Ontario Arts Council is an agency of the Government of Ontario.

We acknowledge the financial support of the Government of Canada.

MAD HATTER

Amanda Hale

GUERNICA
EDITIONS
TORONTO • BUFFALO • LANCASTER (U.K.)
2019

Michael Mirolla, general editor
Seán Virgo, editor
David Moratto, interior and cover design
Guernica Editions Inc.
1569 Heritage Way, Oakville, (ON), Canada L6M 2Z7
2250 Military Road, Tonawanda, N.Y. 14150-6000 U.S.A.
www.guernicaeditions.com

Distributors:
University of Toronto Press Distribution,
5201 Dufferin Street, Toronto (ON), Canada M3H 5T8
Gazelle Book Services, White Cross Mills
High Town, Lancaster LA1 4XS U.K.

First edition.
Printed in Canada.

Legal Deposit—Third Quarter
Library of Congress Catalog Card Number: 2019930421
Library and Archives Canada Cataloguing in Publication
Title: Mad hatter / Amanda Hale.
Names: Hale, Amanda, author.
Series: Essential prose series ; 164.
Description: First edition. | Series statement: Essential prose series ;
164 Identifiers: Canadiana (print) 20190049057 |
Canadiana (ebook) 20190049065 | ISBN 9781771833905 (softcover) |
ISBN 9781771833912 (EPUB) | ISBN 9781771833929 (Kindle)
Classification: LCC PS8565.A4313 M33 2019 | DDC C813/.6—dc23

You return to that earlier time armed with the present, and no matter how dark that world was, you do not leave it unlit. You take your adult self with you. It is not to be a reliving, but a rewitnessing.

—MICHAEL ONDAATJE, *Warlight*

*To all those loving women who cooked, cleaned, kept house,
cared for us children and taught us to read:
Mrs. Fern, Lydia Hope, Mrs. Ward, Mary Simpson, Miss Dixon,
Amy Barrowdale, Vera, Elsie, the Nicoles, and Kati Kunz.*

DISCLAIMER

I have followed as closely as possible the events as they are known. However, this is a work of fiction and I have freely invented scenes, dialogue, and motivations, filling in the blanks in the historical record where necessary. In some cases details have been changed or imagined to serve the purpose of the narrative. Scenes involving actual persons, living or dead, are written with absolute respect for those people's roles and involvement in historical events.

The head of our family was missing, drowned they said, and I, a slow but persistent swimmer and a believer in magic, spent my childhood diving for him, over and over, coming up gasping for air, not knowing whom I sought.

I lived in his body before I became myself. I was with him when he was arrested; I was with him in the holding stall, and in his cell, adrift in that lonely sea of which I still dream—a fathomless expanse without a shore. This thrills and terrifies me in equal parts, a creature suspended, who must imagine her world.

I was with him at Ascot camp and at Latchmere; and when they let him out on overnight leave I made my escape. A swimmer from the outset, I entered another body and took root there, throbbing with the blood I fed on—blood that made me who I am—until I was expelled into this world, through which I have moved for fifty-seven years, pulsing to the rhythm of my mother's heart.

Yet a part of me remains with him in that prison cell, observing and recording. He lives in me—as I lived in him—more insistent perhaps than for the rest of my siblings, though each one of us is, in our own way, haunted by the enigma of that man.

Imagine a day—sun rising on a palimpsest of shadows so dense and peopled that not even its noontime brilliance can dispel the throng. We remain, my father and I, entwined in shadow. His presence lingers like the perfume of a woman long after she has left the room. This perfume is memory—my memory of unconditional love for a man I scarcely knew.

ONE

The Home Secretary today has power to detain on suspicion anybody, from the Archbishop of Canterbury to the humblest labourer in the land. These are powers which would make Himmler green with envy.

—Commander Robert Bower, M.P.,
in the House of Commons.

Chapter One

LIEBESTRAUM: JUNE 4TH, 1940

Imagine a day, a warm summer's day. Christopher is playing with his children in the back garden. He is just throwing the ball to Jimmy as a man rounds the corner and strides down the path, crushing fallen wisteria blossoms under thick-soled shoes. Cynthia happens to glance from the upstairs window of her bedroom. She sees the man and immediately notes that he is wearing one of the wide-brimmed fedoras currently in vogue—a hat like Christopher's—brown with a darker matching band, made of soft rabbit fur, creased with a teardrop crown. She always recognizes a Brooke hat and feels a flush of pride to have married into the family. She hears the low hum of bees buzzing round tangled clumps of blossom still covering the south wall of their house. Her brow furrows slightly as she wonders who the stranger could be, but her heart is full and she begins to sing softly: *"I'll never smile again until I smile at you ..."*

She loves the popular songs, this one newly released by Tommy Dorsey and his band. She turns away from the window as Christopher begins to converse with the man, and she waltzes around the room in her own embrace, her bare arms cradling her body. As she reaches the open door the smell of roast meat reminds her that she must see to the lunch; her housekeeper has joined the war effort. She wonders if she should set an extra place for Christopher's friend. She runs back to smooth the counterpane on her bed—Chris has already done his—he's such a tidy man, so much attention to detail, she thinks with an edge of irritation. Then she smiles and hurries downstairs.

Christopher goes quietly, first taking the children inside—Jimmy gasping with upset because their game of catch has been interrupted—putting them in the charge of their mother while he packs an overnight bag. Pyjamas, socks, underwear, a clean shirt, a hand towel, toothbrush and shaving kit. Cynthia sets the children up with colouring books and crayons at the kitchen table and runs upstairs to hover at her husband's side. He tries to reassure her, telling her that he is confident of his return within a day or two, but she holds onto him, her nails digging into the soft flank of his palm. Before they go downstairs he kisses her, taking from her the fragrance of her perfume. Arpège by Lanvin clings to his shoulder during the long journey to Liverpool.

He removes his hat for the journey, placing it on his lap, and tries to strike up a conversation with the Detective-Inspector, but the man is uncommunicative. In fact, he is rather brusque, even rude, Christopher thinks. No matter. He contents himself with a study of the passing scenery. The rolling hills of Cheshire give way to an industrialized cityscape as the driver turns westwards towards the market town of Warrington where the Mersey River marks the border between Cheshire and Lancashire with its textile and steel mills, breweries and factories. The sun shines through the clouds creating brilliant rays of light evocative of Blake's water colours, but the city of Liverpool with its tall Victorian buildings obliterates the vision until their car emerges on the other side, in suburban Walton.

The gates of Walton Gaol are flanked by massive stone pillars. The gates open and their car passes through and purrs to a halt in front of a long, low building. Christopher is told to get out. The Detective-Inspector, still wearing his hat, accompanies him into the building, where he is registered, then handed over to a prison guard, who escorts him down a long corridor to a metal door at the end. The guard pauses a moment, searching amongst the many keys hanging from his belt, then he unlocks and throws open the door.

As Christopher steps out onto the gravel path he looks up at a cloudless blue sky. It is a short distance to the Reception building where he is passed to a prison officer in a white coat who tells him to deposit his possessions on the counter. He hands over his watch, keys, wedding ring, wallet, a handkerchief, and a roll of mint imperials. The officer places them in a brown envelope and writes, *Christopher James Brooke*, followed by a number. He is asked to surrender his hat, coat and overnight bag, which he does, placing them on the counter. Christopher looks directly into the man's eyes. "One day you will feel ashamed," he says, "that you took part in the imprisonment of men who seek only to avoid war." The officer averts his eyes as he swings the bag over the counter.

Christopher is led down a corridor lined with what appear to be storage lockers, or even the stalls of a public lavatory. To his amazement he is pushed into one of these and locked in. There's no room to move. He is forced to sit bolt upright on a narrow wooden plank. He twists his neck and looks up. There's no ventilation. He calls out, asks how long he is to stay there, what is to happen, but there is no reply. He hears footsteps pacing at the end of the corridor and calls out again. He feels short of breath in this fetid box and remembers a BBC program he heard on the wireless about live burials and how common they were until the advance of medical science. Instructions had been given on how to survive such a situation by breathing steadily and avoiding panic or shouting, so he decides to remain silent and await his release, of which he still feels confident.

But his hunger has begun. He tries not to think of the Sunday lunch Cynthia had been cooking in the oven. The thought of crisply roasted meat with tangy mint sauce causes him to salivate and swallow rapidly and repeatedly to avoid choking. The leg of lamb had been costly, purchased fresh from the farm behind his house. Meat rationing had been enforced three months ago to cut down on the amount of food brought in from abroad as German submarines started attacking British supply ships. Just one more consequence of the government's foolish decision to go to war, Christopher thinks as he lapses into a kind of half sleep from which he is roused by a rattling of padlocks.

A guard prods him with a group of fellow detainees towards yet another building where they are stripped of their clothing and directed to a single shower equipped with a dirt-veined bar of carbolic soap. Christopher steps in first and turns on the hot tap which seems to produce only cold water. He begins to scrub himself vigorously—he feels soiled since entering this place—but his efforts are cut short when he is yanked from the bath-house to be medically examined by another white-coated man, who pushes roughly, first into his mouth and then his anus, with a gloved finger.

Finally, bereft of everything that has identified them, the men are given each a mug of cocoa and a hunk of dry bread and are allowed to stand for a moment while they chew hungrily. They wear coarse grey prison shirts and loose trousers made from material that scratches the skin. The guards, Christopher notes, are armed with pistols in hip-holsters, while some have rifles slung over their shoulders. The real-ization dawns on him in flickers of delayed reaction, that this is not a scene from a film but a real situation to which he himself is subject. Everything is suddenly in the present tense.

The men are taken to their cells on the top landing four floors up, and Christopher notes on the way the nets that span each of the land-ings. For a moment he thinks himself at Bellevue Circus with his par-ents and Alice, watching the trapeze artists fly through the air, always a safety net beneath them. He hears gates clanging one after another as the men are locked up, and then it is he who is being pushed into a cell and locked in as the remaining prisoners march on.

He stands a moment, taking stock, then he begins to pace—four-teen feet by eight—he looks up, gauges about twelve feet. He inhales deeply, forcing his ribs outwards, flared into the barrel of his broad chest. The air has a mouldy, mushroomy smell; something rank and sour about it. The floor is thick with grime and the ceiling and walls are be-dewed with flaking distemper, white-washed from ceiling to shoulder height, continuing down in green, speckled with black mould. There is a small window high up, almost opaque with its coagulation of soot and pigeon excrement, but Christopher detects a patch of blue and is unaccountably pierced, his throat swelling with the threat of tears. His impulse to control is immediate, but he cannot quell an insistent memory of bluebell-carpeted woods; he and Alice picking bunches of the slippery-stemmed soldiers of spring for their mother; how she dunked them in pale vases that revealed their drinking and quivering.

He sees a Bible lying on the shelf above a rickety wooden table, government issue with a faded burgundy cover. He drags the table to the window and climbs up. From there he can see through the bars a blackened brick building and beyond that something that could be a patch of green grass, a football field perhaps or a cricket pitch. He lifts his arm to touch the ceiling but quickly withdraws it when flakes of distemper fall on his face and shoulders. He brushes them off and looks down at the bed with its thin mattress, canvas sheet, grey blanket folded at the foot, and a clay-coloured pillow of coarse material.

He climbs down from the table and takes the few steps necessary to reach his bed. He lies down on the wooden bed-board, his hands cradling the back of his head, and tries to float above his feeling of desolation, but he is overcome, a small child again, taken in the night by a power much greater than him. When the metal grating scrapes open and a tin mug is pushed through, he jumps up. It is a full measure of tea that gives warmth to his cupped hands. He drags the chair over to his table, sits, and drinks thirstily. When he's drained his mug, and has massaged some of its warmth into his hands, he sits erect at the table and lets his fingers play from memory Franz Liszt's *Liebestraum*.

Chapter Two

MARY BYRNE SPEAKS

July 1940

The year was nineteen thirty-nine,
the sky was full of lead.
Hitler was headed for Poland,
and Paddy for Holyhead.
    —POPULAR IRISH SONG

Mary Byrne saw me in my father's palm when I was barely conceived, and she saw my father in mine long after he was lost to us. Mary has her own story, and without it my story would never have been told.

IT WAS MY Da advised me to get out of Ireland. Mam was worn out with the raising of us all. My sisters and brothers were gone and I was the last one left at home, except for Patrick who is the youngest and must help with the farm. I was expected to marry like my sisters, but all the good looks had been used up by the time I arrived.

"You'll never find a man here, especially not with this war on," Da said. "And I'll wager it's not the convent you're wanting. Go across the water and make a life for yourself, Máire. You're a brown bunny, darker than the rest, but they'll not notice over there."

Is there something of the tinker in me, the travelling people? I wondered.

"You're destined to cross the water," he said, looking into my palm. "It's written there, you see?" I'll admit I felt the pull of England, as though something was waiting for me there, but I could never have guessed at it, even with what I'd inherited from my Nana on Da's side. *An da shealladh.* My sisters got the beauty, but I had the Sight, and I was to have the adventure too, though I wept the day I left. "You're best gone," Mam said, "with the TB epidemic and all."

I took the boat from Dun Laoghaire, south of Dublin, and slept that first night in a room the size of a cupboard, near the wharf where we docked at Holyhead. Next day I took the bus to Bangor, bought a paper and searched through the *Help Wanted* columns. My dream was to become a switchboard operator, but there was no call for that in the paper, so I was out of luck. There was a few openings for housekeepers and nannies, but I didn't bother with the ones requiring references. I was in a hurry to find a place before my money ran out, and she was desperate too, as it turned out.

"I need a housekeeper," she said. "Can you cook?"

Bless you, Mam, for teaching me! It's been my saving grace.

She told me to take the bus to Chester right away and she'd come to meet me with her motor-car.

It was July of 1940 when I started working for her, and I soon found out it was more than housekeeping and cooking. There were three children to look after. I'd grown up looking after our Patrick who had the devil in him, and Mam too tired to be bothered, so I was used to it, and I didn't mind, though the lady of the house—Mrs. Brooke I was to call her—expected a lot from me, but then I thought, that must be how it is in service. It's all new to me so who am I to know? I think myself lucky to have a job in England. That's how I talked to myself alone in my room at night before I fell asleep—the first room all to myself which should have been a wonder, and I wrote home about it, but I didn't tell them how lonely I felt in that room.

The children were my only comfort in those early days, Jimmy and Birdie especially. He was four years old, and Birdie was the baby at two. Charlotte, the firstborn, was six years old, and already a little mother to her siblings. With the war on and their father away they were bound to be needing more love than usual, but there was something strange about those children, something that troubled me and which I came to understand as time went on.

There was a circle of grass in the back garden, taller and greener than the rest, and I told them about the fairy circles all over the fields surrounding our farm in County Cavan where the grasses grow higher to make a place for the fairies to dance. Next thing you know I see them circling, clustered together in the back garden. They seemed so alone in their little group, the way children have of separating themselves from the adult world, Charlotte bent down, whispering to Birdie, and Jimmy smirking and scuffing his shoe in the grass. Then they each stretched out their arms, joined hands and began walking—not dancing as you'd expect of children—but walking with slow deliberate steps, and all the while their lips moving. I was curious to know what they were saying, so I opened the nursery window upstairs where I was making the beds, and this is what I heard.

"Come back fairies, come back soon, hold the circle under the moon ..."

And here they all looked up at the sickle of a new moon hanging in the daylight sky, then Charlotte's voice like a bell—"We gather here to summon you, please come back to one three two."

That was the number of their house—132 Chester Road. The children raised their arms, hands still joined, faces staring up into the sky and, just as suddenly, they dropped them all together and bent over, hair flopping on the grass. Birdie started jumping up and down shouting: "One three two, one three two!"

It's too much for her, I thought, the seriousness of it. She's a wild unruly child and will have to be tempered someday.

Chapter Three

A FIREBALL

Walton Gaol—July 1940

I'M HERE TO see my husband, Christopher James Brooke."

Cynthia stood defiantly before the uniformed man who sat behind his desk cradling a mug of tea. He raised his eyebrows and appraised her briefly, then turned his back, revealing a line of dandruff along his collar, and addressed an elderly man sitting at a desk facing the back wall of the cramped office.

"Brooke file," he barked at the old fellow who bent to a filing cabinet, his fingers crawling like a half-dead spider over the grubby folders.

"'Ere we are, Mr. Sharples," the old man said, proffering a slim folder, which Sharples flipped open as he swivelled to face Cynthia. He made a show of studying the file and shuffling the few papers within it before he looked up, pausing even then.

"There'll be no visit today," he said finally, snapping the file shut, and leaned back in his chair with an air of satisfaction.

"Why not? I telephoned last week and you said ..."

"The prisoner's been transferred."

"But that's impossible! You said quite clearly, Tuesday at ten fifteen ..."

"Not me." He wagged his finger. "You didn't speak to me."

"Well ... whoever it was." She tossed her head impatiently. "I must see my husband. I've driven a long way."

"Nice for some as has cars."

"That's beside the point. Christopher Brooke is my husband and you're holding him illegally."

"He's not here." Sharples sniffed with an air of finality.

"Well, where is he?"

"I'm not at liberty to say." He paused, enjoying his command of the situation, and then, just as Cynthia opened her mouth to speak, he scooped her. "Classified information. You'll have to make an application to ..."

"For God's sake, you must tell me where he is! He hasn't done anything wrong."

"I must caution you, madam ..."

"I won't stand for it! I want to speak to your superior."

Cynthia's cheeks flushed, and her dark eyes glistened as Sharples pursed his lips and, moving with a deliberate lassitude, pulled a sheet of paper from a large brown envelope on his desk, circled a number in red pencil, folded the paper and placed it on the sill between them.

"What's this?" she snapped.

Sharples leaned back with folded arms. "That there is the telephone number of the person you need to talk to," he said, slow and deliberate.

"This is no way for the British government to treat its own people. My husband is a gentleman. He's a director of Brooke's Hatters. I demand to know where he is!"

Sharples' hand rose, poised in a gesture between caution and a slap.

"Calm down, my lady, or I'll have to call a female warden."

"How dare you threaten me! What is my husband charged with? Tell me that. But you can't, can you, because he's not guilty of anything. You can't hold him without a charge."

The old clerk had turned from the back wall, his neck twisted to observe the scene. A teacup rattled in a saucer held in his trembling hand. He raised the cup to his lips, watching Cynthia as he slurped a noisy mouthful. She saw him staring at her over his spectacles, and felt humiliated by her audience.

"You haven't heard the last of me. My father will be making a formal complaint to the Governor of this gaol."

With that she turned and walked away before they could see her tears welling. The click of her heels echoed down the slate-tiled corridor, and there was a final slam as she banged the door behind her.

"She's a fireball," the old man croaked, breaking into a phlegmy cough.

"Oh yes, and much good it'll do 'er," Sharples drawled.

Chapter Four

OFF TO ASCOT

Walton Gaol — July 1940

Floating in darkness, I feel a vibration spiralling through my body in circles of sensation; I am held by a desire that propels me on a hurtling journey to a place where I might hear those sounds.

CHRISTOPHER WAKES STARTLED by the clang of metal juddering through his body, leaving a sick feeling in his throat and stomach. He suffers that temporary disconnection of not knowing where he is, searching with bleary eyes for something familiar—Cynthia's discarded clothing on the corner chair, the rose-patterned curtains of their bedroom—then he hears a tin plate sliding into place, a cup slopping liquid, another clang as the metal flap drops. He sits up and swings his long legs off the bed, in two strides he is there, hunkered down, lifting the flap, grasping his plate and cup. Porridge, every morning, thin, grey and lumpy, already congealed around a spoon so soft it would bend if you gripped it hard. He wolfs it down but doesn't drink the tea; there's bromide in it.

At first he'd been tempted to huddle on his cot and give in to the sedative, but it was forbidden to use your bed between 7 a.m. and 4 p.m. so he'd had to fight his tiredness. Now it is thirst he must fight, with his tongue furred in his mouth, thick with the silence of the long night. He tosses the tea into his toilet bucket and fills the cup with water from the sink. The taste is foul, and later there will be knife-stabbing pains and diarrhoea.

He begins his daily pacing, back and forth, counting his steps, estimating the miles that accumulate with the hours and days and weeks. They have only half an hour in the prison yard each day, not enough for a man accustomed to the vigorous exercise of tennis, boxing, cricket and swimming. More than anything he misses ballroom dancing, with the lightness of a woman held in his arms. Before his marriage he had frequented the dance halls of Manchester and won prizes for his foxtrot and quickstep.

In his determination to keep himself fit he has done step-ups on the rickety chair until it collapsed under his diminishing weight. He has lain face down on the floor and done push-ups until his shoulders and arms ached. Now his limbs have begun to twitch; his muscles cramp in the night, waking him in agony so that he has to grit his teeth and pace the cell until the spasms pass. Then he lies there, afraid to sleep, his feet hanging over the end of the bed as he feels his flesh trying to crawl out of his skin. He is losing strength, losing muscle mass from lack of nutrition.

During the first weeks of his imprisonment Christopher has made daily requests to speak with a solicitor. He has asked for permission to telephone his wife, to speak with someone, anyone who can enlighten him about his situation and tell him what is to become of him. Though he has been in Walton Gaol far longer than he had anticipated, and with no explanation of how exactly he is charged, he still believes it to be temporary. He is keeping a penciled record of the days on the Bible flyleaf, striking a line through the completion of each week. He is a patient man filled with the conviction that he will soon be home again in the bosom of his family.

When shadows gather on the darkening walls of his cell he busies himself with routine activity, placing and aligning his shoes under the bed, squaring his Bible on the shelf, folding and refolding his clothes, preparing for the night. But as he lies down on his wooden bed-board it is impossible to avoid a creeping feeling of desolation. There is no music, no children's voices, no laughter, only the rattling of the warder's keys against his belt buckle as he makes his rounds, peering through the door slots.

Christopher tries to summon Schubert's C minor impromptu with its loud opening chord followed by a four-bar statement of theme repeated in haunting and inventive variations and changes of harmony. His fingers move on the rough grey blanket, but the day's thoughts intrude, crowding his head with rumours snatched in whispers during the brief exercise period in the prison yard. Yesterday there had been an unexpected medical inspection and instantly a rumour had swept through the prison that they were all going to be shipped to Canada, a terrifying prospect given the news of the Arandora Star, sunk on the 2nd of July by a German U-boat off the coast of Ireland. The ship had been bound for Canada with a cargo of 1,500 Italian and German internees, many of whom had drowned when British soldiers shot holes in their lifeboats to prevent their escape. Some days it is rumoured they will be transferred to another prison, or to a concentration camp to work alongside Jewish German internees.

One day there had been talk of a mass release, but each night Christopher finds himself lying on the same board in the same cell, waiting for something to happen and fearing what it will be. He prays as his mother taught him to long ago, though he does not kneel. He lies in prayer, eyes closed, praying for his wife and children, praying for his parents, praying for blessed sleep to come and relieve him of the uncertainty of his existence. And when he sleeps he dreams that he is in Cynthia's embrace, pressed against the perfumed softness of her body, and he awakens in dark ecstasy plunged suddenly into such loss that it is like falling from a mountain top.

Jangle of keys, metal inserted, lock turned.

"Movin' on today." Musgrave's cheery voice, his cockney twang.

"Going home?"

"No, mate, you're off to Ascot. Dust off your top 'at. Put your best foot forward."

"Ascot? Is there a prison there? Am I going to have a hearing?"

"Nah. They've converted the winter quarters of Ringling's circus into a camp for you blokes. You'll be rubbing shoulders wiv Jerries and Eyeties. Enemy aliens, the lot o' them. You're not alone, mate."

Christopher runs a hand over his cropped head. "But why Ascot?

It's so far from my home. It would be a more appropriate journey for you, Musgrave."

"Right enough. *I'm* far from my 'ome because they can do what they want wiv ya if you're not fit for war," Musgrave says, slapping his gammy leg.

"But would you fight?"

"Darn right I would. The Jerries are banging at our front door, mate. They've got France, 'aven't they? Pictures in the paper of those ruddy Krauts marchin' up the Champs Elysees. Now they're fighting us in our own English Channel!"

"But you don't understand, Musgrave. Thousands of young Englishmen will die in this war if we don't ..."

"*You* don't understand, mate! Your sort finks you can talk the 'ind leg off a donkey."

"I'm only trying to tell you ..."

"And I'm telling you we can't let them win or we'll all be talkin' German."

He sees the fear in the guard's eyes, and it silences him.

"I'll be back to take ya to the main gate at eight sharp, alright?" Musgrave says.

The door slams shut with a violence that echoes inside Christopher's head. He stands a moment until his nerves settle, then he begins to prepare for his journey. He can't help thinking of his last visit to Ascot, for the Royal Ascot Races with Cynthia in the first year of their marriage. He remembers her excitement, her shining eyes, and how he had impressed her by recognizing each of the Brooke Toppers—the grey plush hats worn in the royal enclosure, the black ones for the commoners.

Chapter Five

TROUBLE SLEEPING

C YNTHIA BROOKE, NÉE BLACKWELL, sat on the hard chair and
smoothed her skirt.

"I need some legal advice," she said, smiling at Ronald Pearson who was an old family friend, and a partner in the Manchester
firm of solicitors that took care of her father's business affairs. "As you
probably know, Christopher is being held without charge ..."

"Yes, yes, dreadful business," Ronald lisped as he smoothed his
thinning hair nervously.

"He's done nothing wrong, Ronald. But they won't let me see him,
and I'm at my wit's end. Isn't there anything you can do? What about
habeas corpus?"

"Ah yes, well you see this is a case of uh ... executive detention —
that is to say, detention at the instance of the executive for an indefin-
ite period without charge and without trial."

"Trial! But what's he supposed to be guilty of? His connection
with Mosley, is that it? He's been going to those British Union meetings
for years and now suddenly ..."

"Yes, well that's it, exactly!" he exclaimed, raising his finger in the
air. "Suddenly we're at war. It's all about context, Cynthia. Very bad
business, very, very bad."

Ronald had an unfortunate inability to roll Rs. But he did have,
Cynthia noticed now for the first time, the most extraordinary eyes.

They were green and fishlike, with a luminous quality that made him seem almost attractive.

"Couldn't we apply through the courts, Ronald?"

"Indeed, yes, we could apply for a writ, but I wouldn't expect it to get anywhere. Unfortunately there is ample precedent for the government's right to do this sort of thing in an emergency. We used it against the Irish, and now their own government is using it under the Emergency Powers Act against the IRA activists."

"Don't I at least have the right to visit him?"

"Technically, yes, of course, but these are troubled times, Cynthia." He nodded his head from side to side like a pendulum, considering with clasped hands before he continued. "The dilemma that faces liberal democracies such as ours in certain extreme situations—let's say in times of emergency, crisis or serious disorder—to wit, war—freedom from executive detention is the first right to be curtailed." He noted the rising flush in her cheeks and he pressed on, drawing on photographic memory. "The democratic challenge is to strike as just a balance as possible between the right of a state to preserve itself and its citizens against the risk of destruction, and the fundamental right of the individual not to suffer executive detention in the sense I have defined."

"Yes, yes, but can we *do* anything? I'm alone you see with our three children and I don't know what's going to happen."

Noting what might have been tears gathering in Cynthia's eyes, and wanting above all to avoid a display of emotion, the solicitor adopted a more cheerful tone.

"I believe it's up to the detainees to apply from within for judicial review. Let's wait and see where Christopher lands, then there may be a procedure laid down for him to appeal his situation. You see we're all rather at sixes and sevens just now, Cynthia, with Hitler knocking at our door." He rose from his chair, scraping it across the floor, and walked to a cabinet in the corner of his office. "Can I offer you a sherry?"

Cynthia opened her mouth in surprise. "Oh ... it's rather early, isn't it?"

Ronald consulted his watch and then with a smirk and a shrug he said: "Fancy that, almost lunch-time. Will you join me for a bite, Cynthia? There's a nice little pub down at Deansgate ..."

"I have to get back to the children. A judicial review, you said. What ... what is that exactly?"

"I'm sorry not to be of more help to you, Cynthia. You see, the usual rules have flown out of the window. I really think the best thing is to lie low for the moment and see what happens. Very embarrassing business for the family, what?" His head was nodding again, up and down this time. "Best to keep it quiet for now and we'll see what transpires."

Cynthia's jaw was clenched as she got up to leave.

"Of course there'll be no charge. Family friends and all that," Ronald said, smiling indulgently. "What about Archer? Perhaps he could help you." Archer was his elder brother, and the Blackwell family doctor.

"Archer? But I'm not ill, Ronald. This is a legal matter."

"Oh, I thought perhaps a sedative ... mmm, trouble sleeping, that sort of thing."

Chapter Six

GIRL IN A BOAT

WHEN MRS. BROOKE took me on I naturally assumed that the Master was away at war like everyone else, and she said nothing to make me think different. But being of an inquiring nature I was always looking for clues as to who exactly she was and what had brought her to her situation. It was while cleaning her room that I came upon the photograph. *August 1930, Cynthia Helene aged 18*, it said. She was leaning back in a boat, her hands resting on the oars. It must have been warm because she wore a strapless sundress, her shoulders dipping where the rounded part meets the collar bone, her flesh smooth and slightly tanned. Her arms rested so lightly on the sides of the rowboat that if they had been wings she could easily have taken flight, rising above the water, nothing to anchor her but the gaze of the photographer. And what a gaze *she* had. I felt she was looking straight at me, deep into my soul.

She was a dark beauty with that thick hair bobbed in a shock around her face, and her brown eyes so deep-set you couldn't see the sparkle, but I knew it was there. Her lips were dark with what I guessed was a deep red lipstick like the ones on her dressing table, and the fashion of the day no doubt. We don't go in for such things where I come from. Her teeth were small and perfect, and behind her smile there was a hint of something. 'Come on, take me. Take it.' No shadows in the picture. I wondered who did take it?

I heard her footstep on the stairs and quickly put the photograph back in the drawer and resumed my dusting. Her dressing table was full of knick-knacks—hairpins and half-used lipsticks scattered about amongst her silver-backed hairbrush and tortoiseshell comb set, a big powder-puff in an open box of face powder, earrings and bracelets spilling from a jewel box. I moved them all onto the bed while I gave the glass a good polish. As she entered the bedroom I glanced up and I saw her differently then. I had finally discovered her—a girl in a boat, not yet married, not yet my employer. She'd come to life, a living, breathing person with a history and a future, who incidentally had become my mistress. I vowed then that I would no longer lose myself in servitude because I knew she was no different from me at heart.

She came into the kitchen one morning with her eyes shining and her cheeks flushed.

"There's been a telephone call, Mary. My husband is coming home, his first leave." Then she hesitated. "He won't be in uniform. He has a special civilian job. It's top secret, so you mustn't ask him anything."

"When's the Master arriving, Ma'am?"

"He'll be here for dinner. You must bake some bread, and make a pudding, will you, Mary? I don't know what we're going to eat."

"There's the pig's liver in the meat safe, Ma'am, that I queued for at the butcher's yesterday."

"Yes, of course. But will it be enough for a homecoming dinner? My husband has a big appetite."

"I'll gladly give him my share," I said. "After all, it's a special occasion, isn't it?"

"Oh, Mary!"

She clapped her hands with joy. She was that excited.

We waited up for him until that pig's liver was dried out in the oven, then she told me to throw it out and she went up to bed. I heard her weeping when I went up later, but first I gorged myself on the liver slices till there was nothing left but the tough parts which I threw to the dog.

Next morning she came downstairs with puffy eyes and her face well powdered. I was in the kitchen with the wireless playing and Vera Lynn singing her lovely song: *We'll meet again, don't know where, don't know when ...*

"Turn that thing off!" she shouted, and so of course I did, but then she apologized for her testiness. "It's this damned war. We're all at sixes and sevens." But she never mentioned her husband directly, only that it was not the first time she'd been disappointed. I thought perhaps he'd been delayed and would come later, but days passed and nothing more was said, except for Jimmy who asked for his father every day.

"I don't know," she'd say. "We'll have to wait and see."

I saw Charlotte staring at her mother as though she'd been betrayed. Of course, I didn't understand it all then. I was in agreement with her. This damned war, I thought, breaking up families.

Chapter Seven

'COLLAR THE LOT'
—WINSTON CHURCHILL, MAY 1940

Ascot Camp—July 31st, 1940

Feel the weight, the trembling ground as elephants glide silently on feet thick as tree trunks; smell the warm air, fetid with rotted vegetation, as those creatures trumpet into the darkness. Sense the caged power as lions pace, claws concealed in soft paws. We dream of tearing at each other's throats, bloody teeth and stinking breath, the sweetness of pale straw. And then my father wakes.

THEY ARE SEVEN hundred and fifty men, all internees for varying reasons, and no-one knows what is going to happen. After the long train journey from Liverpool's Lime Street Station, they arrive tired and hungry on a blazing hot afternoon. They have marched from the station to the Ascot racecourse, and into a compound behind the camp buildings, where they are made to stand for several hours until the last of them has arrived. Then they are counted and recounted until it is finally determined that one man has escaped. A medical examination follows, in which the men are made to strip naked. It is late in the evening by the time a meal is forthcoming and then it is only bread and margarine with a thin slice of bully beef.

The Camp Commandant appoints Christopher leader of his hut which houses fifty-two men. He shoulders the responsibility eagerly —after all, leadership is familiar to him—he was a school prefect at Malvern Boys' College and at the age of nineteen moved into industry as a Director of the family hat manufactory. It is a tremendous relief to be in the company of men after the isolation of Walton Gaol where he'd been in solitary confinement for twenty-two hours of each day. This is the company he has craved; like-minded men with whom he can discuss the vital questions of Churchill's mistaken war and Oswald Mosley's efforts toward appeasement with Germany. Some think it too late with the so-called Battle of Britain already commenced and Churchill's heroic call to arms with talk of "their finest hour," but Christopher is optimistic.

"We stand for peace in England!" he declaims. "Fascism is the greatest crusade ever undertaken, against the evils of war, poverty and wasted lives. It is aimed at the creation of a world fit for the twentieth century man and woman, in the words of our Leader, Sir Oswald Mosley whose intelligence, courage and oratory are unmatched in Britain today!"

He does notice a shifty-eyed turning away of some of the men, and he resolves to single them out and engage them in persuasive discussion. He is aware of his own privilege, and of the generally downtrodden, undereducated condition of the British working class. He must help them.

They sleep on paillasses in three-tiered wooden bunks. Their pillows are stuffed with straw and their only covering is a coarse army blanket. The smell of the circus animals lingers and on that first night slipping into the month of August comes a dream of lumbering elephants and pacing lions.

The next day, August 1st, Christopher discovers something marvellous. There is a piano at Ascot Camp. It is a honky-tonk excuse of a thing with several dumb keys and horribly out of tune, but he is in heaven, playing from memory the classics in which he has been trained. He organizes musical evenings for the men where he plays waltzes, foxtrots and quicksteps. He plays *April in Paris, Begin the Beguine,* and *I Got Rhythm,* his face creased with merriment as his right foot pumps the pedal. But the men will not dance without women, so he turns to the classics, playing the *Moonlight Sonata,* and his own favourite, *Liebestraum.*

The hall is filled to capacity, all the men hungry for entertainment, and with the warmth of their bodies, with the applause and the vibration of the piano, a pungent odour arises, of circus animals perhaps, their urine soaked through the wooden floor. It is a primal smell and it arouses in Christopher a feeling of urgency at odds with his patient demeanour. He is afraid that he might suddenly lose control of himself.

Then another musician comes forward, an accordionist with a baritone voice and a Douglas Fairbanks aspect.

"I have my own band in Manchester," he says, "We're all of Italian background and we've been arrested now that Italy has declared war on Britain. They've separated us, in different camps."

He asks Christopher to accompany him as he sings *O Sole Mio,* and *Sorrento,* switching from Italian to English and back, drawing applause from the grinning men. He tells Christopher about the attacks on Italian restaurants and businesses all over England, but especially in London's Soho district where his cousin ran a café-bar.

"They ransacked the place," he says. "Ripped the awning from the front of the building and took down his sign. I was born here. Never set foot in Italy. The only reason I speak Italian is because my mamma insisted."

He sings *Blue Moon,* but when he asks Christopher if he knows the Tommy Dorsey number, *I'll Never Smile Again,* Christopher excuses himself and leaves the soloist to continue *a cappella.* He is overcome with longing for his wife but finds it best not to dwell on such emotionalism and switches his thoughts to other matters. He is disturbed that Italy has declared war on Britain, especially since Mussolini has been a strong ally of Mosley and British Union. What has happened to the supporters of appeasement? he wonders. Nobody is thinking clearly. France has surrendered and the Germans are now dangerously close to England. He must seek an opportunity to explain the situation to someone in authority before it's too late.

On August 15th Christopher is selected for special treatment at Latchmere House, which is rumoured to be an MI5 outfit, situated at Ham Common near Kew Gardens. There has been talk amongst the detainees about Latchmere, where men are said to have been sequestered for weeks at a time, returning pale and thin and sometimes emotionally ill.

Christopher is squeezed into the back of a van with thirteen men, six of them British Union colleagues and the rest foreigners. They are made to squat on the floor and are ordered not to talk to each other. They are followed by armed guards in a military lorry. Christopher is confident that he will be able to convince his interrogators of his sincerity as a pacifist and make them understand finally the rationality and humanity of the British Union message. Having written many unanswered letters to politicians and church leaders in the months leading up to the declaration of war, he now welcomes the opportunity to state his case in person to someone in authority, and to defend himself as a loyal Briton.

"I expect us to walk out of Latchmere as free men," he whispers to Cliff Byrd, a man he is acquainted with through the Manchester branch. Cliff gives him the thumbs up as they lurch to a halt with a crunch of gravel, all the men falling against each other, eager to get out into the fresh air.

Christopher steps down from the van and almost loses his footing as he looks up at an imposing building adorned with a scattering of dwarf palms along the driveway. Latchmere House looks like a comfortable Victorian family mansion, the kind of home that would be full of servants bustling and polishing and dusting, with a grounds man, several gardeners, and children running on the lawns.

As they enter the house Christopher is separated from the other men and is hurried up the broad staircase to a first-floor room, smaller than his Walton Gaol cell, but better furnished with a camp bed and two army blankets, a towel, a chamber pot, and a sturdy wooden chair. There is a window, covered with barbed wire, overlooking some outbuildings at the back. Clearly the house has been modified and the rooms partitioned to accommodate the maximum number of inmates. He waits and waits, alone in his cell, but no-one comes, except a guard who pushes a mug of thin soup through a metal grille and returns later in the afternoon with a call for "Exercise!"

The men file out of their cells and troop downstairs, out onto the back lawn where they are ordered to walk in silence at a distance from each other. He feels a tap on his shoulder and turns to see Cliff Byrd grinning.

"Keep your spirits up, Brooke," Byrd says with a wink. "I got the scoop on Latchmere."

As he leans in and begins to speak a young soldier runs over and shoves the muzzle of his revolver into Byrd's back.

"No talk between inmates!" he barks.

"I was wearing three stripes in the RAF when you were still wearing nappies!" Byrd shouts back.

All the men are staring now, and Christopher sees that there are guards spaced around the lawn, armed with revolvers, and a couple of police dogs snarling and straining at their leashes.

"You'll change your tune when you're up against a brick wall facing a firing squad," the boy shouts and he jabs again, catching Byrd in the kidneys this time, with the butt of the revolver, causing him to wince and double over.

Christopher walks on, an endless circle around the trampled lawn which is about the size of a tennis court. He glances back to check on Cliff who is walking painfully with clenched jaw. A roll of barbed wire tops the fence, but beyond it, behind a cluster of shrubs and bushes, he sees the backs of row houses. He hears a radio from an open window and sees a woman pass by and children at an upstairs window. He feels a sharp pang in his throat as he thinks of Cynthia and his own children.

The first night he sleeps soundly in his camp bed, but then they leave the lights on in his cell—bright lights, night and day. He complains, but they take no notice. He ties a handkerchief over his eyes and huddles under the blankets but still it is difficult to sleep, and when he does drift off he wakes with nightmares that terrify him. He remembers what Cliff had whispered in the exercise yard—that Latchmere had been leased to the War Office during the Great War to house officers suffering from shell shock. The place might be haunted, he thinks. Normally he doesn't hold with such nonsense but his dreams are vivid and completely unaccountable. He tries to imagine a happier time with children's laughter filling the house—the chatter of dinner guests—anything to take his mind off the horrors he sees in the night.

An orderly comes to inquire if he has any complaints. Of course he has complaints! His cell is stifling, he can barely breathe because the window has wood blocks screwed into the runners to prevent it from opening, his eyes are stinging from the glaring light, he is constantly hungry, the rations are half of the already meagre ones he received at Walton Gaol ... The light in his cell is switched off. A guard comes with a hammer and nails to board up his window and Christopher is left in total darkness, feeling his way around the walls, dressing and tying his shoelaces by feel, eating without knowing what it is they are feeding him and, worst of all, unable to read the tattered Bible he has smuggled out of Walton Gaol and in which he continues to track time, along with minutely written notes scrawled in the dark.

He thinks of escaping, of running to the nearby Thames and stowing away on a river vessel, or hiding out in the woods bordering Ham Common, but the exercise yard continues to be patrolled by armed guards and Alsatian dogs, as are the corridors of the old country house which seems to be a warren of impenetrable rooms and passageways. They move him every few days, from dark cell to bright cell, back and forth, round and round, until he loses all sense of his placement. The house seems enormous, an unfathomable maze of rooms, each the same as the last, shrinking in on him, squeezing him. He begins to lose hope, and this is when the interrogations begin.

They come in the night, faceless men, every night a different one, waking him from his only refuge. At first they are polite, then they switch to threats and bullying which reminds him of his boarding school days, though he had not recognized it as cruelty when he was a boy. It had seemed normal. And there had always been plenty to eat at school, even though the food was bad.

"When did you join the British Nazi party?"

"British Union is not a Nazi party. We stand for peace and for a new and revolutionary form of politics that will serve the British worker and preserve our Empire against ... "

"What d'you know about Mosley's visits to Germany?"

"I know nothing of this."

"Arms trafficking? D'you know about that?"

"Of course not, I ..."

"How much are you paid for your part in the Movement?"

"Are you accusing me of espionage?"

"We ask the questions here, Mr. Brooke."

They threaten him with the firing squad.

"Or the hangman if you prefer, Mr. Brooke. Come on, speak up or we'll have to decide for you."

"I have the right of habeas corpus."

"Oh no you don't." The man laughs. "No-one knows where you are."

They never lay a finger on him, but he wishes for it, for physical pain to distract him from the torment of his confused thoughts. He embarrasses himself by scratching in front of them, his skin flaking off, leaving bloody streaks under his nails. He's been suffering with bed bugs since the first days in Walton Gaol and now the bites have become angry red bumps that weep and itch incessantly.

Byrd has gleaned some information about the director of Latchmere House — "Colonel Robin Stephens," he whispers to Christopher as they're herded downstairs for exercise. "Nicknamed Tin-Eye for his monocle. He's an amateur psychologist with a vile temper, but don't worry, they say he never uses violence — except for the occasional execution."

He wonders how Byrd manages his sleuthing. He admires his friend's rebellious spirit. Christopher requests a meeting with Stephens. He has always believed in going to the top.

"Colonel Stephens is too busy for the likes of you, unless you *really* have something to tell him."

"I do. I have an important message," Christopher says emphatically.

Though he is exhausted Christopher finds himself resisting sleep, straining for the sound of plimsolled footfalls in the night — a guard coming to take him to Colonel Stephens. But all they do is move him to yet another cell and subject him to a numbing repetition of the same wrong-headed questions. He is interrogated in the most irrational manner, completely without context to his situation, and this infuriates him, but he manages to maintain a gentlemanly comportment, except for the one time when they wake him yet again and he humiliates himself by crying out for his mother, then weeps with hunger and exhaustion. The interrogator is kind to him that night. He puts his arm around Christopher's shoulders and he almost surrenders, but in reality there is nothing he can tell the man, only that he is sorry for the outburst. It is deeply disturbing to him, to revert in that way to childhood, to feel manipulated in the night.

One morning he is told that he is to have an hour of "association" with a fellow inmate. They take him to a room at the far end of the house and lock him in with Cliff Byrd, who is looking dreadful. He hasn't seen Cliff at exercise for more than a week and has been worried about him. Christopher begins to speak, all the pent-up words tumbling out, but Cliff silences him with a cautionary double wink. He points to the ceiling and mouths "microphones."

"Ah," Christopher says, and they begin a cautious conversation about their pre-war work, about Christopher's time as a Director of Brooke Hats, where he would join the men on the factory floor, rolling up his sleeves, donning a leather apron and sturdy boots to work alongside the hatters. When their hour is up they clasp hands with the intensity of all that has been unspoken, and part with the British Union salute.

The worst for Christopher are the hoaxes.

"Pack your bags. You're going home today."

"You mean it this time, no joke?"

"Scout's honour. Weekend pass. You applied, remember?"

"What date is it?"

"Your wife's expecting you."

"You telephoned her?"

"Oh, we had a little chat, me and Cynthia. She's co-operating nicely. Better than you, Mr. Brooke."

"What do you mean?"

"She'll put you straight, you wait and see."

"What time? What time can I go?"

"When we come to get you."

He waits and waits until by evening he is hopeless and angry, his head pounding, blindness clouding his right eye. And then they come in the night and move him to yet another cell, indistinguishable from the last, with no-one to talk to but the ingratiating interrogator who turns suddenly and threatens harm to Cynthia and his children. He knows their names, their ages—Charlotte, Jimmy, Birdie.

It is the middle of the day, near the end of his third week at Latchmere, and he can't stop scratching—his arms, his legs and ankles, the trunk of his body. There is no soap and very little water. Christopher can hardly bear his own stench. He wonders if he will ever feel clean again or eat enough to do more than taunt his hunger. Then he is summoned to the carpeted rooms of Colonel Robin Stephens.

The monocled man has a penetrating gaze. He is clean-shaven and immaculately dressed in full uniform with rank insignia on shoulder, collar and cuff. "Mr. Brooke, my invisible guest. We meet finally." He gestures to Christopher to take the seat opposite. Christopher attempts to offer his hand but has a sudden unbearable urge to scratch his left shoulder, which he grasps in a paroxysm, shamed by the filth and stink into which he has descended.

"I'm very glad to meet you at last, Colonel Stephens," he says through clenched teeth. "I have an urgent message which perhaps you can convey to the right people. You see, war is not the answer ..."

"But what of the social niceties, Mr. Brooke? I know all about you, but you know nothing of my background. Aren't you curious?"

"Well, no ... I suppose ... if you wish ..."

"I was born in Egypt to British parents in 1900. I was educated at Dulwich College in London before being commissioned. I earned these in the Indian Army." He points to a row of medals over his heart. "I fought in a number of campaigns and was mentioned in dispatches. You haven't had the pleasure of combat, have you, Mr. Brooke? A hatter?" He chuckles with mouth closed, deep in his throat, and Christopher feels shamed somehow without knowing why. "Languages, Mr. Brooke? You speak German?"

"No, I don't. A little French ..."

"I speak German, French, Italian, Urdu and Arabic. I am widely travelled, Mr. Brooke, but my travels have not led me to respect foreigners, nor do I like Jews, but most of all, Mr. Brooke, I despise the Hun."

"War is not the ..."

"Hear me out, Mr. Brooke," Stephens says, his right finger in the air, his face a mask of implacability. "We have one objective here at Latchmere—truth, in the shortest possible time. I hope you are not going to waste my time."

"Indeed not. I have vital information for you, Colonel Stephens. War is not the answer, as I have repeated countless times to my interrogators. And as I have written in letters to Chamberlain, Churchill, Attlee, and to my local Member of Parliament. *It is the working men of England who will be killed,* I wrote, *the poor working classes who have no choice and will be sent to the front as cannon fodder.*"

"No cannons in this war, Christopher," Stephens says with a pitying smile. "We have Spitfires now. You're confusing facts with rhetorical propaganda, modeling your oratory, I suspect, on that of your hero, Oswald Mosley." Again he chuckles deep in his throat, his face barely moving.

"That is beside the point," Christopher says, his fists clenched at his sides as he tries to clear his mind.

Stephens leans forward, his eyebrows raised and says with an edge of impatience in his voice: "I'm listening."

"That's what I'm here for, isn't it? To tell you what I know to be true."

"Tell me what your plans were as leader of the Stockport division of the BUF."

"To follow our Leader and build the membership of British Union. There's strength in numbers. Sir Oswald has a massive following. He should be leading our country."

"Well now, he'd have to be elected for that job, Mr. Brooke, wouldn't he? We live in a democracy here in Britain."

Christopher remembers how Cynthia too had looked at him in silent judgment, as her brother went off to war. She was clannish, gripping tenaciously to the bedrock of her Welsh family, loyal to them and their values.

"Sir Oswald will be proven right. You'll see. One day he'll be the leader of ..."

"You have nothing to tell me, do you? But I have something to tell you, Mr. Brooke." He leans forward again, his monocled eye narrowing. "If the Hun were to invade our country not one of you and your kind would leave this house alive." He pauses, watching for Christopher's reaction. "Dismissed," he barks the order, picks up a pen and bends over his papers. Then he looks up again. "And Brooke? Watch your back. First rule of a soldier."

"But you don't understand. I have much more to say."

Stephens is shaking his head. "You're not a bad fellow, Christopher. You're just a nobody." He lifts his hands in the air and the corners of his mouth pull down in a gesture which Christopher cannot quite interpret but which unsettles him unaccountably. He can think of no retort. A sudden feeling of exhaustion assaults him, so deep that he can barely stay on his feet. They have used my body against me, he thinks.

Two days later Christopher is released. He has been held at Latchmere House for twenty-one days—not much to bear in retrospect, but he had not known how long it would be and so it had seemed interminable and has taken a toll on him. His first night back at Ascot Camp he weeps silently into his straw pillow, for the comfort of his fellow men, and for the longing he harbours for his family. He hopes he has not failed them. He'd had nothing to hide. But he feels somehow that he *has* failed because he was unable to hold Captain Stephens' attention.

Christopher turns his face and burrows for a comfortable place in the pillow, remembering the air of lightness around Cynthia as they'd stood under the wisteria on the Cartwrights' veranda. How magnetized he had been by that light, dazzled and confused because Cynthia was in fact a dark and earthy girl with her deep-set eyes and shining bobbed hair that seemed to float like a dark halo around the whiteness of her face. Everything about her seemed contradictory.

When his old school friend Eric Cartwright had become engaged to Cynthia's cousin Adèle, the Cartwright family had hosted an engagement party. All the Cheshire Set were there, and Christopher had moved easily from one group to another, champagne glass in hand, toasting and chatting, quite oblivious to his own charm and good looks. Even before Eric introduced them, he had seen Cynthia, glimpsed between bare shoulders and dinner jackets, and had become inattentive to the chatter of the beautiful women around him. When he saw her move onto the veranda with Adèle, he waylaid Eric and asked for an introduction.

"Of course, old boy! That's Cynthia Blackwell. Lucky for you she's only just back from France and still unattached. Adèle can fill you in. They've grown up together."

Adèle's honeyed voice trickles in the background as their eyes meet and we surge forward, baby oh baby, me and my siblings clamouring for our existence, bundles of cells striving to assemble, oh joy the chance to create our living bodies from that glimmering exchange of light in their eyes.

He invited her to dance and she moved easily into his arms, her cheeks flushed as she smiled up at him. They hardly spoke as they waltzed to the haunting melody of Irving Berlin's *What'll I do?* He found himself stumbling a couple of times despite his skill as a dancer. As the music ended Cynthia asked him if he would give her a badge to pin on her French beret.

"Some political group you belong to, they say?"

And so their conversation began.

He had proposed to her and presented her with a diamond and sapphire ring after only three months. They were both eager to celebrate their engagement, but because Dick Blackwell was leery of Christopher's involvement with British Union he had warned his daughter against him, and it was several months more before familiarity and the credentials of good breeding had prevailed and Christopher had won the Blackwells over.

"He'll grow out of it," he'd heard Dorothy Blackwell whisper to her husband. "Let's move ahead with the wedding, Dick, and make these young people happy. He'll have no time for Mosley and his gang once he's married."

After the wedding, which took place in January of 1933, he lay beside her and gazed in wonder at her beauty, but he found himself unequal to her desire. She would cling to him, wanting more, more than he could ever give. He would have liked to play the piano for her — the baby grand, a wedding gift from his parents that took pride of place in the living room — or to take her in his arms and dance her around the room, but she held onto him fiercely, wanting something she could not name.

When morning comes and the alarm sounds for the men to "rise and shine," Christopher cannot believe that he's slept, though of course he must have, his dreams haunted by all that has passed.

In the fading days of autumn the men play cricket on the racecourse with improvised bats and an old flat tennis ball. They're all rattled by disturbances in the night which they learn through the camp grapevine is heavy bombing of London only twenty-five miles away. Christopher's sister Alice lives in north London with her husband and small child. He feels desperate and useless, unable to do anything to protect her. When rain sets in the men improvise a boxing ring inside the old circus quarters, and one of their number, a former heavyweight boxing champ, coaches the men. They spar against each other, but Christopher finds himself flagging and stumbling. He curses the meagre camp rations that leave him constantly hungry and weak.

In October a number of detainees, including Christopher, are sent to York Racecourse Camp, others to Huyton near Liverpool, and so their network is broken. But before they go the men celebrate the eighth anniversary of the foundation of British Union. Christopher is one of the organizers of the event and he gives a speech, along with Charlie Watts, District Leader for Westminster.

"Hail Mosley, and fuck 'em all!" shouts Watts, giving the fascist salute as a portrait of Oswald Mosley is unveiled to a tumultuous wave of applause. Christopher is deeply affected by this unrepentant demonstration of loyalty. It bolsters his own faith in Mosley and everything he stands for. He is overcome and has to turn away and wipe his face with a large handkerchief, a gesture that reminds him of his father's tears at the dinner table over port and cigars, and his mother's embarrassment as she excused her husband to the dinner guests and hurried him up-stairs. It had started, his mother told him, after his father had been brought home as a survivor after the sinking of the Lusitania in May of 1915. Christopher had been five years old at the time and oblivious to his father's emotions, and to his drinking. In truth he had been less afraid of his father than of his mother, despite the fact that it was James Brooke who held authority in their house. It was Nancy who had rapped Christopher's knuckles each time he stumbled over the piano keys. "For your own good, dear," she would say, smiling with that slight nod of her head, but from so far away that it frightened him to look at her, whereas his father was a substantial presence—a portly joker with a sandy moustache and penetrating blue eyes.

The hall is echoing with the men's defiant cries, and Christopher joins in.

"Hail Mosley, and fuck 'em all!" The crude word feels alien in his mouth and rather daring. He's never been one to swear. He wishes he were going to Huyton Camp, closer to home, even though it is reputed to be a nightmare of a place situated on a half-built housing estate covered with rubble and surrounded by anti-aircraft guns. He longs for a visit from his wife. He dreams of her almost every night and wakes sticky with semen. He feels soiled and diminished, forced back into a second adolescence.

Chapter Eight

THE PHOTOGRAPHER

December 1940

IT WAS THROUGH no action of mine that I won her confidence. She was desperate. Shortly before Christmas, and just after the terrible news of Coventry being destroyed by German bombs, Jimmy had a full-blown asthma attack. We had to call out Dr. Pearson to give him oxygen, and though the lad improved after that he still wasn't right by Christmas day, so I stayed home with him while Cynthia took the girls to her parents' house. The Blackwells had a big family do but without, I suppose, the usual Christmas fare because of wartime shortages, though it was nothing then compared with what was to come. If we had known how long it would last we would have been quite discouraged, but we thought then that the war would soon be over and that the Jerries would go back to Germany where they belong.

'Twas a lonely Christmas—my first in England—but at least I had little Jimmy to care for. I sat in his room with our gas masks handy just in case, and I listened to him wheezing and struggling for breath while I stroked his head and told him the story of how the Giant's Causeway came to be. How the gentle giant, Finn McCool, in love with a lady giant who lived on the Scottish isle of Staffa, built the Causeway to bring his lady love safely home to Ireland. My story seemed to ease him a little until he fell asleep and started to breathe normally.

She came back in a foul humour, but when the girls were safely in bed she invited me into the front room. She was drinking from a crystal glass and smoking one of her Turkish Abdullahs. They were flat squashed-looking cigarettes that she kept in a silver box on the coffee table, and as she waved her lighted one in the air her diamond bracelet caught the light and shed rainbows all around the room.

"Will you join me in a gin and tonic, Mary?" she asked.

"Thank you, Ma'am. I'll fetch a glass." Who was I to say no to a nip of gin?

"No, no, sit down. Let me serve you for a change."

There was a slight slur to her speech, and when she rose and walked over to the cocktail cabinet to pour my drink, I saw she was a bit unsteady. There was fresh lipstick around the end of her cigarette, and a shred of tobacco clinging to her upper lip. Her mother smoked like a trooper. I'd seen her in the scullery of their big house giving instructions to the cook with a cigarette hanging from the beak of her lip, a long ash on it and a swirl of smoke rising in the air. My Da didn't smoke, couldn't afford it, though my brother Brendan, the eldest of us and the wildest, managed to maintain the habit. He'd smoked his first Gold Flake in the school playground, he told me, at twelve years old.

She cut me a slice of lemon, poured a good dollop of gin and splashed some tonic into it. Then, as an afterthought, she took the silver tongs and dropped a couple of ice-cubes in. You could see she wasn't accustomed to mixing her own drinks.

"Thank God that's over," she said, sinking into the sofa. "Here's to the future, Mary, to a Happy New Year and an end to all this turmoil."

We both had a drink of our gin and when I looked up she was staring at me as though she'd never seen me before. She'd forgotten her cigarette. It was smoldering away in the ashtray, nothing now but a long grey ash with the red tip of her lipstick just visible.

"Thank you for looking after Jimmy. You've worked wonders with him."

"It was nothing, Ma'am. He slept most of the day after the doctor gave him the sedative."

"Oh please, call me Cynthia. We're in it together, aren't we, Mary? Thrown together by this war. We must see it through as friends."

I felt my face flush even though I knew she was right and there was no difference between us. She took a large mouthful of her gin, the ice cubes clinking against the glass. Crystal is like a musical instrument, I'd discovered, for when I ran a wet finger around the rim at the kitchen sink, it made a sound so high-pitched that the dog ran into the corner whining. I'd never seen glasses like that before. In our cottage we had thick, serviceable ones, with chips in them from rough handling. I could see Ma's hands all red and slippery dunking our glasses in soapy water, her legs planted apart at the sink; and beyond her, through the scullery window, the turf stacked along the stone wall of our barn. We burned that turf for our warmth and it gave off a scent that is in my nostrils forever, the smell of Ireland. They say the English toffs like the taste of peat in their whisky, but how they get it there I don't know. It's a mystery, how you make a smell into a taste.

"You must miss your family, Mary. With all the bustle of the day I never thought to suggest you telephone them. Is it too late?"

"Oh, I'll not use the telephone. They'll all be in bed." My face flushed up again because now I had nothing to call her. I couldn't use her name, not yet; it didn't seem right, and I felt quite adrift without a name to put to her.

"Tomorrow then."

I was ashamed to tell her we had no telephone. I didn't want her to know how we lived. She probably pictured a big house in Dublin.

"Charlotte and Birdie had a nice Christmas then?" I asked.

She leaned forward to reach for another cigarette and I saw the shine on her silk stockings. There was a ladder starting at her left ankle, running up the calf towards her knee. She must have snagged her bracelet on it, or one of her rings, not the smooth gold band of her wedding ring, but the sharp diamonds and sapphires of her engagement.

"To tell you the truth, Mary, it was a dreadful day," she said, her chin trembling as she took another swig of her gin and drained the glass. She pulled on her cigarette and blew out a cloud of smoke, but none of it helped. She was ready to break down and blubber. But what came first was the anger.

"They were cruel. My mother nagged at Father all through lunch about how he should never have let me marry Christopher. 'Sitting pretty in prison,' she said, 'while my son is on the battlefield fighting for England.' My brother Jack was at Dunkirk in the summer," she explained. "But, thank God, he was safely evacuated."

She leaned forward and flicked her ash into the silver ashtray, which I would have to be polishing soon enough, I thought, removing those brown stains.

"I was so ashamed, Mary, and nobody spoke up for me, neither Father nor my sisters nor any of the aunts and uncles. Eighteen of us round the table, and not one of them raised their voice. They just let her go on and on shaming me in front of my children."

She was sobbing now, hunched over with her hands covering her head and the cigarette burning her hair. I jumped up and grabbed it from her hand and stubbed it out in the ashtray. I knelt to stroke her poor singed hair. "There, there, it'll be alright," I said.

"Oh, how terrible for you to see me reduced to this."

Her face was wet with tears, and her mouth all twisted. She must have seen the puzzlement in my face because she said: "You don't know what I'm talking about, do you?"

"I don't understand, Ma'am ... I mean, Cynthia." There, I'd said it. "What's all this about prison? The Master is in the Secret Service, you told me."

"I lied, Mary. My husband has been detained for his bloody politics!"

Her face was white now, despite her crying, and she looked at me like a frightened little girl, as though I was going to slap her. I shook my head and I said: "No matter. He's your husband, and you must love him so, and the little children."

Then she wept and threw her arms around me, quite drunk.

"Don't tell anyone, Mary! You don't blame me, do you? You'd have found out eventually, but the children mustn't know."

"There, there, blow your nose, and let's get you up to bed."

I was all in myself, and the gin was going to my head too. We staggered up the stairs and I bid her goodnight at her bedroom door. I would have gone in and tucked her into bed as I did with the children, but we weren't on those kinds of terms yet.

After that night she often asked me into the sitting room of an evening. She was lonely and I was glad of her company. Although we did not refer directly to it, the knowledge of our Christmas conversation was between us and all our discourse was built upon it.

It was clear she was a collector, for the house was crammed with stuff—clusters of china dogs and fancy figurines jostling each other behind the glass of the sitting room cabinet, knick-knacks on every shelf, and lacy handkerchiefs piled high in her underwear drawer. It turned out that's how she met him. That was the hook. It was early in the New Year when I asked her one evening: "How did you meet the Master?" She hadn't invited me to call *him* by his Christian name.

"Cousin Adèle told me about him when I came home from France. 'You must meet Christopher Brooke', she said. 'He'll give you a badge for your collection. He belongs to a political party called British Union, always talking about it. He's from the right sort of family, and *very* good-looking.'

"I remember dancing with him for the first time, and feeling that I was home, unquestionably home after all the sadness of leaving France. He did give me a badge the next time we met. It was red with a blue circle and a white streak of lightning zig-zagging across the middle. The badge said B.U.F. British Union of something or other. I didn't know then. It sounded good, patriotic. We married two years later on a crisp January day, shortly before my 21st birthday. Christopher named our first house Briuni, for Sir Oswald Mosley's British Union."

I got up to stoke the fire. The coal scuttle had only two lumps in it, but that would see us through, it was nearly time for bed.

"Briuni was smaller than this house, but I was so happy there, Mary. It was wonderful to have my own home finally. I could hardly believe it. I remember unpacking my wedding presents and thinking, I'm the happiest girl in the world! I stood in front of our dining room sideboard, arranging the cut-glass whisky tumblers, placing them one by one on the polished wood, thinking how fortunate it was that I had obeyed Father, leaving France to come home when all I'd wanted was to stay and marry Roger, then leaving my job in Manchester to help Mother in the house ..."

"You had a job?" I was shocked to think of her going out to work. That was reserved for the likes of me. And who was Rojay, and what kind of strange name was that? But I couldn't ask two questions at once. That would have seemed nosey.

"Oh yes," she said with a toss of her head, as though she were proud of it. "I was secretary to a solicitor, until Father came into the office one day and said: 'On your feet, Cynthia. No daughter of mine is going to work for another man.' When I protested he yanked me by the arm and marched me out onto Prince's Street to catch the tram. I cried all the way home. I liked my little job, and I'd worked so hard to learn shorthand and typing at Mother's insistence—I think *she* wanted me to be independent—but Father was used to having his own way, and I realized later that he knew best and I'd been right to obey him, even though I was bored out of my mind sitting around the house. Mother didn't need my help. She's always had servants."

"And who was Rojay?"

She coloured up right away and started babbling and laughing at the same time, gesturing with her hands in what I took to be a continental style.

"Oh, I met him in France. I'd been sent there, you see, to learn French, and I lived with Monsieur and Madame Plasse. Their daughter, Mireille, introduced me to him, and he joined us when we went on a trip with the family to Marseilles. It was August and so hot; everyone leaves Paris for the month of August. Mireille and I went everywhere together, but I don't know what's happened to her now. There's been no news since the Germans occupied Paris. I do hope she's all right."

She reached for a cigarette, but she never lit it, only played with it, rolling it round and round between her fingers.

"Roger wanted to marry me, but Father wouldn't hear of it. 'You've misunderstood me, Cynthia,' he wrote. 'I did not intend for you to settle in France, but simply to learn the language. And as to the money …'—I'd asked him for money, you see, I had none of my own …—'I'm not a millionaire yet. I'll let you know when I attain that status.'"

"How did you manage then?"

"I gave English lessons. Mireille found me some students, and when I thought I'd saved enough I invited the family out for lunch. Madame Plasse chose the restaurant. It was modest, but all through the meal I was on tenterhooks, calculating the prices in my head, down to the last centime, praying that Monsieur and Mireille, both known for their sweet tooth, wouldn't order *choux* or *gâteau* after the meal. And then they did! But Madame and I only had coffee, and Mireille fed me *petit gâteaux* from her fork. It was delicious and when the bill came and I was able to pay, with almost half a franc to spare, I was so proud! I left a generous tip and floated out of the restaurant on the arms of Monsieur Plasse and Mireille!"

As she told her story I could see her as the carefree girl she'd been in France, and later, sitting in the morning room of her father's house with a pool of sunlight circling her feet as she painted her fingernails and carefully outlined the half-moons that I could see now on her lovely hands as she flourished her still unlit cigarette. Was it Rojay she was thinking of, remembering the French words he'd whispered in her ear? Or was she thinking of Mireille, who she seemed equally fond of?

"I remember those first weeks in Paris when words were indistinguishable from each other, when I felt bowled over by the strangeness of France, its foreign smell and the rich buttery-garlic food. Being abroad makes you feel like a child, Mary, with no choice but to trust. I remember the day that everything became clear. Mireille was chattering to me about her latest romance and I so wanted to understand and have a proper conversation with her, then there it was like a miracle, words emerging from a stream of sound, and I was able to understand and speak! I was like one of those children who are silent for years, then say an entire sentence, then another and another. And I could converse with Roger without feeling a fool."

I'd seen no photographs of Cynthia and Rojay together. Perhaps he was the man in the boat, the photographer. But then perhaps it was Mireille who'd snapped her. Rojay had wanted to marry her, she said, and in her locket she carried a tiny picture of a man, a dark foreign looking fellow. I'd seen it on her dressing table and now I knew who it was, for it was a different man from the handsome one I'd seen in her wedding picture.

I was getting the measure of her bit by bit, despite her slippery ways. She had a habit of skittering along and changing direction suddenly just when I was catching up to her. I felt the struggle inside her. She had a great desire for friendship, but she didn't want to be known, as though she couldn't quite trust me. I was angry when she gave me the slip, but who was I to care? Without the war we never would have become friends. She had no-one else to turn to at that time, and neither did I.

One afternoon I chanced upon a bundle of photographs in a hatbox in the back of the wardrobe in my bedroom, and with what I saw there and the stories she'd told me I was able to match things up and travel a fair distance towards imagining her life and making it my own. There was little enough room in the cupboard for my things so it was just as well that I had nothing to speak of in the way of belongings—just my travelling clothes, a good serviceable working dress, and a skirt and cardigan for my evenings in the sitting room with Cynthia. At the bottom of the cupboard, in front of the hatbox, I had placed a pair of sturdy walking shoes, my comfortable slippers, and my everyday house shoes which were worn down by then. I was saving for another pair for I've always been hard on my shoes.

Mam would scold me for my heavy footedness. "Don't scuff, Máire," she'd say. "You'll wear out your shoes, and my nerves along with them."

Cynthia had taken the children out for the day to the Brooke grandparents who lived in a big house called Dinglewood and in spring, she'd told me, there would be a carpet of bluebells as far as the eye could see. I had all my chores done and was changing into my slippers when something about that hatbox piqued my curiosity. I sat on my bed, which was higher than most, so that my legs dangled over the edge, and I opened it. The first photo was of their wedding. There was the Master beside her, quite the toff in his pin-striped trousers and a cutaway jacket, with a white carnation in his lapel, and his hair parted just off-centre. Oh, he was handsome, and she was like a little girl beside him, a big bouquet in one hand, and the other hand holding up her dress to show off her dainty white shoes. Her train was so long it took three little bridesmaids to hold it with the help of the bigger girls behind, five of them, her cousins and sisters I would guess.

There were a few photos of a family which I took to be the French people for there was a different look about them, and about the place. It looked warmer than England, with palm trees and a scantily clad older couple sitting on a beach. That must have been Mr. and Mrs. Plasse. There was one quite dog-eared, as though it had been handled more than the others, of Cynthia with another young lady—not exactly beautiful but with the brightest eyes, and a big smile on her as though she had nothing to hide. Cynthia had her arm draped around the girl and at first I thought it might be her sister, but then I thought no, we're in France aren't we, it must be Mireille, and that *she* was the real reason Cynthia hadn't wanted to leave.

Mam always teased me about my flights of fancy. "Making up your stories again," she'd say. My brothers called me a plain liar, but unless you allow your imagination to wander you'll never find out anything. There was a small photo of Cynthia on her own, perhaps just home from France for she was plump and innocent, smiling for the camera, but you could see in her eyes that she was sad.

I noticed a different look to her in the photos taken with Christopher Brooke, and no wonder, for there he was like the devil himself with shiny shoes and his long legs—he must have been six foot two—in tails and a wing collar holding a young lady in his arms. They were dancing, I'm sure of it for Cynthia had told me he won prizes for his ballroom dancing.

"His partners were working girls he paired up with at the Academy in Manchester," she'd said. "But there was nothing going on, Mary. Christopher's always had a reputation as the perfect gentleman. And he would never stray outside his class."

Perhaps he would inquire after their mothers' health, compliment them on their intricate footwork, or discuss the weather. But I could see that he had a smile to break a working girl's heart and make her long for elevation to a higher station. Cynthia was born to it. She knew nothing more of the working world than her brief time as a secretary. It was her birthright to have Christopher Brooke, and you could see it in the next photo I studied. It must have been their engagement for she looked like the cat that got the cream. There was a look of ownership and contentment as though her whole life was set before her, smooth as the satin of her wedding dress. But I saw a wildness in her eyes too, and I felt a clamour around the two of them even though it was not there in the photograph.

I could imagine how she would take hold of her new life with him and begin to plan their wedding. By the time he requested her hand and received her father's blessing, she likely had a picture of the event firmly imprinted in her mind, with every detail clear: the dress, the bouquet, her bridesmaids, the cake, his handsome form in top hat and tails with the soft fur of the hat fashioned in his father's factory. And she would have grown thin with excitement, for by the day of the wedding I could see in the photo it was only her lips that bloomed, full and fleshy, smeared with that dark red lipstick she favours. I imagined a longing swollen inside her as the big day approached, consuming her like a hungry animal.

I collected the pictures in my hands and leafed through, making a moving picture of them as one image flickered into another. In all those photographs from their long engagement she was gazing up at him with her hands clasped, sometimes a little dog in her arms, and she was always smiling with her dark, deep-set eyes that turned down at the outside edges, giving her a look of sadness even though she was smiling. And him leaning towards her as though pulled by a hidden force.

There was Mr. Brooke in a separate pile, with his sleeves rolled up, standing with the men in what I took to be his father's factory, for they were working on the forms of hats which did not yet have their brims. In another he was standing before an avenue of leafy trees, all in white, with tennis shorts and his legs naked but for white socks. Beside him was a fellow with a moustache wearing long white trousers. Cricketers and tennis players they were, men of privilege, but he was trying to do it all, to run the factory and hobnob with the workers, just like his wife using me as her servant all day and then expecting me to keep her company in the evenings.

Later I was to take some photos myself, of her and the children, with a little box camera she gave me as a gift. I still have those photos though the camera is gone. Cynthia stares solemnly at me, her cheekbones jutting, her mouth and eyes dark as blood, as though she were herself being sucked into her own darkness. And the children are clustered around her, each with their own manner of coping: Jimmy smirking with a kind of embarrassment, Birdie with that impish grin until the later photos after she's decided to be a good child and manage in that way. Charlotte is sitting up straight or standing to attention, always on guard, taking care of the others. And the baby, when she arrived like an afterthought, just sat there absorbing it all. But I'm getting ahead of myself.

Chapter Nine

THE DREAM OF BRIUNI

April 1941

I WAS POLISHING the silver at the kitchen table, shining up her ashtray and cigarette lighter, meanwhile keeping an eye on the children through the window as I worked. They'd clamoured to go out even though it was a blustery April morning with showers gusting across the field behind our house. Charlotte home from school with the sniffles, and Jimmy with another asthma attack, though the truth of it was that Cynthia didn't want them going to school. One of the children had said something to Charlotte, something she'd heard from her own mother about Mr. Brooke being in prison. Well, no harm in missing school. I'd been a bit of a truant myself, and I thought the children were better off playing in the garden in their own magic world. I'd bundled them up, especially Birdie who was a skinny little thing but full of pep, and I'd wrapped a woollen scarf around Jimmy's neck and whacked each one of them on the bottom. That always made them laugh. But there they were again, circling slow and solemn with their arms raised and their faces turned to the grey sky. Charlotte's lips were moving and the others seemed to be repeating whatever it was she was saying.

I picked up a silver tennis cup and began to scrub with a toothbrush at its tarnished filigree. The house was filled with the Master's trophies—cups and shields for tennis, cricket, ballroom dancing and boxing—I should know for I was the one had to polish them. There were framed certificates too on the wall of his study—he was quite the sportsman. But what's the use of prizes for being the best? It's daddies who invented prizes, I was thinking to myself. Mammies would never be so cruel, for we're all good at something and not only the prize-winners. Nine months I've been here, I thought, long enough to grow a baby. And I remembered as a little one watching Mam's belly swell up with Patrick and wondering how it could take so long when our dogs and pigs could produce their young in a matter of weeks.

"What are you doing, Mary?"

"Oh, you gave me a shock!"

She'd crept up behind me barefoot, still in her dressing gown. She must have slept in; God knows she needed it. When I'd gone down the corridor in the night to check on Birdie who'd been crying out with a bad dream, Cynthia's light had still been burning, and I'd seen when I got back to my room that it was three in the morning.

"Can I get you a cup of tea?" I asked. Her hair was tousled and unbrushed, quite unusual I thought for one who was often primping in front of the mirror.

"I'll get it."

"There's a pot freshly made in the scullery," I called after her for she was already gone.

The children were circling the other way now and Charlotte was singing. She had the poetry in her, that one, and it came out effortlessly. I had moved on to the tea set and was rubbing hard at the spout of the milk jug when Cynthia came and sat down beside me.

"I dreamed of Briuni last night," she said, folding her arms under her ample bosom and cradling herself against the chilly morning.

"Oh, then it must have been a happy dream."

"No, it wasn't. There was something sinister. It was both Briuni and my father's house, the Woodlands, because Mother and Father were there too."

The English gentry have a fancy way of presenting themselves and their property. I would smile to myself as I pushed Birdie's stroller along Chester Road at the names they dreamed up—Primrose Park, The Spinney, Cedars of Lebanon ... And the Brooke house named Meadowside because of the cow pasture in the back. In our townland of Carrigan the farms are known by family names; ours is Odhrán Byrne's, and that was my great grandfather's name.

"Father was sitting in his armchair reading the newspaper," she said, "and Mother leaned down to whisper in his ear. There was a rumbling noise, like a tank breaking through the fence and coming into our garden. And through the rumbling I heard Mother whisper something about the BUF, Mosley, politics ..." — her brow furrowed with remembering — "... a young man, he'll grow out of it ... good family, financial security, and so on. Then Ruby came bursting in and she said: 'I'm going! I'm going!' The Red Cross, I suppose. She's determined to join up and go to the front as an ambulance driver even though Father forbids it. Mother encourages her, you see. Ruby's always been a spoiled brat."

Cynthia has that way of mixing up her dreams with real life, like me. Perhaps she's got the Sight too, though I doubt it. She's flighty.

"I wish Ruby would get married and settle down."

"Fat chance with all the men away," I said.

"You don't know Ruby. She always gets her way." She slammed her cup down in the saucer. "She's been nothing but trouble since she was born."

I'm the youngest girl in my family, so I don't know what it is to be jealous of a sister, but I'd bet that's what it was with Cynthia, the first-born, and her sister Ruby coming to displace her. Never got over it. *She* was the spoiled brat.

I heard the children running, a clatter of footsteps on the path, and Birdie's voice pitched higher than the others. That child could have broken a crystal glass with her screaming. Cynthia jumped up when she heard them and was already at the back door as they burst through.

"Mummy, Mummy! We did the Magic Circle, and Charlotte says the fairies are coming to save us!"

It was Jimmy, panting and wheezing from his running. And Charlotte behind him reaching out her hand.

"Ouch!" he squealed. The little minx had pinched him.

"Save you?" Cynthia said laughing. "Save you from what?"

"From ... from ..." He looked at Charlotte, seeking help, but her eyes were on the kitchen linoleum, her lower lip pushed out. "Don't know," he said with a snicker.

"Birdie biscuit, Birdie biscuit …" the little one chanted. I picked her up and took her to the cupboard where the biscuit tin was. I could see Cynthia was in no mood for the children this morning. She came from a world where children were presented to their parents at the end of the day, their faces pink and shiny from the bath, and all ready for bed. She told me she'd had a nurse and a housekeeper, and when war was declared those patriotic women had gone off and joined the WAF. Now she was looking for a governess so the children wouldn't have to go back to the local school and hear the evil rumours about their father. I don't know how she managed before I came along. I felt her reliance like a heavy weight on me. Birdie was scattering crumbs everywhere and Charlotte was at the table trying to polish the teapot, spilling Silvo all over the cloth.

"Come on, Jumbo, you can help me get dressed."

She took Jimmy upstairs with her and I turned on the wireless and found some music for Charlotte and Birdie to dance to while I finished the polishing. *The Children's Hour* was on and they played *Ring a Ring o' Roses*. Birdie had just fallen over laughing when the telephone rang. That shrill sound always frightened me. I've never got used to it and am thankful after all that I did not become a telephone operator. Five rings and then I heard her voice in the front hall, cautious at first, before the excitement bubbled up. What could it be, not another false alarm? They walked into the kitchen together, her eyes shining and Jimmy with a big grin.

"Daddy's coming home!" he said in his husky voice.

Charlotte grabbed Jimmy's hands and they jumped up and down laughing so hard that their eyes were reduced to slits in their chubby faces.

"It's real this time, Mary," she told me. "The Superintendent himself telephoned me. Christopher is on his way. And he doesn't have to go back to Ascot, or to prison. He's being moved to a camp on the Isle of Man."

She was almost weeping.

Chapter Ten

A WHOLE LOAF

Ascot Camp, April 1941

We are swollen with desire, heading towards freedom, ready to leave this prison. I am carried on a drowning wave, swept away, though all my longing remains with him. He longs for a whole loaf, we are longing and longing for something.

THE MEN ARE packing. Spirits are high. Though some have no homes to go to, no family to visit, they welcome the move to the Isle of Man, a holiday destination dropped into the Irish Sea. They will meet up in Liverpool in three days' time to take the Mersey steamer, and Christopher will be himself again, renewed by the visit with his family. He feels as he did at the end of term, going home for the holidays, excitement rising in his belly. He sees Cynthia's lips parted, her hands twisting nervously as she opens the door, and then her tight embrace, the fierce grip of her hands on his arms. He will hold her loosely like a dancer, the way he was taught at the Manchester Academy, with Carrie inside the circle of his arms, her stiff dress standing out from her malnourished body, rippling as he turned her in circles. And her friend Lydia on the sidelines, watching, waiting her turn.

He strips down with the other men and runs shivering into the shower where the shock of cold water splashing his body numbs the flesh. He soaps his armpits, genitals, anus, scrubbing with a nail brush until he is pink and tingly all over, his grinning face raised to the shower nozzle. When he is dried he buttons up his shirt which is grey with repeated washing, steps into his flannels and buttons the fly. A whole loaf. He will have a whole loaf to himself at the kitchen table, cutting into it with the serrated blade of the bread knife. He will consume the spongy whiteness, crumbs falling from his lips with the freshness of it. His mouth fills with saliva.

Chapter Eleven

A SOUVENIR OF DADDY'S WAR

WE WERE READY for him with the dining table laid for lunch and as good a spread as we could manage in wartime. I was upstairs making the beds when I heard the commotion. I must confess I was more and more curious and for this reason I'd sneaked another look at the hatbox of photographs in bed the previous night. There they were, standing together in a garden, Cynthia gazing up at him, and in her arms a fluffy white dog. That would be Gigi. Her father had bought the pet for her, she'd said, shortly after her return from France, perhaps to make up for the damage he'd done her. If there is indeed a line of destiny to a life, Cynthia's father had much to answer for in obstructing hers. But what is destiny but the path we take regardless? I found something amongst the photographs that I had missed before. It was a faded newspaper clipping with a picture of Cynthia, her hand on her husband's arm as they stepped off a boat:

Prosperous British hatter seeks new business opportunities

Mr. and Mrs. Christopher Brooke arrived in New York yesterday on an extended vacation. British hatter, Christopher Brooke combines business with pleasure as he meets with Cornelius Van Dusen, President of Macy's. Accompanied by his wife, Cynthia Brooke (née Blackwell), Mr. Brooke seeks new business contracts in the United States.

It was dated January 1933. She had a radiant smile and was wearing a Persian lamb coat and hat to match. They would have been entertained by all manner of important men, and perhaps by some of their wives as well, American women like Mrs. Simpson who caused such a scandal when she made off with the King of England. I wonder what Cynthia thought of those Americans. I'll bet she enjoyed showing off her diamond engagement ring and her shiny platinum wedding ring while her husband talked business.

England and its troubles would have seemed far away as she looked through her hotel window at the streets of New York. They say it's cold over there and thick with snow all winter long. She would have felt protected by her husband and by his importance in the business world. Even though her father disapproved of the Mosley movement, she must have felt in that moment that she'd made the right decision, coming home from France as he'd asked her to, leaving her little job and marrying Christopher Brooke to secure her future. I could see that she was—to use her own words—"the happiest girl in the world" at that time. But how could she not have known the truth of her husband's political life? In Ireland we may turn a blind eye, but we all know what's going on.

I was in the lavatory when I heard them tumbling up the stairs. She was laughing softly and I heard his voice, deep and gentle, then their bedroom door clicked shut, and I flushed and hurried downstairs.

The children were cranky with hunger, disappointed that their father had disappeared so quickly.

"He needs a nap," I said. "He'll be tired from his journey."

I sat them down and we ate our lunch, then they started on a game of snakes and ladders while I cleared our plates and took them into the scullery. There was the wash to be done as well so I was a good while out in the back kitchen with the wringer washer. 'Twas a new-fangled thing that I knew my mam would not have given house room. It had taken me a while to get the hang of it and I'd suffered a trapped finger in the wringer, bandaged up for a week, but now we were friends.

I ran in to check on the children and sure enough there was a fight in progress with the board upended and tiddlywinks all over the carpet.

Birdie was screaming at Jimmy, and Charlotte trying to make the peace. I brought out the big tin of marbles and that diverted them until Birdie began cramming them into her mouth and wouldn't stop until her cheeks were all swelled up and she almost choked. I was so preoccupied with the children that I didn't even know they were downstairs until we heard laughter from the dining room next door.

Cynthia came into the sitting room, her cheeks pink, her eyes sparkling—Oh, she looked beautiful—and I was feeling quite flushed myself. A man in the house will do marvels for the lifting of the spirits! I was glad for her, but I will confess I felt a twinge of jealousy at that moment. I was jealous of *him*, for I was accustomed to having Cynthia to myself. But that was all to change.

"You can clear the table now, Mary. We're finished with lunch."

I could see she'd hardly eaten a thing—her lipstick was still fresh, and there was a breathless feeling about her. I supposed him to be upstairs again, or in the cloakroom perhaps, refreshing himself. I hadn't yet set eyes on him and I was bristling with curiosity as I loaded up my tray and headed down the corridor towards the kitchen.

When I saw Christopher Brooke for the very first time, he was sitting at my kitchen table slicing a loaf of bread. It was a fresh loaf I'd baked that morning, and he was eating his way through it, slice by slice, ever so slowly. When he turned his head, sensing my presence, he was blinded, for I was standing in the doorway with the light behind me, flooding through the scullery window.

"Is it the Master?" I asked. "Is it the Master, home for a spell?"

He stood up, brushing crumbs from his lap, and walked towards me like a blind man, one hand reaching out in front of him, the other at his brow to block the sun. He saw me finally as he entered my shadow, and he extended his hand. He was so close I could smell his skin —a stale smell of neglect mixed with a manly, animal smell. I didn't have a free hand because of the tray I was holding, so I bobbed him a curtsy as I had seen the servants do in the moving pictures.

"Mary Byrne, Sir," I said, "at your service."

I don't know what he said in reply. He was so close I couldn't think. I felt the heat of his body, and blood was pounding in my ears, deafening me. He must have addressed some kind words to me, because he was smiling, his face so handsome, but pale with being shut away from the world. I wished there was something I could do for him, but he walked back to the kitchen table and I turned and went into the scullery. I dared not look, but I could hear him brushing up the crumbs and sucking on them. After he'd gone I went to give the table a wipe with a wet cloth, but there was nothing there. It was as though no-one had been there, and I wondered if I had seen a ghost. But, despite my confusion I knew I had seen something in that extended hand, something I was to remember when the time came.

He was gone next day, and it was me had to deal with the consequences. The children had been that excited and now it had all gone too fast and they were inconsolable. Charlotte was sat in a corner weeping and sulking, Jimmy with a full-on asthma attack, and Birdie screaming: "Where's Daddy? I want my Daddy!"

That was when she started the business about the spider, wrestling her clothes off and turning them inside out.

"There's a spider tickling me," she'd say, laughing and crying all at once. "I know there's a spider but I can't find it."

Cynthia was nowhere to be seen, up in her room, I suppose. I wished he would never come back. If his whirlwind visit was to cause such turmoil, we were better off without him.

Charlotte threw something across the room and hit me right on the temple.

"What's this?" I said, picking it up, something hard and brown like a dried turd.

"Oh sorry, Mary," she said, brightening up from her snivels. "I didn't mean to hit you, honestly."

"It's Daddy's ginger pudding from the war," Jimmy said, gasping. The poor child could barely breathe. "He saved it for us."

"It's a paperweight," Charlotte said primly. "A souvenir of Daddy's war."

Chapter Twelve

VOYAGE TO THE ISLE OF MAN

Peveril Camp, Peel, Isle of Man

*A different body of liquid now, larger, permeated with blood and light;
I am floating in a scarlet globe engorged with it, my father abandoned
at Fleetwood Docks, unprepared for the cat-calls as the men aboard the
boat stare defiantly into the jeering crowd. But he keeps his head down.
Imagine him leaning on the railing of the steamship as it carries him
across the Irish Sea, shadowed by a naval vessel. Imagine him in ecstasy,
leaving me with her, haunting me with his absence. This is the beginning.*

"IS THIS HOW we treat them Fascist thugs?" shouts a scrawny woman
in a headscarf. "Sending them on holidays to the Isle of Lucky
Men to frolic on the beaches in their bathing trunks!"

Christopher ducks just in time to avoid being hit by a spray of
gravel thrown by a red-faced man on the dock. He is scooping up
handfuls of it, hurling it at the men on deck with a string of his own
abuse. Christopher is shocked by the crowd's fury, and for the first
time feels grateful for the protection of his internment.

The men are kept under close guard, restricted to a roped-off area
on the upper deck. They are to disembark at Douglas and take transport across the island to Peel where they will be housed at Peveril (M)
Camp. The Manx people have been moved from their homes to make
way for the many camps that will house German, Italian and Finnish
enemy aliens, and British fascists, with separate camps for the women
and children.

Christopher studies the gunmetal waves churning in the wake of the ship. He is full of Cynthia, filled with a vibrancy that comes to him only in her presence, naked and intimate. This feeling is like a drug to which he has become subject during their eight years of marriage. Her body has restored him, reminding him of the days when he was free to go where he pleased—like the time he was to leave for a mass rally at the Free Trade Hall in Manchester, unable to find his tie-pin, and Cynthia, rather than helping, had tugged at him, not wanting him to go. He remembers her sudden question: "Can I come too?" Watching Charlotte and Jimmy playing in the sandbox in the back garden, the leaded panes of his bedroom window framing them in rectangles. Birdie in her pram, three months old.

"Nurse Brown will look after them," she'd said quickly.

He hadn't been able to think of a good reason, only that he must keep his life ordered and calm. Mosley himself was to speak at the rally and as District Leader of the Stockport branch Christopher was to welcome him personally. He knew he wouldn't speak well if she was there; her presence unbalanced him. Early evening sunlight had spilled across their twin beds. Her dark eyes as she watched him, her red lips moist and parted.

His stomach lurches with the roll of the waves and he closes his eyes and tilts his face upwards, welcoming the sting of salt spray on his cheeks, the wind forcing itself into his lungs. He feels that he is being scoured in preparation for what is to come. But still the past echoes in him, the memory of a time when he'd felt vital and full of purpose.

He'd been waiting in the lobby of the Midland Hotel in Manchester, going over his speech. A Persian carpet formed an island where he sat and his feet scuffed restlessly on it, disturbing the nap.

"Hello there, Chris. What are you doing in town tonight?"

Eric Cartwright, his Best Man and life-long tennis partner. They still played three times a week in summer and paired up for the annual doubles tournament at the Cartwrights' weekend house party in late August. Eric was one of those nondescript Englishmen with no remarkable features—sandy hair and pale lashes, fair skin that became mottled in moments of excitement, a man of medium stature, medium weight—

and yet he seemed a combination of everything solid and comforting about English culture. His conversation was made up of truisms and clichés, but behind those meaningless words was a wealth of camaraderie. Though he and Eric had never discussed anything remotely intimate during their long friendship, their bond was strong and Christopher counted on him.

"I say, are you alright?" Eric inquired.

"Of course," he'd answered, springing to his feet and shaking hands vigorously.

"How about a drink?"

"Oh. Well, thanks Eric, but ... I'm not actually thirsty."

"To pass the time, old chap," Eric said, laughing. "What's up? Waiting for your paramour?"

A line of perspiration beaded Christopher's upper lip. His trouser was creased where his knee had pressed into the damp pulse of his crossed leg. There was a moment of embarrassment as his friend's joke fell flat.

"I have a meeting at eight—British Union."

"Ah." Eric's head tilted back slightly as his guard came up. "Well then ... See you on the court Thursday."

Eric walked away towards the bar and Christopher strode quickly across the lobby towards the revolving door, single-mindedly focused on the prospect of meeting Sir Oswald Mosley in the flesh and conversing with him for the first time, man to man.

He resumes pacing now, the short distance within that roped area of the deck—up and down, back and forth. It is a longer crossing than he had thought—nearly three hours—and he's still fighting nausea and the turmoil of memory.

"Cynthia, if you could have heard Sir Oswald speak!" he'd said when he'd returned later that night to find his wife in her nightgown, waiting up for him. "We had to wait almost four minutes for the crowd to stop cheering. And he clasped my hand firmly and thanked me for my leadership of the Stockport branch."

"Oh Chris, you're like a schoolboy," she had said. "Where will all these meetings lead, Darling? You should use your own initiative instead of following Mosley."

Her mother's words. He'd heard them before.

"He spoke for almost an hour and a half to a packed ..."

"Was it as boring as his Southport speech?"

"Don't belittle the man. He's a veteran of the Great War. He fought on the Western Front and was transferred to the Royal Flying Corps. That's how he got the injury that caused his limp." Cynthia shrugged, unimpressed. "He paid tribute to all the British veterans and to the young men of his generation who died in great numbers. He praised Chamberlain for his efforts towards appeasement with Germany as we see the threat of yet another war looming on the Continent."

He had removed his cufflinks and placed them carefully in a small leather box that bore his initials in gold—CJB—a gift from Mother on his twenty-first birthday. Cynthia meanwhile had tucked herself into bed and lay back on a couple of plushy linen-sleeved pillows.

"He spoke rousingly of our warriors and working men and of how they've been betrayed again and again by politicians. 'Let they who remember the mighty past now join hands with the new generation. Lift up your voices at this great meeting in the heart of England!'" He was quoting Mosley's very words so that Cynthia would understand and be inspired. But all she'd done was *shush* him, reminding him that the children were asleep in the nursery next door.

"A fine trumpeter played the National Anthem," he'd said in a lowered voice, "And we all stood, Cynthia, every one of us stirred to the core."

"What about the rabble-rousers? The newspapers say that Mosley is becoming extremely unpopular."

"Oh, there were a few thugs trying to cause trouble as usual, but our Leader parried their jibes like the expert swordsman he is." Trouserless now, in his stocking feet with shirt-tails flapping, Christopher had struck a fencing pose, parrying and thrusting at Cynthia with a big grin on his face. She'd jumped out of bed then, ducked under his arm and pummelled his chest with her fists, and when he'd wrapped his arms around her body to restrain her, she had burst into tears. Like a sudden summer storm, it came and went, and then she was smiling up at him.

"Darling," she said, "Oh Darling." Her red lips parted. He'd felt the softening of her body, the trembling of her belly against his groin, an exquisite feeling, like butterfly wings, but dense and full of promise. They stood by her bed, where a pink-shaded lamp threw a circle of light on the pillows. He had raised his hand to stroke her hair, inadvertently brushing her nipple, taut against the pink satin of her nightgown. There had been a moment of stillness as he took a breath, then she had begun clawing at him. She had torn the buttons off his shirt, raked his chest with her red nails. He'd had no choice but to meet her there, trying to calm her but, surprised to find himself erect, he penetrated her roughly as they toppled onto the bed.

Christopher remembers their wedding night, entering her for the first time, shocked by the magnetic pull of her body that had enveloped and held him like a bitch in heat. There'd been nothing in his life to prepare him for this, for the smell and taste and hunger of his wife. At boarding school he'd captained the football and cricket teams, swum record-breaking lengths and won the junior tennis tournament with Cartwright. He had become one with his body; a healthy, uncomplicated youth on a clear path of goal-oriented sports, with the expectation of sex as a similar sport. But Cynthia had confounded him with her passion; she had thrown him back into the shadow of Nanny Darlington.

He'd been four years old when Nanny first took him into her bed. Half asleep, he'd been bundled into her arms and carried across the room. Christopher could still hear the soft breathing of Alice in her crib in the corner, and he felt the thud of Nanny's footsteps rippling through his body, indistinguishable now from the nausea he feels as the *Viking* lurches from side to side.

"*Shush, shush*, my little laddie, don't tell Mother," she had crooned, her cheeks wet as she nestled into him. She'd held him like that every night, her body shuddering as strange sounds came from her throat. Afterwards she would push him out.

"Get back to your own bed, you naughty boy," she'd say, and he'd scurry across the cold floorboards in the darkness. Alice saw him once, and she gurgled and waved her arms at the breakfast table next morning, but Mother only nodded and smiled at Nanny whose eyes were red-rimmed as she turned her face away and made herself busy with her handkerchief.

Cradled in Nanny's arms at night, Christopher would feel a dreadful sadness come over him, and sometimes he woke startled from a dream where he'd seen terrible faces in the darkness; hands reaching out of the mud, clawing at the air. But all would be silent and still in the nursery except for the comforting sound of Alice's breathing, and sometimes Nanny's sniffling.

As the boat docks with a great shudder the men crowd towards the gangplank and Christopher joins them, feeling the absence of his friend Cliff Byrd who has been detained at Huyton Camp. Why couldn't we have stayed together? he wonders, remembering the bond they had formed at Latchmere. How could anyone ever understand the humiliation we shared in that place?

Now he is going back to boarding school, wondering who he'll be sharing a dorm with. At least then he'd known it would be only three months until he'd be home for the hols. He walks down the gangplank with small steps, held up by the slow-moving line of men ahead, and has a sudden déjà vu, a postscript to the memories that have flooded him on the sailing. He's a small boy again, holding Alice's hand as she waddles beside him, learning to walk. Nanny Darlington holds onto her other hand, and his parents are up ahead, Mother floating as though she has no feet, her gloved hand on Father's arm.

Christopher steps onto solid ground with mixed feelings, unsure as to whether he is going on holiday to this wild, green-mountainous island, famed for its Celtic and Viking history, with castles and ruins abounding in witness to the past, or to be a prisoner here, reviled and feared by his own people. He has nothing to hold onto, not even his own dignity. He lost it somehow in that carpeted room rumbling with Stephens' throaty laughter.

Chapter Thirteen

A DAY IN MANCHESTER

June 1941

IT WAS ME she came to when she found out. It was not a complete surprise for I had seen it in his hand, though you don't always trust your vision until it's proven.

"How will I manage, Mary? I can't have another child in the middle of a war. And with my husband away. Do you know someone?"

What did the war have to do with it? Babies continue to be born, especially during wars, for life must go on. I reckoned she had doubts about her husband, that was the truth of it. My mistress was married to a man she did not understand, and the baby made her feel she was wading in deeper. That's why she was afraid to tell her mother. But how could Mrs. Blackwell not know? When our Deirdre was pregnant with her first, Mam knew it before she did and I saw on her face a troubled feeling, as though she didn't want for Deirdre the life she'd had herself. That's when I realized what it must have been like for my parents just starting their life together before we all began to arrive. I knew that we had drained her, seven of us coming one after the other, not counting little Cliodhna who died before I was born.

Cynthia sent the children to her mother for the day, and told her she was taking me into Manchester for an appointment. I don't know what kind of appointment that would be, but it was none of my business. I left it to her. She's good at lying.

"Only a white lie, Mary," she said, flipping her hand as though she were tossing a coin, but I could see that she'd be caught in her own web someday.

I took her to the midwife on the Walkley Estates, and her hand gripped mine so tightly as we left the motor-car I thought she'd break my skin with her nails. On her arm was a handbag with a wad of five-pound notes. I'd seen her stuff it in there.

"A caravan!" she exclaimed, stopping at the bottom of the steps. What did she think it would be, a private clinic with fashion magazines and a potted plant?

"Come on," I said. "Meg's waiting for us."

By chance I'd met this lady in the queue at the grocer's in Bramhall village and she'd given me her coupon for a pot of jam.

"My Lennie's away at war," she'd said, "and I don't 'ave much of a sweet tooth m'self."

I'd thanked her and told her it'd come in handy for the little ones to slather on their toast, especially now with the scarcity of butter. It was a long queue so we'd had time to talk and just before we'd reached the counter she confided to me that if I knew of a girl in the family way who needed help I could take her over to the Walkley Estates to Camp-site number five.

So there we were in Meg's kitchen, and I was thinking surely she can't go through with this, it's his little baby she's carrying that's scored on his hand. And sure enough she baulked at the last minute, whether out of fear or something nobler I couldn't say, but Meg was none too pleased. For myself I was relieved. It would have been a heavy weight to carry if something had gone wrong, and me a Catholic.

I doubt my mam would have borne us all if she'd had a choice. I would never have entered this beautiful world if it were not for the Catholic Church and its edicts. I would never have walked on the springy grass of those fields surrounding our farm, nor seen the mist rise like breath in the morning and felt the sun warming my face as it burned through the whiteness. I know I am not a beauty like Deirdre and Siobhan, and even Caitlin in her way, but when the sun shines on me I *feel* beautiful. If you were never to see a mirror you could live a happier life, fooling yourself that you were the most beautiful woman in the world. That is how I pictured myself when I was a little girl, out in the pastures in my own world.

I could not help it. I was already in love with her, nestled under her heart, pulsing to its beat. And if she flushed me out how would I ever find him again? It was the first threat, and I kicked and triumphed, exultant as I felt her feet descending the steps of that caravan, the slam of the car door, the rev of the motor as we drove away.

We had the rest of the day to ourselves, and indeed we did go to Manchester, so she wasn't a liar after all. She bought me a slap-up lunch in Kendal Milne's restaurant, because there was no rationing yet for restaurants, though that was to change as people grew resentful of those who could afford to eat in such places and save their coupons to trade for petrol and other luxuries.

It was her that broached the topic of the Master's involvement in politics.

"I never went to the meetings, Mary, not after that first time," she said.

I could tell she had something niggling at her that she wanted to confide.

"I went with my husband to hear Mosley speak at the Southport Floral Hall. It was almost seven years ago, in July during a hot spell, just after the big rally at Olympia which had been in all the newspapers because it turned so violent. Thank goodness Christopher hadn't been there. So many Blackshirts were injured. It was reported that there were twelve thousand supporters and another two thousand rabble-rousers outside—mostly Communists and Jews—who ganged up on them."

She laid down her knife and fork and reached into her handbag for one of her Turkish cigarettes, a sure sign that she was upset. She was so beautiful with her cheeks flushed and her shining eyes. She had a beauty like my sister Deirdre, but different because she's English. Why is it that people look like who they are—Mireille with her Frenchness, me with my Irishness, and Cynthia so very English?

"There was a big crowd in Southport and everybody chanted as we waited—Mosley! Mosley ..."

She clamped her hand over her mouth and looked around to make sure that no-one had heard, then she whispered his name—"Mosley!" and giggled. She continued but in a quieter voice: "When he finally entered the Hall there was a hush, as though we couldn't believe it was really him, then a gasp from the women as he mounted the steps and marched across the platform. He paused a moment with arms akimbo and his chin jutting, in front of a union jack and the British Union bolt of lightning, then he came to life with that infectious grin, like a little boy playing at soldiers. Everyone was jostling for position, and I had to hang on tightly to my handbag because there were some unsavoury looking types in the crowd. A huge banner on the stage behind him said: *"Mosley Speaks,"* and that he did, for more than an hour in his plummy voice, punching the air with his fist. I've never seen anyone so sure of himself. I just knew that he could have anything he wanted, and I could see the crowd being drawn in, feeling that they could have what they wanted too, and live a life they hadn't even dared to consider. So you see, Mary, I began to understand how my husband was influenced by him."

"What did he say?" I asked, all ears, as though I too were drawn in by his spell.

"I don't remember exactly," she said, shrugging. "Something about appeasement, I suppose. Everybody was talking about appeasement in those days, trying to curry favour with Hitler and the Germans." She puffed on her cigarette, threw back her head and blew a stream of smoke into the air. "Oh yes, I remember! He talked about women, all the women involved with the BUF, like Mary Richardson who'd worked with Mrs. Pankhurst for women's suffrage and had then become Chief Organizer for the Women's Section of the BUF. He talked about the Lancashire cotton mills and the Party's plans to boost industry, and ... oh yes, he said this dreadful thing I'll never forget. He was talking about ... hmm ... international finance, the economy, that sort of thing, and he made mention of ..."

Here she paused, for effect I felt, now that she was in full swing and remembering it all after she'd claimed not to. "... 'the grasping little tradesmen of Whitechapel.' He was referring of course to the Jews of London's East End. Well, that's not the sort of thing you say in public. We all have our opinions, but some of them are best kept between ourselves. My father says that's what did Mosley in, letting Jew haters join the BUF. They caused the violence that turned public opinion against him."

She paused to light another cigarette from the stub of her previous one before she crushed it in the ashtray and looked directly into my eyes. I felt she was waiting for me to speak, but I had nothing to say. I was thinking only that perhaps our tinkers are the closest we come to having Jews in Ireland, but as Cynthia had remarked some opinions are best kept under cover.

"My husband is not ... of that opinion, Mary. Christopher is a good man, a decent, upstanding man."

She looked intently at me, waiting again for some pronouncement.

"What happened next?" I blurted.

She sighed and leaned back in her chair, disappointed in me perhaps. She sucked on her cigarette and blew a stream of smoke before she continued.

"Oh, we all crowded into the back room of the Hall. It was a dingy place, but there were sandwiches and urns of tea. Christopher was terribly excited, trying to push his way through to talk to Mosley—they'd met, you see, here in Manchester and were quite pally. Or so he'd like to think," she said with a dismissive wave of her hand. "But then I lost sight of Chris, and it was I who ended up standing across the table from the great man. I was holding a cup of tea in my hand and was about to drink when he caught my eye. I thought he was going to speak to me, I'm sure he was, but just then a young woman came up behind him and addressed him boldly. 'Sir Oswald?' she asked, as though she couldn't believe it was actually him. He turned towards her, a sandwich in his hand, half way to his mouth. 'I was just going to ask you if ...' she began. Then, with his free hand he reached out ..." Cynthia leaned across the white tablecloth, her eyes locked on mine as she continued in a whisper. "He reached out and stroked her bottom. He cupped one buttock in his palm and pulled her against him. 'Vote for me,' he said, 'when the time comes.' I heard him quite clearly though his voice was low and intimate. 'Vote for me and I'll think you as I make love to my wife.'"

"He said that?"

"Yes, Mary. And then he released her and bit into his sandwich and chewed hungrily, holding her with his eyes. I've never seen such cheek! He's a seducer of women as well as crowds. And just think, it could have been me if that girl hadn't intervened. You know that his wife's name was Cynthia, or Cimmy as they called her?"

She crushed out her cigarette, the tip of it moist and red.

"The odd thing is she had died the previous year, a few months after Christopher and I were married. But by all accounts, he'd been carrying on with Diana Mitford so that's probably who he meant when he talked about 'making love to my wife.' Diana and her sister Unity were pally with Hitler. Mosley married her after a decent interval and they had their wedding in Germany at Goebbels' home where Hitler was a guest. It was in all the papers, an absolute scandal! I'd felt so sorry for his first wife. They say he was having affairs with all and sundry —with the Mitford woman, with Cimmy's sister, and even with her mother. How can Christopher admire such a man?"

I still had no answer for her, but by then I'd realized she wasn't expecting one. She only used me as a sounding board because she had no-one else. I wondered did she secretly admire Mosley, for all her words, but it was not my business, the strange affairs of the gentry. Oswald Mosley was a toff and a charmer was what I'd heard, handsome and full of himself, even on his way to prison. I'd seen his picture in the *Daily Mail*.

"First it was the meetings," she said. "Then Walton, Ascot, Latchmere House, and now he's stuck on the Isle of Man where I still can't visit him."

She talked as though he was on a tour of England. She couldn't even say the word. Prison! He's in prison! I almost shouted, my mouth pursed to hold the words in. In our house we always called a spade a spade.

Kendal Milne's is a big shop on Deansgate with any number of floors and departments. After our lunch we went down in the lift to the second floor where there was more clothing than I'd ever set eyes on.

A green scarf caught my eye, and I was fingering it and thinking of my mam, for she had a dress of that colour she wore for special occasions. I wished I could buy it and send it to her in a parcel, but before I knew it Cynthia had whipped it out of my hands and taken it to the cash register. She's going to buy it for herself, I thought, the selfish bitch, and then she paid for it and told the shop assistant: "No, no, I don't need it wrapped. She's going to wear it. Look, it matches your beautiful green eyes, Mary." And she draped it on my shoulders and smiled at me in that way she had. I'm sorry to say that I blushed. And I was speechless, especially after my wicked and mistaken thoughts, but it didn't matter because she chattered on about how she loved to buy presents, and how she'd never had money of her own until she married, her father keeping her on a tight budget and all. She must have handed over a good few of her precious clothes coupons for my scarf.

I will just wear it for a while, I thought to myself, then I will send it to Mam. This way, we both can benefit from Cynthia's generosity.

As we drove out of Manchester I saw the damage that had been done in the bombing. There were children's toys scattered amidst the crushed bricks, bedsteads sticking out, chair legs and tables. It was terrible to think of people being attacked in their own homes, terrorized for hours by the bombing, and then buried in those piles of rubble and their families desperate to get them out. I could not bear it. I prayed silently to keep my brother safe, for Seán had joined up despite the fact that de Valera had declared Ireland neutral. Mam had wanted Seán to join the LDF and stay in Ireland, but he was determined to leave. There were thousands of boys needed work and took the opportunity.

"You'll never see me fighting for the bloody English," Brendan had said.

"Not *for* them, *with* them," Seán replied, though we all knew he hadn't a leg to stand on. But, I'm no better, am I, working for them, making their beds and raising their children?

"You go to hell with the rest of the mercenaries!" Brendan shouted at our Seán. "I'll be here at home fighting to end the partition of our country."

Brendan's the eldest of us and he remembers the war of independence. He was fighting down in Kerry when I was learning to walk. I'd grown up on stories of that war and here I was in the middle of an even bigger one. Brendan never gave up his loyalty to the IRA, though it had lost popularity with the threat of German invasion. And I'd heard that the more active members were being interned without trial, so I worried all the time for our Brendan.

"If the Germans win we'll be rewarded for our neutrality with a united Ireland," Seán said.

"And I'll stop calling you Alice when you stop living in Wonderland," Brendan replied. "Wake up, Seán! This is not a war against Hitler. It's not to prevent the partition of Poland. It's to protect the bloody British Empire! And there you go, you mad eejit, laying down your life like a fool for stuttering George!"

My brothers were always fighting—giving each other bloody noses and black eyes. War drives families apart, it does. Look what happened in this very house. Cynthia would never have wanted to kill her baby if it hadn't been for the war.

Just then, as though I'd brought it on with my wicked thoughts, we heard the sirens. We were on the outskirts of Stockport when Cynthia turned the wheel suddenly and took a left turn.

"We're close to the hat factory," she said. "It's in Offerton, only a mile or so. We'll take shelter there until the raid is over."

"But it's the factories they go for," I said, clutching at my handbag. Lord knows where I thought I was going to run to with it, and nothing of value in it anyway.

"The last I heard they were targeting munitions and aviation, not hat factories. We'll be in more danger here on the street, Mary. Come on!" she shouted at the car in front of us, and she swerved so violently that I had to brace myself with my arms and legs stretched out rigid while she overtook him. I thanked God for my thick, strong ankles.

We spent the rest of the afternoon drinking tea in her father-in-law's office where I kept my place in the corner and continued to pray for the safety of my family. Dublin had been bombed on January 2nd, by accident they said, "a navigational error," but it happened again, didn't it, and then a third time when they bombed the railway station in May, and I'd thought to myself, three times in a row could hardly be a mistake, and Ireland neutral in this war. But we'd heard Lord

Haw Haw in his broadcast from Germany warning that the Amiens Street Station would be bombed because there was a stream of people arriving from Belfast, trying to take refuge with us. Someone must've been giving the Germans information and I could bet that my brother Brendan and his IRA cronies were in on it.

We would listen in on the wireless at night and Cynthia said Lord Haw Haw, who was an Irish American, had been a member of the BUF too and had fled to Germany so he wouldn't be interned like her husband. The news we heard was terrible during those months with all the big cities being bombed in the Blitz, and people killed and injured in great numbers. It was my introduction to England and a dreadful one. Many a night Cynthia and me would huddle together in our air-raid shelter with the children and I would wonder if we were going to survive, and if I would ever see my dear family again, though we were safer in that small base-ment room with its four bunk beds and a narrow space in between than most people with those flimsy Anderson shelters in their back gardens.

I didn't even know where my brother Seán was with the war mov-ing from country to country. We were all in danger, wherever we were, neutral or not. I had grown up in the bosom of my family with a feeling of great security. I was never alone unless I wanted to be, and I always felt safe as houses. If Brendan and Seán started their ructions I could escape to the fields where the mossy ground was a cushion under my feet, catapulting me into the air as though I were as light as a fairy join-ing my folk in the wild. Now it had all changed and I was in a foreign country that was being blasted to pieces, all the houses burning and falling, just piles of smouldering bricks. Is this what it means to grow up, I wondered? And as that led me to thinking of the children, I glanced at Mr. Brooke senior, their grandpa, who was sat behind his big desk mopping at his moustaches where some drops from his teacup were clinging. I could see him, but I was invisible. I wondered if Birdie and Jim and Charlotte were safe with their grandmother in the air-raid shelter under her house.

Near the end of June news came of the German invasion of Russia. Cynthia and I sat up late listening to the wireless as Mr. Churchill broke the news to us.

"At four o'clock this morning Hitler attacked and invaded Russia," he said. "Suddenly without declaration of war, without even an ultimatum, the German bombs rained down from the sky upon the Russian cities, the German troops violated the Russian frontiers, and an hour later the German Ambassador, who till the night before was lavishing his assurances of friendship, called upon the Russian Foreign Minister to tell him that a state of war existed between Germany and Russia."

We neither of us knew what to make of it. The Germans had shown themselves to be dirty turncoats. The war seemed to be spreading like a disease, with no cure but to rage and rage until the end. "A bloodthirsty guttersnipe," Mr. Churchill called Hitler; "pillage and devastation," he spluttered, sounding more and more angry as he told us about the poor Russian peasants valiantly defending their native soil, only to have their daily bread stolen from them. Well, that was a crime against the Lord's Prayer if ever I heard one. I could hardly bear to listen. It made no sense to me, for I'm an uneducated girl, but neither did it to Cynthia for all her boarding school studies. I was clipping my fingernails while she was painting hers, and then in the middle of all those words he said something that put the fear of God into us:

"Hitler's invasion of Russia is no more than a prelude to an attempted invasion of the British Isles."

I nicked my thumbnail down to the quick and made myself cry out.

"He hopes, no doubt, that all this may be accomplished before the winter comes, and that he can overwhelm Great Britain before the fleet and air power of the United States will intervene."

We sat there staring at each other. What was going to happen to us, all alone with the children and not a whit of support from our neighbours who took us for traitors along with the Master.

Mr. Churchill's opposition to communism had faded away, he said, in the light of the day's events, and he pledged Britain's help for the Soviet Union in any way possible.

"Let us redouble our exertions, and strike with united strength while life and power remain," he concluded, just when we were hoping for an end to it all and the return of the Master to his family.

Chapter Fourteen

ST. BARBE BAKER

Peveril Camp, October 1941

H E SLEEPS ON the third floor of a five-storey boarding house facing the promenade. There are fifty-seven men in the house, cut off from the sea and from the town by a barbed wire fence fifteen feet high and six feet deep. The ruins of Peveril Castle stand on a promontory jutting out from the bay. The old keep is like the Pharos of Alexandria, Christopher thinks as he stares from the bay window —the way it stands apart from the town, heralding its presence. He and Alice had been photographed holding hands on the Corniche that curves around the bay of Alexandria, much like the curve of Peveril Bay. Alice had been twelve years old, and he a teenager, still innocent, before the school trip that autumn to the east end of London, where he had been shocked to see the conditions in which people could live. Perhaps the same poverty had been evident in Alexandria; if so, he had not noticed because he had been in a foreign land where everything had assaulted his senses, clamouring for his attention. Mother and Father had spent their days on the veranda of the Cecil Hotel and had sent their children out with a guide.

He turns from the window to see Ben Glover bent over his bed, folding back the sheet, tucking in the blanket. Though only in his mid-forties, Ben has the comportment of an old man, moving slowly, carefully, around their cramped room. Ben sees him watching and nods in his desultory manner. Christopher learns that Ben, like so many of the

Peveril Camp detainees, is a veteran of the Great War and has suffered shell shock.

"It's affected my working life, you see," Ben says in his broad Lancashire accent.

He's from the industrial town of Bolton, a depressing place in itself, Christopher thinks.

"We never 'ad much where I come from, but at least I 'ad me ambitions. It's m'wife who's kept me goin'. We were walking out together before I went over to France, and she waited for me. But we've not 'ad children. I'm not strong enough."

Christopher clears his throat as he searches for words. "Now look here, Ben Glover. You had the gumption to join British Union and stand behind the Leader. That counts for a great deal."

"I 'eard 'im speak once," Glover says, his back straightening. "'E's a great man. 'E stands up for the working class and that's why I'd follow 'im to the ends of the earth. When 'e speaks there's sparks fly from 'is eyes."

Glover is a Catholic, though less of a believer since his war experience, he says. Suspecting that his room-mate may be semi-literate, Christopher reads to him from the Book of Matthew, a passage marked in his stolen Bible, and read to boost his own faith during the darker times in Walton Gaol and at Latchmere:

> And when he was entered into a ship, his disciples followed him. And behold, there arose a great tempest in the sea, insomuch that the ship was covered with the waves: but he was asleep. And his disciples came to him and awoke him, saying, Lord, save us: we perish. And he saith unto them, Why are ye fearful, O ye of little faith? Then he arose, and rebuked the winds and the sea; and there was a great calm.

Glover listens poker-faced, and when Christopher attempts to engage him on the topic of faith, with a critical view of the Church leaders who have failed to speak out for Peace, he changes the subject. It turns out that Glover was the night watchman of a three storey warehouse for textile and hat-making machinery, Bolton being one of several Lancashire towns with their own hat factories.

"I would've been a hatter like you," he says, "But I was already damaged from the mustard gas, and I didn't need the mad 'atter's disease on top of it, did I?" He summons a half-hearted laugh, referring of course to the tremors and mental instability caused by mercury poisoning. "Boss wouldn't 'old me job at the warehouse. So Gladys is doing it for me. But it's too much for 'er, traipsing up and down all them stairs, and the air-raids on top of it. She's not young any more. She'll be in a state of collapse if this goes on much longer."

Christopher thinks of Cynthia and their children huddled in the air-raid shelter. "We must see this war through together, Ben, as soldiers for justice and truth, building a future for our children. Let us take solace in our fidelity to Sir Oswald Mosley," he says, beginning to pace back and forth across the creaking floorboards. "Ours is an honourable stance, not to be relinquished for our own comfort or convenience. The Leader has been proven right in his analysis of the situation and his push for appeasement because look, Hitler is sweeping across Europe."

"'E's winning," Ben says, nodding.

"You're right, Ben. He does appear the man of destiny, battling it out with the Communists. His troops have taken Kiev and now they're laying siege to Leningrad in the north. And do you know, I'm tempted to applaud. But my feelings of patriotism for King and country are deeply rooted, even though we're now allied with the damned Soviets."

"War is a cruel animal," Ben says, "biting at its own 'eels."

Christopher nods. "It gives everyone cause for reappraisal of their more simple-minded opinions."

He begins to prepare summaries of the daily news bulletins broadcast by the BBC which he hears at one of the many boarding houses requisitioned for their five-acre Camp. That particular house is fortunate in having a loudspeaker and Christopher listens to the news with a group that includes Thomas St. Barbe Baker, another war veteran and an interesting fellow, Christopher thinks. And there's George Unsworth, a rather withdrawn man with a shock of unruly dark hair, and apparently a man of privilege like Christopher himself, judging by the regular parcels he receives filled with expensive foodstuffs.

During the month of October, with the help of daily newspapers and BBC bulletins, Christopher is able to inform his companions on many topics ranging from Mahatma Gandhi's urging of passive resistance to British rule in India to the heavy losses suffered by the RAF during the October 7th night bombings over Berlin, the Ruhr and Cologne.

Christopher attended Church with his parents throughout childhood and still remembers the weekly collects he memorized from the Book of Common Prayer, to be recited for his mother on Sunday afternoons before tea. If he was word-perfect she would nod her approval and give him an extra slice of cake, the sweetness of it filling him as he munched proudly. When he begins to air his religious beliefs for the benefit of the men peeling potatoes in the camp kitchen, he is flattered by Thom Baker's attentions. Unsworth listens quietly, nodding from time to time, but Baker, a fervent Christian, applauds Christopher's opinions in a loud and somewhat embarrassing manner. His applause is verbal, his hands being crippled with arthritis, he claims.

"The Great War, Brooke, did me no good. Affected all my joints. I did not like that war, Sir, not one bit. Buried alive during the shelling when I was a junior officer, fought my way up to 2nd lieutenant in the Royal field artillery, ended up a Captain in the Royal Flying Corps."

Baker's narrow chest puffs with pride. When he proposes their collaboration on a lecture entitled "Is Biblical prophecy being fulfilled today?" Christopher jumps at the chance.

"I used to sport a walrus moustache," Baker says. "But I had to shave it off when I was on the run. Dammit, they caught me anyway!"

Christopher laughs with him, showing the lucky gap between his front teeth. It is a long time since he's had reason to laugh.

"I've grown quite partial to the clean-shaven look," Baker says. "I've nothing to hide, Christopher. I stand unrepentant for the truth."

Thom Baker is as enthusiastic and confident as Ben Glover is dour, Christopher thinks. He looks forward to Baker's company, and only in the night now, with Ben Glover snoring across the room, does he allow himself to succumb to that feeling of futility that assaulted him at Latchmere.

Under the wet slap and slosh of my mother's heart I feel a scraping of stones pulling, sucking in waves that burrow pathways beneath the splashing organ that threatens to drown us even as it feeds me.

He listens to the pounding of waves and is haunted by the smell and touch of his Cynthia, so alive in his memory of their honeymoon at Rhosneigr that he can almost feel her there beside him. He prays for something to happen, something that will take him home. And then the news comes of his father's heart attack. He immediately requests permission for leave. When the Advisory Committee approves his leave, a grinning Baker shakes Christopher's hand vigorously and says: "God was listening when I interceded on your behalf."

By the time he arrives at Dinglewood, his father is home from the hospital and recovering well. Nancy Brooke asks her son to keep his visits short and to avoid talking politics. She communicates her wishes by euphemism, smiling as ever. She has survived an identical twin who died at birth, and her mother who died three years later. She has walked miles and miles beside her father, a strict Victorian clasping the hand of his only child. And when she turned twelve he gave her a brooch to wear with the name "Frank" picked out in precious stones, to commemorate her dead twin. Then he remarried and Nancy became subject to a rather cold stepmother. She has learned through loss to live at a safe distance.

Christopher offers to go down to the factory and check on wartime progress of the business. James Brooke declines his offer. As early as 1936 the tide of public opinion had turned against Mosley, and Christopher had received an ultimatum in writing, signed by his own father, informing him that he must choose between his membership in the British Union of Fascists and his position as Board Director of Brooke Hats. Christopher feels relieved not to have to face what would surely be open hostility from the men at the factory. He strides up the pebbled drive of his own house and raps on the door. The children are thrilled to have their daddy home for a whole week.

Chapter Fifteen

GIVE ME A PUSH, SIR

October 1941

CYNTHIA TOLD ME that when war broke out in earnest, after eight months of the phoney war with hundreds of children evacuated and sent home again just as the bombing started, they had interned all the Mosleyites. Sir Oswald himself was sent to prison, and his beautiful wife Diana in Holloway Prison for Women, separated from her little children.

"What a comedown for the high and mighty," Cynthia had said.

But the Master was a loyal man and wouldn't give up his convictions. I'd heard Cynthia shouting at him the first night he was home after visiting his father.

"Give it up! Give it up!" she shouted. "You men and your bloody politics!" And him *shushing* her like a mother with a child, but she wouldn't have it. There was something untouchable about him, and that was what taunted her. It was a circle of light in him, shining on another world where no-one else could go. He held it there and it sustained him, but perhaps in this world it's not a good thing to be held aloof. We all have to get down to it together, none so high and mighty as to be apart from the dirt of life.

Next morning the children were kneeling on the floor, bent over a game of Snakes and Ladders while I was dusting the piano lid, so dark and shiny you could see your reflection in it. Jimmy's chin rested on his bunched-up fists, his bottom up in the air as he studied the board, and Charlotte was sitting nicely, her skirt tucked in around her, while Birdie fidgeted impatiently.

"My turn, my turn," she chirped, and then we heard the front door slam.

It was the Master back from visiting his father. Cynthia had gone with him this time. She wouldn't let him out of her sight and clung onto his arm, gazing up at him. She was well into her pregnancy now, and riper than ever with her round belly. The children ran circles around them, getting Percy the dog overexcited and causing him to bark and jump up, but they soon settled again to their game, and I was about to leave the room, feeling myself an intruder in this rare family gathering, when Cynthia said: "No, Mary, don't mind us, finish your dusting." So I was witness to what happened next.

The Master had the newspaper spread on his lap and was leaning over it, his brow furrowed. "Germany is making headway in the Soviet Union," he said. "An official state of siege has been announced in Moscow, and the city is under martial law. Kharkov has fallen. And look here, they've reached Sebastopol in the Crimea. At this rate the entire area will have to be remapped."

He looked up expectantly, but Cynthia only sat there tight-lipped. He rustled the newspaper and turned to the next page.

"Hmm, I see that Japan has elected a new prime minister, a former general of the Japanese army, so we can expect some sparks from ..."

"Why can't you be here with us?" she said, slamming her fist down on the open page of the newspaper. "It's too much for me, all alone with the children."

Birdie's eyes started rolling as she tugged at her dress, trying to find that spider again.

"Darling we've been over this before. You know I have no control over the situation."

"Ask them again, Chris," she pleaded. "Make a petition, tell them about our special circumstances."

She meant of course her pregnancy, and she began to cry, big tears welling up as she reached across him for a cigarette.

"Please, Cynthia, not now, you know I don't like to see you smoking."

"I *will* smoke. I *want* one."

She flicked the cigarette lighter and sucked on the blue flame. Jimmy started coughing and wheezing.

"A six! I got a six," he exclaimed. "I'm going up a big ladder! Your turn, Charlie."

"Don't call me that!" Charlotte hissed.

The Master had his arm around Cynthia and she turned her head away, blowing a stream of smoke into the corner. She didn't inhale. It was all for show.

"Oh no!"

"Ha, ha, longest snake on the board!" Jimmy shouted. "Go on, back to the beginning. I'm going to win this game." But on the next round he was crestfallen because he landed on the very same snake. He tried to bluff it and move his marker one more space, but Charlotte caught him.

"Oh no you don't," she said. "I saw you cheating, Jimmy."

He tipped up the board and all the markers went flying.

"It's not fair!" he shouted, and punched the carpet.

Birdie began to cry and when her mother told her to be quiet she clenched her teeth hard into her lower lip and made it bleed. Cynthia turned away and stubbed out her cigarette. Her hand was on his arm, gripping it. They disappeared upstairs soon after that, leaving me in charge, and they must have sorted it out because the next day, my birthday, passed without incident. In fact I'd even go so far as to say we had some fun.

The game started at Sunday dinner over roast beef. What with wartime rationing we were lucky to have it, from the farmer in the field behind our house. It was a tough piece of meat, but I had soaked it in red wine from a corked bottle I'd found at the back of the pantry, and I added several cloves of garlic from our own garden. Cynthia said it reminded her of the lunchtime fare in France at Madame Plasse's house, and I was flattered, and thanked my mam again for teaching me what she knew of cookery, but truth be told it was the necessity of softening the old cow that led to my success. My mam certainly never wasted good drink in the cooking pot.

"Let's see who can get through the hatch quickest," Jimmy said, full of glee with his father home.

Our hatch was a small opening between the kitchen and dining room, meant for the passing through of food, not for the scrambling of children, but they all went through and were timed, leaving Jimmy in the lead at 20 seconds. Then Charlotte tugged at me and said: "Come on, Mary. You have to go through. And Mummy and Daddy."

My first thought was to hang back, but there was such a feeling of jollity that day that I allowed myself to be lured into the game, as though I were one of the family.

I went around to the kitchen where the Master was waiting to help me up onto the counter. The hatch was a very small space to be sure, and I started to feel short of breath at the prospect of forcing myself through there.

"Give me a push, Sir," I said, red-faced already with the effort of climbing up onto the counter, and I turned redder yet with the pleasure of his hands on my backside, and the embarrassment of my stockinged legs sticking out behind me. The Master gave me a mighty shove, and the first thing I saw as my hips burst through was Cynthia doubled over, clutching her stomach, with tears streaming down her face. Jimmy and Charlotte had their hands over their mouths, shaking with laughter, and Birdie, too young to know any better, screamed with joy to see me floundering on the serving table beside a dish of chocolate blancmange bunnies circled with green jelly. Here I am, a brown bunny like Da said, I thought as I wriggled into a sitting position and slid off the serving table, getting my skirt smeared with beef fat.

"53 seconds!" His laughing voice, head through the hatch. "Your turn, Darling!"

Cynthia waved her hand, helpless with laughter, and her face as red as mine. She wouldn't go through, not with the new baby growing inside her, already five and a half months gone. What would it be this time, I wondered? Jimmy needs a brother. He's surrounded by females with the Master away all the time.

They all went out to the garden to enjoy the fine autumn day and left me to clear up the dirty dishes, even though it was my twenty-third birthday and they'd sang to me over the blancmange bunnies.

If you could have stood beside me at the window that day and seen the Master tossing Birdie up in the air, Cynthia pushing Charlotte on the swing, and Jimmy swiping at the grass with his cricket bat, you would have thought they were the perfect family, but you would have been wrong. All you had to do was watch those children in their Magic Circle. It was not play they were at, but something desperate and dark with a terrible innocence about it.

Get on with it, Mary Byrne, I told myself, plunging the dishes into soapy water and grasping the pan scrub firmly. Standing there at the sink, lamenting my humble situation, I had to confess that his presence in the house stirred me up, with heat rising through my body from between my solid Irish legs. All I'd ever wanted was a man in my bed to keep me warm, a good dinner in my belly, and my own babies to hold, and here I was 23 already with time slipping away from me, witnessing other people's lives while mine was at a standstill. Did I cross the channel for this, to want and want and never get?

I had been surprised to find him in my kitchen again that morning, though I had thought at first glance it was a tradesman come in on an errand—or any one of the poor rejects who'd been turned down for enlistment and were taking their pick of odd jobs. He was sat at my kitchen table staring at the pile of potatoes I was to peel for the roasting pan with the tough cut of beef. He had looked up at me, smiling, and said: "That's one of my jobs at Peveril Camp. Can I help you?"

"Oh no, Sir," I said. "This is women's work." I bit my tongue, thinking what a daft thing to say. But he seemed not to take offence. Perhaps he hadn't even noticed. He told me there was Irish blood on his father's side. "County Monaghan, Mary, bordering on Northern Ireland."

Well, I didn't need a geography lesson, did I?

"Ah sure, Sir, isn't that where I'm from, near the town of Cavan. Monaghan is the next county over."

"Look in the telephone book there and you'll find my name."

He didn't know that the likes of us don't have call for telephone books, and I didn't enlighten him. He was trying to make me feel I was his kinswoman, and it was a warm generous feeling, to be sure, though his family were likely displaced English or Scots planted there, pretending to be Irish because they live on our land.

I wanted to take his big hand in mine, lay it palm up on my knee and smooth it with my own hand, running my fingers across the soft pads of his fingers, tracing a circle to the centre of his palm where all the feeling is. I'd glanced at his hand without him knowing and I'd seen enough to determine there was nothing good in his future. I was to read it more clearly at a later date. But for now I knew his heart would be broken, and I wished that I could save him, but there's nothing to be done when it's scored in your hand.

I looked down at my own hands all red and wet, still grasping the pan scrub which was greasy from the roasting pan. I saw a long life and perhaps two children, but they wouldn't be his. I knew that. I saw myself living with some rough fellow. I could see his face, brown like mine, but he was a sharp little weasel, eyes close together, narrow shoulders, not a healthy man. All this way to live with a man like that —Why didn't you keep me home, Da, where I'd have been satisfied with my life? You can't escape your destiny, but you can dream. That's all I had, my dreams of glory.

I would lie under my weasel man, I thought, a brown bunny, and dream of my Master. I'd have given up all my dreams for a day in Cynthia's shoes, those fancy shoes she wore on her dainty feet. What must it be like to have hips so slim and a tight little bottom? She has a big bosom like mine, but on her it looks different with her slender body and the bones jutting in her white face. I'd seen her eat, ravenous like an animal since the baby had rooted itself in her. They say you can tell how a woman loves by watching her eat; famished, as though the Devil himself was driving her. But the Master ate like a gentleman, slowly, savouring his food and dabbing at his lips with a napkin. Who could have seen how it all would end? In truth I never have stopped thinking about him, even after all these years.

I had dried one batch of dishes and went to clear the last of them, hauling them through the hatch, when I saw her in the back garden with her dark eyes flashing, setting off sparks all around her. That's what he wants, I thought. He needs her fire because he's like me, always holding back. It's not my nature to be a mild-mannered servant, it's my position calls for it— "Clear the table, Mary, polish the silver, dust the sideboard ..." But what prevents him? And why does God favour the wrong ones? Why does He give her all the beauty and I get nothing but my brown skin and my solid sensible body like a comfortable walking shoe, with no-one to make up a pair?

When I'd dried the last of the dishes I glanced out again and that's when I knew it must be time for him to leave, because Charlotte was clinging onto his arm and Birdie was running circles around him squealing, and there was Jimmy with his hang-dog look, and Cynthia bunched like a thundercloud with her arms folded across her bosom and the new baby swelling out underneath.

There was bound to be an argument—it always happened before he left—then she'd run upstairs and slam the bedroom door and I'd be left with her children—Birdie screaming, Jimmy hunched over like a wounded animal, and Charlotte all buttoned up, trying to pretend nothing was wrong. What could I do with them? There was no fighting in our house. Da was the peacemaker. Couldn't get a rise out of him with a pound of yeast.

I would take the children to the air-raid shelter, where it was safe, and we would light the candles and pretend we were on a camping holiday in an underground cave. I'd hold Birdie on my knee and bounce her up and down. "We're in your little birdhouse, love," I'd say. "A small place to be safe in, to take shelter."

I ran back to the scullery and made up a packet of sandwiches with thick slices of beef left over from our dinner and horseradish sauce slathered all over the way he liked it. They didn't feed him enough in that camp. You could see his ribs standing out under his shirt. If I was a man I'd still love him, though in a different way. He's what I came to England for, I know that now. The feeling I'd had of something waiting for me, the first advertisement in the *Help Wanted*, the first telephone call, as though God was pointing the way from Heaven with His Big Finger. He treated me like an equal from the beginning. Not her, not until later, and then only when it suited her. Even though she acted friendly and confided in me I didn't fool myself it was genuine. She had no-one else to talk to, that was the truth of it. Meg had cottoned onto her right away.

"She's spoiled," she said. "Got no heart."

And I thought to myself, she's just angry at Cynthia for backing out, especially after she'd seen that wad of money sticking out of her handbag. Meg was always hard up in spite of her work as an angel-maker. She was too soft-hearted with the girls.

"Never mind, lovie," she'd say. "Pay me when you can." And of course, she'd never see them again—until the next time they needed her.

But Meg was on the right track about Cynthia, though she wasn't quite correct. Cynthia does have a heart, but it's damaged. We need to care for one another and she's not had what she needed. If she had she would've been able to take care of him. He was a lost soul. I would've taken care of him if I hadn't been held back by my station in life, and by my fat behind and thick legs. You'd never know from my plain face what goes on inside me. You're not supposed to have strong feelings unless you're beautiful, or at least pretty. I'd seen his future and I would have changed it, except that I couldn't, because I couldn't change my own any more than I can change this moon of a face.

Chapter Sixteen

NEW SHOES

CHRISTOPHER RETURNS TO face his first winter at Peveril Camp, with the inevitable storms that begin to buffet that small island stranded in the Irish Sea. He imagines himself at war, being attacked from all sides by a faceless enemy, which is how nature can manifest, like the plagues and pestilences documented in his Walton Bible, that book accompanying him everywhere now, talismanic, tucked into his jacket pocket. He has brought with him from home some sturdy winter wear—woollen pullovers, socks, gloves, and rubber wellington boots, together with several shirts and pairs of trousers which he distributes to the men eager to replace their worn clothing and down-at-heel footwear. Christopher has replaced his own shoes with a pair of brown leather brogues from his well-stocked wardrobe and has provided a similar pair for Ben Glover who shares his foot size. Thom Baker's feet are smaller, but he claims the black oxfords Christopher has brought and cheerfully fills the extra space with two pairs of thick woollen socks.

"Let's hope it's a boy," Baker says, when he hears about the new baby on its way. "I have a son myself, and a devoted wife in Norfolk. Muriel writes frequently on my behalf to Herbert Morrison at the Home Office. She signs herself 'Your Most Humble Servant,' in an ironic sense of course." He winks. "Women can get away with the semblance of subservience, but don't be fooled, Christopher. They're all demons under their angelic exterior." Christopher chuckles along with Baker, feeling quite daring.

As winter draws on the men are driven indoors where tempers become testy, and Christopher finds himself defending Baker when the physically inferior man is threatened by a group of BUF supporters.

"You're not one of us," someone shouts when he greets them at breakfast with: "*Sieg Heil!* Good news, my hearties ... bombs over Bolton last night."

Ben Glover is particularly upset and Christopher has to explain to him Baker's peculiar sense of humour. "He was damaged in the Great War, you see, Ben. Buried alive, shell shock, had a breakdown."

"Don't try to tell me about shell shock! I was in that bloody war myself. I know all about shell shock. The lads are right. 'E's not one of us. 'E only joined British Union two years ago because the Nordic League went under. And our Leader said 'e wouldn't have nothing to do with that League on account of its 'extremist rhetoric,' his very words. 'E warned against it. And I warn you against Baker. Watch out for him, lad. 'E was a member of the Right Club. Jew-'aters, every one of 'em. 'E's looking for rich company, you mark my words."

Chapter Seventeen

A BIG BLACK CROSS

WITH THE ADVANCE of her pregnancy Cynthia leaned on me more than ever until I began to feel I was the man of the house. She would do that—make you into the one who felt responsible. She made the decisions, but she couldn't do it without someone to kick against.

It was a long winter and we had the opportunity of many nights huddled together in the dark with the glow of the coal fire flickering on our faces, and the dusty tar-smell of the coal so different from the aroma of burning peat I was accustomed to. We felt safe there, close to the air-raid shelter where we had candles and matches stored, with a jug of water and a tin of biscuits, as well as a chamber pot for emergencies. And sometimes, when we'd been warned to expect trouble, we all slept downstairs in our clothes with a flask of hot tea at the ready.

But often as not the sirens would go off in the middle of the night when we were asleep upstairs. It was a terrible sound that entered my throat and made it thick with wanting to cry, but there was no time for that. I would get my dressing gown and slippers on and busy myself with rounding up the children and getting them downstairs to the safety of the shelter, trying all the while not to think about what might happen and whether these were my final moments on earth. There is nothing like an emergency to bring you into the moment. I didn't have time to pray, but the care of the children was a kind of prayer, and they brought me more comfort than God or Jesus ever could. We got used to the air-raids. And of course, we were accustomed to the roar of aeroplane engines because the A.V. Roe factory where they made the Lancaster bombers was just down the road towards Wilmslow.

In the beginning of December, just as we were beginning to think about Christmas and what we could do to make it nice for the children, something terrible happened. The Japanese bombed Pearl Harbour, and declared war on Britain and the United States, which brought the Americans into the war in earnest. I thought to myself there'll be no toasting a speedy end to the war this New Year's Eve. Cynthia and I listened to Mr. Churchill's speech on the wireless and I must say he sounded rather pleased.

"The Cabinet has authorized an immediate declaration of war on Japan," he said in that measured way he had of speaking with lots of pauses for his great thoughts, and his mouth full of something thick, as though his tongue were too big for it. He told us that the Japs had attacked British territory in Northern Malaya and that our soldiers were there waiting for them.

"No time has been lost," he said, and I could just see him puffing triumphantly on his big cigar. Cynthia said his mother was American and that's why he was pleased that the Americans were coming into the war as our allies. "We'll stand a better chance now, Mary," she said.

It was in early January on one of the coldest of nights that she went into labour. I woke with a start and heard her calling down the corridor.

"Mary! Call the doctor! My water's broken!"

The children were already out of bed and clamouring to get into her room. Charlotte stood staring inside the open door, her eyes so big and frightened, but she wouldn't let the other children past her. I picked up Birdie and tried to take hold of Charlotte's hand, but she pulled away and crouched down by the door jamb, so I let her be.

"Come on, Jimmy," I said. "We're going downstairs."

I telephoned Archer Pearson and he came with the midwife. They were there right fast—he only lived a mile down the road—and he took the stairs three at a time with his long legs, but by then she was calling for Christopher. You'd think it was her first baby the way she moaned and wailed. There was no getting the children back to sleep, so I kept them with me in the kitchen while I boiled up four big pans of water.

"How's the baby going to get out?" Jimmy asked, and Birdie thrust her tummy forward, pointing at her belly button. Charlotte had come slinking downstairs when the doctor arrived, and she had a long face on her, missing her father I expect. We hadn't seen him since the October visit which had coincided with my birthday. It had been a quiet Christmas with Cynthia refusing to go to her mother's house and just the two of us with the children. The Isle of Man was too far away for Cynthia in her condition, though some of the wives had been granted visiting rights. She waited every morning for the postman to come—Percy would start barking to sound the alarm—it was the only time she didn't shout at him, the poor miserable creature—and it was a wonder to see her face light up as she recognized the Master's handwriting and held his letter to her heart.

It was seven in the morning when we heard Cynthia's scream, then a thin wail, swelling into full-blown protest. Jimmy's face broke into a grin and Birdie jumped up and down.

"My baby! My baby!" she shouted. "Mummy says I can look after it."

Charlotte brightened then and said: "Let's go up and see if it's a boy!"

We all trooped upstairs and stood quietly outside the door while I knocked.

"Come in!" boomed Dr. Pearson. He was a big slop of a man with loose lips that foamed with spittle at the corners. He had a reckless look about him with his hair drooping in his eyes and his hands all bloody from the birth. The midwife had likely done all the work but he was intent on being the hero. Cynthia looked pale and tired. I walked around to the other side of the bed and took her hand.

"Are you all right now? You've done a grand job. It's a miracle to be sure!"

I saw the little one, tucked into the crook of her left arm, a crop of dark hair all wet from the waters, and a red face scrunched against the world. The children were quiet now, tip-toeing over to the bed.

Birdie was licking her lips and chewing at them and Jimmy's grin had shrunk to a smirk.

"I can look after it, Mum," Charlotte said. "Is it a boy?"

"She's a girl," Cynthia said, with a gentle smile. "I'm going to call her Katharine. Take her, Mary, show her to the children."

I leaned down and took the bundle from her and my heart took me by surprise. The child had unlocked me and I had to turn away and sit in the rocking chair beside the bed, keeping my head down to hide my tears as the children clustered around me. Jimmy started counting her fingers and toes while Charlotte laid her hand on the baby's chest. She was all bundled up in a white shawl like a shrunken old lady.

"Me, me, I want to hold her!" Birdie shouted, jumping up and down impatiently.

"No, Birdie, you can't hold her yet, darlin'," I said. "She's too small and new in the world." I could feel the tiny heart beating under the palm of my hand and I watched her mouth working and her neck wobbling as she began to root at me. I wished they'd all go away and let me rock with her. I'd have put her to my breast in a minute and guaranteed she'd find milk there. As I held her I had a taste of the freedom she'd brought from that place she'd come from, on loan to us for a spell. Cynthia was softer than I'd ever seen her, the way people are when they've had a brush with the other world, and I understood then how it was that her husband loved her. She asked me to telephone the camp and send word to him.

A girl answered and put me through to the superintendent, a fellow with a gruff voice. He heard me out, all dewy-eyed as I was after holding the new babe, and he said he'd give the message to Mr. Brooke.

"Will he be coming home?" I asked.

"That's not for me to say," he replied.

"But you're in charge, and it's not every day a man becomes a father. We're all women here, apart from little Jimmy. It's a crime keeping an able-bodied man there at a holiday resort, when he should be home with his family."

The line went dead before I'd finished, but I felt better for giving him an earful. Of course, the Master didn't come home, not for several months. It was cruel of them.

I'd become a dab hand at the telephone after all my nervousness. I hardly remembered the first time I'd used it, to inquire about the *Help Wanted*. Somehow when you're new to everything you just get on with it and you don't remember how you did it. We spend a lot of time worrying about things that will take care of themselves. Though I do remember my first telephone call in Cynthia's house. She had gone to her mother's down the road in Poynton village, and Jimmy fell on the slippery steps by the coal house and cut his head open. Oh Lord, I thought his skull was cracked the way head wounds bleed, but by the time I'd mopped up the worst of it I could see it was only a small cut, but perhaps needing a stitch or two. So I'd picked up the telephone and asked the operator for the number, thinking that could have been me, a switchboard operator sitting on my behind all day talking with strangers in distant places.

I held the receiver at a distance from my ear because I have acute hearing, and when I heard Cynthia's voice I started babbling, but she couldn't hear me, because the mouthpiece was too far away. "Hello? Hello?" she kept on saying and finally, with a combination of shouting and common sense I got the message through and she came home immediately. She always responded to a crisis, I'll say that for her. It seemed to bring out the best in her, to draw the real caring from her heart. But then the whole wartime was a crisis, wasn't it? It wore us all down, too long and drawn out to sustain any kind of caring.

She was a quiet baby with a dreamy look as though she was still in the other world, and reluctant to enter ours. She needed coaxing to feed at all. If we hadn't paid her so much attention, picking her up at all hours and the children buzzing around her like a swarm of honey bees, I think she might have drifted away. Katie had no real presence in the world in those first months. She was far away like her father, with something untouchable about her, as though no-one could ever love her enough to make up for what she had lost. I liked to hold her and sing to her when Cynthia was resting, and I'd watch the movement of her eyes under those pale lids that were almost transparent.

Later on, when she began to focus, she would cast around as

though she were looking for someone who wasn't there. She would stare into the shadows, entranced with the darkness she found there. The Master's family came to see her—his sister Alice, all the way from London, and old Mr. and Mrs. Brooke. Cynthia's sisters came, Ruby and Margaret, two such cheerful girls, and Margaret with her camera, snapping pictures of the new baby. It was a good while before Mrs. Dorothy Blackwell graced us with her presence and even then she was all pursed up as though she did not approve of another child in the house. But who can resist an innocent baby?

She was a wakeful child and in her third week she began to cry urgently until I'd pick her up and carry her downstairs. Once I'd put her into Cynthia's arms she'd lay there wide-eyed, staring up at her, trembling and hiccoughing in that way that babies have when they've worn themselves out.

There's one night sticks in my mind forever. The children had only just settled in bed, and Cynthia and I were having our supper in the sitting room. That had become a habit with us. After feeding the children at the dining room table with the gas fire flaring and popping, I'd clear up while she got them to bed, then I'd carry our meal in and we'd eat with trays on our knees in front of the coal fire.

The siren started at 7.35—I remember looking at the clock on the mantle. You do that in wartime, never knowing if it will be your last minute. We abandoned our supper and rushed upstairs to get the children. Cynthia grabbed the baby and ran down to the shelter while I got the other three.

"Don't bother searching for your slippers, Birdie," I said. "We've got woollen socks in the shelter."

I could hear the planes flying ever so low, with explosions all around us, and I was so frightened I could hardly think. Jimmy had his hands over his ears and couldn't hear me, so I slapped at his hands and then I felt terrible, adding to the boy's distress when I should be helping him. No sooner had we all crowded into the shelter and closed the door than there was a ... I can't say it was a sound, although there was a roaring, like a lion, or an engine revving up ... no, it was more like the feeling of an impact, as though the house had been struck, and the walls shook around us, they did really. We were all speechless. I looked at Cynthia and her face was chalk white. Will we roast in here, I asked myself, buried alive? Oh God that I had stayed on the farm, safe with my own dear family. I got down on my knees and I began to pray like an eejit, but I had got no further than "Hail Mary, full of grace, the Lord is with thee," when there was a terrible whining sound and an almighty crash. It was deafening. Then everything went silent and at first I thought I *had* gone deaf. But then I heard the planes receding into the night, and Birdie beginning to cry.

"My bones are shaking," she said, weeping, and I got up off my knees and took her in my arms.

"Is it safe to go out, Mummy?" Jim asked.

"Let's wait a bit longer, Jumbo," she replied and she reached out her arm and snuggled him into her, the baby crooked in her other arm. That left Charlotte all alone so I held out my hand to her, but she turned the other way.

"Cuckoo, cuckoo," she said, and I knew what she meant. She and Jimmy had been learning from a library book about birds, and he'd told us at supper that the cuckoo is a bird that makes its home in other birds' nests. It pushes them out and takes over. That's how Charlotte felt about me, that I had moved in and pushed her father out, though she had it backwards of course but she had to have someone to blame. And perhaps there was a grain of truth in it now that I was getting thick with Cynthia, but that wasn't my doing. It was her that controlled it, turning to me instead of to her children. But when he came home it all changed at the drop of his hat on the hall stand. At bottom of it I felt Charlotte was suspicious of me. We were peas in a pod. She read me as I read her, but she wanted to be the only one in the house who could see it all.

"Cuckoo, cuckoo," Birdie started up, and then Jimmy joined in. "Cuckoo, Mary Moo."

"Oh be quiet," Cynthia snapped, though she didn't understand what Charlotte had started. It was just that her nerves were frayed. I went up the basement steps and ventured outside by the French doors into the back garden. That's when I saw the scattering of brick cracked all over the stones of our crazy paving, and there was a wicked stink in the air, raw and harsh, the smell of bombs.

When I looked up at the back wall of the house and into the sky, which was dark but for a brilliance of stars, I saw the outline of our chimney broken like a jagged tooth and I thought, Lord, how could that have happened? And I realized how lucky we were to be alive. It was a miracle to have come so close, to be touched by the enemy and to be spared. I heard a crackling sound and I turned and saw it, a big blaze on the edge of the woods that bordered the field behind our house. There was a heap of twisted metal with flames leaping from it and a wing sticking up out of the ground and on that wing was a big black cross. It was the symbol of the Luftwaffe, as I learned later, but all I could think of in that moment was an ambulance with the red cross burned black in the fire, and I realized I was crossing myself as though I were in church and praying that the men had parachuted themselves out before the crash.

I ran inside and told Cynthia to call for the fire brigade. As she was talking on the telephone the all clear sounded so I brought the children into the sitting room and I went upstairs for blankets and pillows and got them all bedded down on the sofa. Birdie fixed me with her big blue eyes, licking furiously at her lips.

"Have they gone away for good, Mary?" she asked.

"They won't be coming back tonight, Birdie," I said. "Now you settle down and get yourself some shut-eye, there's a good girl."

At the other end of the sofa Jim and Charlotte lay pressed together like sardines, she the little mother with her arm around his shoulders. I checked his breathing because I thought he might be after having an asthma attack with all the excitement, but he was breathing gently in Charlotte's arms.

"Why are we sleeping here, Mary Moo?" he asked in his husky boy voice.

"So we can all be together," Charlotte answered before I could get a word in. Well, she was right. That was exactly it. Not a word had been said. We just knew we needed to stay together after what had happened.

There were china pieces in the cabinet had broken with the trembling of the house, and Cynthia found two cracked tiles by the fireplace. The grand piano had shifted on its wheels—I could see from the indentations on the carpet—such a big instrument yet it was sensitive, its wire strings vibrating from under the lid as I shoved it back into place. I even thought I heard a distant music—then Cynthia said: "I hope Christopher is safe."

By that she meant, I wish he was here with us, looking after us. I always picked up her thoughts, especially about him. I tucked her and the baby in with a heavy woollen blanket covering them from shoulder to ankle. She insisted on sitting upright in the big armchair, so I settled myself on the second sofa next to her. I'm a short woman, only five foot two, and with my legs pulled up and my knees touching my breasts, I'm small as a child. It felt good to be all together after the emergency, all breathing the same chilly air, our breath vaporizing as we whispered, and the warmth creeping around us as our bodies heated up under the blankets.

I lay over her splashing heart, which had softened now to a lub dub, my head cushioned on her breast. When she spoke her voice flowed through me, a river. We were joined still, but everything was different; a blurred world of confusing dimension after my cave of blind longing. When she left me alone I was desolate, for although I could not feel her I was with her, part of her. Where was she? Where was he?

"We must get a man over tomorrow," Cynthia said, "to repair the chimney."

I went to the window and pulled back the curtain. The plane was burning in the field and I thought what if it's still carrying a bomb and it explodes? I closed the curtain and then I began to shudder violently, my teeth chattering so hard I had to clench my jaw to control it. I must be calm for the children, I thought, meanwhile a scream was gathering in me and it took a great force of will to restrain it and keep my silence. I went over and over in my mind how it could have happened.

"Did you hear me, Mary? The chimney."

I turned and looked at her leaning forward in her armchair beside the dying fire. I saw the chimney directly above us, travelling through the ceiling into Cynthia's bedroom, reaching past the picture of Jesus that hung over her bedroom fireplace, emerging onto the roof—the breath of the house, shattered by its brush with the enemy. I would go over to the Walkley Estates in the morning and look for Reg. He was a handyman who lived in his own caravan behind Meg's. She said he was related to her, second cousin several times removed, that's how he'd been introduced to me as I'd sat supping my tea in Meg's kitchen. There'd been something familiar about him and it had niggled at me though I couldn't tell at that time exactly what it was. Perhaps I'd seen him in Bramhall village.

"Why aren't you at war then?" I'd asked.

"Weak lungs," he'd said, his shoulders held high and a slight wheeze to his breathing, but he smoked, didn't he? That wad of Gold Leaf tobacco sticking out of his shirt pocket, and a packet of cigarette papers worrying at his hand. He had long fingers with big raw knuckles.

"Failed me medical, so I volunteered for the Home Guard," he'd said, with a toss of his head, bright eyes twinkling, and then he'd told me about his fire-watching and his sentry duty at the A.V. Roe factory, so I reckoned he'd be game to run up a ladder and tackle our chimney.

"Remember that play we listened to, Mary?" Cynthia said, interrupting my thoughts.

"About the albino chimney murderer?"

She nodded as Jimmy stirred in his sleep and coughed a couple of times, but then he settled. The girls were sleeping soundly.

"Remember how frightened we were at the end?" she asked. "You didn't want to go back to your room."

Of course I remembered. We'd been listening to the wireless in her bedroom because she couldn't sleep. "It's a long corridor, Cynthia," I had said. "And it's already past midnight." "Oh come on then, curl up on his bed," she'd said. And I'd done it. I'd slept inches from her on the Master's bed, not inside the sheets mind you, but on top of the counterpane with the eiderdown thrown over me and all my clothes on. What did they do—push the beds together? Or did he slide in with her and return to his own bed when it was over?

"I have a vivid imagination, Cynthia," I said. "I could see his naked white figure sliding down the chimney into our house like Father Christmas, creeping upstairs to ..."

"Don't! I can't bear to think of it. All those bodies they discovered, one after the other, drained of blood ... it was the mystery, the not knowing that made it so ..."

"Then the last night, with only the housekeeper left, and the detective arriving in the nick of time. Can you wonder that I was afraid for my life for I'm a housekeeper too."

"Oh you're more like my friend now," she said, with her beautiful smile and her eyes so warm and brown. She always drew me in and made me feel like one of the family, but I'd be cut down to size in a flash when the temper came on her. It wasn't personal, mind you. It's just the way Cynthia was. She wanted me to be her friend and her servant too. Well you can't do that in England. It's not on, as the toffs say, it's not cricket.

We were silent for a while and I thought she was nodding off, then she leaned over and whispered: "Mary, have you ever had a boyfriend?"

"Me?" I felt my face flushing up. "Where would I find the time for that?"

"Before the war, in Ireland, wasn't there someone?"

"It's very quiet where we live ... out on the farm ..." I was flustered. I could hear myself stumbling over the words, grasping for excuses.

She leaned in even closer, her face only inches from mine. "Have you ever been ... kissed?"

"There were boys at school ... behind the schoolyard ... but it was more like teasing ... bullying ..."

She leaned back with a sigh, and I wondered if she was disappointed in me.

"One afternoon Mireille and I were on the bus in Paris," she said. "We were standing because the bus was full, then a man stood up and offered me his seat. Of course I took it, but the seat was still warm and I was terrified until my next period that I would be pregnant. I knew nothing, you see." She laughed, but more from embarrassment than mirth. "I'd never been ... intimate with a man till I married Christopher. It's the most marvellous thing, Mary," she breathed, clasping her hands together, "Better than anything you could imagine—the feeling of intimacy—no end to it—like floating in the sea."

Oh, I could imagine it alright. And I did, in my bedroom at the end of the corridor.

"The first time he kissed me was at a house party at the Cartwright's, out on the veranda. The wisteria was in bloom with that sweet fragrance it has, and all the flowers hanging from the trellis, pale mauve, with delicate tendrils, like wisps of hair. I'd never felt like that before, not even with Roger, and he had kissed me right away, on both cheeks. The French are different, you see, very bold and forthright. But Christopher is a gentleman."

She cupped her face and slowly drew her hands down, folding them under her chin as though in prayer.

"I think it was his first time too because he was hesitant. We'd been dancing together and I could tell he was nervous. But as soon as we began talking it was as though there was a force outside of us, like a third person driving us together. All the feeling came flooding in from somewhere mysterious, and I began to understand that longing I'd felt in France, a longing for something that my body did not yet know. It was a craving, Mary, that couldn't be satisfied by French pastries. Once I met Christopher I was in a constant state of longing ... until our wedding night."

"And where were you on your wedding night?" I asked, for I wanted to steer our conversation in a more geographical direction. It was too embarrassing. I hardly knew what to say.

"Rhosneigr, on the island of Anglesey, in a big hotel on the front. Christopher loved to swim. He plunged into the sea as though it was his home, and he swam and swam while I watched him with the fishy smell of the seashore filling my nostrils, and the sharp grasses of the sand-dunes lashing my legs. He came running up the beach, all wet and salty, his feet *thunking* on the sand. I remember watching his footprints, how the sand would hold them for a few seconds before they disappeared. He was such a tease. He stood there shivering and grinning at me, then he threw his arms around me and picked me up. I screamed because he was so cold and wet!"

She leaned forward and rattled the poker around, setting the glowing coals alight with little blue flames.

"He told me about the Druid priests who'd lived on the island of Anglesey in round stone houses, growing wheat for the Celtic armies of Wales. Then the Romans had come and cut off their heads and burned the wheat fields. He held my hand as we walked amongst the remaining rings of stones—circles like heads with skinny-necked entrances stretching and yearning. I remember the rustle of our feet in the dry grass, the lightness of my body as he lifted me and carried me into the sand-dunes. My hands, Mary, my hands."

She held them up to me.

"These hands hold the memory of his neck, firm as a pillar. At night as we lay in bed we heard stones scraping on the beach as the waves sucked them back. To tell you the truth the first night was a disappointment, but next day, well then it was easier, and it got better and better as we became used to each other. I miss him terribly, Mary. I'm in that state now ..."

"A constant state of longing?" I asked.

"Yes."

"Well perhaps they'll give him leave soon."

She clicked her tongue and turned her head away abruptly. There, I'd broken the spell with my stupid remark, and I felt the anger rising in her, just like when he was home, wanting him and fighting him, but she couldn't do that with me. I wasn't going to play the Master. She'd sit up all night talking with me, but when he came home it would be: "Bring the tea, Mary, fetch the biscuits, keep the children quiet, cook the dinner and set the table ..."

I'd be her servant again, lying alone in my bed by ten o'clock. I knew she wanted me to say something, to tell her something wonderful, to enter into the spirit of it, but I couldn't. It was a private area of which I had no experience. Truth be told, the boys had never kissed me behind the schoolyard. They would only kiss the pretty ones, but I live in a constant state of longing too. I would've liked to tell her: "I understand that state." But what could we do about it? We had to wait for the Master to come home and receive all our longing in his fateful palms.

It was mid-morning of the next day when a grimy-faced fellow knocked at our door. He was from the Auxiliary Fire Service, he said, and he wanted a statement from the lady of the house who had telephoned about the crashed Luftwaffe. But it was me he needed to talk to because I was the one had seen it, so I answered his questions and he told me they'd been up all night putting out fires in the neighbourhood.

"What about those Germans?" I asked.

"No sign of 'em. Must've escaped. Don't worry. They won't get far in this country. Those Krauts don't even speak English. There's one body, prob'ly the gunner back in the fuselage, burnt to a cinder. Makes the wreckage into a war grave, doesn't it?"

He said they had likely been aiming for the A.V. Roe factory but had missed it and gone off course.

"He was flying too low, you see, snagged himself on the tethering cable of a barrage balloon. We found it all tangled up. There's several of them guarding the factory. Must have thrown him into a spin and caused him to crash, clipping your chimney on the way down. You were the lucky ones, believe you me."

He was making out a report as he spoke and he asked me to sign it which I did willingly, but I was thinking of that pilot and his crew, running through the woods in the darkness with the flames crackling behind them while their mates pulled on their joysticks and took off into the sky, home to Germany. I could only imagine what it was like over there for I'd never been in Europe, and still haven't to this day. I'd never set foot out of Ireland until the day I sailed over to become a servant in Cynthia's house. It is strange to remember how I had thought England to be, and to realize how absorbed I have been by the place and all my prejudice lost. That is why when you've left home—left your family and your country—you go back a different person and cannot find there who you were any more than you can turn the clock back or pretend that the war never happened and didn't change everything, for everyone.

Chapter Eighteen

WEASEL MAN

ON MY AFTERNOON off I'd walk over to Meg's and have a cup of tea with her. Then there was that fateful day, about a month after our chimney had been repaired. It was Jimmy's sixth birthday and we were still in the grip of winter with no sign of spring, though it was mid-February. There'd been a hard frost the previous night, but a weak wintry sun had softened the ground, so I arrived at Meg's caravan all muddy.

"Take off those filthy shoes," she said, "while I give you a pair of slippers."

"Thanks, Meg. I can always rely on you for a warm welcome."

"Oh, get away with you, girl. You can't stay long, I've a client coming at four …"

I could see her instruments on the kitchen counter—shining metal clamps and scissors. What could be worth risking those going up inside you? Sex must indeed be a marvellous thing, I thought, to make you throw caution to the wind and gamble with your body. Meg had never forgiven me for Cynthia's backing out. It's not often you get the gentry coming for such services, able to pay a decent sum for it. The working girls that came to Meg had most often got themselves in the family way with soldiers on their way to war, and ten to one were lying dead in foreign places. Cynthia's wad of money would have given Meg a holiday in Blackpool, which was where she liked to go.

"You should have seen the Illuminations before the war, Mary," she said. "They'd switch them on at dusk and the whole promenade would light up. You'd see the curve of it at night, and the stalls and sideshows lit up. It's all gone with the blackout." She sighed. "But that's where I'm going when this damned war is over, off to see the Blackpool Illuminations."

"And when will that be, d'you think?"

"When my Lennie comes home."

Her lips tightened as she busied herself with the tea kettle, pouring boiling water into the pot. Lennie's picture stood on the window sill —a freckled lad with sandy hair and an impish smile.

"He's got the gift, Mary," Meg had whispered to me when she'd first shown me her son's photograph. "Six toes on his left foot, five for the road and one for the devil."

He was in the RAF and I shuddered to think of the danger he was facing, especially after our crashed Luftwaffe and those German boys perhaps lying dead in the woods.

"How's Madam today?" Meg's lip curled. She was a mistress of sarcasm.

"She's taken the children to her mother's house in Poynton village. It's Jimmy's birthday party."

"Nice for them as 'ave cars, and petrol to run 'em."

"Don't be so hard on her, Meg. She can't help it. She's different from us."

I found myself defending Cynthia for the charm she held over me. Sometimes it made me long to be like her and live in her world, but then it was a torture living in her house, being part of the family but quite apart from it when push came to shove, as I would see. Looking back on it now I was used in the most despicable manner, without my permission and even without my knowledge. But I had been happy enough in my fool's paradise, loyal to my mistress who said she was my friend and had me sit up with her in the front room through the wartime winter evenings, listening to her stories. She was a fine story-teller, I'll give her that.

I was stirring a spoonful of sugar into my tea when there was a tap at the window. I looked up and there was Reg with his grinning face.

"Now why wouldn't he come to the door like any normal person?" I asked.

"Oh, Reg, he always wants to surprise me," Meg said casually. "He's a back-door man and a tease." She motioned him around to the front and opened up for him. "What you doing sniffing around 'ere?"

"Wondering 'ow chimney's 'olding up," he replied, peering past her at me.

"Well enough," I called out, because of course I could hear him from where I sat. Meg's caravan was small, just the one narrow room, and her bed curtained off at the end.

"Well aren't you goin' to ask me in for a cuppa?"

Meg sniffed and tossed her head, and Reg pushed past her with a wink and sat himself next to me. I knew he'd had his eye on me the day he came to repair our chimney, but there'd been no more than a look and a sparkle.

"You can tell your missus if she needs a chimney sweep I'm good at that too. I'll turn me 'and to anything. Man of all trades, that's me."

He was full of questions about Ireland, about my family and whatnot. A cheerful fellow, friendly to a fault, though I had the uncomfortable feeling that he was trespassing on my life without permission, but I couldn't find a good reason to resist, so I kept on talking, and himself grinning at me like the cat that got the cream. Well, then he had to attend to his tea, didn't he, so I watched him as he blew on it with his lower lip puckering outwards as he slurped a mouthful.

Reg was a slight man, with a hunch to him as though he was caving in to protect himself, holding his heart from harm's way. He had big hands with long fingers like the Master, for *he* was a piano player, but Reg only used his hands to smooth his hair off his forehead where it flopped into his eyes, which were small but twinkly, and a bit too close together. He was always ready for a laugh and that's what I liked best about him, that and his long snaky body as he sat slumped at the table with a feeling that he might slither across it at any minute.

I shuffled in my chair, painfully aware of my sturdy Irish legs and broad beam. I tried to pull in my stomach and tighten my buttocks into a tidy package like Cynthia's, but Reg seemed not to notice. His eyes were riveted on my face. It is not my best feature but with the way he looked at me I began to see myself through him—green eyes that could melt your heart, my Da used to say, and the curve of my eyebrows that didn't need pencilling in like Cynthia's, and my mouth with full lips and strong teeth.

Meg was at the sink, busy with her instruments when Reg lurched forward suddenly and gave me a wet kiss, just missing my mouth. I was shocked, and I realized in that moment who it was he reminded me of —the Weasel Man I had seen in the palm of my own hand. A feeling of doom came over me then, though I have to say that at the same time I felt flattered by his kiss. Why would he choose me? A reject could take his pick in those days with all the men gone to war.

"You'll 'ave to carry on outside," Meg said, down to earth as ever. "My visitor will be 'ere any minute and I don't want you two frightenin' 'er away."

That was my cue. I hurried to the door and put on my muddy shoes, hoping to escape before Reg could follow, but there he was at my side, taking my arm, guiding me down the steps as though I couldn't manage on my own.

"D'you like the moving pictures?" he asked and then without waiting for an answer: "There's a good one comin' to the Tudor next week. Will you step out with me?"

"Oh I'm very busy—I have the three children to look after, and a new baby ... but I'll think about it, I surely will. I ... I'd like an evening out."

My face flushed and I was disgusted with myself for the hot feeling between my legs. Truth be told I'd rather an evening with Cynthia, listening to her stories. But I could keep him at arm's length was how I looked it at then. I hurried away so he'd not get the chance to kiss me again. I knew he'd want my lips next time. The incident set up a whirl of confusion in me. This war has made us all lose perspective, I told myself. Although perhaps Da was right and I'd found myself a man where I never would have had a chance at home. But I wasn't ready yet to settle for a Weasel Man.

Chapter Nineteen

LEO KAUFMANN

IN MID-MARCH the first signs of spring appear at last with new growth forcing through the earth and birdsong waking the men at dawn. Christopher is hired on for potato planting at a farm outside Peel. He wonders if he will still be at Peveril Camp when it's time to harvest the potatoes he is to plant. He is heartily sick of potatoes and bread which make up the majority of the camp diet. There's salted fish three times a week, a horrible amount of cabbage and turnip, and sometimes a lump of maggoty meat to accompany the ubiquitous bread and potatoes. He's lost all sense of discerning appetite and eats like an animal, to abate his hunger and keep his strength up, taking comfort in the knowledge that he shares this privation with his fellow Britons.

He is driven with several of his sturdier mates past the village of St. John's on the Douglas road to a farm where they are issued shovels and work boots. The earth is soft, clinging to foot and blade in clods of heavy brown clay, making each step heavier than the last. But underneath, the earth is crumbly and easier to turn, and he begins to enjoy his task, working up a steady rhythm.

After the first day he is stiff and aching; he longs for a bath, but they're on a strict schedule of one bath a week in his house, so he pushes himself for the next couple of days until the stiffness is gone. Even his back moves smoothly as he bends to drop the eyes of the potatoes into the ground, covering them with the darkness of newly turned earth squirming with worms.

"Not so bad this work," a voice says, and Christopher looks up to see a handsome fellow, covered in mud like himself. He has compelling eyes and a wide mouth with a full lower lip. Above the cupid's bow is a deep furrow. Christopher remembers Nanny Darlington laying her finger into his own childish indent, telling him: "This is the place where the angel laid her finger when you were born, Christopher, to remind you never to tell the secrets you know."

"What secrets, Nanny?" he had asked.

"Secrets from the other world, my little man. The secrets to be revealed as you leave this vale of tears."

"Leo Kaufmann," the fellow says, taking off his glove and offering a clean hand.

"Brooke, Peveril Camp (M)," Christopher says, shaking Kaufmann's hand.

"I'm with the enemy aliens at Hutchinson Camp in Douglas," Kaufmann says. "Don't look so worried!" He laughs. "I'm not dangerous. I'm a German Jew, and I've learned to 'minimize my foreignness,' as I was advised to do when the Anglo-Jewish community sponsored me as a refugee in '38. Don't speak German in public, they said. Never draw attention to yourself."

"Your English is excellent."

"I learned as a child in Berlin. I must say I expected better hospitality in Britain, not to be detained in a camp for enemy aliens."

"Ah well, we're all in the same boat," Christopher says coolly and returns to his planting.

But at lunchtime he finds himself sitting next to Kaufmann. He eyes him suspiciously as they cradle their mugs of tea and chomp down on bully beef sandwiches.

"And you?" Kaufmann asks, his eyes bright with curiosity.

"I'm a pacifist," Christopher says curtly.

"Ah, then we have much in common."

"I don't think so."

"Oh, you English, so ... how do you say ... standoffish?"

"Britain for the British," Christopher says, seeing in his mind's eye Sir Oswald declaiming those very words from platforms all over the country.

"But Britain likes to export her presence all over the world," Kaufmann says. "To India, Asia, the Middle East ..."

"Look, nothing personal, old fellow, but you people need to find your own home."

"You're quite right. We Jews have become a global problem, even an embarrassment. Canada, America, so many countries falling over themselves with excuses—no room, no money, no jobs. Mr. Churchill would like to send us all back where we came from, but of course he can't." He wipes his hands and brushes a couple of crumbs from his lap with fingers long and elegant—a pianist's hands, Christopher thinks. "This camp is my survival. Remember the Arandora Star? I missed a random selection for that death boat. And here I am, a lucky man, planting potatoes in England with you, Mr. Brooke. Many of my fellow Jews have been released, but for some unknown reason, of which incidentally I find very little in England, I have not been released. As you say, we're in the same boat. Can't we be friends?"

Christopher is not accustomed to the company of Jews, at least not to the flaunting of such an identity. Kaufmann is not the only foreigner in the potato fields. There are Italians, Finns, and of course more German nationals, but none that insist on Jewishness. Most disturbing to Christopher is a reluctant liking of Leo Kaufmann. There is something provocative yet irresistible about him and Christopher finds himself looking forward each day to resuming their conversation. By the time they near the end of their planting he has become drawn to the fellow in a personal way that jiggles the structure of his thinking. As a pacifist he does not hold with anti-Semitism but, like the Leader, wishes to solve the problem of international Jewry by establishing a national home for the Jews.

"But I have a home, Christopher," Leo says. "I don't want to go and live in someone else's home. When this war is over I will return to Germany."

"And if Germany wins?"

"This is our fear, that the British will surrender and we'll be handed over to the Germans like rats in a cage. It happened in France."

They walk in silence to the canteen to eat their lunch. "L'chaim, to Life!" Kaufmann says, clinking his tea mug with Christopher's. "If we were in the same camp I would invite you tonight to a concert. There are two musicians in our camp who play Sephardic songs in the flamenco-fado tradition—songs of hope and love and pain sung here on the shores of the Celtic sea."

"My wife is Welsh," Christopher says, "one of the dark Welsh, who mixed their blood with the Spanish from the Basque region they say. They're a clannish group."

"Perhaps the clannishness has more to do with class than ancestry. You British are bound by it."

"Her family has rejected me for my political beliefs."

"Which are?"

"I am not a warmonger, Leo. I stand for peace and the true Christian gospel."

"Ah, if you were a Jew you would be a Rabbi." Two fat gold molars are visible as Leo Kaufmann laughs. He seems to Christopher an intensely physical man with his vigorous gestures and the kind of flamboyance often seen in foreigners. Leo's words come quickly, unconsidered, and yet are wise and witty. At lunch the following day Christopher inquires about the concert.

"Exquisite," Leo says, bunching his fingers to his mouth and throwing a kiss. Then he begins to sing, his face transformed as the melancholy music releases him, but he quickly senses Christopher's embarrassment and stops. "Poorly attended I'm afraid. We are diminished."

"Diminished?"

"There have been several suicides in our camp. Men who have lost hope of regaining their former lives. We were many—musicians, academics, a Nobel writer, architects, scientists, Rabbis, doctors, lawyers—all men of note—and women too, segregated in their own camp. Now many couples are reunited and have their freedom, such as it is. I hope for my own release shortly. Priority has been given to the married men, I'm told."

"You have no wife?"

"I am a widower."

"I'm sorry."

Leo smiles and bows his head.

"And if Germany loses this war will you stay and marry an Englishwoman?"

"Perhaps." He shrugs his shoulders with a wry smile. "Perhaps I will teach German Literature in a British University and publish British books about this nightmare we are living. It will be easier to write about in retrospect, yes?"

When Christopher returns to his billet that afternoon he is faced with a problem which as house leader he has to resolve. Thom Baker has received a parcel from his wife and, as with all parcels sent to internees, it had to be opened in front of an officer. There had been materials in the parcel considered to be Nazi propaganda, which had been removed and dispatched to the Commandant's office, and Baker had reacted badly to this—in the words of Ben Glover: "A full tantrum, ravin' and shriekin'."

Christopher hurries to his friend's side. "Look, Thom," he says, "I really think you should let this matter go. If you cause trouble here at Peveril they can send you to prison."

"And then I'll have to throw a double six to get out!" Baker shouts, his pale eyes wild, almost luminous.

"Do calm down," Christopher says.

"With my arthritic joints? You have no idea how they're torturing me!"

Christopher pats the man's shoulder gently. "I'll speak to the Commandant on your behalf and see what I can do."

He has thought in any case to speak with the man on his own account, requesting leave to see his new daughter, already two months old. With the coming of spring and the hardening of his body in physical labour he is filled with a sense of urgency and a belief in the power of his own will.

Chapter Twenty

A FRIGHTENED RABBIT

JIMMY WAS SICK as a dog after his birthday, and of course it was me had to stay up all night with him. His uncle Richard had given him a carpentry set for his birthday and he'd hammered a row of nails into Grandmother Blackwell's parquet floor, which was quite a feat for a six-year-old, but there was hell to pay for it. He was punished with a good smack-bottom on a full stomach—three pieces of cake and two helpings of jelly and blancmange, Charlotte told me.

By the time they got home he was wheezing like a steam engine and he vomited three times in the night. Next morning we called Doctor Pearson out; another asthma attack, he said, likely from overexcitement. The second night he coughed so hard I couldn't sleep, so I sat in the rocking chair in his room to keep an eye on him. Around two in the morning I woke from my dozing to find him burning up with fever. I packed him around with cold cloths, then I woke Cynthia and she called the doctor out again. He arrived with his spectacles askew and his pyjama top showing under his overcoat, and I took him up to Jim's room where Cynthia was hovering over the boy with her hand on his brow.

"Archer, thank goodness you're here! Save my little boy, please, please save him!"

He sounded Jimmy's chest with his stethoscope, then we lifted the child up and leaned him forward so the doctor could sound his back. He listened, then he thumped with two fingers.

"I'm afraid it's bronchitis," he said. "Mary, go and boil the kettle. We'll give him a mustard poultice and a Friar's Balsam inhaler. Bring clean towels and a pot of boiling water."

Cynthia began to weep. I left the doctor to comfort her while I went down to the kitchen, half my attention taken up with Cynthia and her frantic worrying. That's how it was when the children fell ill. She would get into such a state that she'd draw all the caring to herself. Jimmy turned around after three days of poultices and inhaling, but how he hated it.

"No, no, Mary," he'd say. "I don't want it, don't make me!"

I can see him still, a towel over his head, bowed over that pot of Friar's Balsam, gulping and wheezing.

"How much longer?" he'd ask, his voice half muffled under the towel.

"Only another minute. There's my brave boy. Then I'll tell you a story."

He'd come up spluttering, his face red and mottled, and I'd mop the condensation off him with the bunched-up towel.

On the first warm day after Jimmy had his strength back I took the children walking in the field behind our house. You could still see the scorched grass from the plane crash—a big black circle on the edge of the woods—as we made our way to the pond, with Katie in her pram, bumping over the tufts of grass that'd had a chance to grow up over the winter with the cows in the barn. The pond was circled by a muddy bank with trees overhanging the water. We squatted at the edge with a jam jar to catch tadpoles, but I was nervous, especially with Birdie determined to get at the water, her little feet squelching in the mud.

"Hold onto my hand, child. And don't go so near the edge."

I'm becoming like her, I thought, like Cynthia with her worrying and fretting.

"When will Daddy come?" I heard Jimmy ask Charlotte.

"He's coming soon, Jim."

"How d'you know?"

"I just do."

When we got back Cynthia said Reg had been to call.

"He was looking for you, Mary. Said he'd come again."

I coloured up right away. "What's he doing here? He should be at war, doing his share like a man." Oh Lord, I bit my tongue to have said such a terrible thing. I might as well have damned the Master. She snatched Katie from my arms and ran upstairs with her.

Charlotte was right. We got the call a week later, at the beginning of April.

"He'll be home for his birthday on the eleventh!" Cynthia said. "A weekend paternity leave, they said. Oh, and I already sent his card off. I'll have to buy another. Can you lend me a couple of shillings, Mary?"

I sent half my weekly salary home to Mam, and the rest I kept in a jewellery box Cynthia had given to me for Christmas, for what jewellery had I? I was saving my money to go home for a visit, though sometimes I bought sweets for the children. And if ever I went to the cinema with my Weasel Man, I would sure as heck pay my own way.

The Master arrived earlier than we expected. Cynthia was upstairs with the baby, and the other children were in the back garden doing their Magic Circle, so it was me that answered the door and stood there like a fool, gaping at him.

"It's ... it's ... the Master," I stammered, "Welcome home, Sir."

"Thank you, Mary."

He remembered my name, and he put out his hand to shake mine, so I curtsied and took his palm, cool and dry against mine. In his other hand was his hat held loosely by the brim and under his arm a rolled umbrella. I stepped back and held the door as he crossed the threshold and stood in the centre of the hall looking around him, as though seeing his house for the first time. There was something different about him as I began to see over that weekend, though at the time I felt simply that it must have been a torture for him being away from home, missing the growth of his children and the comfort of his wife.

He removed his raincoat and handed it to me so that I felt the warmth of his body in it. That's when I heard her, the flopping of her slippers across the bedroom floor upstairs. He heard it too and looked up, and then the children came running in from the garden and threw themselves at him, Jimmy tugging at his sleeve.

"Daddy, Daddy! We've got a new baby. Come and see."

"You'd better go ahead, Mary, and tell her I'm here. I don't want to surprise her."

The baby was asleep in her cot and Cynthia was at her dressing table. Her face lit up when I gave her the news, and then she was across the room in one leap as it seemed, and the breath leaving her body as he clasped her. A slight moan escaped her, and those little noises in the throat where your longing lives. They leaned over the cot together and he smiled and touched the baby's head with his fingers. I had to leave because I couldn't bear it, the whole room filled with feeling. It was more than a person could stand because I knew it would all turn bad.

My head swelled with his touch, gathering a burst of stars and planets tingling between my ears. I opened my eyes and saw their blurred shapes hovering above me. I could not see his features, only the taut fibres joining him to my mother and the riot of dark matter in his groin.

I bustled the children out with me and closed the door. Jimmy was beside himself with excitement, so I sent them all outside to run around the house ten times and let off steam. It was Saturday and we celebrated the Master's thirty-second birthday with a rabbit stew for lunch and my attempt at a cake which fell flat with only one egg and a scrap of margarine. But there was a feeling of spring in the air and the joy that it brings, all of us hoping for an end to the war, which has always seemed to me a winter activity, though I grew up in Ireland where war knows no season.

The Master held his little girl, already three months old, all through that first evening, and it was he who received her first smile. Isn't that always the way? Those who do for you every day are taken for granted, then along comes a handsome stranger and hits the jackpot. He gazed at her in wonder, making up for lost time, although it was clear he would have preferred a second son. He must have been going a little strange even then because he wanted to christen the baby

Helga—a wrong choice in the middle of a war with Germany—but Cynthia insisted on Katharine and wouldn't hear of anything else. She was all over him and the children too though by Saturday afternoon I could feel the tension building.

"Do you have to go back tomorrow, Chris?" she asked.

"I'm afraid so, Darling."

"But what if you just didn't turn up?" she said, teasing, almost flirting with him.

"They'd send someone here to get me, and then I'd be in solitary again."

"We could hide you in the coal-house. They'd never think of looking there."

Was it a game she was playing? The children were all ears, but they knew enough not to interrupt.

"Or you could escape through the garden into the field and hide in the woods."

"What would you say to them?" he asked, humouring her, for to be sure they were wild and impractical ideas she was putting forth. Though perhaps she was only joking.

"That you'd gone! That you'd taken the bus to the train station and were on your way back to the Isle of Man."

"I've given my word, Cynthia, and I must live up to it."

"What about us? Don't you think we need you here? Every minute of every day I miss you, the children miss you. Your damned politics have saved you from the battlefield, but for what—to dig potatoes in some godforsaken field on the Isle of Man?"

He started to protest, but it was no good, she was off on one of her rants.

"You're a coward, Christopher. You won't go to war, and you won't look after your family like a man. Oh God, I wish I'd never married you!"

Of course the children heard it all. Birdie started plucking at her dress and before we knew it she had it off and turned inside out searching for that spider. Jim had slunk behind the sofa—I could hear his laboured breathing there. And Charlotte just sat on the sofa with her hands in her lap and her head down, her lower lip pushed out in that sulky expression. Finally they went upstairs to battle it out, and I got the children rounded up for a game of tiddlywinks. It was teeming with rain outside.

"Imagine running through the field in that," I said. "Sloshing through the mud, slipping and sliding. Even the cattle are in today in a nice dry barn munching hay to make their milk sweet."

"What about Uncle Jack?" Charlotte said. "He's over in France fighting the Germans. I bet he's sloshing through the mud."

Guess where she'd heard that? She's the apple of her grandmother's eye. And how must she feel, the one who loves her daddy the most?

"You're quite wrong, Darlin'," I said. "France is occupied by the Germans. I don't know where your Uncle Jack is, but sure enough he won't be there."

"He was at Dunkirk," she said, "sloshing along the beach."

The day passed without further incident until I went to collect the children and get them ready for bed. It was their bath night and I had the hot water already drawn. When I entered the sitting room Cynthia and the Master were sat together on the sofa and I sensed that strange mixture of desire and discord between them, and I wondered if it had always been so, or had come about with the war and his disgrace. He was as usual intent on the newspaper and Cynthia watching him in what I took to be her "constant state of longing." I traced the curve of her neck with my eye, and I remembered a blind horse I'd seen once at the livestock market in Butlersbridge, its nostrils flared and quivering, searching for the water trough.

"The Americans have lost the Philippines. And Japan is sweeping through Southeast Asia—Thailand, Malaya, Hong Kong ... "

"Can't you talk about anything but the war?"

"But you do know, Cynthia, that Singapore surrendered in February? I only mention it because of the Andertons ..."

"Jenny and George? Will they be alright?"

"I expect they've been evacuated. You see how important it is to understand what's going on when our friends are ..."

"I understand only too well. All the men are gone and we're left here to look after everything on our own. What would I do without Mary?"

"Mary?" he said, bemused, and I cleared my throat and called to the children for bedtime, though I knew that Cynthia had seen me and was in her usual way playing me off against him. Birdie was at the piano tinkling away at her fairy music, while Charlotte and Jim were twiddling with the knobs of the wireless, making crackling noises with snatches of loud music in between. It was a wonder that Cynthia and the Master could carry on a conversation over the noise. He held Katie in his arms like a loaf of bread, hardly aware now of what he held. He was a strange man for he could give his full concentration to the baby for minutes at a time, and to a cricket game with Jimmy, whom he'd found pale and thin after his bronchitis.

"Come on Jim, let's get you back into training," he'd said in the morning before the rain threatened, and he'd tied cricket pads onto the boy's legs and bowled at him for a full half hour. And when Jimmy took his turn bowling the Master restrained himself, batting the ball exactly so that the boy could catch him out.

But when he started talking it was as though his body did not exist. His mind took him miles away, across the sea to other countries. Singapore, where is that? And all Cynthia's desire was for his body, to have him there with her in her bed each night. It was a mistake for him to talk politics with her. It always ended in a fight, and sure enough the shouting soon started, even before the children were out of their bath. We could hear from upstairs Cynthia's voice raised, and the steady drone of the Master's voice under her.

"You bloody coward!" she shouted. "You're a frightened rabbit!"

I remembered that because it seemed a strange insult for a tall handsome man. There was nothing at all rabbit-like about him. His teeth were broad and straight with a lucky space between the two front ones, which Charlotte had inherited. I was drying Birdie off when she slipped away from me and ran from the bathroom stark naked. I started after her but she was too quick for me and was down the stairs and into the sitting room before I could stop her.

"There you go ... nag, nag, nag," she said, hands on the place where her hips would grow one day, her head bobbing like a chicken and her little bottom stuck out to catch the breeze. Cynthia was on her feet in

a flash and slapped the child so hard and smart we were all paralyzed
with the force of it. The baby started wailing before Birdie did, then
all hell broke loose. I gathered Birdie in my arms right quick and tried
to comfort her. Then I saw Jimmy and Charlotte in the doorway bundled in their towels, wide-eyed and shivering.

"What d'you think you're looking at?" Cynthia shouted at them.

"A cat can look at a king," Jimmy quipped, and Charlotte dug him
in the ribs causing him to smirk and hang his head.

"Get upstairs to bed this minute!" Cynthia shouted, and we all
scurried out and left the two of them with the screaming baby.

When I came down next morning to start the fires, I got the shock of
my life for he was sitting at the kitchen table like a ghost with his head
in his hands.

"Oh, Mr. Brooke," I said, "you gave me such a start. What are you
doing up so early, Sir, and on a Sunday? Would you like a cup of tea?
I'll get the fire going and put the kettle on to boil."

He was miles away again, I could tell, because he looked up as
though he was seeing right through me. What a pair we were, me blab-
bing away, and him off with the faeries. But he came to then, and he
stood up and smiled a most charming smile, and I was undone.

"Let me help you, Mary," he said and he came forward and put his
hand on my shoulder which, even though it was there only seconds, set
up such a turmoil in me I did not trust myself to speak again. He got
down on one knee, took the poker and began rattling out the cold
ashes into the pan under the grate.

"Is there a bucket?" he asked, looking up at me with his clear blue
eyes. I hurried out to the scullery and fetched the bucket from the back
corridor where the washing machine lived, and I was in such haste I
almost tripped on the doorsill as I came back into the kitchen. He was
waiting for me with a shovelful of ashes which he tipped into my bucket, causing a cloud of ash to rise around us and settle on our clothing.

"Let me do it, Sir," I said. "It's no work for a gentleman."

"I must make myself useful, Mary. My life depends on it."

When we'd finished laying the fire he set it alight and it gave him great satisfaction, I could see, to watch the flames leap around the kindling, consuming the newspaper, licking at the black coals with little sparks and explosions as it burned up the coal dust. The kettle was soon bubbling and I ran to the scullery and made a pot of strong tea. When I returned with the tray he was standing with his back to me, staring out the window, perhaps looking across the field to the pond and the woods beyond, thinking about disappearing.

For all their talk of a "war grave," the men from the Auxiliary Fire Service had cleared the wreckage with no mention of the missing Germans. That was the feeling of Christopher Brooke, a missing person, a fugitive you can't get a hold of. No wonder Cynthia was driven mad. He was a wraith, like one of the faery people that dwelt in the fields and in the woods. My da had warned me about them when I was little.

"They will steal you away to ward off their own death, Máire," he'd say.

The Master turned then and looked at me strangely, as though he had forgotten I was there and felt intruded upon.

"Will you take a cup of tea, Sir?" I asked, and a smile of recognition lit up his face, as he sat at the big square table with me and waited while I poured.

"Is it too early for the mistress?"

"Oh yes, we mustn't disturb her yet."

He stirred two heaping teaspoons of sugar into his cup, lifted it to his lips and sipped. Then he replaced his cup firmly in the saucer and turned to me. I thought he might confide in me about their disagreement the previous night, but no, all his concerns were for the impersonal.

"Mary, I must tell you that I stand for peace and socialism. That is why I have been detained, uncharged and untried. Do you stand for socialism?"

"Oh sir, where I come from we are for a united Ireland and a good square meal on the table each day."

"Of course, your life is a hand to mouth existence so to speak."

"Indeed, sir, or why else would I be here, far from my home and my family?"

"We have much in common, Mary. I've come to understand this

kind of life in a very personal manner since my detainment."

He stared intently at me with his sharp blue eyes, the pupils small and black like those of a bird. There was a world behind that blueness. It was like looking into the sky.

"But how can we level the playing field and attain true socialist values?"

"I don't know, Sir. I only know that it is important to care for the children and bring them up to feel loved."

"My children are indeed blessed in having you as their nanny."

"I am not a nanny, Sir. I was taken on by the mistress as housekeeper."

I took a gulp of tea and almost choked I was so embarrassed at speaking out of turn, but he carried on unruffled. It was impossible to offend him, as I learned later. He was a man so removed as to be entirely protected from a feeling of hurt.

"And what of your religious convictions? Are you Catholic?"

"Yes, Sir."

"And do you not think it strange that the Catholic Church supports this war?"

"I don't know about the Catholic Church, Sir, but I can tell you that our government does not support this war. Mr. de Valera has declared Ireland to be neutral."

"Mary, we must put an end to the hypocrisy of a Church that says 'Thou shalt not kill,' the first of our Commandments, and yet supports the killing of thousands in this mad warfare." His face lit up as though he'd had a grand idea, and the way he leaned towards me I thought he was going to say something wonderful. "Come to Church with me this morning and speak out, will you?"

"I ... I can't, Sir. It's ... it's not right for the likes of me to ... to ..."

"But Mary, you're the salt of the earth. If all your kind were to rise up ... "

"But you don't understand, Sir, what it is to be ... to be ... an ordinary person. I do not have the power to speak as you do."

"Perhaps this war is the leveller. You take refuge with my wife and children in the air-raid shelter during the bombing while I cower in my attic room without shelter or protection, and we both know our worst fears."

His foot touched my calf as he swung one leg over the other, and I forgot what he was saying. For a moment I thought it had been intentional, that he had wanted to touch me, but as he ranted on, all his passion held in the brightness of those eyes, I realized that any such thoughts were my own, and I felt closer to Cynthia and her frustration than I did to Christopher Brooke and his political passion. Nevertheless, it was a tender moment we shared in the early morning, warming ourselves over our tea, and I took what I could from it.

"Is your father fighting?"

"No, Sir, he has the farm to run."

"Do you have brothers?"

"I do, Sir, and two of the three are enlisted." I did not mention what Brendan was fighting for. He bowed his head a moment, and then suddenly he thumped the table so that our cups and saucers rattled.

"You see, I must make myself useful! If only they'd let us serve in a peace-keeping capacity instead of planting potatoes, digging them up, peeling them, eating them! I'm a man in my prime, Mary."

As I knew only too well from my observations. I busied myself with the teapot to distract myself from blushing, and at such an innocent remark.

"There is a famous painting by Vincent Van Gogh of the Potato Eaters. Well, we are the potato *peelers*, me and my kind." He laughed, an empty sound that seemed to echo around us. "Before the war I was a director in my father's hat manufacturing business, but I renounced my directorship. I spent my time on the factory floor, Mary, labouring alongside the common man, working up a sweat instead of dandling a pen."

"Then why wouldn't you want to be alongside those men in the war, Sir?"

"I've told you, Mary, I stand for peace."

He spoke with that same patient tone he used with Cynthia and the children.

"But, Sir," I said, leaning forward, "we can't let Hitler march across Europe taking all the land for Germany."

"Adolf Hitler has always been in favour of a negotiated peace with Britain, and the British leaders know this. We can only hope for a change of government to rid us of Churchill."

"Mr. Churchill seems to know what he's doing, Sir."

"He's duplicitous, Mary. He is governed by ego and self-interest, and he has made some dreadful mistakes which have affected all Englishmen. I make a study of the newspapers for my daily news broadcast at Camp Peveril, and I tell you that despite his popularity Churchill is a heartless man. If we'd had Sir Oswald Mosley for Prime Minister we'd be living in peace now with the rest of Europe."

It was a little tedious to be lectured at, and in truth I felt his words were wasted on me, an audience of one and a humble one at that. I did not fill my head much with politics but more with visions of the future. I don't know what came over me, but without thinking I took hold of his left hand and stretched it out palm upwards. He surrendered his hand and kept on talking, but I hardly heard a word, so powerful was the force of his flesh on mine. He had beautiful hands, large and square with long fingers for his piano playing. All the music was in those hands and all his future too in crisscrossed lines like railway tracks running along, unstoppable.

"What fortune do you see, Mary, in my palm?"

I don't remember what I said, but I was duplicitous like Mr. Churchill. Perhaps I told him there was another child in the palm of his hand, but I didn't tell him she'd have a different mother, and I certainly didn't tell him about the ending I saw moving towards the veins of his wrist.

Chapter Twenty-One

COUSIN ADÈLE

IT WAS A relief when he returned to the camp and we were able to get back to normal. Those visits unsettled us, and the Master put Cynthia in a fever without having the cure for it. She questioned me about our early morning conversation. She did not like her people to talk to each other, "behind her back" as she put it—she liked to keep us all separate and for herself, playing us off against each other. I was glad when she softened up and began to treat me like her equal again; I had grown accustomed to our evenings in the sitting room, to the pretence we made of being like sisters. Our game did not bear the intrusion of outsiders, and fond though I was of my handsome Master I found myself resentful of him.

It was soon after the visit that my dreams started, not about our Luftwaffe pilot as you might expect, even though I lay awake wondering about him escaping through the woods, helmet in hand, and his companions running on ahead, then he'd turn back to look at our house and I'd see his white face covered in burn scars with the pale skin puckered and his mouth a dark hole. But I wasn't afraid, and I'd follow him until I drifted off and dreamed instead of a large white rabbit—not the kind you'd see in a children's story-book, but a wild albino thing with red eyes and fangs.

It was trapped in the vegetable garden behind Cynthia's greenhouse, desperate to escape, but the fence was solid, unlike the real fence there, which was a flimsy affair of thin sticks joined by a couple of lines of wire. What struck me about the dream was the rabbit's fear and the strength it gave him, for it was definitely a male rabbit, or perhaps a hare, very large with long legs that could have injured you if it had kicked. The creature ran around and around the borders of our garden, and there was a cuckoo calling from up in a tree—*cuckoo, cuckoo*. Finally the rabbit ran at the fence and leapt over it, and as I watched it disappear into the field a shot rang out and its white fur was streaked with blood as it dropped to the ground and lay there darkening the earth.

I woke with a sick feeling in my stomach, wanting to make it better, so I pictured the rabbit getting up and running off into the woods, alive and healthy with its wounds healed. But my waking dream must have taken control of me, for that night the rabbit loped back through the darkness and hid in the coal shed and got coal dust all over its white fur. I tried to clean it but the fur was slippery and the creature slid through my hands and escaped. I remembered the albino chimney killer, and Cynthia shouting: "You're a frightened rabbit!" And the story she'd told me about her father shooting rabbits and hanging them in the shed—how she'd remembered blood dripping from the open eye onto the wooden floor where it was soaked up, darkening to a rich mahogany, and I thought, we're just a clamour of stories getting mixed up, it's all nonsense.

The dreams I had in that house, they did not belong to me, but to some other realm where people spoke to me in voices forbidden to them. Everything unspoken in that house entered my dreams and deafened me with their noise. Those dreams stayed with me all day, sitting heavy on my shoulders, weighing me down with their puzzlement.

We didn't have many visitors to the house. The neighbours knew about Mr. Brooke's detainment and they shunned the family, Cynthia told me. She said she would not be bothered with such cruel people, but sometimes I wondered if it was *she* who shunned *them* because she was ashamed. She was over at her mother's house several days a week with the children, especially Charlotte who was Grandmother Blackwell's favourite. Jimmy and Birdie always wanted to stay with me and play in the garden, and sometimes she let them, but of course the baby went everywhere with her. She wouldn't let Katie out of her sight.

Cousin Adèle came over faithfully every week to drink coffee with her in the sitting room. She was beautiful like Cynthia and resembled her remarkably, but with a lighter spirit. You could see it in her dealings with the children; she was sweet and generous with them, leaving room for the little ones to be their true selves. I liked her visits for she brought out the best in Cynthia too, and she spoke well of the Master and put things in perspective.

"Don't worry, Darling," Adèle would say as she stood in the hall arranging her hat in the mirror. "All this will soon be over and you'll have him home where you can nurse him back to health."

"Oh Addie, do you think so?" Cynthia asked.

"Of course, Darling. Christopher was never like this before the war. He's had a breakdown, that's all. He needs your loving care." She turned from the mirror with a radiant smile. "Remember the Fun Fair we went to with the Merry-Go-Round? I'll never forget your face as you came into view, riding your wooden horse with that carnival music playing, and Christopher on the horse next to you with a big grin on his face. You flung your arms up in the air and shouted: 'We're going to be married!' It was so romantic. I remember turning to Eric and saying: 'There you are, Darling, I told you so.' We were just waiting for it."

"Were you? Oh Addie, those were the days! And remember the Cinderella Dances, how we'd all dress up and take the train into Manchester?"

I was holding Adèle's coat for her, so I heard their conversation, and I saw Cynthia's face, young and fresh as it had been in that photograph of her in the boat. Adèle had been in Europe with her too, they'd been reminiscing only the previous week about a skiing holiday in Switzerland and how they would drink hot chocolate in the ski lodge to warm up and how Adèle had lent her engagement ring to Cynthia to discourage the unwanted attentions of the ski instructor.

"He had hair growing out of his ears," Cynthia had said, screwing up her nose. "I couldn't *bear* the thought of being kissed by a man with hair in his ears."

They were always laughing like schoolgirls.

"Any news of your friend Mireille?" Adèle asked.

"I had a letter from Madame Plasse, routed through Portugal," Cynthia replied. "She said they're alright and not to worry. They have enough to eat. But it was odd what she said about Mireille."

"What? What did she say?"

"Mireille ne parvient pas à écrire pour l'instant. Elle est trop oc-cupée par son travail, mais elle envoie ses pensées affectueuses et dit de continuer à sourire, Cynthia."

"Too busy with her work ... Hmm, I wonder what she's up to ... sends her love ... and says keep smiling. Was that a special thing for you two—keep smiling?"

Cynthia laughed, a bit embarrassed it seemed. "Mireille always said: 'I'd recognize you anywhere by your smile, don't ever lose it.' That's all."

I thought she was going to cry, but she did that about-turn she was famous for and switched to another topic altogether.

"Any news from Eric? Where is he? When's he coming home on leave?"

"He's in Libya, Darling, quite safe. He loves the desert," Adèle said as she slipped her arms into the sleeves of her elegant coat, not forget-ting to thank me. "He's been dilly dallying in Tobruk almost six months now, having a frightfully good war. The most action he's seen so far is cocktail hour in the Officers' Mess!"

Chapter Twenty-Two

MAD HATTER

CAPTAIN BAKER HURRIES to keep up with Christopher as they battle their way along the Front. It's a windswept day with whitecaps surfing the waves and Baker has to shout over the din.

"When this damn war is over we'll buy a large freehold, Christopher, and assemble a community of like-minded people," Baker says, the light in his pale eyes reigniting Christopher's spirit.

Since his last visit with Cynthia he's felt impotent in every way, her verbal insults affecting him deeply. How do other men manage? he wonders. Is it cowardly to remain stoic in the face of Cynthia's haranguing? He confides in his friend, who is of the opinion that wives should be shared and in this way such problems would be minimized.

"And the children, whose paternity can likewise be shared, will be raised by an entire community with revolutionary values," Baker says. "We will create His Kingdom on earth! These are the last days of the Mammon world, Christopher! We must keep the faith and prepare ourselves."

They discuss the first lecture in their Biblical Prophecy series, to be presented the following week. When Baker reveals his surprising belief in Adolf Hitler as God's Chosen Instrument to destroy the old Mammon system, Christopher, only momentarily taken aback, confides confirmation from a most unlikely quarter.

"I was able to buy a copy of the Spectator while on paternity leave," he says. "And I read an article entitled *India at the Cross Roads*, documenting Sir Evelyn Wrench's interview with Mahatma Gandhi. And do you know, Thom, the old man said—and I quote: 'Hitler is a scourge sent by God to punish men for their iniquities.'"

As they turn homeward out of the wind Christopher feels blessed to be living at a turning point in world affairs in which he is now able to play an instrumental role. He has discovered the secret; do not long for what you cannot have; awaken to the angel in your midst. He will persuade Cynthia. She will meet Baker when their internment is over and then she will understand, as he has come to understand, the mysterious ways of divine intervention.

Their lecture is well attended, largely due to Christopher's good-nature and promotional talents. He has been teased by the working-class men at Peveril about his role as a Captain of Industry and has taken it in stride, like a cuff on the chin. They called him the Mad Hatter behind his back, tittering and nudging each other as he passed, but the nickname has gradually become a term of affection. Now the men address him directly: "'Ere comes the Mad 'Atter! Mornin' Sir. 'Ats off to yer."

Christopher smiles with genuine warmth, remembering his days on the factory floor, working alongside the Brooke Hats employees, moulding hats on wooden forms. A sense of self-respect has begun to bloom in him. He has gained the attention of his fellow prisoners, and has become popular with the men. They've come to listen because Christopher has promised them a lively exchange of ideas. But Baker too, who is to be the opening speaker, has played his part. His wife has made the difficult journey to the Isle of Man, accompanied by their son, a boy of ten with an unsightly birthmark on his forehead that Baker claims is a swastika marking the boy for a divine destiny. This visit, thanks to the wild-haired Mr. Unsworth—a barrister and former racing car driver—who is now contributing weekly to the upkeep of Baker's family, is to be a demonstration of the boy's gifts as a healer. The men have been invited as witnesses to the laying on of small hands, but when the boy steps out in front of the crowd, urged forward by his mother, his healing powers beg credibility, for he is a stunted specimen, pale and sickly looking himself.

"Come on, lad," Baker says, gritting his teeth and hobbling across the stage, one hand supporting his right hip. "You see your poor old dad crippled with arthritis. Can you ease my pain?" The little fellow nods his head. "Witness," Baker says, turning to the audience, "witness this symbol of divinity emblazoned on my boy's forehead—the swastika, a timeless icon of ancient spiritual significance seen on the streets of India, in Eurasia and beyond. My son is stamped by God, who is everywhere!"

Baker lowers himself gingerly onto the chair that Brooke has placed centre stage, and beckons to the boy with a crooked arthritic finger. The child looks to his mother, who gestures with a flap of her hand. "Go, go!"

Still uncertain, the boy shuffles forward, circles the chair and stands behind it where he cannot be seen. His two small hands appear on Baker's shoulders which begin to relax with a dramatic exhalation as Baker's eyes close and his jaw goes slack. Next the hands travel down Baker's right arm, lingering at the wrist, and onto his knee where they clamp on the knobbly clump. Immediately a growl of satisfaction comes from deep within Baker's throat as he throws back his head.

"Agh," he says, "the pain is leaving my tortured joints!"

Encouraged, the small hands continue on their healing journey, the nails flecked white with a calcium deficiency suffered by so many war-time children. Only minutes later, with a great sigh, Baker is able to rise from his chair in a spritely manner, throwing his arms into the air like a champion. George Unsworth, sitting up front and centre, begins the applause and soon all the men are cheering the boy, who smiles sheepishly as Baker begins to speak to a captive audience.

"Biblical Prophecy, my hearties!" he says. "It's all here." He holds up the Bible that Brooke had placed on his lap during the healing. "Everything we need to know in order to understand this mess we're in. Take heart from the miraculous demonstration of my healing, and know that we're all bound for freedom!"

"What time's the train coming?" shouts a heckler from the back row. Christopher notes a general scepticism in the men's eyes as they all begin to laugh.

"We are united in our love of God and England," Christopher shouts. "Martyrs to Peace in our time."

"You have witnessed the marvellous healing powers of my boy," Baker says. "Come lad, come."

The ten-year-old approaches shyly and, seeing him again, Christopher thinks of Charlotte. They must be about the same age, he thinks.

"How many of you are fathers?" Baker's pale eyes scan the hall as the men shuffle and raise their hands. "Well then, it is for our sons that we speak. Suffer the little children to come unto me." He lifts his son high in the air. "See how he has healed my pain and given strength to my arms! Our children are living miracles to remind us of God's plan. Our corrupt government sends the flower of British boyhood to the battlefields to be slaughtered, all over again, as in the Great War of which I myself am a veteran. I tell you, my hearties, I've seen the face of Death, and I bear witness now that a scourge has been sent by God to cleanse the world of wickedness and his name is Adolf Hitler!"

There is an immediate cry of outrage, one voice after another accumulating into a wave of protest.

"Ha! There's life in you yet, my friends, but hear me out. Go sweetheart, go to your mother," Baker says, patting the boy's bottom. "Today we witness the Antichrist in our midst: International Jewish Finance!"

The response now is a mere rumbling, disgruntled but undecided.

"Every one of us knows poverty in this camp. Poverty, poverty, yes, poverty! Going to bed hungry, waking hungry, walking in leaky boots. We eat wormy potatoes and watery cabbage, saltfish that pollutes the temples of our bodies, but a better day is coming when the evil Mammon system will be scoured from the face of the earth."

"Thy Kingdom come! We are comrades in Christ," Christopher chimes in, noticing that some of the men are leaning forward curiously now, their eyes opening to the message.

"Comrades indeed," Baker says. "Each and every one of us on this

Island has surrendered himself to the British Government, and here we sit, red-blooded men living like monks."

The crowd surges and Baker has to raise his voice above them to be heard.

"Crowded like schoolboys into dingy dormitories, able-bodied men without an honest day's work to be proud of, bored out of our skulls!"

"You can say that again," comes a high-pitched whine.

"Bored out of our skulls by that numskull Churchill's skulduggery!" Baker shouts, launching his gadfly words into a pot that is beginning to bubble. "Rule 18B is a game, my men, and we are the pawns, to be pushed around at will and locked into a box at night."

A few scuffles are breaking out on the floor and Baker raises his voice even higher above the discord, seizing the moment to focus the energy of his audience.

"But how to gain our freedom? How about it, lads? What? I don't hear you." He leans towards the audience, hand to ear. "Wake up, wake up! Who can give me the answer? Come on, my brave hearts, a show of hands. Come on, come on!"

"Get a boat and make a dash for it," a young fellow sitting behind Unsworth says.

"Who's rowing?" Baker says. "*I'm* healed." He waves his Bible-free arm. "I can take an oar."

And the men as one begin to wave their arms, shouting enthusiastically about their rowing and fishing skills.

Baker lets them go for exactly 12 seconds and then he shouts, "NO!", raises a rigid index finger, shakes it back and forth, and suddenly all the men fall silent. He holds them in suspense a moment, his hypnotic eyes scanning theirs, then his body slumps and he shrugs and smiles benevolently. "In order to be free we must surrender to God, and to his son Jesus Christ who has walked in our midst on this very earth only 19 centuries past." He pauses a moment, opening his Bible at the red marker. Then his right arm sweeps an arc in the air like a fairground touter: "I give you the words of John the Apostle written all those centuries ago — Chapter 21 of The Revelation:

Then I saw a new heaven and a new earth, for the first heaven and the first earth had passed away, and there was no longer any sea.

I saw the Holy City, the new Jerusalem, coming down out of heaven from God, prepared as a bride beautifully dressed for her husband.

"Was he drunk?" shouts a heckler, but this time the men *shush* him. They are captivated, Christopher sees, all listening intently.

And I heard a loud voice from the throne saying: 'Now the dwelling of God is with men, and he will live with them. He will wipe every tear from their eyes. There will be no more death or mourning or crying or pain, for the old order of things has passed away.'

He who was seated on the throne said: 'It is done. I am the Alpha and the Omega, the Beginning and the End. To him who is thirsty I will give to drink without cost from the spring of the water of life.

He who overcomes will inherit all this, and I will be his God and he will be my son.

But the cowardly, the unbelieving, the vile, the murderers, the sexually immoral, their place will be in the fiery lake of burning sulphur. This is the second death.'

"Hear hear!" shouts Unsworth, raising his right arm in the Nazi salute. "Well said."

"Well read," echo voices around the room, some of the men on their feet now applauding as Baker smirks and bows, darting forward suddenly with a faux lion's roar that causes an outbreak of laughter amidst the cheering.

Baker signals for them to sit down and when he has everyone's attention he says: "And now I give you my partner in crime, companion to my March Hare, my Cheshire Cat, my Dormouse, my White Rabbit ... The Mad Hatter!"

In this way Christopher is winning even before he launches into a Bible verse from memory—"The kingdom of God on Earth will rise triumphantly and to the eternal happiness of regenerated man under the leadership of God-guided rulers." He moves on to an idea posited during happier days to the Stockport Rotary Club. "We are all men of industry here whether we peel potatoes or plant them. Were we to observe our world from another planet we should be amazed at the stupidity we see. In an age where science has made it possible to abolish poverty, it is still tolerated. Yet God has not created this poverty; it is not His Will that unemployment, slum dwellings, trade booms and depressions persist. Man has created these things ..."

Baker was on the floor signalling to the young fellow seated behind Unsworth. The men shuffled along to let Thom in and he reached out his hand. "Arthur Kern," the man responded, clasping Baker's small hand. "The lad with the boat eh?" Baker said. "The very same," Arthur said. "My sisters would like to meet you, Sir. You're a fire and brimstone man." There was a tinge of foreign accent to him, Baker noticed. He liked the sound of the sisters. And Arthur was young and strong. Good grip. They would need such people after the war for their freehold —agricultural workers, domestics, breeders. He began a spontaneous round of wild applause, interrupting Brooke's speech with an avalanche of cheering from the crowd.

Chapter Twenty-Three

A SUMMER PICNIC

1942

IT WAS A hot summer. When I think back on it I see myself inside a golden bubble of sunshine trembling with the children's laughter, and Cynthia is at my side in all my dreams. It was a shimmering bubble, like those the children blew through little hoops dipped in soapy water, reflecting all the colours of the rainbow as the sun shone on it, and soon to burst. That's where the sadness and the beauty lay, in my knowledge that it would have to end even though I felt that summer to be timeless.

When we heard on the wireless that Tobruk had been taken by the Germans, Cynthia got on the telephone to cousin Adèle and talked for more than an hour, then she ran upstairs and only came down at dinnertime, with her eyes swollen from weeping. I didn't dare ask, but I found out later that night that Mr. Cartwright was safe, though his cocktail hours had ended.

In that first week of August we went for a picnic in the field behind our house. It was Charlotte's idea. She helped me make the sandwiches—spam with lettuce from the garden inside crusty rolls, five slabs of Battenberg cake—Birdie's favourite with the pink and white squares and the marzipan covering, a flask of tea for me and Cynthia, and another with lemonade for the children.

"Wouldn't it be grand if Daddy was here?" Jimmy said in his husky voice.

Charlotte gave him one of her *shushing* looks, and he put his head down and studied the grass as we trudged through the field. Cynthia carried the baby because the ground was too bumpy for the pram, and Birdie hopped ahead and ran back, covering twice as much ground as we did, with Percy lolloping along beside her. That child had the freest spirit I've ever seen. She was a sprite to be sure, but she was crushed and all the magic wrung out of her by what happened later. I wasn't there to witness it and if I had been perhaps I could have helped her, or perhaps no-one could. One crime in so many. Who can judge?

I spread the blanket and Charlotte helped me to lay out our picnic.

"Be careful not to lay the blanket on a cow poo," Jimmy said earnestly. He had a healthy dread of it since stepping in a fresh one the previous week.

"Don't go near the pond, children," Cynthia said.

"I want to look for tadpoles," Birdie said.

"They've all grown up into frogs and hopped away," Charlotte said.

"But I want to go anyway," she said, whining.

"Me too!" Jim exclaimed. "I'll look after her, Mummy."

"Alright, but be careful," she said. "And don't be long. We're going to eat our picnic soon."

'Course they came back covered in mud, and it was Charlotte got in trouble for it.

"You're a big girl now. You should be looking after your little brother and sister," Cynthia said sharply, and she slapped Charlotte's leg and left the white imprints of her fingers on the reddening flesh.

"But it wasn't my fault, Mummy, the cows have been drinking and they've churned up the bank and made it all muddy."

"I don't care for your excuses. Come on you two."

She grabbed Birdie and Jim and marched them to the pond. They disappeared down the steep bank and we heard splashing noises as she cleaned them up with the green slimy water. Charlotte sat hunched on the edge of the blanket sulking, while the baby lay gurgling and staring up into a cloudless sky with eyes blue as her father's.

"There now." Cynthia was back with the children. "Dry your hands on the grass, and we'll eat our sandwiches."

When I handed her a cup she blessed me with one of her beautiful smiles and I could see that she was happy in that moment, as happy as ever she might be under the circumstances. It was as though someone had snapped a photograph for I can see us now, our teacups steaming beside us on the blanket, the sun in my eyes as I stared into the sky, and the musky smell of the children, their skin glistening with pond water, and the sucking noises of Katie's rosebud mouth as her baby lips smacked together in contentment. If a German bomber had come over at that moment I would not have believed in the reality of it, the shadow it cast with its great wings, a bird of death with a black cross, because nothing was as strong as our happiness that day, nothing could touch us.

Chapter Twenty-Four

QUINK VISTA BLUE

T HE CAMP COMMANDANT drains his teacup and hunches over the stack of papers piled before him. Repeated petitions for release from Baker, complete with empty threats against the Commandant's own family for God's sake! And a couple of more courteous petitions penned in an elegant hand from Christopher Brooke. He has respect, even empathy for Brooke, a gentleman if ever he saw one, though sadly diminished by his circumstances. But the Commandant is wary of Baker. There is something calculated and cunning in his attitude — a bit of a fox, he thinks, or even a blackmailer.

"It is perhaps significant that most of the detainees to whom Baker has paid particular attention are men of means," he writes. "One of these, George Unsworth, is already contributing to the upkeep of the Baker family."

The Commandant refills his Parker fountain pen from a fresh bottle of Quink Vista Blue, and resumes his report with a recommendation that Baker be kept on in detention, though he strongly recommends his removal from Peel Camp ... "where he is exercising a most pernicious influence on some of the weaker-minded brethren," he writes. He does however recommend Christopher Brooke's release, a matter which will have to be reviewed at length by the Advisory Committee and which will require Brooke's appearance before them in London. The Commandant thinks it unwise to mention the matter to Brooke yet, since it will undoubtedly be a drawn-out affair and could result in yet another disappointment for the man.

Chapter Twenty-Five

THE BIRTHDAY CAKE

CYNTHIA AND I sat up late listening to the wireless almost every night that summer. She was desperate for news of Mireille, but there was seldom anything about France, except for the brave activities of the Resistance there, and the brutal German reprisals. At the end of August we learned about the failure of the raid on Dieppe and the terrible losses suffered on the beach. Less than half of the five thousand Canadians who embarked on that raid were returned to England. They say there were two thousand taken prisoner, and God knows how many dead and wounded. It made no sense to me—boys dying in a foreign place they'd never seen before. I wondered about my brother Seán and I prayed fervently that he had not been in Dieppe with the British commandos.

I'd had no news from home in more than a month. Mam and Da were not letter writers, and Patrick neither, besides which after a full day of work on the farm they were likely thinking more about their beds than putting pen to paper. I knew that if anything happened I might feel it or see it in my dreams. Being in the middle of a war is like being in the dark. Afterwards, when we learned about the death camps, they said that even the people living close by never knew what was going on, because it was unimaginable. And if they had known, what could they have done? There is a force of history that paralyzes us and robs us of our humanity. How else can you explain the madness? In the 1940s that force was Hitler, an upstart who chanced upon fertile ground and grew rampant there, poisoning everyone around him with his disease.

The memory of our summer picnic warmed me as autumn drew on and Cynthia pulled back, for she would do that—come up close, then pull away for no reason. I turned to the children for comfort. Birdie would sit on my knee and play horsey, her little body bouncing up and down. I loved it when she flung her arms around my neck and kissed me full on the mouth. She was a darling child with the wildness still in her, and Jimmy was a darling too, though a bit cautious until that night I woke to hear him whimpering. I jumped out of bed, wrapped my dressing gown around me, and got my slippers on for the floors in that house were always cold. When I entered his room I found him sat up in bed, staring into the darkness.

"Now what's the matter, Jimmy?" I asked, and then the floodgates opened.

"I had a dream," he said, sobbing. "Daddy came home and Mummy wouldn't let him in. He had to stand outside the front door all night, and then he went into the coal shed and got his coat all dirty." He broke down entirely with the telling of it.

"There, there," I said as I rocked him in my arms.

"I'm frightened! I hate sleeping alone."

"Well then, I'll just lie down here with you till you go to sleep."

"No," he said. "It's this room. There's a ghost!"

"Is that so? Well, what about my room?"

He looked up at me then, finding his vision in the darkness. "Can we try it?"

I wrapped him in a blanket and lifted him from the bed. He snuggled into me as I carried him across the corridor; it was not often Jimmy had his way, and I could feel the little smirk on his face. We settled down in my big bed and I began to tell him the story of Connla of the Fiery Hair, son of Conn of the Hundred Fights, who was one day stood by the side of his father on the height of Usna when he saw a maiden clad in strange attire coming towards him ... But the lad had fallen asleep right quick so I shut up and lay a while savouring his little boy smell, bitter and spicy.

In the morning I left him sleeping soundly while I went down to start the fires and, wouldn't you know it, that was the one morning Cynthia decided to look in on her son and when she found his bed empty she looked in my room and found him there. Well, she hit the roof! I heard her shouting from downstairs, and Jimmy's sudden wailing as though she'd slapped him.

"Get back to your room, you naughty little boy!" she shouted.

I ran upstairs, but before I could get a word in she turned on me.

"What d'you think you're doing, taking my son into your bed?"

"He was frightened. He had a bad dream."

"I don't care. He must learn to be a man."

"But he's only six years old, Cynthia."

"You'll make a namby-pamby of him, just like his father."

"What?"

"You heard me. There are things you don't know. I can't discuss it with you, Mary Byrne, but if I ever find you spoiling Jimmy again I'll, I'll ..."

"You'll what? And what d'you mean by spoiling?"

I had a dirty feeling in me and the shame of it drove me to challenge her for the first time.

"I think you need more time off, Mary. I ... I've expected too much of you."

I should have challenged you earlier, I thought. You're just a coward at heart.

"Why don't you take the evening off? ... a couple of evenings a week ..."

"What for?"

"To go out with your young man."

"What young man? What're you talking about?"

"The one who repaired my chimney."

That's how it started. I was so angry with her that I accepted his invitation finally. Reg had been pestering me all summer long and I'd avoided him for there seemed something fateful about stepping out with such a man. But now I thought, I'll show her. At least I have someone to pay me attention and he's not complicated like your husband.

We sat in the back row at the Tudor Cinema and he held my hand and pressed his palm into mine. When he put his arm around my shoulders I let it rest there with his fingers rubbing back and forth over my collar bone. I still had my face turned to the screen, watching the pictures there and the shifting streams of light from the projector with cigarette smoke curling through them. I could tell he wanted to kiss me. He smelled of tobacco, and something oily and woody, a man's fragrance. I felt his warm breath on my neck as he leaned into me, surprisingly sweet, so I turned my face slightly, my eyes still on the screen, and he found my mouth and fixed his onto it. There was nothing special about the look of Reg's mouth which was small with thin lips, but he turned out to have a shockingly strong tongue. His lips too were like living things from the feel of them moving energetically on mine, and there were tiny bristles on his face scratching me and, oh my God, I felt desire rising in me in spite of everything. And when he clamped his hand on my breast the feeling shot through my nipple like a bullet and down between my thighs to the secret place. I felt something melting inside my belly and a wetness seeping into my knickers. I only wished it could have been the Master and not Reg from the Walkley Estates. There's a sadness to feeling such beauty with the wrong man.

Jimmy was right. There were ghosts in that house and we all felt them. Cynthia had a tale about Charlotte at five years old, standing in the open doorway of her parents' bedroom which faced down the length of the corridor to the lavatory at the end, flanked by Jimmy's room and mine.

"I was sitting at my dressing table, Mary, when something made me turn. Charlotte was pointing down the corridor. 'Look, Mummy,' she said. 'A dwarf lady in a long white dress, and an old man. They're calling me.' I rushed over, but there was no-one there. I was angry with Charlotte for telling fibs, but she insisted and as I listened my skin broke out in goose bumps. She was describing the people who had lived there before us—an old couple, the woman legless with her white nightgown collapsed around her stumps—apparently she'd had both legs amputated as a consequence of diabetes. They had died there in the house within a few days of each other. That's all the estate agent would tell us. How could the child have known that?"

I had no answer for her, and neither could I argue. Children will tell inconvenient truths, to be sure, especially Charlotte who had the Sight and called me cuckoo. I wondered if the old couple had died in my room or in Jimmy's, or perhaps one in each for my dreams were strange and vivid as day under that roof. My head was so full of stories about Cynthia's life, about the Master and the children that I couldn't tell the difference between what I'd dreamed and what I'd heard.

Sometimes I saw my brother, and hers, their heads down, rifles slung across their backs, running through muddy fields, and I didn't know if they were hunting rabbits in Ireland or fighting the Germans in Europe, or even what country it might be in that patchwork of a place. Sometimes I'd see the Master standing alone in the garden in the centre of the Magic Circle, and all the children running around him, Birdie squawking like a blackbird, and Cynthia sitting on the swing with the baby on her knee, her face white and her eyes burning like beacons. Always in those dreams there was a darkness, like water pressing in on me, threatening to drown me. And sometimes there were cities destroyed by bombs, and I'd be running through the streets trying to find the children and take them to safety, and I'd wake in a sweat and tiptoe down the corridor to make sure the children were safe.

There was one nightmare I'll never forget. It woke me with a start and left me chilled to the bone. All day I carried it with me, planted in my gut like a bad seed. It was soon after Jimmy's birthday, I remember, because we had a scramble to bake him a cake, begging sugar and eggs from the neighbours who were reluctant enough to share. I almost had to get down on my knees, but then Mrs. Arnold across the road revealed her Irish heritage on her mother's side and when I said I was from Cavan two eggs appeared with a cup of sugar besides, and it was all I could do to get out of her house within the hour.

When I remember that nightmare now all I can see is Cynthia's face as she walks towards me. "My children ... my beloved children," she says, and she leans forward, trying to tell me something. She beckons and I follow her down the corridor into the kitchen. She is so beautiful, her brown eyes liquid, her face filled with a love that shines all around her. I reach forward to touch her, but she moves away towards the kitchen table where the three children sit. It is Jimmy's birthday and he has on a paper dunce's hat with the number six on it. Charlotte sits rigid, her eyes fixed on the table, while Birdie is colouring in her Cinderella book, her tongue at the corner of her mouth where the sores are, caused by her licking and chewing.

Cynthia moves towards them very slowly. She's chanting over and over — *Bake a cake, Bake a cake, Bake a cake and Fix your Fate ...* to the tune of Birdie's fairy music. Then she turns to me and says she's been to the shops but there are no cakes on offer, and with the rationing she has no sugar or eggs to make one, so she's going to make a joke of it, for Jimmy's sake. Though she doesn't actually say these words, it's just that I know it, the way you do in dreams, like mind-reading.

She has three pieces of cloth laid out on the table and she pours something on them and wraps them around the children's mouths, one by one, very slowly. I feel afraid for the children and I want to run forward and help them, but I can't move. Everything is so slow, it's like moving through treacle. Cynthia is smiling now, and she's struck a match. It flares blue, then orange. I can see the red tip at the centre of the flame. And the match becomes a burning torch in her hand as she touches it to their mouths, one by one — first Birdie, then Jim, then Charlotte — lighting them like candles until their mouths are circled with fire.

She begins to sing, *Happy birthday to you ...* I open my mouth to scream but no sound comes out. My feet are stuck to the kitchen linoleum. The children don't move. It is the strangest thing, all three of them sit there staring at me, and I can't bear it. I close my eyes tight and when I open them Cynthia is still smiling as she unwraps her children. The blackened cloths crumble between her fingers and their faces are revealed, the mouths sealed with fresh pink skin as though they had been wounded and are now healed.

"Don't you look at me like that," she says. "I'm their mother. I love my children."

I feel the force of her anger and I know I shouldn't have seen this. She lunges at me and I wake with my heart pounding. How will they eat? How will they speak and make their way in the world?

Chapter Twenty-Six

KINGDOM HOUSE

I am pulled into the pages of my father's slim volumes, given to me by Auntie Alice, the only words of his I have, because our mother burned everything—except for the Walton Bible. As I read I am confounded by my own memory of those prison cells, collapsed into one solitude, stronger than his words. We are fused like burnt flesh imprinted with his life in whorls and worm-silvered patterns, forever indecipherable, only to be felt in dreams.

CHRISTOPHER IS CALLED to the Creg Malin Hotel and informed by Inspector Blunt that the Advisory Committee has summoned him to appear before them in order to assist the Home Secretary in reconsidering his case.

He travels with a group of fellow detainees in the autumn of 1942 and is held in Brixton prison while awaiting his hearing. This is his third petition. He feels sure that Captain Baker's intercession on his behalf will make the difference this time. After one week he and a fellow prisoner are taken early in the morning to Burlington House. He is shocked to see the extent of bomb damage in London as they pass in a saloon car along the Thames Embankment, through Trafalgar Square and around Piccadilly Circus. He resolves to request permission for sister Alice to visit him in Brixton. Upon arrival they are shown to a small basement room which is blacked out and only dimly lit by a forty-watt bulb. They spend the morning here awaiting their call. When the Advisory Committee has reassembled after lunch Christopher is called in to face three judges and a plump, pretty stenographer who records their exchange. At his first opportunity he speaks up.

"There appear to be two grounds for the detainment of British Union members—a suggestion that we are traitors who would take up arms and fight with the Germans if they landed. And that our propaganda undermines civilian morale."

"You can entirely dismiss the first suggestion, Mr. Brooke," the judge says in a deep, melodious voice.

"Then I can only assume that we have been detained because of our campaign in favour of a negotiated peace."

"Yes, Mr. Brooke," the judge intones, "That *was* the case, though hardly relevant now in the midst of war."

After an exhaustive review, during which he is questioned on the complete history of his activities during his membership of British Union—an interrogation that continues for more than an hour—one of the younger judges speaks up cautiously. "We realize, of course, that the Government has made mistakes. We all do, Mr. Brooke." He smiles apologetically and clears his throat. "But if you *were* to be released, it would not be tactful of you to say so." His tone is diffident, almost pleading.

Christopher can barely suppress a smile as the sing-song judge weighs in with his baritone. "Your testimony has been most informative, Mr. Brooke. If only the world could be as you perceive it, but sadly times have changed, and I'm sorry to say that the change may not be temporary, hmm?" He looks up, removes his spectacles and focuses intently on Christopher before continuing. "An adjustment, Mr. Brooke? An adjustment in perspective perhaps, for the good of your family?"

"When may I expect your decision?" Christopher asks, unmoved by the judge's suggestion.

"These decisions are never made quickly, Mr. Brooke. The soonest one could hope to hear would be in four weeks, and could even stretch to twenty weeks."

"But my family has already suffered from false hope and inaccurate information. There have been several occasions when I have been told that I was to be released, when I have awaited that release daily, with my wife and children expecting me home at any moment, only to be informed by the Home Secretary that I was to be further detained."

"Really?" the senior judge says, raising his eyebrows and staring over his spectacles at Christopher with genuine concern. He confers briefly with his colleagues, flips through Christopher's file, but finally shakes his head. "No record of such an incident here, Mr. Brooke."

"Well, certainly at Latchmere. Several times I was informed ..."

"Ah, Latchmere. MI5 operations are outside our jurisdiction, I'm afraid." He closes the file with a decisive gesture. "Please be patient, Mr. Brooke. All this will come to a close eventually. We're all waiting for closure." The corners of his mouth twitch upwards, into a kindly smile—a signal Christopher recognizes as dismissal.

Early on the following Wednesday he is informed that the Home Office has requested his immediate return to Peveril Camp where he is to await the Home Secretary's decision regarding his release from detention. He is to leave that very evening for an overnight journey to the Isle of Man. He will miss his visit with Alice. Only now does he realize how *much* he misses Alice. She is perhaps the only person with whom he feels able to be his true self, a feeling that rests upon the bedrock of their childhood play and shared innocence. He had always been kind to her, trying to live up to her little-sister adoration.

He slumps at the table in his prison cell, cradling his head in his hands. He's worn down with false hopes continually dashed. He's sick of being played with, like a mouse tormented by a grinning cat. He has to remind himself that his request has in fact not been turned down and that he must simply wait out the war and his inevitable release.

Just as he returns to camp the news comes that Tobruk has been retaken by British troops, and he wonders about his old friend Eric Cartwright. Cynthia has told him in her letters that Eric had been waiting out the war in Libya, enjoying the desert experience until the Germans blundered in. He wonders if he and Eric will resume their friendship after all that has occurred. He scours the pile of newspapers Ben Glover has saved during his absence, looking for news on the

British attack at El Alamein and Rommel's subsequent withdrawal, and about the progress of the ongoing battle at Stalingrad where he finds himself cheering for the German side. He and Thom Baker begin to plan in earnest for the purchase of a property. They will call it Kingdom House.

Chapter Twenty-Seven

TWENTY-FOUR AND STILL A SPINSTER

"You've made a happy man of Reg," Meg said as she greeted me at the door of her caravan.

"What's he been telling you?"

"There's no need of telling, my girl. One look at 'is face is enough. Grinning ear to ear and whistling like a bird in springtime."

I shrugged my shoulders even though I felt myself colouring up. "Sure, it was only a trip to the cinema."

"I'll bet you can't tell me 'ow the picture ended?" Meg exploded with her throaty laugh which soon turned into a spluttering fit.

"Meg, go on with you!" I said as I thumped her on the back to ease her coughing. She came out of it breathless but with a wicked grin on her face that embarrassed me no end. I was new at this game for sure and didn't think of myself in that way, except in my dreams of the Master, but they were only fantasies and never to be told.

"Well, are you going to marry 'im?"

"What? I've only been to the pictures with him, for mercy's sake!"

"You take my advice, Mary. Snap 'im up. 'E's sweet as a lump of sugar on you and 'e's not a bad feller."

"But I hardly know him ..."

"Reg Wilkins will stick with you and 'e'll be a good provider. 'E'll get you out of Lady Muck's 'ouse and you can 'ave some kiddies of your own instead of looking after hers."

"Well, aren't you counting your chickens? He hasn't even asked me."

"'E will. You mark my words. I've known Reg since 'e was a nipper."

"But he's not a strong man, Meg. He can't even join up and fight."

"That's the beauty of 'im, love. You won't be widowed in a week like most of the girls around 'ere. And it's only 'is lungs. I'll wager 'e's a strong man where it counts."

Her own lungs got her then in another spasm of laughter turned to coughing. When she was done she gave me her parting shot.

"And 'e doesn't drink. That must mean a lot to a girl from Ireland."

I didn't want to leave Cynthia's house, but between her and Meg, they'd planted something. I spent sleepless nights in bed thinking about my future. Twenty-four and still a spinster. Was I to dream about the Master all my life, or should I be realistic and settle for Reg? I knew with a bit of encouragement he would broach the subject. I was holding back in spite of my body wanting to loose the reins and run headlong at him. I didn't know how it was for other girls.

Cynthia had told me about her passionate feelings for Christopher Brooke, and of course her friendship with Mireille, and I knew about that all right, because I felt the same kind of friendship for her when I was in her good favour, but I had not the freedom to show it being a servant in her house. It was all one-sided, with Cynthia in control of how it would be. She was the lucky one, but perhaps not so lucky seeing the turn things had taken with her husband. I wondered would they manage to get back to normal when it was all over. I was naïve. Any fool could have predicted what was to come. But I was too involved, you see, my life lived through them. I couldn't see what was going on in the house, let alone in the prisons and camps, on the battlefields and at conferences where Mr. Churchill was meeting with Josef Stalin and Mr. Roosevelt.

Chapter Twenty-Eight

NEW MOON

WE WENT A second time to the Tudor Cinema and I'll admit I was nervous, not of Reg, but of my own feelings and the turmoil he could set up just by touching me, even though it was another man I was thinking of. I wonder now if that isn't the case for many people, women and men alike. They say that men operate differently from us on account of their private parts being outside the body, and therefore more public than private, making them incontinent and entirely out of control of themselves.

My thoughts and fantasies are important to me and I wouldn't want to lose them, for without them I'd be indulging in the same kind of animal behaviour, but perhaps that's not so bad either once in a while. I reckon there was a lot of that going on during the war with the men coming and going between long periods of deprivation, and the women soft-hearted and soft-headed enough to indulge them. It was Meg's busiest time, a regular boom at the Walkley Estates in those war years.

Reg bought me a Cadbury's Ration bar which was not as good as the Dairy Milk chocolate, but the use of fresh milk had been banned and the Cadbury's factory had to use skimmed milk powder instead. We sat in the back row, right in the middle. I can see it now, and smell it too, for the floor was like an old ashtray, and Reg adding to it with the droppings of his hand-rolled cigarettes. But when the projector started its whirring and a shaft of light appeared like a giant fog light dancing with dust, I was transported to another world as I watched that crowing white rooster herald the Pathé News. The newsreel was all about Monty's forces attacking Rommel at El Alamein in Egypt. A very excited gentleman gave us a special report from British Headquarters in Cairo. He told us how they'd cleared the mine-fields inch by inch to make way for the Allied soldiers to move forward.

"This triumph is the beginning of the end for Adolf Hitler in North Africa," he said.

Reg remarked that all those lucky lads were having a chance to travel finally, though it looked to me like a dusty desert of a place with nothing of interest in sight. Perhaps he wanted to impress me with his wish to go and fight for the travel and adventure of it so that I wouldn't think him a slacker. Well, I didn't. I was grateful there were a few men left in England, even if they were weaklings, though you could hardly call the Master a weakling.

They finished up with a message from the King himself congratulating the Allied Commander in Egypt.

"The 8th Army has dealt the Axis a blow of which the importance cannot be exaggerated," he said in that halting way, not at all excited as the reporter had been. Then we heard Vera Lynn singing to the troops in Egypt, a lovely song called *The White Cliffs of Dover*. And finally came the feature presentation, *Goodbye Mr. Chips,* and it was a marvellous film though Reg was soon pawing at me so that I had to fight him off to keep up with the story. After the death of Mr. Chips' young wife I was overcome with a surprising grief and Reg put his arm around me for comfort. I let him do it, because I asked myself, what's more important, a pretend film in moving pictures, or a real flesh and blood man sitting next to me?

Afterwards he wanted to take me for a cup of tea, but there were no cafés open, so he walked me home from the village, going out of his way past the Walkley Estates. I said no, don't do it, Reg, I'll be alright on my own, but he insisted, and held my hand all the way and pointed up at the new moon as we came to the corner of Chester Road. It was so thin I could barely see it, for I am short-sighted and hadn't wanted to put on my spectacles in front of Reg. The film had been a bit blurry, but I had caught the gist of it. Da says that my Second Sight makes up for it.

"Let's make a wish on it," Reg said, looking up at the faint moon.

"What kind of a wish?"

"Up to you, but you can't tell or it won't come true. I know what I'm wishing for."

I could guess well enough what he was after from his suggestive tone.

"I wish for an end to this war," I said, just to show him that my mind was not full of smut like his.

"No, no, you mustn't tell," he said. "Go on then, make another. I've already made my wish."

I stared up into the sky. There were a million stars, just like at home on a clear night, and I thought how small we were, and how close, all of us crowded together under that huge sky. And I wished fervently that I might go home to Ireland and find myself a man there. But perhaps that was my mistake, to wish for two things at once.

He wanted to see me right to the door, but I told him we must part at the gate. It was a long goodbye with my back up against the gatepost and his slippery tongue in my mouth, getting me all stirred up, but I finally broke away and left him there, alone in the darkness.

I opened the door ever so carefully and locked it behind me, then I saw that the light was on in the sitting room.

"Who's there?" came her voice.

I was half-way across the hall when she appeared at the door, her face white and pinched looking.

"Oh, Mary, you gave me a fright. I thought someone had broken in."

There was a tinge of disappointment in her voice and I realized that she was waiting for him, for the Master to come home unexpectedly. But she recovered herself quickly and invited me to sit with her for a while, though it was late.

"Was it a good film?" she asked.

I babbled on about Mr. Chips and his poor wife who died in childbirth, and before I knew it I was blubbering like a baby, Lord knows why. Cynthia shuffled up beside me on the settee and put her arm around me, just as Reg had done in the cinema.

"What's the matter, dear? Did your young man upset you? Did he say something?"

I felt like a teenager being questioned by her mam, though there was a mere five years between us. She was cleverer than she knew for it was true that Reg had stirred me up but without saying anything, only his nonsense about wishing on the moon and me wishing something quite different from him. She poured me a drop of gin and offered me one of her Turkish cigarettes. There were already two cigarette butts in the ashtray, rimmed with her red lipstick. I soon cheered up with the gin slipping warmly down my throat, and we laughed about poor Mr. Chips and his schoolboys. It turned out that she and the Master had seen the very same film in Manchester before the war so we were able to discuss it, though Cynthia was more for telling me what happened after.

"We left the Odeon and went out dancing at a nightclub. A group of our friends were there and we joined them at their table—Adèle and Eric Cartwright, and my old school friend Jenny Anderton with her husband George. They were about to leave for a posting in Singapore —George is in rubber—and I remember thinking how lucky I am to be settled in England, close to my family with no need to travel for anything but pleasure."

She paused, gone far away suddenly, and I held still, not wanting to break the spell. There was nothing like her stories. I could smell the richness of the club with its mixture of fine wines and ladies' perfumes, and I saw the big round table where they sat with its crisp white linens and crystal glasses. The lights were dim enough that everything simply glowed and throbbed like a slow fire warming them, and the Master spinning in circles on the dance floor without ever taking his eyes off Cynthia.

"Christopher held me so lightly, yet masterfully. I've never been much of a dancer, Mary, always stumbling and tripping, even as a child. But in his arms I felt like Ginger Rogers! Of course he had to dance with all the ladies, so I sat out and watched him. There was a foxtrot, his specialty, and he manoeuvred Jenny around the dance floor with such ease. D'you know, I felt intensely jealous, even though there was such pleasure in watching him? I've never been able to get my fill of him. He always leaves me wanting more." She stubbed out her cigarette suddenly and viciously. "Now look at us—a houseful of females with one asthmatic little boy."

I blurted something to cover my embarrassment for I could well understand her frustration after feeling my own so recently at the front gate with Reg.

"This war will soon be over, and perhaps Mr. Brooke will be home even before the end of it."

"D'you think so? D'you think we'll dance again?"

She turned to me with such childish hope that I felt terrible for speaking out, for what did I know of it? Though in truth I do know that you can't quite recreate the past no matter how hard you try. All you can do is remember it and move forward with it inside you. Every day is a new one, informed by the last. I hadn't a chance to voice my thoughts for she soon skittered away from the topic and started on about Reg again, turning the tables on me, teasing.

"Well, what did he say? Did he pop the big question?"

I blushed and spluttered as I searched for words, and Cynthia went full steam ahead with her mistake.

"Oh Mary, I'm so happy for you," she said. "But what will I do without you? The children will miss you so."

She'd jumped the gun and I couldn't stop her any more than I could keep up with her. The entire subject of me and Reg seemed to please her, and of course it had been her suggestion that I step out with him after she'd discovered little Jimmy in my bed that fateful morning. Here she is trying to comfort me, I thought, when she wouldn't allow me to comfort a little fellow that was having a nightmare. There was something strange about it. Could she be living through me? I wondered.

That whole house was filled with uncertainty, with voices and ghosts clamouring for attention. Perhaps all of England is like that, I thought to myself. After all I'd hardly had the chance to get out of the house, only to the village with the children, or to the Walkley Estates to visit with Meg. And my one day in Manchester with Cynthia. Perhaps it was the war had made everything strange. A girl of my limited experience was in no position to understand such things.

We all make our opinions on the flimsiest of grounds. But at the bottom of it I knew I had gained Cynthia's approval by walking out with Reg. And I do believe it was the reason I was invited to her family's house that Christmas of 1942, for I was presented there as a girl engaged to be married, which was a complete lie, though I believe it did lead me into that condition, for when you tell a lie, or even go along with someone else's pretence, you begin to believe in it yourself.

"Here, Mary," she said, sitting me down at her dressing table one morning in front of her jewellery box. "Try this ring, no, no, your left hand, come on, your engagement finger. Look, it fits perfectly!"

'Twas a fancy ring of sparkling little diamonds with a tiny emerald in the centre.

"There. It's on loan until your young man can afford to buy one for you."

It was an uncomfortable feeling, being caught up in her web of pretence, but I couldn't help feeling quite grand with that ring on my finger and a green woollen dress she loaned me for Christmas day at the Woodlands. It was loose on her but fit me like a glove, and if I say so myself I looked grand in it, especially after I took up the hem a few inches.

We all crammed into Cynthia's Hillman Minx and motored the two miles to her parents' house. Jimmy was already feeling sick as we arrived, so I got him out of the car right quick and made him gulp big mouthfuls of fresh air. We were greeted at the door by Cynthia's sister Ruby, and a lively spark she was, who shook my hand and said: "I'm so pleased to meet you finally. Where's Cynthia been hiding you?" She laughed, as though it was a joke, but she whispered to me later on: "Don't let her make a slave of you. You're entitled to a day off every week, and two evenings out."

Of course she *had* met me before, right after the baby was born, when I'd opened the door to her and her sister Margaret, but domestic help are invisible people in England. Mind you, I couldn't take Ruby amiss for she had a warmth and enthusiasm that Cynthia lacked, as though the one stood in sunshine, and the other in shade.

It was a grand house with a front hall big enough to dance in.

There were statues on pedestals, and paintings hanging all over the walls, and parquet floors covered with patterned carpets. Cynthia had told me that her father travelled in his business and sometimes took his wife with him, to Egypt and India, to Persia, Turkey and other faraway places. Ruby pointed me towards the cloakroom where I took the children while we hung up our coats and changed from our outdoor shoes, for we weren't to dirty the carpets.

Cynthia sent me to the kitchen to help Mrs. Fern, the housekeeper, with the lunch, and to give her the Christmas cake I had managed to bake with Mrs. Arnold's contributions, despite our own shortage of sugar and eggs. Birdie had scattered silver balls on the icing, and Charlotte had put Father Christmas in the middle of it, riding in his sleigh, so at least it looked good, though I was afraid of how it would taste, especially in this grand house.

It was a sitting of seventeen adults, and our children at their own small table in the corner. I was to sit with them which pleased me because I could feel part of it without the responsibility of making conversation out of my depth. I had the baby beside me in a highchair, eleven months old and quite a handful by then. I helped Mrs. Fern to carry in the turkey, a twenty-pounder with all the trimmings—bacon, sausage, and stuffing. Lord knows where they got it all with the wartime rationing. The rich are not affected by hardship like the rest of us. They can buy what they want on the black market, even during a war.

It was Cynthia's mother, Mrs. Dorothy Blackwell, who was in charge that day. Her husband sat quietly and did not say much except for the occasional joke, and a cruel one at that. He called his wife Dotty and I wasn't sure if it was an affectionate term or an insult. How could a man stand happily by and let his wife rule the roost? I could see that Cynthia adored him, so then I understood how it was that he'd been able to take her away from her job in Manchester. She would have followed him anywhere.

But it was different with her mother and her sister Ruby. They made fun of the old man, and with each other they were quite snippy. Mrs. Blackwell embarrassed Cynthia with a comment about Christopher Brooke enjoying another Christmas at the expense of His Majesty's

Prison Service, but Mr. Blackwell silenced her with a fierce look from under his bushy eyebrows. He had the carving knife and fork poised at the time. Then Ruby burst out with the news that she'd been accepted by the Red Cross—just like in Cynthia's dream—"I'm going to the Front as an ambulance driver!" she announced with great importance.

"No daughter of mine is going to war," Mr. Blackwell said, and Mrs. Blackwell replied: "Nonsense, Dick. Ruby will make us proud. Besides, unmarried girls are being conscripted now so you can't stop her."

The other sister, Margaret, was studying for a career in photography, and it was likely her who had taken some of the photos I had been studying. After the meal she was up with her camera snapping away at us—not me of course, for I was not part of the family—but she took many photos of the children, and no doubt I was caught in one or two of them, though I never did see them. They were a close family in spite of everything. "Blood is thicker than water," Cynthia was fond of saying, when she wasn't complaining about her family.

We were short on men that day for the one brother, Jack, was fighting at the Front, and some of the cousins too. You could tell that Jack was his mother's favourite. She hardly stopped talking about him all through the meal, or perhaps she was only trying to shame Cynthia. The youngest brother, Richard, was only a lad, though a tall one with the beginnings of a moustache. He tried to take Jimmy and Charlotte down to his basement workshop between the turkey and the pudding, and Jimmy was ready to go with him for the promise of hammering more nails, but Charlotte held onto the boy.

"No, Jumbo, no," she said, with such a fierce look in her eye. But I could see she was frightened behind her bravery, and I wondered what it was that had frightened her. Teenage boys can be bullies. I knew a bit about that from defending myself against my own brothers. What is it about men that makes them that way? Is it the world we live in, or something they're born with? Even Jimmy would be bullying Birdie when I wasn't looking, but she could stand up for herself. She'd bite him, usually on his bottom, then it was him would be screaming, and Birdie getting punished.

After the Christmas pudding we listened to the King's message on a crackly wireless that Mr. Blackwell brought in from his study. There was more talk about the King's stuttering than about his message, and no wonder for he didn't say much of anything, just to be strong and patriotic until the end. Easy for him to counsel from his comfortable palace, though they say he never wanted to be king. It was his brother that let him down by running off with a twice-divorced American.

As soon as we'd eaten my cake, which turned out to be quite palatable with a strong cup of tea, Cynthia bustled us into the car, but not before she'd announced in front them all that I was engaged to be married to a young gentleman.

"Take care of my Cynthia," Mrs. Blackwell said to me as we stood at the door. "Don't leave her in the lurch." Those were the first words she had spoken to me. No doubt she thought my intended was a soldier fighting alongside her son, which made me worthy of her notice at the last minute.

"You were a tower of strength," Cynthia said after we'd got the children off to bed and were sitting with our stockinged feet up on the coffee table, laughing about it all. My heart warmed to her then because I'd seen how diminished she was by her family, even amidst that sense of belonging she must have felt. And aren't we all like that, receiving the mixed blessing of kinship and thick blood?

Chapter Twenty-Nine

A POSY OF WILD FLOWERS

THE NEW YEAR began with another visit to the Tudor Cinema, but to tell you the truth I don't remember what film we saw. It was the Pathé newsreel commanded my attention with a report on the battles being fought in distant places that neither Reg nor I had ever heard of. The cheery tone of the commentator made it sound more like a Saturday afternoon football game than a war, with both sides scoring goals against each other. He said the British troops had taken Tripoli which looked like a sunny place with palm trees rustling as though there was a breeze blowing through. We saw soldiers marching with rifles over their shoulders and cartloads of foreign people dressed like Irish tinkers with mules to pull their wagons while they stared at the man behind the camera who must have been as foreign to them as they were to him. The American and Australian forces had attacked a place called Buna, and the Japanese were at it all over the Pacific and becoming more unpopular every day. How our war with Germany could have got so out of control I couldn't fathom.

Meanwhile Charlotte was waging her own little war against me. I'd thought I might win her confidence, but she was a stubborn child and wouldn't let up. She told her mother that I'd stolen money from Miss Dixon's handbag, Miss Dixon being the elderly lady who came every morning at nine to give the children their lessons. She wore spectacles and a tailored grey suit with sensible shoes like my own. Charlotte would run and hide from her because she didn't want to learn. Jimmy was Miss Dixon's favourite. He called her Dik Dik, and they would sit all morning over their books while she taught him patiently how to read. Birdie joined in sometimes, for as long as she could sit still. She was going to be five years old next birthday, and was eager to keep up with her brother.

I didn't rise to Charlotte's bait, though I felt saddened to be accused of theft, and by a child. There was no winning her. But Cynthia, to her credit, supported me and told the girl not to tell fibs.

"This is not a white lie, Charlotte," she said. "It's a slander."

"Like what they said about Daddy at school?" she came back, smart as a whip.

Cynthia's face changed then. She pressed her lips together and took hold of the child with such force that I thought to myself it would have been better to have shouted at her. I'd seen it time and again, those children taking it all into their bodies and not understanding what it was about. Charlotte tensed up and glared at me as though it was all my fault.

"Jimmy did it!" Birdie shouted. "Jimmy took Dik Dik's money!"

"I did not!" Jimmy protested and began to wheeze.

"I'm sick to death of you children!" Cynthia said. "There'll be no pocket money for two weeks."

It was a mere storm in a teacup, as I thought, and the gentle Miss Dixon herself telling Cynthia not to worry about it.

"A matter of two half-crowns, Mrs. Brooke. Perhaps I've been mistaken after all. I'm sure the dear children would not ... "

She trailed off, perhaps implying me as the guilty party, for she did set herself up as a rival for the children's affections. It was my hope that she was indeed mistaken, but the following week, on the day that I was paid I discovered a theft from my own bedroom. I had been saving part of my salary for a visit home, and it was a great satisfaction for me to place a crisp ten shilling note each week in the jewellery box in the top drawer of my dresser.

On this occasion, as I went to count my savings and add another note, I found myself five pounds short. At first I could not believe it, for my heart sank to think that anyone would trespass into my room. I had no lock on my door and therefore no hope of security if there was indeed a thief in the house. I thought again of the albino chimney murderer, lurking always in my imagination, burrowing his way into my thoughts and holding me hostage, but of course it was not money he was after.

I took the rest of my notes and hid them under the mattress. But then I thought, no, that is an obvious place, and I took the wad again and shoved it into the corner of my pillow slip where it was hidden by the bulk of the pillow itself and by the thick cotton of the cover. Cynthia was very particular about her own pillow cases, which were linen, nicely ironed and starched, while the rest of us made do with cotton which was quite good enough for me because at home we'd had the most threadbare of bedding.

Though I tried to keep it at bay the picture of Charlotte sneaking into my drawer would not go away. I knew she had been there and that she had taken my money. There was a boldness to it, and a challenge too, for the child would surely know that I was onto her. I said nothing and tried to act normally though I felt her watching me. I checked my pillow case each day but there was no further theft, and as the days passed I began to sense a change in Charlotte's attitude. She stopped her cuckoo teasing and even offered to help me with drying the dishes.

Jimmy was the one who began making fun of me now, trying to imitate my accent — "Darlin's, it's a grand day for a walk in the fields," he'd say, strutting around, wiggling his behind, but it was all in fun and we'd usually end in a chase with tickling and fits of helpless giggles. As spring came with wild flowers growing in the gardens and fields there was a new feeling of hope for us all. We endured the dark mornings for the blessing of longer days with double British summertime, and I was comforted to think of Mam and Da enjoying the same brightness, though poor Patrick would be getting up in the dark to stumble around feeding the animals. And Brendan out there doing whatever it was he was doing to free Ireland from the yoke of British rule in the north. There was no news of Seán so I knew he was still alive; bad news will surely reach you faster than anything.

One evening towards the end of May I went up to my room to fetch a cardigan, for though the day had been sunny and the children out in the garden playing until teatime, there was a sudden chill in the air. I had stopped my daily checking of the pillow and only added my ten-shilling note on Fridays, but something made me lift the bedcover, and there was a posy of wildflowers lying on my pillow. I knew immediately it was Charlotte had placed it there for it was a posy picked from the children's Magic Circle, with clover, dandelions and cowslips. Tears pricked my eyes as I thought of her tiptoeing into my room, insisting on entry into my private place, sending me a message of trust finally at nine years old. I said nothing, any more than I had blabbed about the theft. I placed the flowers in a glass of water and put them on my dressing table so that she'd know I treasured them. And after that I left my door open a crack to let her know she was welcome.

Chapter Thirty

HOSPITALITY

CHRISTOPHER IS CALLED to the Commandant's office on a blustery morning in late May when the flush of spring is once again belied by a series of squalls that lash the islanders with stinging needles of rain.

The Commandant greets Christopher with a broad smile. "The Home Secretary has approved your release, Mr. Brooke," he says, and when Christopher stares blankly at him, he hands over the letter with its Home Office letterhead embossed in royal blue.

Christopher holds the letter a moment before dropping his head to read it, and even then the letters swim before his eyes in a blur of disjointed digits. All he can think is that the typewriter lacked a new ribbon; the secretary should have replaced it before typing this important letter with a pale worn-out ribbon that has left traces of red where the shift key has been sloppily operated.

"When am I to leave?" he asks in a tone of bewilderment.

"When would you like to go?"

"Is Captain Baker to be released?"

"No."

"Why not? If I am to be released, surely ..."

"You are free to go whenever you wish, Mr. Brooke. Perhaps there are matters you wish to ..."

"Does my wife know?"

"Of course, she will have received a copy of the letter from the Home Office."

"This is not a trick, not like before when ...?"

"You have the proof here, Mr. Brooke." The Commandant places the palm of his hand firmly on top of the letter where Christopher has abandoned it on the desk. "You are a free man. And let me take this opportunity to say that you have been an exemplary member of this Camp. But now you are free to go and to regain your health in the comfort of your own home. And let's hope that we will soon see an end to the war. Then we will all be able to close this unpleasant chapter and move on with our lives."

Christopher sits rigid, his eyes staring into the middle distance.

"Is there anything I can do for you, Mr. Brooke, anything you need?"

"I have many matters to attend to—my daily broadcasts, my plans for the future with Captain Baker ..."

The Commandant clears his throat. "I would caution you against further involvement with Baker," he says, but he is interrupted smartly by Christopher who seems suddenly to have regained his clarity.

"I have the utmost respect for Captain Baker and I thank God for the opportunity to have allied myself with him here at Peveril Camp. He has interceded on my behalf on many occasions and no doubt I owe my freedom now in part to his good opinion of me."

The Commandant shrugs. "As you wish, Mr. Brooke, but surely you can see that you have only yourself to thank for this new development."

Christopher stares steely-eyed at the Commandant. "I need a little time. There are friends with whom I must part, business matters to conclude ... The guarantee of perhaps a fortnight more of your hospitality?"

"Indeed," the Commandant says, nodding, "you have it, Mr. Brooke."

Chapter Thirty-One

MANURE FOR THE ROSES

T WAS JUST before the homecoming that Charlotte knocked on my door and entered, looking curiously around the room as though she had never been in there before. And that is when she asked for my help in a matter of great importance to her.

We had received news that the Master was to be released on June 11th and Cynthia was beside herself with joy, though I could tell she was nervous about her family's reaction to Mr. Brooke's freedom, for she would be between them now, and that would be an awkward place and a test of her loyalty. We certainly hoped we would see him changed for the better and not so strange as on his last visit, ranting about politics and so on. How little we knew as we went into a frenzy of spring-cleaning, and the children sent out to pull up weeds from the driveway at sixpence a bucketful.

I confess I was filled with confusion myself, excited about having the Master home, but unsure as to how his presence in the house would affect my position, for rather than have me in conversation with the Master she would want to turn me against him by making me jealous of the notice he gave her, and then she would have us both in her grasp, on opposing sides. It made me tired to think of her silly games so I turned my attention instead to Reg and the serious matter of my future, and whether I should go home to my family or accept his offer and make my bed here and lie in it. And this is where Charlotte and her theft took a role in my destiny for to be sure if I'd had the money when that dreadful day dawned I would have fled to Ireland without looking back, so shamed was I by my own behaviour.

She knocked on my door early in the morning when I was barely dressed and intent only on hurrying down to get the kettle on and start breakfast.

"Now what is it you're wanting, love?"

She stood there with a smirk on her face, almost embarrassed I'd have thought if she weren't such a bold one.

"I've had an idea," she said. "I thought ... we could decorate the garden for Daddy's homecoming."

She was hesitant, as though she expected me to make fun of her idea. It seemed a thing of the utmost importance to her but she was no longer capable of that spontaneous outburst that is the signal of a happy child presented with a joyous occasion.

"That's a grand idea you have, Charlotte," I said, taking hold of her hands. "Of course I'll help you. We'll go down to the shelter and get the streamers and drape them among the trees."

We had decorated the shelter with Christmas streamers so that Birdie and Jimmy wouldn't be so afraid of going down there during the air-raids.

"And I'll make a big sign saying WELCOME HOME DADDY," she said.

After breakfast we got the paints and crayons out and sat ourselves down at the kitchen table to make the sign on a piece of cardboard I'd saved. We kept everything during the war, down to the shortest length of string. We strengthened the cardboard with tape and punched holes to make a loop with the string from the butcher's parcel, and I fetched the scissors with some strips of coloured paper and a pot of glue and set Jimmy and Birdie to making paper chains to mix amongst the streamers. The Master was to come home the following Friday, so we delayed the hanging of our decorations until Friday morning in case of rain.

Well, on Thursday didn't the telephone start ringing, and it kept up all day. It was the reporters, Cynthia said—from the *Daily Mail* and the *News of the World*. They'd found out about the release and they wanted an interview with Mr. Brooke. I had not thought that the Master was such a celebrity. Reporters are like bloodhounds when it comes to getting a story, as I would learn.

"It's just like when he was arrested three years ago, Mary. They were at my door, peppering me with questions, and I felt such a fool. I didn't know what to say. The *Daily Mail* is a rag. They publish hate letters from people saying that Mosley's fascists are cavorting on the Isle of Man and that they should all be shot!"

"Don't answer," I said. "Just let it ring. They'll soon tire of it."

But it was too much for her nerves. She'd lift the receiver and slam it down in a fury, and sometimes she'd shout at them: "Don't you dare dial this number again, or I'll call the police!"

On Friday morning after breakfast we were out in the front garden bright and early. It was a beautiful day with the roses and azaleas beginning to bloom, and the pampas grass sending out feathery white plumes. Jimmy went up the ladder and hung the streamers all across the front of the house, from the cloakroom window to the corner of the garage. Charlotte put her Welcome Home sign over the front door, and Birdie had made her own daisy chain that she draped over the front gate while we spread paper chains between the tree branches, and especially around the spiky branches of the monkey-puzzle tree where they held most easily. Birdie had the job of keeping Katie off the road, running after her and struggling back indoors with her, but by ten o'clock we were all set with nothing to do but wait. It was a long day with the children running in and out to see was he there yet.

"Darlin's, your daddy won't be here at least until teatime," I said, and after they'd eaten their lunch I sent them out to the back garden to play in the Magic Circle, so we didn't see the intruders come, sly like foxes to the chicken house, and the damage they did.

Cynthia was nervous as a hen. I heard her pacing upstairs in her bedroom for I was down in the sitting room doing a final dusting with special attention to the Master's grand piano. I hoped he would play for us every day now that he was to be home for the duration. I thought to myself what a comfort it would be to have a man in the shelter with us when the next air-raid came. That was my thought—I remember it well, and the shine I had put on the piano—as Charlotte opened the door and stood staring at me. Her face was red and she was trembling all over, with something clenched in her fist which she hurled at the piano, then she burst into tears.

"My goodness, child, what is it?"

She couldn't speak, she just stood there sobbing uncontrollably. She was a passionate soul to be sure when she allowed herself the indignity of it. I heard Birdie with her high-pitched squeal and in that same moment I smelled the burning and I rushed past Charlotte into the hallway.

"They've spoiled it all! They've spoiled our welcome for Daddy!" Birdie screeched. She had Katie by the hand, the child's eyes big and round as she looked about then started to wail. Jimmy ran into the house through the open front door, trying to tell me something but the poor boy was wheezing and spluttering so much he couldn't get the words out.

"I ... I can ... read," he said, finally getting it out. "I can read ... the word they painted."

Just at that moment Cynthia came dashing downstairs wanting to know what on earth was going on, and we all went out together through the front door.

They had desecrated the garden. They had pulled up the roses and azaleas, and they had set fire to the streamers and trampled on Charlotte's Welcome Home sign. There it was, all crumpled and ground into the gravel of the pathway. And our paper chains were hanging in tatters from the trees. But worst of all was the whitewash on the brick wall. TRAITOR, it said, in big letters all across the front of the house— TRAITOR, TRAITOR, TRAITOR—and across the garage door too.

Cynthia's face was ashen. She gathered the children to her and hurried them indoors. I went around the back and got a bucket of water and a scrubbing brush and I set to, scrubbing away at that horrible word until every writing of it had all but disappeared. It was a word I had heard often enough in Ireland, and a word my own brother Brendan had used against our Seán when he joined up. I took the garden hose and sprayed the brick until it was clean and red again, and the garage door too. Next I got a spade and replanted the roses and shrubs and that's when I received the final insult—a great big turd in the centre of the rose garden. Well, I shovelled it in—good manure for the roses, I thought.

I don't know who it was that did such a cruel thing—surely not the reporters who were only looking for a story, and surely not the neighbours' children who were forbidden to play at our house. We never did find out and that was the worst of it for when you don't know who your enemies are you're always looking over your shoulder, unable to trust anyone.

When I went back into the house I suddenly remembered the shattered thing under the piano, so I took the dustpan and brush and got down on my knees to sweep up the fragments. It had been something of great beauty judging by the colours and patterns I saw in some of the larger pieces. I looked up at Cynthia with her children on the settee, all holding onto each other like survivors of an accident. Even Birdie was quiet with her head nestled up against her mother's breast, and I felt a pang of jealousy run through me like a knife for I realized that's what it is about families—they will herd together like a pack of animals when there's trouble, and there was I on the outside in spite of my living with them.

What was it that Charlotte had thrown? She wouldn't look at me. She was entwined with her mother and holding onto Jimmy with her other hand. Then all of a sudden I saw it, the beautiful paperweight we'd looked at in Bramhall Village, and Charlotte so taken with it. She'd used my money to buy it for her daddy—a real paperweight instead of that dried up ginger pudding from Walton Gaol. Hot tears scorched my eyes as I felt the pain of that word 'Traitor' she'd read before Jimmy had mastered it.

I lay in bed that night feeling homesick for my own mam, and for my da and my sisters. But I resolved to move forward and create my own family with Reg, who was a stranger but who might become familiar to me through time and habit. That was the tenor of my thoughts even then, though I admit I was still skittish on the topic of Reg.

Chapter Thirty-Two

'I AM WITH MY HUSBAND IN EVERYTHING HE DOES AND THINKS'

S O IT WAS that the Master's homecoming was a subdued affair and not at all as we had planned it. It was me who opened the door to him at five o'clock in the evening with the sun still flooding the newly planted garden, and the shit well hidden under the earth.

The children came running and Birdie clung to his leg while Charlotte and Jim reached up to kiss him, but cautiously I could tell, burdened by the knowledge that their father was not well thought of by everyone.

Cynthia appeared in the sitting room doorway with Katie in her arms, and her smile was so warm as she greeted him. She never did tell him about the destruction done to her house, and the children didn't breathe a word of it. Perhaps she had primed them to spare him, or perhaps it was Charlotte after all who had silenced the young ones. We slept well that night knowing there was a man in the house, and not only for the weekend. But at eight thirty in the morning the doorbell rang and there they were, a gaggle of reporters and a man with a camera and a big flash on it. He snapped me as I opened the door and I was blinded and stepped back onto the Master's foot. He cried out and surprised me for I hadn't known he was there. Next thing I knew he took me by the arm and said: "Go back to the kitchen, Mary. I'll deal with this."

If Cynthia had said that it would have sounded like an insult, but

Christopher Brooke had a way with him. Perhaps his distance was a blessing for there was kindness and respect in his tone, even for his servants. How he could maintain that while living with her I don't know, and perhaps that was part of the problems that were yet to come. It is strange that I had all those thoughts, quick as lightning in that moment of invasion at our front door, but you remember those things, don't you, and every time I remember it I am standing again in that front hall with the open door and the Master striding forth bravely to face the reporters.

He pulled the door to behind him so that they would not peer into our house, and he was gone a good while, telling them what they wanted to know I suppose, but that wasn't the end of it. There were more came badgering him on Sunday morning, from the local newspapers this time. He seemed to enjoy the limelight, but Cynthia was furious.

"Don't talk to them, Christopher," she said. "You'll only encourage them."

"They're just doing their job, Cynthia," he replied. "The press can help me in spreading my message to the people of England."

He invited them in, two reporters, though he made the photographer stay outside under the front porch out of the rain. They sat themselves down at the dining room table and I brought a tray of tea with digestive biscuits so I heard the questions they asked.

"What are your plans for the future, Mr. Brooke, now that you're released from detainment?" inquired a fresh-faced young fellow with a head of curly brown hair.

"A group of us have formed an organization called the Legion of Christian Reformers," the Master began, but he was rudely interrupted by a sharp-featured foxy fellow with a pen and notepad in his hands.

"Is this part of British Union?" he asked.

"It is a non-political organization," the Master replied. "Essentially religious in nature. The people we are aiming to show up are the Church leaders."

"And the basis of your campaign?" asked the foxy one, his pen poised to scribble the Master's words.

"We regard Adolf Hitler as a scourge sent by God to cleanse the world," he declared, causing me to gasp, and the reporters to raise their eyebrows at each other. "Mahatma Gandhi, a deeply spiritual and peaceful leader who also has spoken out against our involvement in the war, has described Hitler in identical terms."

Only Cynthia remained expressionless as though she had not heard his shocking words as she busied herself with the handling of the milk jug and sugar bowl.

"Thank you, Mary, that'll be all," she said with a smile, and gave me a gesture of dismissal. But I heard a little more as I stood outside the door with my ear to the crack.

"D'you think your new crusade will suffer from your reputation as an ex-member of British Union?" I heard the voice of the fresh-faced lad.

"And from this unpopular stance on Hitler?" the foxy one said.

There was a dull thump followed by the rattling of teacups as the Master's fist came down on the table.

"Hitler is a man I have never met, so I can only know what I have read and heard about him, but I believe that all men are essentially good. We must all surrender to God's will in how he wishes to use us for the greater good."

I had to scurry back to the kitchen then because the door opened and he strode out, but I watched him from the kitchen corridor, searching in the hall cupboard for his briefcase. All I could hear as he returned to the reporters was his voice rising and falling as though he were reading from a book, and I dared not venture closer in case he burst from the room again. But I was called on to see the reporters out when the interview was over, so I witnessed their last shot in the front hall. It was the fox who questioned Cynthia, with an impudence that she had to suffer.

"Where do you stand on all this, Mrs. Brooke? We haven't had a chance to hear your voice."

She looked like a trapped animal herself and for a moment I thought she might go for him, tooth and nail. But she pulled herself up and said: "I am with my husband in everything he does and thinks." She hesitated a moment, then continued in a lower voice, but more truly felt. "Don't think he is mad. He isn't."

It was lunchtime Monday when he started on his wild ideas again, and this time I heard it all because I was invited to sit with them and tend to the children, especially Katie who was a fussy eater. She would turn her face away as the spoon approached and close her mouth tightly. I had learned to make a game of it and was the only one could coax her, with the spoon a choo-choo train going down the red lane, though there was often more food sprayed on her bib than consumed with all the giggling our game set up.

Birdie and Jim were chattering away with their nonsense—they bickered a lot for he would try to bully her but she could stand her ground. Charlotte had a big smile on her face, thrilled to have her daddy home, though he paid little attention to his children this time. I could see the change in him even then. He was intent on convincing Cynthia of his mission, and truth be told the way he spoke made me very uncomfortable, for the tone of it reminded me of the conversation we'd had at the kitchen table when he'd asked me to accompany him to church and bear witness to the corruption of the Catholic Church.

"My internment has enabled me to study the Bible more deeply than ever before," he said. "So that I have come to understand the Truth through my own mystical experience. Only two and a half weeks ago, on May 29th to be exact, I received a message as I worked alone in the fields hilling potatoes: 'You are the chosen instrument of God, to help in the regeneration of your people.'"

Cynthia said nothing, but she was clearly impatient with his religious talk. She'd said she supported him but I knew it was only because she hadn't known what else to say, or perhaps had not fully understood what he'd said. It's a marvel how we will deny things to ourselves to protect the ones we love. I had to leave the room to refill the water jug so I missed part of his sermon, but when I came back he was in full swing, his knife and fork laid down, his dinner congealing on the plate, and his eyes shining as though he had seen a vision.

"I want you to meet him, Cynthia. Thom Baker is a veteran of the Great War, decorated for bravery in the field. His life was spared so that he might preach the Kingdom of God on Earth to all who ..."

"Chris, you're home now and we must start a new life and forget about all this," Cynthia said. "Let's go on a holiday, all the family, and Mary can come too. We could go back to Rhosneigr."

"I'm not permitted to travel more than five miles from home, Cynthia. I'm under house arrest until this war ends."

"Well, we could go somewhere. Lyme Park ... or Macclesfield, a nice hotel ..."

"Just the two of us, Cynthia." He reached out and took her hand. "I have so much to tell you."

"Oh yes! Mary, will you ...?"

She jumped at the idea of leaving me at home with the children. My holiday had been short-lived.

"Thom and I are going to found a centre. We've already gathered a group of followers and our friend George Unsworth is willing to contribute handsomely to the purchase of a property. My real work won't start until ..."

"Surely you're not talking about moving?"

"No need to give up this house immediately. We can travel back and forth and you can help us, Cynthia. We're dedicated to the salvation of Britain."

"Talk, talk, talk! You're always full of talk, Chris."

She had tossed her napkin aside and was halfway out of her chair, the legs scraping on the parquet floor, when he urged her to sit again, his hand on her arm as he began to speak very gently, his blue eyes fixed on her as though she were a child in need of care.

"When we pray 'Our Father which art in Heaven, hallowed be Thy Name, Thy Kingdom come,' we either want it to come or we don't."

Birdie and Jimmy jumped in and began to recite along with their father, for they had been learning the Lord's Prayer with Miss Dixon and were proud of their recitation.

"If you don't," he said, "you should not pray for it. If you do, you must more than pray for it, you must live for it!"

He leaned into her, gazing intently into her eyes as though he would hypnotize her and convince her in that way.

"I quote John Ruskin," he said. Lord knows who that might have been, and I don't think Cynthia knew any more than I did.

"Be quiet, you children!" she snapped, cutting the children off at 'those that trespass against us,' and Jimmy lapsed into his wheezing while Birdie began to roll her eyes and chew at the insides of her cheeks.

"And stop your silly clowning!" Cynthia said to Birdie, who crossed her eyes then in the most alarming manner, but Cynthia was already gone, her footsteps quick on the stairs. We were silent as we finished our meal, the Master himself chewing steadily on the tepid tripe and onions, for it was all I had been able to find at the butchers.

"Daddy, can we play cricket after lunch?" Jimmy asked.

"Later, Jim, later. I must see to your mother first and persuade her of my plan. Then we'll all have a jolly game, shall we?"

The children started their chatter again, like musical boxes wound up and released, and the Master surprised me with a smile as he picked Katie up from her highchair and dandled her on his knee. When he was present there was no denying his charm, but you had to catch him when you could for he was a feather caught in an ill wind.

Chapter Thirty-Three

A STROKE OF BAD LUCK

I T WAS WHILE they were gone on holiday to Lyme Park that I received a letter from home. The children were at the dining room table having their lesson with Miss Dixon so I was able to run upstairs and read my letter in private, not that I expected bad news, but you never knew, so my heart always beat a little faster as I recognized my father's writing on the envelope handed to me by our postman, who was a weakling like Reg, unable to serve, and put on Home Duty delivering letters and parcels, though he was a cheerful fellow and we sometimes drank a cup of tea together while he told me about his wife and children.

I sat on my bed and began to read. The words were Mam's though written by my da for Mam had not received the schooling she deserved and had never mastered the art of writing. She told me first about the farm and Patrick's care of the livestock. "Six lambs born," Da wrote, "and all the shearing done. Milk cows producing well, only one calf sickly."

It gave me pleasure to think of him at our parlour table with the pen in his hand and Mam pacing back and forth in her apron reciting the words to him, a pot of tea on the hob and their two cracked cups together on the table. Sometimes we'd steep the same leaves three or four times when money was scarce. It was only at the very bottom of the page that she told me. "Your sister Deirdre has had a stroke of bad luck, Eamon has met with an accident on the road and she is left a widow with her two little ones and the new baby."

All the breath went out of me, and my first thought was, an accident on the road or an execution? Eamon had been in the police force and likely would be labelled traitor by the revolutionaries for his work in seeking out arms caches. And if it was the IRA did for him was it my brother Brendan had a hand in it, making murderers of us all? But there was no mention of Brendan, only about our poor Deirdre and her grief at Eamon's funeral.

My next thought was a stupid one and quite impractical given my sister's situation. I wished she would come to England and let me take care of her. It was a selfish thought to be sure because I missed Deedee more than any one of them. She was a beauty with raven hair and deep blue eyes and it was she had taken me to the fields when I could barely walk and given me a feeling for the land and the spirits that inhabit it. Only eight years old, she would take me by the hand and dance me, a fat little five-year-old, over those grand hills, and we would play hide and seek behind the stones that jut out of the earth all over Ireland. I began to blubber at the thought of it, so I had to find a fresh handkerchief and give my nose a good blow before I went downstairs to prepare the children's lunch.

I heard Miss Dixon's voice as I passed through the hall, low and steady as she instructed the children. Charlotte had become a better student. Now that her father was home she was a different child altogether. You might think that life on Chester Road was improving for us all but I felt a foreboding, though as yet it was a fog in my mind that I could not see through to what lay beyond.

The newspapers were piling up in their absence, and I was afraid of the trouble they would cause, for the reporters were cruel in the way they had portrayed the Master as a crackpot. He'd been damaged by his internment, any fool could see that, but from what they wrote they'd taken him seriously, but not so seriously as to dodge making the fool of him that Cynthia had so often accused him of being. They had twisted his words and taken advantage of his sincerity, making him appear as someone sinister, though at the same time a figure of fun to be jeered at. So it was both a relief and a surprise when they returned all smiles, and the children overjoyed to see their parents arrive at the door together just like a normal family.

"Oh Mary, we had a marvellous time!" Cynthia said. Her face was glowing and she seemed to me that day the most beautiful woman in the world, like an actress you would see up on the big screen with her red lips and wavy hair and her long slim legs and dainty feet. I blushed at the turn of my own thoughts for it seemed to me they'd had a second honeymoon, and I was glad then that I had been there to mind the children for them, though jealous too, but of what or whom I was not clear, for there was no realistic place for me in that house but as a servant.

They went upstairs to unpack their suitcases, but he was down directly to play with the children, a game of croquet this time with hoops set up on the back lawn and big coloured balls to whack through the hoops with wooden mallets. I opened the French doors from the sitting room onto the back veranda for it was a beautiful sunny day and the back garden felt like a haven for us all, the vandals not having reached it, and nothing but fields stretching as far as you could see to our picnic place by the pond, the farm buildings in the distance, and sometimes a rabbit or a hare hopping across the turf.

Later on they came into the sitting room and he played the piano for the children—I could hear from my kitchen as I made pastry for the gooseberry pie I had planned for their dinner with the fruit picked from our very own bushes beside the greenhouse. I heard Birdie playing her fairy music for him, then Charlotte had a turn, and Jim. He was teaching them all, telling them about the world of music, his voice steady like Miss Dixon's.

This is my last memory of that house for I was soon to be an outcast, but I will not forget the contentment of that summer afternoon, and Cynthia upstairs at her dressing table, no doubt admiring her jewels and lipsticks, singing to herself which was a good sign for I had not often heard her sing before and she had a beautiful voice, full of feeling.

I'll never smile again until I smile at you ... I'll never laugh again for what good would it do ...

It was a popular song, often played on the wireless. One day it had come on the air while we were in the kitchen together discussing the menu for the week, and she had run out of the room suddenly as though she were unwell. But there now, she was singing it to herself, and in such good spirits.

Looking back on it I have to say I had felt something building in me and I should have paid attention and given myself a talking to. I did go up to my room for a brief spell before I served dinner and I paced up and down a few times, but then Jimmy was calling for me and I had to cut my time short and help him to find his pyjamas and bedroom slippers. I never minded helping the little lad, he so loving and, like his father, without any unkindness in him, though perhaps he would change after all the troubles.

It was later that night I had my outburst—God only knows where it came from—it wasn't my true feelings at all. I had settled the children, except for Katie who was wide awake from napping all afternoon, so I took her to her parents' room. I was in a hurry to get the potatoes on for dinner, but as I stood there about to knock on their door I heard him talking and his tone caught me off guard. He was excited, as though he'd come to life, and Cynthia's voice softer than usual, compliant, as though she hadn't the energy to argue with him anymore. He was on about that Captain Baker again and the house they would have in the countryside, and how they would fill it with people and live off the land, sharing everything. It sounded much like our life on the farm in Ireland.

"This is the answer," he said. "This will be the beginning of a new life for us all, Cynthia," and I could hear it in his voice that he was deluded in some way—by that Captain Baker, or by his feeling for Cynthia and his belief in their future.

I dished up the dinner and they came down together, him carrying Katie all fresh from her bath. I was jealous, that's the truth of it. I'd always loved his visits, loved the smell of him, his presence in the house, the children's excitement. But this time was different. I was part of the family, and here was himself, home for good, holding my little baby that I'd fed with a bottle and held to my heart. I'd set the dining table with the best cutlery and clean linen serviettes, but my face was flushed and my feelings in a confusion as I served them their dinner and took Katie from him. I had her with me in the kitchen and left her for only a moment while I went to clear the dishes before the sweet.

"Will you be wanting cheese with your fruit pie, Sir?" I asked, meek as anything, trying to keep my place in spite of wanting with all my heart to be part of the family as I had been with Cynthia, sitting with her those long evenings in his absence, her light shining on me. But it was all different now, and I didn't know which one to look to for comfort. I was jealous of him, *and* of her. Then we heard it, a shocked wail from the kitchen, getting louder by the second. Katie, still unsteady on her feet, must have taken a tumble. Cynthia frowned. I knew she didn't want to be bothered with it, but before I could move the Master jumped up.

"I'll fetch her," he said and left the room.

You could've cut the air with a knife at that moment, as though I were an intruder and a dirty slut the way she looked at me. My face coloured up right away for I was confused with everything uncertain and unspoken. But that's how it was in her house—either silence and mean looks, or: "Come on Mary, you're my best friend, let's have a glass of gin and a cigarette." And when he was home she'd be all smiles until she was at him, shouting about his bloody politics. But not this time, oh no, she was meek and mild with him, not a squeak out of her, because she'd had a nice honeymoon, hadn't she, had him all to herself while I looked after her children and her house.

He came back with Katie in his arms, patting little circles on her back to soothe her. And he walked straight past me as I stood there like a fool, my arms loaded with their dirty dishes, and sat at the table with his back to me. Cynthia gave him such a smile, then she glanced at me with one of her looks, as though I were a piece of dirt and hadn't listened night after night to her complaints. That's when it happened, taking me completely by surprise.

"You Nazi! I'll tell them about you," I said. "I won't work in the house of a Nazi! Do your own dirty dishes!" And I dropped my armful with a great crash and ran from the room, shocked by the damage I had done. I heard through my sobs Katie screaming as I ran up the stairs to pack my bag.

I believe now that I was used; that those words came out in my voice but did not come from me at all, as though I'd been swept up in the haunting of that house, which was an unlucky house to be sure.

I'd seen it all in his hand, that beautiful hand that I only touched the once. I'm sorry now for those cruel words, but perhaps they had more truth in them than I knew. What I do wonder is, whose words were they?

TWO

... to the British citizen interned under Regulation 18B ... a stigma must necessarily attach not only to himself, but to his children and his children's children. We cannot get away from that fact.

—FLIGHT LIEUT. BOOTHBY,
in the House of Commons, November 26, 1941

The power of the Executive to cast a man into prison without formulating any charge known to the law and particularly to deny him the judgement of his peers is in the highest degree odious and is the foundation of all totalitarian government whether Nazi or Communist. Any such power was a response to emergency that should be yielded up, when and as, the emergency declines ... This is really the test of civilisation.

—WINSTON CHURCHILL,
explaining his decision to release
a number of people detained without trial
under wartime regulations. November 21, 1943

Chapter One

THE KING'S DAUGHTER

I had found him, the man with whom I'd shared a prison cell, a straw paillasse at Ascot inhaling the pungency of ghost elephants and lions in our sleep, the hopelessness of Latchmere, not knowing if we would ever escape, and now I lay in his lap exhausted from a bout of crying. Mary Byrne was gone, and the story was mine to pick up and tell. Charlotte might better have spoken up but she was biased. She had knowledge of him and I had only longing, without the capacity yet for opinion, though now I have the benefit of maturity and reflection, and know more than Mary who could give only the factual report allowed her as the Brooke family's housekeeper, involved though she was, especially in her friendship with my mother. In any case Mary will return to the narrative, perhaps not within it quite as before, but as a vital artery branching from the heart of it.

As to who put those fateful words into Mary's mouth, it could well have been Cynthia for she was a woman of powerful psychic energy with the ventriloquist's ability to speak through people such as Mary and myself without owning up to it. Now I speak for Mary in a way that I think she would not have minded for it was a good life she led, leaving each of us with a clear memory of her goodness and care. Our darling Mary, exiled from paradise by her own vulnerability, left us children with the legacy of her whole-heartedness during that terrible wartime which turned out to have been a far better time for us than what came later.

The head of our family was missing and I, a slow but persistent swimmer and a believer in magic, spent my childhood diving for him, over and over, coming up gasping for air, not knowing whom I sought. Eventually I began to mould a head, shaping it with my hands, as my father had manufactured hats on the factory floor, shaping them to the various forms. My hands must have retained some memory—the feel of my father's body, his shoulders, his neck, the skin of his face—because, in the making of Head from the Ocean, *my heart recalled the love I'd felt for him, and up from the ocean he came finally, swaddled in sheets of kelp, lit from within by a golden bulb illuminating the blood writing of my mysterious yearning on the stretched translucence of his skull.*

In this making I followed the trail beaten by my siblings and entered the earth beneath that Magic Circle of our childhood; descending step by step, year after year, I walked that long subterranean tunnel to find him standing at the end, in the deepest recess, waiting for me. As I approached I became again the one-and-a-half-year-old I'd been when he came home to us, my legs barely free of their dimpled chubbiness as I learned to walk without wobbling; and he so tall, his face kind but impassive as he leaned down to lift me, the King's daughter, and hoisted me onto his shoulder, Princess of his realm.

I won't pretend that my story is factual. I imagine a man I never knew, creating what I cannot uncover, adorning him in top hat, bow tie and winged collar, a Mad Hatter. In dreams my silent father stalks me, insistent as he crosses the prison yard and turns slowly to reveal a ticking clock embedded in his crushed head. Our dead enter us and take root. They are determined to have a voice.

How to distinguish the living from the dead, the blood we share, our rhythms and perfumes? It has taken me a lifetime to untangle this web of bewildering desires and passions, one thread inextricable from the other, woven as we are into a collective fabric; the connective tissue of a family of restless souls jostling for governance.

Christopher and Cynthia are dead. Now it's my story, and I must return to my childhood to relive it, tethered to my adult self by the memory of a time that can only be understood in retrospect. They all

live in me: siblings and parents, Mary Byrne and Mosley, a clamour
of souls demanding a voice, echoing from my father's cell.

"GOOD RIDDANCE!" CYNTHIA said as we heard the front door slam
and the crunch of gravel as Mary trudged her way down our
driveway. She would have turned left at the gate, towards the
Walkley Estates, hardly knowing where she was going, and there might
have been tears running down her cheeks, though perhaps a part of her
was relieved to be finished with us. I sprawled, half dozing, across my
father's lap, in that drugged state that signals emotional exhaustion.

"Good riddance," she said again, fumbling for a handkerchief as
she began to clear the dishes. "You'll have to help me, Christopher, until
we find another housekeeper."

But it was Charlotte who helped, and who looked after us until
Vera came, and by then it was her habit and she continued with it.
Charlotte was in her tenth year and with the prospect of two digits to
her age she seemed grown up way beyond the rest of us.

Jimmy cried his eyes out at bedtime when it became clear that Mary
would not return to tuck him in. He couldn't sleep without the feeling
of safety he'd had from her presence across the corridor. That night he
came down with a severe asthma attack which turned into bronchitis,
and Charlotte had to be moved into Mary's room to be close to him
until another housekeeper could be found, which was not easy with
the war on and no-one wanting to work in the house of a traitor except
the most desperate, which Vera was; and the loyal Dik Dik who continued to coach my siblings in their reading and writing. Birdie asked
every day for Mary until she was silenced by our mother's sharp words,
and finally a slap. Cynthia had been much more affected by the incident than had our father, who was preoccupied with his plans for the
purchase of Kingdom House.

"Where are you?" she asked. "I can't find you, Chris."

He spread his arms with hands palms up. "It has all been revealed,
Cynthia. I am ready to fulfill my life's mission. We have a marvellous
future ahead of us, Darling."

She wanted to trust him. She wanted to put it all into his hands and be taken care of, but she needed reassurance and with Mary gone she felt uneasy, as though that poor Irish girl had been her anchor and she'd never realized it until now.

Chapter Two

MONOPOLY

IT WAS VERA who brought Monopoly into our house and that's how she won Jimmy's heart. It was a new game, she said, from America, a present from one of her GI friends.

"You know why they're called GIs?" she asked, and without waiting for an answer she burst out: "Government Issue! It's stamped on their uniforms!"

Jimmy wanted to play all the time and he wanted to win. Birdie and I were too young, Vera said, so she and our mother would set themselves up around the board with Charlotte and Jimmy, while our father sat in his study writing letters requesting the release of Captain Baker.

Vera was quite different from Mary. She wore red lipstick and dressed in a pencil skirt with a tight pullover that showed off her bosom. Her legs were long and slim, encased in sheer nylon stockings the colour of milky tea which she received as favours from her GIs. Our mother said that Vera'd had a hard time and needed a home more than Mary Byrne who had not appreciated the cushy place she'd had with us. The mention of Mary set Jimmy off wheezing and Birdie chewing at her lips. But Vera and Mum were always laughing, and that was the best thing about her — she was company for our mother during her own hard time.

Vera would pick me up and squeeze me so hard and when I protested she'd say: "Oh don't, baby, don't leave Mummy, I miss you so much."

She'd had a baby of her own, we learned, and had to give her up because it was wartime and too much for a woman alone. Vera talked a lot about her GIs, but in a jokey way as though they were just playthings. "They're overpaid, they're over-sexed, and they're over here!" she said, warbling.

"Look, I've landed on the Angel Islington!" Jimmy shouted. "I'm going to buy it!"

He'd no sooner handed over his money and got his ownership card than Charlotte landed in prison. "You'll have to throw a double six," he said. "Or buy your way out. You don't want to stay in prison too long."

"I'll buy the Isle of Man and go there for a holiday," Charlotte replied.

Mum leaned across the board and hit her so fast that none of us knew what had happened. We just saw Charlotte jump up and run from the room, her face bright red.

"Can I have her money?" Jim asked. "She won't come back and play now."

"Why don't you throw a party to celebrate your husband's homecoming?" Vera said.

"Oh, he's tired of the Cheshire Set after what he's been through," she said, reaching for one of her Abdullahs. Vera took one too and they lit up together.

How can I know all that I'm about to describe? I don't have a real answer, not one that would satisfy the sceptics. I was not present, and yet I have been there—though long after the actual events—informed by membership in the Brooke family, threaded through with family nuance and emotional memory. I am a believer in magic, as I've said. I have found my way back, and I know that these scenes, painful as many of them are, approximate the truth.

Cynthia remembered the dinner she'd organized at Lyme Park Hall a couple of weeks earlier. Eric Cartwright had been home on leave, triumphant after the allied sweep of North Africa, and the Andertons had returned to England after their evacuation from Singapore to

Australia in January. When they'd met in the cocktail bar at seven Adèle had been the first one to embrace Christopher with her customary warmth, and Eric had shaken his hand vigorously.

"Good to have you back in circulation, old man," he'd said, somewhat over-enthusiastically.

Jenny and George had been more restrained, though friendly enough, and everything had gone smoothly over drinks, continuing with catch-up chatter as the waiter showed them to their table. Eric had spoken about his enjoyment of the desert, with Adèle's hand on his knee to keep him from talking directly about the war. George Anderton had spoken at length over the hors-d'oeuvre about his work in Malaya, and the abundance of the rubber industry there.

"Bad show we had to leave, eh Jenny?" he'd said, turning to his wife who smiled and shrugged. "Doing jolly well until the Japs had to ruin it all."

Adèle had cut in with what she thought to be an innocuous statement: "It must be wonderful to be reunited with your children, Chris."

There had been a moment of silence as Christopher laid down his fork and faced Adèle.

"At the end of this war we shall have learned a great truth—that a healthy child with the living spirit of God in his eyes is to be preferred to all the empires and massed material wealth that men ever wrested from their fellow men and held down by aggression." His voice rose and he'd begun to gesticulate as he continued. "So shall we abandon the values that have cost mankind millions of lives and all but submerged our very souls in blood and tears."

The silence that followed his speech had been quickly broken by a fevered conversation in which everyone had stumbled over each other like bomb victims. Cynthia had struggled through her meal, and vowed never again to subject herself to such embarrassment.

"We have a different set of friends now," she told Vera, who had risen to toss the contents of their ashtray into the fireplace. "And we're all going to buy a house together in the countryside. You can come with us when we move. I'm going to need help."

"Where will it be?"

"I don't know, probably down south somewhere."

"I can't move down south. That's too far away from my little girl. I'm hoping to get her back, you see, when ..."

"Don't do that! Look, you've got your apron all dirty."

Vera was polishing the ashtray with the corner of her apron.

"I can wash it."

She was a strange girl, Cynthia thought, generally quite slovenly, but then surprisingly meticulous about little things like ashtrays.

"You could bring her along. There'll be other children there. Christopher wants us to live communally, you see, as one big family. It's all part of his idea for our future, that we should all share in ... " She saw Birdie listening, her blue eyes wide with curiosity. "Little pigs have big ears," she said, wagging her finger. "Come on Jumbo, let's finish this game. I have to go over to the Woodlands."

Granny had telephoned that morning and said she had something important to discuss, so Jimmy was allowed to win the game in order to speed things up, and then we all had lunch and waved to her as she drove off.

Chapter Three

A PUBLIC EMBARRASSMENT

S HE DROVE THROUGH Poynton village in high spirits. Now that she had Vera she was enjoying a renewed sense of freedom, and with Christopher home, despite his strangeness, life felt almost normal. She held him close at night and forgot about his religious and political ranting. It would pass, she told herself. And soon, surely, the war must end. How long could people go on hating?

When Dorothy Blackwell opened the door instead of Mrs. Fern, Cynthia knew that something was wrong.

"What is it, Mother? Is it Jack?"

"No. Jack is safe, thank goodness. On leave in London for a few days. He'll be home for the birthday party."

"Whose birthday?"

"Your brother Richard. Had you forgotten? Come along, dear, we'll have a cup of tea."

Dorothy ushered her into the drawing room and called for Mrs. Fern to bring a tray of tea.

"Richard is going to be eighteen and he's decided to apprentice with your father at the Engineering Works."

"Is Daddy here?"

"No, it's just the two of us, Cynthia. We need to have a serious talk." She paused, considering her words. "Ruby will be home on leave too. She's been promoted to driver for the ambulance service."

"Yes, mother, I know that," Cynthia said. "Get to the point, will you."

"We'll all be here for Richard's coming of age—of course it's not his twenty-first, but in these times young people must grow up fast and take their responsibilities for the war effort." She rocked on her heels, standing in front of the Chinese fire screen. "Naturally you are invited, and the children ... but Richard does not want Christopher here."

Cynthia leaned forward on the settee. "Why ever not?"

"My dear, he's a public embarrassment. Apparently he's been raving about fascism and all sorts of confused religious ideas."

"How d'you know?" She clasped her hands, gripping her knuckles.

"It's the talk of the village. He's been seen in the Poynton café on several occasions, holding forth in a most appalling manner." Dorothy joined Cynthia on the settee and tried to take her hand, but she pulled away.

"Richard *must* invite him. He needs our support, especially now. You wouldn't believe what he's suffered during his internment."

"It is you who needs our support, my darling, you and the children. We have to think very seriously about what you're going to do."

"It's none of your business!" Cynthia jumped up and began pacing between the bay window and a mahogany side-table covered with Dorothy's china figurines. "We're managing very well. We have plans to move down south."

"What!"

"A change of location will do him good. It's just a matter of ..."

"You can't move away from your family, and in the middle of a war ..."

"It's temporary, Mother. When the war's over and everything's back to normal, Christopher will ..."

"Will what?" Dorothy was on her feet now, following her daughter as she continued to pace. "Go back to the hat factory and carry on as though none of it happened—the disgrace, the shame, the embarrassment—and then, to go and have another child with him! What were you thinking?"

Cynthia turned to face her. "He's my husband! In spite of everything, I love him. I thought you knew that, Mother. Remember what you said to Daddy? 'Let's make these two young people happy. Let's give them our blessing.'"

"That was before war broke out, my dear. September 3rd, 1939 changed everything."

"Christopher is ill, Mother, that's all. He's been badly treated and he's ill from it. Archer Pearson recommends counselling and I think he's right."

"Counselling? It's the first I've heard of it."

"It could be very helpful for Christopher, but we need support. Please help me to make him better, Mother. Tell Richard. Explain to him that he must invite us all, as a family."

Dorothy turned and looked out the window at her garden for a full thirty seconds, then she turned back to face her daughter. "I can't do that, Cynthia."

"Why not? You control everything in this family."

"I don't agree with you. And even if I did I'm powerless to go against the wishes of my son. He's a man now."

"So why doesn't *he* go to war?"

"One son at the front is enough. Your father needs Richard at the Works."

Mrs. Fern entered with a tray of tea and laid it down on the table in front of the settee. She smiled at Cynthia. "How are you, Mrs. Brooke?"

Cynthia had to bite her lower lip to avoid disgracing herself by crying. She merely nodded and focused on a vase of pale pink gladiolas on the sideboard. There was a circle of fallen blossoms gathered at the foot of the vase and she began counting them in the awkward silence while Mrs. Fern fussed with the tea tray, laying out linen serviettes.

Dorothy waited for the housekeeper to leave before she continued. "How do you think Jack and Ruby would feel if we invited him? Imagine the terrible injuries they've witnessed over there. Think of someone else for a change."

"I'm going to speak to Father about this."

"Don't waste your breath, dear. He's absolutely against the presence of Christopher Brooke in this house. Your disgraceful husband is no longer a pacifist. He has chosen to associate himself with Nazi sympathizers and ..."

"He has not! He's ill, mother. You have to help."

Dorothy gave her a pitying look and spoke now in a low voice. "Wake up, dear. Mrs. Fern's husband heard Christopher in the Poynton café talking favourably about Hitler."

And that's when Cynthia did disgrace herself. She broke down and sobbed.

Chapter Four

HARVEST FESTIVAL

WE DIDN'T GO to Uncle Richard's birthday party. We were invited instead to Granny and Grandpa Brooke's house where we ran in the woods and walked on stilts through Granny's flower garden. Birdie got lost in the box-hedge maze; we heard her wailing, but we couldn't find her. Charlotte ran down one pathway after another with Birdie's voice getting louder and fainter until she finally found her curled in a ball under the hedge with her mouth all red and itchy from chewing. I tumbled into Granny's pond trying to catch a goldfish and our mother pulled me out while Vera ran to get a towel. Then we had tea and I had to sit on Grandpa's knee. He smelled funny when he leaned down to kiss me with his bristly moustache, and he lit a big cigar which set me off coughing again because I'd inhaled pond water.

Daddy sat at the end of the table with his chair pulled out to allow room for him to cross his long legs. His foot pulsed gently up and down and a white plume of smoke rose from a cigarette held dangling in his right hand. Cynthia reached over and touched his other hand which was resting on the table.

"What is it?" he asked in a surprised voice.

She shook her head and smiled.

"I don't suppose our boy could work again at ..." Granny began in a whisper.

"No, Nancy, no," Grandpa said with a growl. "Out of the question."

"Well, come to church with us, will you, dears? There's a harvest festival service tomorrow at ten."

"You go, Chris," Cynthia said. "Take Charlotte and Jimmy." She turned to Granny apologetically. "I have the little ones to look after, and Vera just settling in ..."

"Of course, dear, I understand. Will you have a piece of bread and butter to take away the sweet taste?" she asked us, offering a plate of thinly sliced bread smeared with the precious butter ration.

"More cake!" Jimmy demanded, and our father smiled from his faraway place.

At nine thirty next morning Christopher took Charlotte and Jimmy by the hand and walked them down the road to Woodford church. The interior was decorated with sheaves of wheat and bunches of golden chrysanthemums, giant pumpkins, baskets of red apples and yellow corn cobs. There was an uneasy shuffling amongst the congregation as Christopher and the children took their places next to the Brookes in the front pew. It was like the rustling of leaves before a storm.

As the vicar entered he took the measure of things, nodding almost imperceptibly in the direction of the Brooke family, then the service began, with hymns and prayers that required much kneeling and rising, sitting and standing, flipping of pages in prayer books, and searching for hymns—so much to keep everyone occupied that they forgot the traitor in their midst. When it was time for the sermon the vicar ascended the steps to the pulpit and stood there, hands looped into the folds of his cassock, his face solemn as he began with a blessing for the soldiers who had fought and died in Europe and in North Africa. He named each of his parishioners' sons who had fallen in the line of duty, and each who was still fighting.

"Let us give thanks for the bravery of our sons in the allied invasion of Sicily," he said, his eyes ablaze. "And for the overthrow of the Italian fascist Mussolini which has enabled our Italian brothers to become our allies."

Jimmy grew fidgety, and Charlotte whispered to him to keep still. But Christopher was riveted, his steely eyes focused on the vicar.

Suddenly he rose to his feet and called out, his voice resounding through the chilly church.

"Hypocrite! None will be revealed as guiltier than the clergy for the misfortunes that have been brought upon the world. You profess adherence to the teachings of Jesus Christ, and yet you promote war and hatred with your every utterance."

There was a shocked silence. Old Mr. Brooke dropped his head into his hands and his wife went rigid, a nervous smile twitching at the corners of her mouth. Nobody moved. Then suddenly they came to life in a rising cacophony of outraged voices turning to each other for comfort, shocked parishioners assaulted in the haven of their own church. But Christopher's voice rang out relentlessly above them all as he raised his right arm in a salute, declaiming: "Heil Hitler!"

Jimmy stared up at his father and pulled anxiously on his trouser leg.

"Love thy neighbour as thyself." Christopher's voice rang out. "It takes two to make a fight, and the Christian role is the pacifist one." He continued above a second wave of protest, and despite his own mother tugging at his sleeve. "You clerics have loved neither God nor your neighbours. You have merely served to assist in the maintenance of the Mammon system as supporters of successive governments that have honoured gold rather than God." His right arm flailed while his left rested on his son's narrow shoulders in response to Jimmy's persistent tugging. "If Christian peace had been won for Europe in 1918 there would have been neither opportunity nor need for a Hitler to redress the wrongs of mankind by force. Blind even to the words of their prophets in the Bible, the churches have consistently courted the disasters foretold for the Judgment of a world that has denied Christ."

"Daddy, Daddy!" Charlotte was pulling at her father's hand. "Jimmy has to go wee-wee ... *now!*"

Christopher was suspended a moment in the now hushed church, then he bent down and picked the boy up in his arms and edged his way out of the pew. Everyone stared in hostile silence as he walked down the aisle with his children—urine already seeping through Jimmy's trousers, and Charlotte smirking shame-faced with sidelong glances at the staring congregation. When they reached the heavy oaken door Christopher turned as though he would deliver a final homily, but then he was gone, the door sending a cold draught through the congregation as it closed.

Chapter Five

TOO EASILY INFLUENCED

IN NOVEMBER OF 1943 Christopher was summoned to appear in Manchester before the Appellate Tribunal for Conscientious Objectors. He had to apply for special permission from the Chief Constable of Cheshire because Manchester was outside the five-mile range of his home, being roughly thirteen miles away. The Tribunal included His Honour, Judge Burgis, Alderman Aveling, and A.A. Kerr, Esq, an elderly, garrulous gentleman. Christopher was immaculately dressed and groomed, his physical person bearing no trace of eccentricity, so when he told the Tribunal of his challenge to the church to face the truth and repent their hypocrisy the men were frankly shocked, and Mr. Kerr delivered a spluttering accusation of blasphemy.

"The future will prove who it is that blasphemes," Christopher said. "A man detained for three years without charge or trial, because he believes that a Christian should respect the commandment and assurance, 'Blessed are the peace-makers,'—or the Churchmen who profess to be ministers of Jesus Christ, and yet make a mockery of His teaching in their ministries."

"Mr. Brooke, while we are sympathetic to your position as a most sincere objector," Judge Burgis intervened in his smooth drawl, "we must emphasize the need to pitch in, in one manner or another. With the entire nation at war, you see, it's a matter of not letting the side down."

"I am for Britain and for the prosperity of our working men and women, not for their slaughter in the name of ..."

"Quite so, quite so, Mr. Brooke. Point taken. Now on the question of your patriotic duty, we see from your file that you were formerly employed in hat manufacturing."

"I am a concert pianist."

Judge Burgis and his fellow Tribunalists looked up in surprise.

"I am no longer employed as a hatter. My corporate interests have been disallowed, together with my attempts to work alongside the British labourer. Nor am I now a member of British Union. I recognize Adolf Hitler as the scourge of God to cleanse ..."

"Please keep to the point, Mr. Brooke," the Judge said, and his head began to shake back and forth. "We were discussing the question of your skills and potential employment of same," he said, pushing his slippery spectacles up onto the bridge of his nose.

"My skills are in music, oratory, and sport," Christopher said with dignity.

"Ah, I see," Burgis said. "Well a man must work, Mr. Brooke. Our government cannot afford to house objectors in His Majesty's prisons. We had two and a half thousand men incarcerated at the beginning of this war for refusal to participate, but with the progress of the war, and with shortages of both prison staff and food, conditions have become so very unhealthy that we have had to conscript our objectors into fire-watching, industry and so on. Do you have any suggestions, Mr. Brooke, as to how you could best serve your country?"

"We haven't much call, you see, for concert pianists," Mr. Kerr said.

"The best service I could perform would be to broadcast my witness to the nation."

Burgis sighed and dropped his head. After a brief consultation with Mr. Kerr and Alderman Aveling, during which they each consulted the listings before them on the bench, Judge Burgis looked up at Christopher and said decisively, "With your sporting skills and your young man's physique you seem admirably suited, Mr. Brooke, for agricultural labour."

And so it was that my father began working for the farmer who owned the fields behind our house where Mary Byrne and my family had picnicked in happier days. It turned out that as well as having a herd of dairy cows Mr. Jones kept pigs, chickens, sheep, and also grew extensive crops of potatoes, barley and corn. My father spent his days in the fields and around the farm buildings cleaning out livestock pens. He came home tired but content, and after supper he would sit down to write his letters: to the Advisory Board requesting the release of Thomas Baker, to the Archbishop of Canterbury, to the Chief Rabbi of the British Empire, and to the Home Secretary, Herbert Morrison.

Cynthia was glad to have him out of the house. She felt disturbed by his presence. Though she wanted to believe in him and surrender to his authority, she found herself humouring him like a child, and that made her lose respect for him. She became angry and impatient with his ranting, but at night she would be drawn in by the virility of his healthy, uncomplicated body and the heights to which he took her. But something in her remained lonely and unsatisfied. There was a place where Christopher Brooke could not or would not meet her.

Sometimes, after their lovemaking, as she lay with her head in the crook of his arm, Christopher would speak softly to her of his dreams for Kingdom House and the new life they would have after the war. She wanted so fervently to believe in it—to surrender to her handsome husband who was after all benign and sincere—that it all made sense to her, and she would drift into sleep and dream of a big country house ringing with the laughter of children, she and Christopher living amidst a household of smiling people, walking through light-filled rooms, climbing a sweeping staircase that curved upwards to a landing with heavily-curtained bedrooms leading off it.

In the light of day however, her dream seemed ridiculous, and her mother's words echoed in her head— "The disgrace, the shame, a public embarrassment, raving about fascism and his confused religious ideas" —but Dorothy Blackwell was wrong. He had dropped fascism and was no longer interested in Mosley, just as Eric Cartwright had predicted before they were married— "Don't worry, Cyn. This obsession with Mosley won't last. Christopher latches onto things, follows them through to the end, then switches to something else. I've known him since we were boys at Malvern and he's always been the same."

But Baker, what about Baker? Was he a Mosleyite? She would meet him and find out for herself.

"It's Saturday, Christopher. Can't you do something with the children?"

"We can't play cricket in the rain."

"Take them to the cinema. Take Charlotte and Jimmy, then I can leave the little ones with Vera and drive over to the Woodlands. I haven't seen my father for such a long time." Since before Richard's party, she'd been about to say.

Christopher stirred himself and rose from his desk. He stretched and yawned, his broad chest expanding as he smiled down at Cynthia. As he drew his arms in he embraced her and she nestled close and smiled as he kissed the top of her head.

"Good idea, Darling. I'll take them to a matinee at the Tudor."

As soon as they'd left on foot for Bramhall village, huddled together under a big umbrella, she cranked up the Minx and drove to the Woodlands.

Dick Blackwell leaned back in his easy chair and lit a cigarette.

"Your mother is up in arms."

"I wish you wouldn't smoke, Daddy. You know what Archer Pearson said. It's not good for your heart."

"This war isn't good for my heart, but it's good for business. They're building a new railway between Egypt and Libya and they'll need our pistons for their engines."

"What's she up in arms about?"

"Ruby. She's planning to run off with an American GI she met in Italy."

"Oh, it'll fizzle out. You know Ruby."

"Don't be so sure, my girl. Ruby's as contrary as you."

"Father!" she exclaimed. "I'm nothing like Ruby. I've always obeyed you."

Blackwell looked at her with raised eyebrows and they both burst out laughing. He reached out for her and without a moment's hesitation Cynthia threw herself into his embrace and wept.

"There, there. It will all come clean in the fullness of time. Italy's on the allied side now and Mussolini's in Germany where he belongs. He was the first Fascist you know, much admired by Churchill as well as Mosley, though that's been conveniently forgotten. When Mosley started his British Union of Fascists it was to be a vehicle for a new kind of British economy based on the Keynesian theory of deficit spending."

Cynthia fumbled for a handkerchief, found one in her cardigan pocket and blew her nose vigorously as Blackwell continued.

"It was a popular movement at the outset, though I don't suppose you paid any attention, Cynthia—your head was full of the frivolities of Paris, enjoyed at my expense." Blackwell chuckled and patted her hand. "Mosley was the up and coming fellow then, little wonder your Christopher was attracted by him—a pacifist like most of the veterans of the Great War—but sadly the BUF became a haven for the lunatic fringe—anti-Semites who had no interest in appeasement. That's how the violence started—at Olympia in '34—which caused Rothermere to withdraw his support—and of course the rest of the press went with him—only months after he'd written an editorial in the Mail entitled 'Hurrah for the Blackshirts!'" Blackwell's arm shot forward in the BUF salute. "Then there was the Cable Street riot a couple of years later —that was the last straw as far as our government was concerned ..."

"But Daddy, all those things happened in London. Christopher was never involved in the London rallies ..."

"He was duped like Mosley himself who created a monster and lost control of it. There's only one thing that unites us now, my dear, and that is the war. It's primal, it's simple, and we must all get behind it, or else." He punctuated his final words by rapping his knuckles on the wooden arm of his chair.

"I hate this bloody war! It's a man's game."

"It's a man's world, my dear. Read all about it! Let's see what they have to tell us today." Blackwell picked up the newspaper and began rustling through the pages. "The Big Three met in Tehran last week. And look"—he ignored the ashes that spilled into his lap as he hit the page—"our allies are making headway, and Tito's partisans are giving the Germans a lot of trouble." He lowered the paper and looked at

Cynthia over his glasses. "Hitler's allies in the Balkans could soon bolt to our side, then we'll have the Germans surrounded, and beat the Russians to it." He chuckled.

"Perhaps Ruby should marry her GI. The Americans seem to be our saviours."

"Your mother won't hear of it. The fellow doesn't have proper table manners."

"You've met him?" Cynthia reared back in surprise.

"Ruby brought him for dinner on her last leave, and he cut up all his food, put his knife down on the clean table-cloth, and proceeded to shovel roast lamb, peas and potatoes into his mouth with an up-turned fork, using it like a spoon." Blackwell's belly shook with laughter. "You should have seen your mother's face!"

"Why don't *we* get invited to anything?"

He levelled his gaze at her, serious now. "My dear Cynthia, if there's one thing the British won't tolerate it's embarrassment, and you have married a major embarrassment."

"But Daddy, it's the war. You know he wasn't like that before."

"He was a member of Mosley's fascist party when I first heard of him and any fool could see where that was going to lead."

"But you gave us your blessing."

"Under relentless pressure, my child, from your mother. For once we were not a united front, but now of course she regrets her romanticism, which was at the cost of her daughter's happiness, and I might say, our grandchildren's well-being."

He leaned forward to extinguish the damp stub of his cigarette, which had left a yellow thread of tobacco clinging to his lower lip.

"Perhaps I bear some guilt myself. I wanted you to be happy, my dear ... my first-born ... the apple of my eye."

"Oh Daddy!"

He stroked her face. "We all hoped he'd get over it."

"Well, he has! He doesn't talk about Mosley now."

"But he *is* a follower. That's the essential problem with Christopher Brooke. By all accounts his allegiance has shifted to Hitler."

Chapter Six

IN THE BACK ROW

December 1943

T HEY SAT UP front in plush red seats that smelled of cigarette ash and toffee. It was a George Formby film, a comedy with lots of singing and ukulele music. Christopher watched his children more than the film which he considered a tasteless parody of wartime, casting the Germans as devils, and stupid to boot. But the children were spellbound, especially Jimmy who chortled his way through the first half and laughed so hard at one point that he had a coughing fit. Christopher took the boy onto his knee and Jimmy quietened down, but in the interval he wanted ice cream, so Christopher gave Charlotte a shilling and sent her to the front where an usherette stood with a tray hanging from her shoulders, piled with tubs and bars of the poor excuse for ice cream that had been developed during the war with a combination of goats' milk and powdered skimmed milk. They had ices on sticks and Jimmy laughed when Charlotte dropped hers and began to cry.

"Here, Darling, have mine," Christopher said, and lit a cigarette instead.

"Can't wait to see what will happen," Jimmy said, wriggling in his seat.

When Charlotte slid her hand into Christopher's, he pulled away.

"No, Charlotte, you're sticky. Here, wipe your hands," he said, offering a large white handkerchief from his trouser pocket.

When the second half started Jimmy and Charlotte fixed their eyes on the screen and never broke their concentration until the final credits rolled and the lights came up on an applauding audience. Charlotte helped Jimmy on with his coat, and Christopher ushered them into the aisle where they joined the throng shuffling towards the exit.

"Look! It's Mary Moo!" Jimmy exclaimed, breaking away from his father and running headlong into the back row where he threw his arms around Mary who was speechless with surprise, fumbling to button her blouse, and then scarlet with embarrassment as she caught sight of Christopher Brooke and Charlotte standing in the aisle staring at her.

"How are you, Mary?" Christopher asked.

"I'm doing very well, Sir, thank you, Sir. And how are Mrs. Brooke and the little ones?"

"We have Vera now, but she's not as nice as you," Jimmy said. "Why don't you come back?"

"Come along, Jimmy," Christopher said kindly.

"I've got a better game now. It's called Monopoly and I always win."

"Well that's grand, Jimmy. Now listen to your daddy. Off you go." She was about to pat him on the bottom as had been her habit but caught herself in time.

Charlotte hadn't spoken. She was looking the other way determinedly which cut Mary to the quick. Reg, slunk low in his seat beside Mary, suddenly jolted forward, half-standing with his hands on the armrests.

"Read about you in the papers, Mr. Brooke. Quite the personality, aren't you?" he called after the little group as they began to move away.

Mary clamped her hand over Reg's mouth, and there was a scuffle, which left her in tears. When she looked up Christopher and the children were already gone.

"Mr. Wu wears a pair of cami knicks to save his Sunday trousers," Jimmy sang in a broad Lancashire accent. "Remember, Charlie?" He giggled and splashed Charlotte who sat at the other end of the bath with the cold tap sticking into her shoulder blade. At nine-and-a-half she considered herself too old to be sharing the bath with her brother and had complained to her mother.

"I don't have time to bath you separately," Cynthia had said. "It's Vera's night off."

She'd arrived home just as Vera was leaving, all dolled up, to go out with a girlfriend, she'd said, though Cynthia had her doubts. Vera seemed to her the kind of woman who couldn't do without a man. Cynthia had just put Birdie and Katie to bed when Christopher and the other children had arrived and there'd been no time yet to sit down with him. She was determined to make him understand her dilemma with the family, to insist once more on the counselling that she and Archer Pearson had arranged for him. She began to soap Jimmy's feet which only made him giggle more.

"Said Mr. Wu what shall I do," he sang in a cracked little voice. "And Mr. Wu's a window cleaner now."

Cynthia hummed along, for it was a popular song she'd heard on the wireless.

"Was it a funny film?"

"No, it was about the war," Charlotte said.

"He polishes the windows with worn out ladies' blouses," Jimmy sang, clowning and splashing at Charlotte until she threw the soap at him and kicked out, almost hitting his privates. Cynthia raised her hand. "You naughty girl." Charlotte cowered. "You could've ruined him for life."

"It's all right, Charlie. I'm not ruined," Jimmy said, grinning. "Mr. Wu had a laundry," he said, looking up at his mother. "But he couldn't make a go of it."

"Just like Daddy and his hats," Charlotte said. "Mr. Brooke's a farm-hand now," she sang.

"He swills the pigs, and smokes his cigs," Jimmy sang, delighted with himself.

"Oh come along now, stop being silly," Cynthia said, laughing in spite of herself. "What was the film about?" she asked, scrubbing Charlotte's back vigorously.

"George Formby playing his ukulele," Jimmy said.

"He was trying to go to Blackpool, but he got on the wrong boat and ended up in Bergen Norway," Charlotte said. "Then he met an undercover agent and helped her to break a Nazi code to stop a ship sinking."

"George sang a song that had a secret code in it."

"Morse code," Charlotte said.

"Count your blessings and smile," Jimmy sang.

"Count your blessings, one two three," Charlotte sang.

"One three two, one three two, we gather here to summon you, remember Charlie?"

"*Shhhhh.* And don't call me that."

"What nonsense," Cynthia said, rinsing the children with a few quick splashes and getting up from her knees to fetch a towel from the airing cupboard.

"Remember when Birdie got shut in there?" Charlotte said.

"Pity we didn't leave her there," Jimmy said. And then he turned a wistful face to Cynthia as she enfolded him in a warm white towel. "We saw Mary."

"Where?" she asked sharply.

"In the back row of the cinema with a weaselly looking man," Charlotte said.

Cynthia was quiet a moment, then she began to rub Jimmy down. "Good place for her," she said.

Chapter Seven

MARY BYRNE'S NEW CAREER

August 1943

WHEN I WALKED down that path I hadn't a thought in my head of where I was going. My feet turned me to the left, and then to the right, until I ended up at the Walkley Estates in front of Meg's caravan. She had no sympathy or kind words, just sat me down with a hot cup of tea, no questions asked, while she curtained off a space for me at the far end beside her kitchen. I didn't have much in the way of luggage, especially since I'd left behind on my bed the presents I'd received from Cynthia, which was the jewellery box and clothing, but of course the green scarf I could not return because it had long since been parcelled off to Mam. I told her as much as she stood in the doorway watching me pack, and I apologized for not returning that gift. Perhaps she was offended that I'd given it away, or that I was returning her other gifts. I don't know. I could hardly look at her, but I sensed a hurt in her as she begged me to stay on.

"He's not such a bad man, Mary," she said. "It's just the war, you see. It's put him off course."

Nothing would have persuaded me to stay in that house a minute longer, but it was her I was fleeing from, not him. And in the end it was the children I missed with a bitter longing for their little hands in mine, and Birdie's sweet kisses on my cheek. And Katie, my own baby girl who I had welcomed into the world.

I slept like the dead that first night as though my whole self had closed down for repairs. In the morning Meg brought me a cup of tea and said: "I 'ave a client comin' today, and I 'ave clients most days, so you'll 'ave to make yourself scarce, Mary. You can't be 'anging about 'ere. I suggest you walk down to Bramhall village after breakfast and find yerself a job."

So that's what I did. I had a piece of toast with margarine and a second cup of tea, then I put on my skirt and blouse, brushed off my shoes, and I walked down Woodford Road to the village. Meg had told me to try at the fishmongers where her son Leonard had worked before the war.

"There's not many girls want to smell of fish," she'd said. "And all the men are off fighting, like my Leonard. So you'll likely get taken on there."

But I didn't want to smell of fish neither. I fancied myself in the haberdashery, so that's where I tried first, but it was no go. So I tried Halstead's, the newsagents and sweet shop, but they didn't need any help. I must have inquired in more than a dozen establishments as I walked down one side of the High Street and up the other. I even tried the Victoria Hotel and the Bull's Head Pub, but there was no need of chambermaids, cooks, nor barmaids.

I suppose my accent didn't help. There's a prejudice in England against the Irish, thanks no doubt to my brother Brendan and his kind. I began to realize how lucky I'd been to pick up that telephone on my arrival on English soil and snap up the very first job I tried for. I'd been spoiled and now I was coming down hard upon my backside, and not on my feet where I wanted to be.

I thought again of my ambition to be a telephone operator, but I did not know where to apply. Then I had a sudden vision of the A.V. Roe factory, which was down the road from Cynthia's house. Why hadn't I thought of it before? I'd seen girls coming out of there wearing overalls, and with scarves tied around their heads, employed in the final assembly of the aircraft before the test flights. It was an aerodrome as well as a factory. We'd heard the engines roaring as they revved up and took off on their test flights. I might as well get my hands dirty in a factory as anywhere else, I thought. But it was a bit of a walk, back to the Estates, and then off again in the direction of Chester Road, so I went into a café for a cup of tea and a sandwich because it was already lunchtime and I was starved. The girl that came to serve me was expecting, almost ready to deliver by the size of her, poor thing, with her hands to her back, leaning into them to relieve the pressure, just like I'd seen Mam do when she was heavy with Patrick, and Cynthia with Katie.

"You're carrying a load there," I said.

"Yes, I'm due in a month. And what a time to be pregnant, in this 'eat. Thank goodness this is me last day at work."

"Have they someone to replace you?" I asked, for I was less interested in her and her baby than I was in my own welfare.

"Mrs. Plumley 'ad someone, but the girl let 'er down. She's begged me to stay on another week, but I can't. I'm afraid for the baby," she said, holding onto her belly with one hand while she supported her spine with the other.

"I could start tomorrow."

The words were out of my mouth before I'd had time to think, so there went my factory job, for Mrs. Plumley snapped me up. I'd barely supped my tea and bitten into my sandwich before she appeared at my side beaming at me as though I were a prize heifer. When she offered me the job I said yes, because as Mam always told me, a bird in the hand is worth two in the bush, besides which Mrs. P. was a kindly woman with a nice manner to her and I could tell she would be grateful for my services. I washed my hair that night and had a good scrubdown in Meg's tub so that I would look my best for the morning.

I was soon paying my way at Meg's what with the tips I received at Mrs. Plumley's, which was just as well for the wages were nothing to write home about. I tried to make myself scarce so as not to interfere with Meg's private business, and to tell you the truth I felt a little strange to be living on her premises with what was going on there, and me being a Catholic and all. But beggars can't be choosers.

On my day off I would go out rain or shine and take a walk through Bramhall village to Cheadle Hulme, or even ride the bus into Manchester and look in the shop windows there. One day I treated myself to lunch in Kendal Milne's restaurant where Cynthia had taken me. I was quite pleased with myself for finding it. By luck and perhaps my own canny sense of direction I chanced upon it without having to ask the way, and after lunch, which was a bowl of vegetable soup—the cheapest item on the menu—I went downstairs in the lift to look at the scarves again, and I remembered what a grand day we'd had, and how I'd felt lifted above my station by her sparkle, for I felt in England that anything was possible, even for an Irish girl like me. I'd lost the magic of our land, but perhaps there were pastures for me in England too if I knew where to find them.

'Twas the night-times were hard. Even though I was stepping out with Reg on Wednesdays, Fridays, and Saturdays, that still left four nights of the week he was on Home Guard and unavailable to entertain me, and as the autumn came and the nights grew shorter, I couldn't be out walking the streets alone in the dark for with the blackout there were no streetlights to guide me and what if the sirens should go off and me far from Meg's Anderson shelter? Meg told me I should take the plunge and marry Reg, and I was beginning to think that I should take heed of her. In fact I had almost reconciled myself to it, then everything changed.

We were at the pictures a few weeks before Christmas and I was feeling homesick again for I had not seen my dear family in more than three years. I knew my absence was a thorn in Mam's side, for sure I felt it myself, and I knew she'd want me home for Christmas, but when I'd asked Mrs. Plumley that morning she'd said: "No, dear, I can't spare you, at least not until well into the New Year." I hadn't told Da of my disgrace. I'd written with my new address at the Walkley Estates, and told him only that I had a new and better situation. Now I had to write and tell him that I wouldn't be at his table for Christmas.

We were in the back row as usual. It was a George Formby film though I missed the best of it on account of being distracted by Reg. He was a very insistent man. When the lights came up and I was trying to button up my blouse and make myself decent I received a terrible shock which was both marvellous and dreadful. Little Jimmy came running at me, calling out: "Mary Moo, Mary Moo!" And as I embraced him I saw in the aisle Mr. Brooke watching us, and Charlotte beside him.

I felt my face flush bright red. I was mortified to be seen in the back seat of the Tudor Cinema with my Weasel Man, so removed from my dreams of glory. It was a humiliation to be brought down to earth so hard, and it was then that I began to regret most bitterly my unbidden words on that fateful night. I wanted so badly to tell him how sorry I was, but there wasn't a chance, for no sooner had Jimmy spotted me than his father called to him and said they must leave, though not before he had greeted me by name, ever the gentleman, and asked after my well-being.

It was at that moment Reg piped up and addressed Mr. Brooke in the most insulting manner, with never a thought for my feelings, and that made me so angry with him that I determined never to accept his offer, for he was harshly revealed in the light of that meeting as the scrapings from the bottom of the barrel.

Chapter Eight

NANNY'S BED

"**W**HAT ARE WE going to do about Christmas?" Cynthia asked. "We're going to enjoy it," Christopher said with a big smile. "My first Christmas at home in more than three years."

"I mean where are we going?"

"Not to church," Jimmy said. "Granny says we're not welcome there because I disgraced myself and Daddy had to ..."

"Oh, be quiet!" Cynthia said. She turned again to Christopher, her arms folded tightly under her bosom. "Mother wants us there. She wants to heal this rift, but you'd have to give your assurance ..."

"I won't be silenced, Cynthia. It is my God-given mission to bring His message to the ears of the world."

"Little pigs have *big* ears," Birdie said.

"How dare you speak to your father like that!" Cynthia lunged at Birdie who darted under the piano.

"Leave her, Darling. I have an idea. Let's go to Dinglewood."

"To *your* parents? Are you sure they want us?"

"Alice is coming down from London," he said with a boyish grin. "I missed seeing her when they transferred me."

"But what shall I say to Mother?"

"Tell her to go to Hell where she belongs."

He said it quietly, gently even. There was rarely an emotional force behind our father's statements. But Mum stormed out of the room and the next thing we heard was her voice on the telephone, low but insistent. When she came back she wouldn't speak to Daddy. She wouldn't even look at him. She sat on the sofa and took me on her knee, holding me tightly against her like a shield.

It was just before bedtime when the doorbell rang. Charlotte and Jimmy were playing Monopoly with Vera, and I was by then on my father's knee at the piano with Birdie beside us pecking at the black and white notes, singing in her high quavery voice. We all looked up surprised, wondering who could be calling so late, but Mum was obviously expecting someone because she ran to answer the door. When she came back we saw Grandpa Blackwell standing behind her, hat in hand, looking worn out, and a bit awkward as though he didn't want to be there.

"Take the children up to bed, Vera," she said.

"But we haven't finished the game," Charlotte said.

"Leave it for tomorrow."

"Oh no!" Jimmy said, wailing. "I'm just about to buy a hotel for Regent Street."

"Off to bed, Jim," Daddy said, rising from the piano and plunking me down next to Birdie. "You can buy your hotel after breakfast tomorrow."

He patted Jimmy's shoulder and ruffled his hair, then they all trooped out in silence, leaving me stranded on the piano stool. I heard them dashing upstairs daring Vera to catch them, but she wasn't the fun that Mary'd been. Vera was always looking in the mirror to check her lipstick, primping and patting at her hair, twisting around to see that the seams of her stockings were straight.

Grandpa nodded to my father and shook the hand he offered, then he lowered himself into the big comfy armchair.

"Tell my father what you said about my mother," she said, looking straight at Daddy. He hesitated a moment then turned to face Grandpa.

"I have no wish to cause trouble between our families, Sir, but since she insists I will tell you that your daughter, Sir, is ruled by the Devil."

Grandpa's hands dropped into his lap in a hopeless gesture. "You've brought me out for this, Cynthia?"

"How dare he? Tell him, Father!"

"It's not for me to reprimand a man in his own house. Now, can I go home?"

"But what will you say to Mother?"

"I shall tell her to get on with running her house, and let the rest run its course. You'd do well to heed that advice yourself."

We could hear her crying and begging as she walked with him into the front hall. She'd left the door open so a cold draught was sweeping through and Daddy shivered and picked me up, holding me against his chest as we went to join them in the hall. When Mum saw him she turned and ran upstairs. We heard the bedroom door slam, and Grandpa Blackwell shrugged and raised his eyebrows with a wry smile.

"I remember when Chamberlain returned from Munich," he said, fixing my father with his dark eyes. "He was the toast of the nation. The streets of London were lined with cheering crowds. We thought he'd saved the world. I was there, Christopher; I saw him leaning from the upstairs window of Number Ten, and I saw all those upturned faces waiting for him to speak. 'It is peace for our time,' he said, echoing Disraeli after the Congress of Berlin. We had common cause in our desire for peace. Nobody wanted to go to war after the devastation of the last one."

"So why did we?" my father asked. "And why do you support the warmongers, Sir?"

"It became inevitable, whether you had the stomach for it or ..."

"Not a question of stomach, Sir. I registered for military service in June 1940 when I was incarcerated at Walton, but I was not at liberty to perform my patriotic duty, a fact for which I now thank God. Christ's teachings of absolute pacifism have become clear to me during my years of detention."

"Is this where you get the hell-fire from of which you accuse my wife and daughter?"

"I love your daughter, Sir."

"*This* we have in common, Christopher, but your Bible thumping and your misplaced alliances—I can't say which is worse."

"Mosley could have saved us, if only he'd been elected Prime Minister ..."

"My point, Christopher, is that Chamberlain was naïve, as we all were in that time, but his position and his public stance subjected him to absolute humiliation when Hitler occupied Czechoslovakia, *and* went on to invade Poland. A humiliated man is a dangerous man. You're right, it could have gone differently, but it didn't and we've had to adapt ourselves to the situation and make the necessary compromises."

I began to wriggle in my father's arms so he put me down. I toddled over to the stairs and sat on the bottom step, sucking my thumb as Daddy continued.

"I'm glad of the opportunity to speak with you, Sir. We understand each other, man to man. Cynthia has no interest in the world situation."

"She's the mother of your children," Grandpa said as he sat beside me on the stairs and took me on his knee. "You must meet her halfway and take some interest in *her* world. Broaden your horizons, Christopher. It may at first feel like a narrowing but try it and perhaps you will reap the benefits."

I must have fallen asleep because the next thing I knew I was in Daddy's arms again and we were in the sitting room beside a dying coal-fire. Then Vera came to get me and carried me upstairs to bed. Later I heard my father's footsteps on the stairs and his careful closing of the door to the bedroom he shared with my mother.

We ended up at Dinglewood for Christmas dinner, wearing paper hats and throwing streamers across the table.

"Mind the candles!" Granny warned, though she never sounded very serious with her high voice, which was like the tinkling of the chandelier ornaments when Jimmy and Charlotte would race around upstairs making the ceiling shake. Auntie Alice doused the flames which had started creeping up a long yellow streamer, then we all laughed and pulled another box of crackers Grandpa had hidden away in the dresser drawer. They popped when we pulled them, and little prizes tumbled out with furled fortunes and riddles amidst puffs of smoke.

"Listen to this one!" Jimmy said excitedly. "What's black and white and red all over?"

"The newspaper!" Charlotte shouted.

"Ohooh," Jimmy said, groaning. "How did you know?"

"I had that one last year."

Auntie Alice was tall like Daddy, and she had the same calm and unruffled manner as him and Granny, which seemed to annoy Mum who was tight-lipped and tense throughout the day.

"Time for plum pudding," Granny said, and in came Mrs. Ward, the house-keeper, tottering under the weight of a flaming ball of brandy-soaked pudding with a sprig of holly on top, its plump red berries already beginning to darken in the heat. We all gasped, and when the flames died down, Grandpa took the decanter from the sideboard and poured a generous dollop into the dish to reignite it.

When Birdie started to choke Mum stuck a finger down her throat. She had almost swallowed a silver threepenny bit with Queen Victoria's head on it, from Grandpa's coin collection. The pudding was filled with such treasures.

"Tie it in a corner of your handkerchief," Granny told Birdie, "and it will bring you luck all through the New Year."

"By next Christmas we'll be celebrating the end of this war," Christopher said, getting to his feet.

"A toast to the end of war!" Grandpa declared quickly, raising his glass high above the table's disarray.

"To the end of war!" we all shouted and the grownups drank while Daddy stood alone, his glass still raised. He never did drink—I was watching him—he just sank into his chair, a sad expression on his face, and became almost invisible, as though he was not part of our family.

The grownups were sitting around like stuffed turkeys, and Grandpa Brooke had disappeared in a haze of cigar smoke and brandy fumes when Cynthia noticed that Christopher was missing—Alice too. Her husband, Maurice, sat contentedly jiggling their two-year-old daughter on his knee.

"Where's Alice?" she asked.

"Oh, I expect she's gone to powder her nose," Maurice replied calmly.

They're all the same in that family, Cynthia thought, cold fish. She felt impatient with the gentility of the gathering and almost wished for a good argument to disrupt it. She left Charlotte in charge of the other children and, excusing herself to Granny Brooke, she left the room. She stood a moment in the main hall, inhaling the richness of old wood permeated with the aroma of family life. Dinglewood was a sizeable house in Tudor style surrounded by an extensive acreage of garden and woodland. She had been impressed upon her first visit there in the spring of 1931 for her introduction to Christopher's parents. She remembered how shy she'd felt, seated at dinner next to old Mr. Brooke who had teased her. "Will you have white meat or dark?" he had inquired as he'd stood poised to carve a large capon resting on a Crown Derby serving dish.

"Dark meat, please," she'd replied, thinking that white meat was the prize and that she should make a modest choice.

"Ah, a girl who knows the best cut," he'd said with a growl. "The leg is by far the richer and juicer choice over the breast," he said, leaning in so close that she could see droplets of wine clinging to his moustache.

"Serve the bird, Daddy," Nancy had said. "Our dear Cynthia must be building an appetite with all this talk of the best cut."

"You do know of course how we come by the capon? How it differs from the common chicken, Cynthia?"

She had looked to Christopher for help.

She hadn't understood Brooke's laughter. It sounded like wet gravel. She had begun to laugh herself, babbling about the roast beef they ate at her father's table.

"With blood gravy from the dish, spooned over the meat, and he always says ..."

"It's made a bonny girl of you," Brooke said.

After the meal she had asked Christopher what a capon was, and he had tried to explain that it was ... an unmanned rooster.

"Oh, how cruel!" she'd exclaimed.

"To make the meat more tender," he had explained.

Cynthia inhaled deeply and crossed the hall to the main staircase which branched on either side onto a long upstairs landing. She climbed the stairs and paused on the landing, listening. A sound of voices came from a bedroom at the far end. She tiptoed down the landing to the door that stood ajar. She heard Christopher's voice, his soft laughter, and saw Alice, the gesture of her long arm. Cynthia pushed the door open, and they turned to her laughing.

"What are you doing up here?" Cynthia asked.

"Reminiscing about old times," Christopher said. "This used to be our nursery.

"I was worried about you."

"My cot was over there," Alice said, pointing towards the window that looked onto the back garden. "And Nanny Darlington slept there." She pointed to a narrow bed with a faded pink chenille cover. "Has Chris told you about Nanny Darlington?" She touched Christopher's arm gently, as though she were addressing him.

"Well yes ... I mean, he's mentioned her ... of course ..." She trailed off.

"Well, as long as you know. It's always fun to come home and remember the old times, isn't it, Chris?" She slipped her hand into his and their long arms began to swing to and fro.

Cynthia stood there not knowing what to do. She felt foolish and acutely embarrassed as though all the focus was on her exclusion.

"You must come downstairs, Christopher."

"Did I ever show you my party trick, Cynthia?" Alice asked brightly. "Look!" She turned her back and with her neck twisted archly so that she was looking at Cynthia from the corner of her eye, she folded her arms across her body until she was firmly clasped in her own embrace. Christopher started to giggle, a hoarse, little-boy sound which set his body all atremble. Cynthia watched in fascination as Alice's hands began to caress her own shoulders, creeping slowly, slowly down her back, all the while smoothing, squeezing, caressing until Cynthia had to turn away because she realized with a shock that Alice had become two people. She was whispering now in a breathy passionate voice—"Oh Darling, don't stop, I love you so!"—and making little moaning sounds. Cynthia's hands rose up, hovering by her ears, wanting to cover them, but unable to. Christopher was bent over, laughing so hard that he had tears running down his face.

"Stop, Alice, stop!" he said. "I can't stand any more!"

"Chris can do it even better," Alice said, laughing and spinning around suddenly. "Go on, show her." Then she saw Cynthia's face. "I hope I haven't upset you." There was an awkward silence, broken only by the tail-end of Christopher's breathy mirth. "Well, I must go and relieve Maurice. I left him holding the baby." Alice laughed again and sauntered out, leaving Christopher and Cynthia standing in the middle of the room. He wiped his face with a handkerchief, little tremors of laughter still erupting as he recovered himself.

"It's so good to see Alice. I've missed her."

"You have me."

He noticed then that something was amiss and he opened his arms to Cynthia. When she turned away he took a few steps towards her and placed his hands on her shoulders. She swung her arms up across her body and grasped his hands, pulling them down onto her breasts, then she turned and raised her face to him, her lips parted.

"I want you here, in this room," she said.

"We can't, not here. They'll wonder ..."

"Let them. You're my husband. Lock the door."

She sat on the narrow bed and pulled him down with her, tugging at his trousers to release him, but he was unwilling and unable to satisfy her.

"What is it? What's wrong?"

"Nanny Darlington made a naughty boy of me in this bed."

"What d'you mean?"

"She was lonely. She made me stroke her, then she smacked my bottom and sent me back to my bed. Told me not to tell anyone."

"Oh for goodness sake, you were a little boy. That's all in the past," she said, nuzzling into his neck.

"It happened night after night."

"Will you stroke *me*?"

Afterwards he felt contaminated and went to the bathroom to wash his hands. When he went downstairs Mrs. Ward was clearing the table, and he found the family in the drawing room eating Christmas cake.

Cynthia was with them, her cheeks flushed and her eyes shining as she smiled up at him.

"Oh, Christopher, there you are," Nancy said. "Just in time for the King's broadcast. Turn the wireless on, Daddy," she said to her husband.

Christopher would have liked to make a speech of his own, the one he'd been ready to make after their toast, but he kept his silence and drifted away, scarcely hearing the King's halting clichés.

Chapter Nine

IN BED WITH THE ENEMY

WE WERE WELL into the New Year of 1944 before Mrs. Plumley allowed me time enough to go home to Cavan. New grass was already springing up through the mud of the Walkley Estates, and everyone said it was the year that would end the war.

I was packing my bag when Meg drew back the curtain of my little room and spoke firmly to me.

"When you come back, Mary, you must either move in with Reg or find new lodgings for yourself. It's been six and a half months you've lodged in this cupboard. You deserve better."

But I couldn't think of my future just then. I was full of joy to be going home to Mam and Da, and could think of nothing but my desire to walk in the fields again, and to hold my dear sisters and brothers in my arms. I allowed Reg to carry my bag to the train station even though I was the stronger one.

"Come back soon, Mary," he said as we stood on the platform. "I'll miss you."

"Well you behave yourself then," I said. In spite of everything I was fond of him. We'd grown used to each other. It was seeing Mr. Brooke again, and in the presence of Reg, that had upset me, like two separate worlds colliding and one of them gets smashed.

"I want an answer from you when you come back."

"I've already told you, Reg, I won't marry you."

"Oh come on, Mary. You know we're made for each other."

He was so sure of himself, and perhaps he was right, but I wasn't ready to accept it. As the train steamed in he gave me a nice kiss on my lips and squeezed me with his strong arms, then he opened the carriage door and gave me a push on my behind to help me up, and handed in my travelling bag through the window for I had almost forgotten it. I felt proud in that moment to have a man seeing me off to Ireland, even though it was only Reg. I remembered my arrival at Holyhead three years and seven months past when I had been all alone, and I marvelled at how we find each other in this world, like ants or beetles, bumping into the nearest one, and perhaps it doesn't matter so much which one it is so long as you get used to him.

The train travelled along the north coast of Wales and onto the island of Anglesey and as I stared out the window at the passing scenery I had plenty of time to think about everything that had happened to me since I left home. I remembered too that it was on Anglesey at Rhosneigr where Cynthia and the Master had passed their honeymoon. Cynthia had told me about it that evening in front of the fire, and so I had a firm impression in my mind of the stony beach and the windswept sky, and the scraping of those stones disturbed by the waves as she lay awake listening to his breath and thinking, he's my husband now.

It was a rough crossing and I had to go up on deck for the benefit of the air, holding fast to my bag for I had presents in there for all the family. I knew Mam would scold me for spending my hard-earned money but I didn't care. It was a grand event to come home from a foreign land, and myself the first one to leave home and return, apart from my brother Seán who was still away at war, fighting his way through Italy, as Da had written.

A bitter February wind slashed at my face, but at least I kept my lunch down, and when we arrived at Dun Laoghaire and I walked down the gangplank I was overcome and wanted to kiss the ground as His Holiness the Pope does when he goes visiting. But of course I didn't. I collected myself and hurried off to the train station and bought a ticket for Belturbet.

It was Da met me at the station, and I wept to see his smiling face and how old he had become in a few years, perhaps because we had never been parted before, and now, coming home, I could see what the years did to a man. Cavan is the county of lakes and drumlins—little hills that rise and fall so frequently that you can never see very far. And it struck me then as I climbed up onto our horse-drawn cart that it's the same with family—you cannot see each other well unless you can see from a distance as well as up close, for you are always in each other's way, blocking the view.

My da is a quiet man but I could tell he was glad to have me sitting beside him again for he had a big grin on his face all through our journey, two and a half miles off the Ballyconnell road to our farm. Mam must have heard the cart rattling down the lane, because she was already standing in the doorway as we arrived. She didn't move. She just held out her arms and I ran at her like I'd done as a little girl when I would bury my face in her apron.

"Oh, Mam," I said. "It's good to be home. You wouldn't believe the adventures I've had."

"Well then, don't tell me about them," she replied, and hurried me inside to her kitchen where the table was loaded with food. There was a plate of fresh scones and a loaf of soda bread beside a slab of homemade butter, a plate of sliced ham with pickled cucumbers, and fat steaming jacket potatoes baked in the stove. You would not have known there was a war on, though I could guess at the sacrifices they'd made for my homecoming.

"The money is a godsend, Máire," Mam said in her tight-lipped way, but I saw that she had tears in her eyes. "The countryside is littered with abandoned houses and farms lying fallow, and all the animals gone, slaughtered for food."

After the meal we huddled by the stove and drank three cups of tea each, though they were weak as dishwater for there was a great scarcity of tea, Mam said. She went upstairs and came down with the green scarf from Kendal Milne's draped around her shoulders like a bride, and it was then I realized I *had* been away, for there was the evidence of it. I can't tell you how happy I felt in that moment to be with my dear parents, and my brother Patrick who'd come in from milking. He'd been a boy when I left and now he was a man, twenty years old and the most handsome of the lot. Too bad I got the dregs of the good looks, and Patrick got the accumulation.

"What about Deirdre?" I asked. "Is she alright?"

"What d'you think? She's a widow now," Mam said, her lips all puckered with little lines running off around her mouth.

"Was it really an accident?"

"Eamon was knocked down by a car, Máire. It was dark. It was night-time."

"But what was he doing out at night?"

"Nobody knows," Da said, "And you'd best not speak about it in this house, Máire. We don't interfere in those matters here. We've been through a hard time with bombs falling on Dublin and Belfast, and not knowing if it was the Germans or the British bombing us. And folk leaving in droves to go over there and work in the arms factories."

I didn't tell him about our hard times in the air-raid shelter, or about our near miss with the broken chimney, or about the A.V. Roe factory down Chester Road. I was dead on my feet so I went upstairs to my old room, the one I'd shared with Caitlin, Deirdre and Siobhan growing up. I wasn't to see them until two days later, and it was Deirdre who came first with the youngest of her three children in her arms. I was surprised by my tears when I saw her face, for she was changed. She had always been the beauty of the family, and now I could see that far from robbing her of that beauty, the grief had somehow ripened her. She handed the baby to Mam and took me by the hand, and in no time we were out the door, running away from the house and the farm, into the pastures.

"I want to show you something, Máire," she said.

I was trying to catch my breath for I was not used to running. To be sure I'd be on my feet all day at Cynthia's house, and now in Mrs. Plumley's establishment, but it wasn't the same as running free, which gave me a feeling of exhilaration, out of breath though I was. Deirdre took my hand again and led me into the shade of a hawthorn hedge. She bent down and disappeared through a small opening, then she turned and beckoned to me. I'm plumper than our Deirdre and I got stuck half way. Crouched there laughing and cursing as the hawthorns snagged on my hair, I was reminded of the time Mr. Brooke had tried to push me through the kitchen hatch into the dining room, and I saw again Cynthia's laughing face and all the children cheering me on. Well it was my own dear sister pulled me through this time, and I burst into a clearing with my hair flying in all directions.

I didn't see them at first for they were buried deep in the turf with grasses growing up around them, but as Deirdre led me around the circle I *felt* the positioning of the stones and then I began to see them clearly. She led me to the centre and we knelt on the damp grass, for although there was a wintry sunshine that morning we were in a dark place where the sun did not reach.

"This is where I come to talk to him," Deirdre said.

"You mean he's not ...?"

"He's gone, Máire. I saw his body. They suspected him of collaborating with the English."

I gasped with the shock of it, my worst suspicions confirmed.

"I'm sorry, Deedee. I've been praying for you and the little ones."

"What good will that do?" she said with a toss of her head, sending her black hair flying like a cloud of doom around her shoulders. "This is a godforsaken country, Máire, and I'll not stay here after what's happened to me. I want to go to England with you." She grasped my hands.

I was so shocked that the words did not come to me at first. "But ... but ... what about the children?"

"Mam will keep them. I need to get away and earn some money. If I don't board that boat I'll be buried alive here. Ireland's a place with no future." She let me go and leaned across to touch one of the stones, pointing up out of the earth like a giant's jagged tooth. "These stones have listened to me and it is here that I have learned where my future lies."

She caressed the stone, running her fingers over its mottled surface, and I watched her with a feeling of panic gathering in me until I found my voice, for I had to speak before she ran ahead too far with her plans.

"You can't come to England, Deirdre. It's too much of a struggle there with the war on. You're better off here with your children where you belong."

"I thought you would help me," she said, all the fire gone out of her.

"'Course I would help you, but the truth is I was thinking of staying here myself."

"Is it that bad?"

"They're not so bad, the English. I know about them now. But there's nothing there for me, Deirdre, neither for you."

"The war will end, Máire, and there will be opportunities in England. I was thinking to train as a nurse."

I didn't know what to say to her for I could see she was determined. Perhaps it would be Deirdre who would leave for England and I would stay home and look after her children, I thought. But it wasn't to be.

When Caitlin and Siobhan arrived next day they peppered me with questions about my life in England, curious as Mam and Da were not, for *they* had hardly said a word about it, being more caught up with their life on the farm and the welfare of the animals. Patrick too. And Brendan we had not seen for he was away from the house on his revolutionary business, Lord knows where. Patrick said he was over the border to Armagh often as not, and that he'd been scarce during the war years on account of the internment of IRA soldiers.

"One war will put another in the shadows," Patrick said. "The IRA has lost sympathy at home since all this started."

He seemed wise beyond his twenty years, and I felt sorry to have missed his growing from a lad into a man.

"D'you have a gentleman friend, Máire?" my sister Caitlin asked me with a wicked look in her eye, then she winked at Siobhan who giggled and I thought they were making fun of me, which is why I told them about Reg who I had not thought of at all as a topic of conversation for my family. But somehow, as I spoke of him he began to grow in my estimation. I started to realize that people could look different and your feelings for them could change depending on who you were talking to. And that made me distrustful of myself.

"Will you marry him?" Caitlin asked.

"He's asked me, any number of times," I said, for in the company of my beautiful sisters I felt once again dowdy and plain with my moon face and thick ankles. But I knew now what I hadn't known before — the feeling of beauty that can come over a girl when she is touched, and that it doesn't matter what or who she's thinking about, it's the feeling that counts, and the way it opens up your heart and makes a human being of you. Our priests and nuns with their celibacy seemed to me then a miserable bunch, deprived and mean with it.

"You'd best accept him," Da said, and he took my hand and smiled at me with great warmth for I know he wanted my happiness. But how could I explain to him my reluctance to marry a Weasel Man?

"You're twenty-five years old, Máire," Mam said, as though I was nearing the end of my life and had to hurry up and make something of it.

I don't know what it was that finally took me back to England, so contrary to my wishes. Was it my missing of the children, even though it was not to them that I would return? It wasn't loyalty to Mrs. Plumley for I knew she could replace me quite tidily, and sure it wasn't my feeling for Reg. I do believe it was Mam's cautioning about my age that tipped the balance—twenty-five years old and still not settled. I did want my own babies to fill my belly and warm my heart with their little hands in mine and soft lips like Birdie's giving me sticky wet kisses. The words of a mother can have a powerful hold on a girl and send her to her doom as easily as to her happiness. I never did tell Da of my plan to live again under his roof. 'Twas only Deirdre that knew and she so caught up with her own desire to get away to England that I doubt she even remembered what I had said.

It was on my last night that Brendan came, and I ran at him and hugged him nearly to death. My big brother, thirty-two years old, and much wilder and less settled than me. We were the ones, the adventurers in the family, and Seán too, off in Italian parts fighting beside the British. "Máire," he said, holding me at arms' length, grinning down at me, handsome as ever, "I knew you'd come back, for this is your true home."

But it was too late. Where was he when I was under the gun to go back to England and marry an Englishman?

"Oh Brendan, I'm right glad to see you. And I wish you'd come sooner for I'm leaving tomorrow, back to Dun Laoghaire."

"For the ferry?"

I nodded, and his face grew dark. He stepped back and pointed his finger at me. "You're a traitor to this family," he said. "You and Seán, in bed with the enemy." I coloured up and turned away from him, but he came after me and spun me around. "What d'you think you're doing, Máire? My little sister, I never thought it of you. Stay here with me and fight for a united Ireland!"

"You know I can't. I have to earn my living, Brendan."

"We'll look after you. We're a family, Máire." He lowered his voice. "Better than *this* family, turning a blind eye to Ireland's situation. Do you know that after Pearl Harbor Churchill offered us Irish unity in return for siding with the allies? But that damned eejit de Valera wouldn't give up neutrality. So close, Máire." He punched his fist into his palm and his voice rose again. "Come on and join us. We have women like you fighting for the cause, and we shall win with their help!"

There was such passion to his words, with his eyes blazing and flecks of spittle gathered at the corners of his mouth, in that moment I wished I could be like him and give up everything and follow him, but then I'd be like Mr. Brooke, wouldn't I, and come to no good end. It was the children, you see, I kept thinking of the children and how someone had to look after them. I'd abandoned Cynthia's children and left them to fend for themselves in that doomed house, but at least I could have my own and look after them properly.

Mam came downstairs then, just as Patrick and Da came in from the shippen where they'd finished milking, and we all sat down to supper together and nothing more was said about my career with the IRA. But Brendan did leave his mark on me, there's no doubting that, for he is my brother and he offered me an open door with his hand held out, and I closed it in his face. You spend your life remembering all the closed doors, the might-have-beens and what-ifs, but when all's said and done it was not my destiny to join Brendan in his struggle—though I love him dearly to this day—for it is not in my hand.

Brendan slept in our house that night and I've always been grateful for it. I lay awake until the wee hours listening to his gentle snoring through the wall, and to the creaking and murmuring of our house. In the morning he came early to my room to bid me farewell, and he sat on my bed and looked long and hard at me, but he said not a word, only took me in his arms and hugged me so tight I almost cried out. I have always remembered that embrace.

Just as I was climbing up onto the cart to make the journey back to the train station with my da, Deirdre came running down our lane. She threw her arms around me and whispered: "I can't go with you now, Máire, but I'll follow you, I promise, when I have the children settled."

I do not like secrets. Why wouldn't she speak out in front of Da instead of whispering in my ear, making a conspirator of me? You're too beautiful, I thought to myself. You'll come to no good with all that beauty. I held her face in my hands and feasted my eyes on her one last time in Ireland, our true home.

On the road to Belturbet we passed a group of tinkers camped out by the side of the road with their caravan drawn by a sorry-looking nag, and a sudden change of heart took hold of me so that I almost grabbed the reins from my da and turned us back towards home. But the moment passed before I acted upon it.

Chapter Ten

WHERE AM I GOING TO LIVE?

WHEN I ARRIVED at the Walkley Estates after my long journey, I found the door of Meg's caravan locked and no-one in sight. I had a sinking feeling in my stomach as though a stone had dropped there. Must be getting my period, I thought, with that heavy pulling on my insides, but it was too early for it. I walked around the caravan, but I couldn't see a thing because the curtains were closed — perhaps to keep the sun out, I thought, for it had been a bright day all over England and Wales, with the sun glaring in my eyes on the train from Holyhead.

I resisted the urge to knock on Reg's door, and I left my bag on Meg's doorstep and walked across the grass to Vancy Lee's caravan. She was Meg's friend and would surely know where she was. Vancy opened the door to me with a strange look on her face, and I noticed that her eyes were red from crying.

"What d'you want 'ere?" she asked gruffly.

"I'm just back from Ireland and I'm looking for Meg."

"You should've stayed there. Now that you're back they'll be calling you as a witness."

"What d'you mean?"

She pulled out a man's handkerchief and blew her nose with a great trumpet.

"They took 'er to Strangeways this mornin'."

I gasped at the mention of that horrible place. To think of Meg locked up in there!

"Two police, a man and a woman. They searched the place and found all 'er instruments along with the bloody towels and a wad of pound notes from two clients just yesterday. They put 'er in 'andcuffs and took 'er away in a car."

I steadied myself with my hand on the doorframe, for the world was spinning around me. "Poor Meg. What will she do?"

"Twiddle 'er thumbs while she waits for her appointment with James Billington."

"Is that her solicitor?"

"James Billington is the 'angman of England, and a busy feller."

"Oh Lord, Vancy, they'll not hang her. It's a crime, but it's not murder."

"Depends on 'ow they look at it, and what the jury thinks."

All I could think was that I had to see Meg and talk to her, my dear friend who took me in when I was in trouble, and now she was in Strangeways, cold and frightened and needing a friend. "Is she allowed visitors, Vancy?"

"I'd not go near 'er if I were you."

"But I must. It's only right."

"And you can't go into 'er caravan. They've locked it up and no-one's to go near. There's more evidence in there—fingerprints and blood spots. It's the scene of the crime," Vancy said dramatically, as though she were the star of a moving picture.

"Where am I going to live?"

"You can't stay 'ere," she said quickly.

"Well I'd best go pick up my bag."

I left her standing there, staring after me no doubt as I walked across to Meg's caravan, which looked different now, contaminated, like the scene of the crime, as Vancy had said.

Reg opened his door right away, and with the warmth of his smile I began to cry.

"Come on, Mary," he said. "You're a sight for sore eyes."

He took my bag and held out his hand to help me up the steps. He never touched me further than that in the weeks that I lodged with him, so it was my decision in the end, though no doubt he thought he had me, with nowhere else for me to go. But I did not feel forced into it. I felt like a free woman deciding my own fate. And that is how I fell in love with Reg Wilkins, for in that time before we married he showed me all the respect a woman could wish for, and kept his passions in cold storage until the time was right.

Mrs. Plumley was glad to see me, and no wonder for she'd let the place go in the short time I'd been gone.

"We've 'ad it rough in 'ere, Mary. Lucky for you, you missed all the excitement. There was a fight last week," she said, leaning into me and pausing for effect. "Bunch of lads 'ome on leave, come in for a cup of tea, one of them second cousin to me 'usband. Then in comes that gentleman from the 'at factory, starts talking to them about 'peace for our time' and 'ow the British government has betrayed its people. Well, 'e's the traitor, isn't 'e? One of them Mosleyites who refused to fight ..."

"He didn't refuse, he was detained and sent to ..." It was out my mouth before I knew it. "I'm sorry, Mrs. Plumley, I ..."

"Is that who you was working for on Chester Road?"

"Well yes, I was taken on by his wife, you see, when he was ..."

"You would have been ashamed to see 'ow he carried on. Told the lads they should make a stand before they got themselves killed. 'Young men in your prime,' he said. 'The future of England.' And then 'e started on like a vicar in the pulpit, preaching to us about God's divine purpose and 'ow Adolf 'itler was his mouthpiece on earth."

"He didn't! I don't believe it!" Even though I had heard those very words from his mouth myself, it was shocking to hear Mrs. Plumley say it.

"Oh my Lord! One of the lads took a swing at 'im, but he was agile, I'll give him that. 'E was on 'is feet in a second, prancing like a boxer, not hitting, mind you, but defending 'imself. Then the other lads joined in and they 'ad him down on my clean floor kicking at 'im. 'E curled up with his 'ands over his 'ead to protect 'imself until they stopped.

"What happened next?"

"It were dead silent in 'ere, with folk at the window peering in to see what 'ad 'appened."

"Was he hurt?"

"'E got to his feet and put his 'at back on, then 'e walked to the door, turned around and threw out his right arm in front of him. 'Heil Hitler!' he said, and before the lads could set on 'im again 'e was out the door and striding down the High Street with everyone staring after 'im."

"Indeed, I'm glad I missed it," I said, but in truth I wanted to sit down and cry. Why had he never come in when I was there, all those months of serving tea and sandwiches to strangers? I could have talked to him. But then perhaps he would not have listened.

Well, I got the café all ship-shape again, got through my day's work, and then I bought some tripe at the butcher's and took it back to the Walkley Estates, and I stewed it with onions for our dinner, and a few mashed potatoes to soak up the slop of it. I could tell that Reg enjoyed his dinner. He didn't even hurry to light up a cigarette after but sat there smiling at me like the Cheshire cat. It was the first of many dinners we would share.

We married on the 15th of May, just as the weather was warming up and the lilac bushes in bloom and laburnum trees dripping with yellow flowers. The roses were tight buds yet, gathering their strength, and Meg still in prison awaiting trial. There was no denying her guilt after all the evidence they'd found—it was just a matter of how long her sentence would be. Reg and I went to the police station to speak up for her and soon after that a solicitor came looking for us.

"I understand you want to be character witnesses," he said as though he had a mouthful of something troublesome that he could not swallow.

"I'll speak up for Meg," I said. "She's an honest woman, and always a good friend to me."

"Were you one of her clients?"

"Not on your life!" I said. "I've never had that sort of trouble."

"I'll thank you not to insult my fiancée," Reg said, coming to life suddenly, and with a tone that reminded me of *his* insulting remarks to Mr. Brooke in the Tudor Cinema.

It was agreed that we would sign our written statements as to Meg's good character and be ready to appear in court if we were called. What more could I do? She was not permitted visitors which I think was an unnecessary cruelty, and her still awaiting trial. How many poor women did she save? And how many souls spared a life of poverty and shame, coming into the world illegitimate to be dragged up by a mother without the means to care for them, and their fathers disappeared in a cloud of dust.

Mrs. Plumley gave me the day off and we went to the Registry office in Stockport. Reg's sister, Beryl, came with us as witness, and she wore a fancy red hat for the occasion, but I had no-one, with Meg in Strangeways and Cynthia gone from my life. Who else did I know in England? Mrs. Plumley had the café to run, so we just said the "I do's," signed the register, and took the bus back to Bramhall. Reg wanted to take me to the Victoria Hotel, but you had to eat something there in order to get a drink and it was too expensive, so we went instead to the Bull's Head Pub and had a pint each of the best bitter.

"Well, I'm the lucky one, ain't I?" Reg said, grinning. "How are you, Mrs. Wilkins?"

He reached across the table and took my hand. I was nervous as a chicken with a fox at the door, and felt myself running in circles even though I was sitting still. I wondered what I should do in his bed that night for it was to be a new experience for me altogether, and one that I had been longing for without knowing what it was. Those strong feelings had deserted me now that I was allowed to give in to them.

But I needn't have worried. It all went smoothly except for the blood on the bedsheet. I should have known to put a towel under me. But I must confess I wondered what all the fuss was about. I'd had more pleasure from our fumblings in the darkness of the Tudor Cinema than I had on my wedding night. But the following night Reg took his time and then I began to understand the pleasures of my body, and I was grateful for his attentions. He may not have been the best prize, but he was just right for me. I wondered if Cynthia too felt the same pleasures that I did and that's why she had been so passionate with the Master.

"I'll take you to see the Blackpool illuminations in September,"

Reg said as we lay there in his little bed, my head snuggled into the crook of his arm.

I felt so beautiful, my whole body thrilled with the closeness of him.

"We'll 'ave a delayed 'oneymoon, a weekend away in a boarding house. Would you like that, Mary my love?"

"Oh yes," I said, and I couldn't think of anywhere I'd rather be in that moment.

"'Appen the war'll be over by then."

"It's dragging on."

"It'll 'ave to end some day. Goodnight, love." He raised himself on one elbow and leaned down to kiss me. "I'd like to stay awake all night looking at my beautiful wife, but we've got to be up early for work, eh?"

I slept deep and dreamless in those days, not like my troubled nights in Cynthia's house with the turmoil of my dreams there.

Chapter Eleven

1944 — BEGINNING OF THE END

WE GOT USED to having our father at home and settled into the kind of routine that children thrive on. Jimmy's bowling improved and Daddy started playing fast-catch with him to sharpen Jim's out-fielding skills. Charlotte was always at Daddy's side, holding onto his arm, and when he was out working on the farm we all knew he was close by, just beyond the pond, mucking out those farm buildings we could see from the edge of our Magic Circle.

Our mother complained about his smell when he came home from work, and about his muddy boots and work clothes which she made him leave on the back porch outside the scullery, so that he had to dress and undress there. When she was angry she would make him eat his meals in the kitchen, but then she would relent and allow him into the dining room.

There was something wickedly alluring to her about his odour. Who would have guessed that I would share my bed with a farm labourer? she thought. But everything was turning out to be different from what she had visualized. She clung to the belief that her life would revert to normal when the war was over. It was, after all, a time of madness, wasn't it, and not to be taken too seriously.

Christopher refused the counselling that Archer Pearson recommended. "Physician, heal thyself," he said during a particularly embarrassing encounter in the sitting room at Meadowside.

"Archer is only trying to help," Cynthia said. "He's gone to all the trouble of setting up an appointment with a very prominent psychiatrist. How can we help you, Darling, if you won't co-operate?"

Christopher continued quoting from the Book of Luke until Dr. Pearson threw up his hands in a gesture of despair. Cynthia bustled him out of the room and into the hall where they stood together in whispered conversation.

"What are we to do, Archer? I'm losing him."

But the man who had known her since childhood, who had attended her at four births, whose family had been friends with hers for two generations, was unable to come up with anything more. "Be patient with him, Cynthia. Be kind. Be gentle."

Christopher feels insulted by Cynthia's insistence on counselling and by her alliance with Archer Pearson who is really an extension of the Blackwell family, a part of their clan ganged up against him. To be accused of psychological befuddlement when he is in full possession of vital and superior knowledge is almost more than he can bear.

Nineteen forty-four has begun with the Soviets' defeat of the Germans at Leningrad, making an end to a siege that lasted almost three years. In trying to understand the starvation the Russians must have endured Christopher remembers his own time of crippling hunger at Latchmere House, and the steady hunger that dogged him throughout his three-year internment. Though he has regained his normal weight and well-being, the memory still humiliates him; he cannot bear to think about the citizens of Leningrad and what they have suffered in their ignorance, robbed of their ability to think as they were consumed by their bodies.

With news of the Allies sweeping north through Italy and the Russians pushing west through the Balkans, reclaiming territories taken by the Germans, Christopher feels quite adrift. On the one hand he longs for an end to the war so that he can reunite with Thom Baker and start their work together at Kingdom House, but he is dismayed by the fall of Mussolini and by the defeat of Hitler's grand vision. He fears for the fate of Europe as the Communist hordes advance. He feels a physical aversion at the thought of the Giant that is Russia with its icy wastelands and barbaric politics.

In mid-June he receives a rare telephone call from Alice.

"I'm so frightened, Chris. I don't want to worry Mother, but we're being bombarded here in London. It's like the Blitz all over again. Maurice is in the City and I'm all alone with our little girl. And the new baby won't stop crying. I pray to God Maurice has taken refuge in the tube station. I can't reach him on the telephone."

He talks to her for over an hour, reassuring her as he'd done throughout their childhood—Little Sis—talking her down from a state of near terror as German buzz bombs explode all around her. Christopher hears the eerie insect sound in the background and he explains: "These V1s are new, Sis. They don't have pilots. They're robot doodlebugs that tumble to earth when their motors cut out." He is aware of Cynthia's pacing, then she stops and stands behind him with her hands resting on his shoulders. She tries to stroke his cheek, but he jerks his head away. "Hold tight, Sis. Everything will come right, you'll see. We're going to be alright."

Cynthia goes up to her bedroom and lifts the receiver on the telephone table by her bed. She hears them praying together, the Lord's Prayer—'Give us this day our daily bread, Forgive us our trespasses, Lead us not into temptation, Deliver us from evil'—their voices together, in harmony. He is smiling now, she can hear it in his voice, and she hears Alice's laughter, all the way from London. She slams down the receiver.

In our house we grew up waiting for something to change: the war, our parents. They were always fighting, either that or kissing—there was no in-between—and we coped with it in our own ways. I was waiting for something wonderful to happen, something that might remove the caul of shame I'd been born inside, though I didn't know it as that. I thought Grace Kelly must be my real mother and that one day she would come for me and take me away to a new life. Charlotte and Jimmy must have known that something was very wrong in our family, and in our country too, because they had lived through a more normal time, before the war, when our father came and went with impunity, moving freely between our house and the outside world; going to work, coming home for supper, then a change of clothing and off to a political meeting, sitting with us at breakfast next day, smiling and joking.

How can you feel comfortable in the world after a childhood like ours? We were all affected, people all over the world, in different ways, two or three generations distorted by that war, by what was discovered after and by what we did in our different ways to come to terms with it. We were marked by our Blackwell grandparents' attitude to the disgrace of our father's behaviour. Had he been broken at Latchmere, and thus fell victim to Baker's manipulations? As Dick Blackwell discerned, Christopher Brooke was a follower. But he was also a leader — at boarding school, in industry, in the Stockport branch of British Union — and that impulse persisted after the war, isolated though he was.

In a more enlightened time the effects of his experience would have been diagnosed. We would have made allowances for him instead of taking on the shame and embarrassment his name engendered. Cynthia and Archer Pearson tried, but they were outnumbered by people who were themselves traumatized by war, unable to recreate a rational society, able only to shout "Traitor!"

Living with a secret makes you duplicitous; your every action feels fraudulent. At the end of each day you think you've gotten away with it again, made it through another mine field, fooled everybody. We children mistook those boggy, fog-ridden mine-fields for acceptable terrain. We turned in circles, trying to find the right place to sit, cowering and dipping, apologetic, fearful of taking a stand, fearful of speaking out, afraid of visibility, discovery, and exposure to ridicule; one crack in the façade and everything could come tumbling out. Such people develop elaborate coping mechanisms rather than risk revealing their secrets. We were emotional illiterates apologizing for our existence while tunnelling further underground for survival.

But what if you don't even know that you're hiding something? What if you suffer the punishment without understanding the crime? Then you must devote your life to puzzling it out, and get beyond the feeling that life is a minefield.

Chapter Twelve

TARRED AND FEATHERED

T THE END of August Paris was liberated and at our mother's insistence we all went to the Tudor Cinema to see the Pathé News. We sat together in the front row and watched crowds cheering and Frenchmen throwing their hats in the air as women kissed the Allied soldiers. Cynthia stared at the screen, convinced that she would see Mireille waving to her from the crowd. She half rose from her seat when she thought she'd caught a glimpse of Madame Plasse, but then the woman was gone and she said, how could you spot anyone you knew in such a big crowd? But the mere sight of the Paris streets thrilled her. She held onto Daddy's arm and nuzzled his neck.

"Is that where you used to live, Mummy?" Charlotte whispered, pointing at the screen.

"Yes, darling, I'll take you there someday," she said, squeezing Charlotte's hand. "And you'll meet your Tante Mireille."

The celebrations were halted by sniper fire from French fascists and a few straggling Germans, and then there was footage of young women being dragged away by crowds of angry French people, and one girl in particular with her head shaved, and with tar and feathers stuck on her.

"Look, Jimmy. It's a chicken head!" Birdie said, and they both started giggling.

"*Shhhh*, it's not funny," Mum whispered. "She's a traitor. She has a German baby in her arms."

When the lights came up and the usherette walked down the aisle and stood in front of the screen Mum told us we could all have an ice to celebrate. There was such a feeling in the cinema; everyone was caught up in it. Charlotte went with Daddy to help carry the fourpenny tubs, one for each of us with a little wooden paddle to spoon out the cold creamy ice. They were first in line so everyone in the cinema could see them and as Christopher paid a little man in rumpled trousers and a too-small sports jacket darted forward and spat on his shoes.

"Watch out or we'll tar and feather you, Christopher Brooke," he said, wiping the spittle from his chin.

Daddy excused himself and returned only when the lights had gone down, just as we were scraping our tubs clean.

With Paris liberated Cynthia expected a letter or at least a postcard, perhaps of one of their favourite cafés—Les Deux Magots where she had learned to smoke Turkish Abdullahs, or Le Dôme where they'd sat outside on raffia chairs at round tables with barely enough room for their *demi-tasse* and ashtray. She could still see Mireille, applying red lipstick to her mouth with the aid of a tiny mirror, and yet there had been no vanity about her.

Surely she would write. Cynthia was dying to know what she'd been up to. All her own letters had gone unanswered, apart from that one reply sent by Madame Plasse more than two years ago. She read in the newspaper of de Gaulle's return to France as leader of the government, and of Dieppe's liberation, along with Brussels and Antwerp; and she waited and waited for news of Mireille.

In mid-October it was reported that Rommel, the Desert Fox, had died from injuries sustained when his car was strafed. Only much later was it revealed that he had been involved in a plot to assassinate Hitler and, because he was a war hero, had been permitted to die by his own hand, with cyanide, rather than being strung up on a meat hook like the rest of the would-be assassins.

The war was coming to an end. There was a feeling in the air, and who could say whether events determined the outcome, or whether this slow rising of national spirit pushed it to a conclusion? Then a renewed wave of attacks came, with V2 rockets, and civilians once again hunkered in terror as nine thousand Londoners died and people began to ask themselves: "What have we started? And how will we ever end it?"

"Thom Baker will be released soon," Christopher said. "And when you meet him you'll understand, Cynthia, and we can begin our plans."

"We'll look for a new house? I do want a fresh start," she said, sighing.

"Me too, Darling," he said. "All I ever wanted was peace by any means."

Cynthia looked up at him in wonder. Archer was right, she thought. My patience is paying off. He's turning around. But Christopher's contrapuntal thoughts sought a resolution as yet unwritten, a slow movement playing within him, one hand out of harmony with the other, moving forward note by note, in search of the final, perfect cadence.

Chapter Thirteen

MEG'S SENTENCE

Autumn 1944

B Y MID-SUMMER we still had not received a letter from Meg's solicitor, nor had I been allowed to visit her. I worried all the time about what was happening to her, so I followed my husband's advice, plucked up my courage and telephoned from Mrs. Plumley's café. The solicitor's secretary said that neither Reg nor I would be called to testify in Meg's favour, and whether that was because they thought us untrustworthy or because they had already decided on Meg's fate I'll never know. We had to wait two more weeks for her case to come before the court, so our trip to Blackpool was postponed until the end of September, and in the meantime Reg was gone several nights a week on Home Guard, watching for the new V2 rockets that were causing so much damage, especially in London, and this coming after the V1 which had already taken many lives in revenge for the allied landings in Normandy on D-Day, Reg told me. They were a cross between a rocket and a plane, he said—a flying bomb that could land anywhere and surprise you.

There was all manner of stories being told during the war, about electro-magnetic death rays being shot by Germans who had parachuted into England and were being harboured by sympathizers; and even about bombs that could chase you around corners. You were either to be afraid all the time or to take a philosophical attitude. "If your number's on it the bomb'll get you," was what most people said, and I couldn't help thinking that would have been Meg's take on the matter.

I was in the courtroom in Manchester the day they sent her down for five years on the testimony of one of her clients who had been frightened when the bleeding wouldn't stop and had told her mother, who'd taken her to the Stepping Hill Hospital in Stockport. But at least she had escaped Mr. Billington's noose, and I was allowed to visit her after the sentencing. I took an apple cake I'd made from the windfalls on the Walkley Estates and I tried my best to hide the tears that came when I first saw her, for poor Meg was a shadow of herself, though with her spirit unquenched.

"I intend to be a model prisoner," she said. "With the time I've already served, and with good behavior I should be out of 'ere in three years."

We ate the cake together and I enjoyed seeing her relish every mouthful. Even there in the prison she continued a generous woman, offering me the hospitality of her caravan while she was getting free board and lodging courtesy of His Majesty's Prison Services. That's when I told her the good news.

"So 'e broke down your door, did he? Good for Reg!"

She laughed herself into a coughing fit. I saw she was smoking more than ever, her apple cake in one hand, cigarette in the other, puffing between bites.

"How do you get cigarettes in here?" I asked.

"You can get anything you want once you know the ropes."

"I'll keep an eye on your caravan, Meg, don't you worry."

"And give it an airing once in a while. You never know, you might want to escape from your Reg for a spell. 'E's been all bottled up waiting so long for you, no doubt 'e'll make a nuisance of 'imself now, wanting it every night. They say the Irish lasses are loose and easy, but you broke the mould with your Catholic chastity."

I didn't say a thing, but Oh Meg, I thought to myself, you don't know me. I've been bottled up myself and since my marriage I can't get enough of Reg. He was far from the weakling I'd thought him. He had a fine endowment, and a great facility with it. And oh, the skill of his hands with those long fingers like the Master's. For a casual labourer and a handyman he kept his hands in remarkably good repair, and he was a hard worker, I'll say that for him. Between us we were gathering quite a nest egg, even though we went over budget on our holiday in Blackpool which proved to be all he had promised and more. As I looked up at the illuminations with a new moon sliced in the sky I vowed that I would bring Meg on holiday to Blackpool when she was released.

Chapter Fourteen

THE SUNNY SIDE OF THE STREET

December 1944

CYNTHIA AND VERA sat by the wireless waiting for their mince pies to bake. Vera was painting her fingernails and chattering as usual, so Cynthia had to *shush* her when the news came on.

"Germany has launched a counter-offensive in the Ardennes," the announcer said in a dull tone as though he were reading the weather report. "The Allies have been caught off-guard and are sustaining heavy losses ..."

Cynthia sighed. She was sick of it. She wanted the damned war to be over, for the bloody Germans to be defeated once and for all, so they could have a fresh start in another house away from her parents and their silent judgement.

"Vera! The mince pies! Can't you smell them? You already ruined a batch last week. We can't afford to keep burning things."

It was an anxious Christmas with everyone listening for news, but by mid-January the Battle of the Bulge, as the press had dubbed it, ended with a decisive victory. The Allies were a united force against an isolated Germany, but though Hitler's defeat now seemed inevitable Christopher was far from discouraged. He had already begun to digest the inevitable in his own peculiar manner, searching his way into a kind of discordant harmony—a symphony that only he could hear.

"The Windsors are back."

He looked up from his desk and saw the glint in Cynthia's eye. She loved news of the Royal Family and could absorb it more readily than the war news which often made no sense to her.

"The Duke of Windsor and Mrs. Simpson, Darling. They've been in the Bahamas since the beginning of the war. They say that David Windsor was too pally with Hitler, so they put him out to pasture as Governor of the Bahamas. I'd call that internment, wouldn't you? If the war had gone a different way he could have ended up on the throne again, as Hitler's puppet." She perched herself on Christopher's knee and draped her arms around his neck. "Just think, Chris, it could have been us. If only you had been more nobly born we could have had a long holiday together instead of enduring our long separation."

"Cynthia, I'm trying to work," he said, a fountain pen gripped in one hand while his left hand hovered over the outline of her thighs held firm in a tight tweed skirt.

"Oh Darling, you're so lacking in humour. Thank goodness I'm here to liven you up." She kissed Christopher's nose and tweaked his newly grown moustache which hovered under his nose like a ridiculous black toothbrush. She was trying to ignore it in the hope that a lack of attention would encourage him to shave it off. "Never mind, I'm just teasing." She jumped up abruptly. "Couldn't get a rise out of you with a pound of yeast," she said as she left the room. One of Mary Byrne's favourite sayings.

As she walked down the corridor to the kitchen she wished she could find Mary there instead of Vera. It just wasn't the same without her. Mary had been a brick, but Vera was ... loose somehow. Cynthia needed someone solid to push against. I'll go to Paris when all this is over, she thought. I'll take Charlotte with me and show her off to Mireille. She began to sing along with Jo Stafford as she swung the kitchen door open—*Life can be so sweet on the sunny side of the street* ... Vera looked up from the ironing board and grinned. She joined in right away, singing along with the wireless in a high warbly voice as she plopped the iron down on its asbestos pad, took Cynthia in her arms and danced her around the kitchen.

On Valentine's Day Vera surprised them all with a big red cake. It was an inedible thing, made from an assortment of red liquid and substance pressed together into a damp, misshapen heart. Vera's hands were stained with cochineal, beetroot juice, bottled raspberries and plums, mixed in with lumps of stale bread and mashed potato for bulk. Jimmy tasted it and made a face.

"Don't you like it?" Vera asked.

"Tastes horrible," Jimmy said, spitting out the red mush.

"Oh, well, it's just for the look of it," she said, pressing her red fingers into the thing, remoulding it. "To celebrate St. Valentine's."

"What will we do with it after?" Charlotte asked.

"We can put it in the garden," Jimmy said. "The birds might like it."

It was reported on that day, as Cynthia and Christopher listened in, that British and US bombers had dropped hundreds of thousands of explosives on the German city of Dresden. The next day, February 15th, the children carried Vera's cake out to the garden and transferred the bloody dripping thing to the bird table where it finally dissolved in the rain, leaving the empty table stained purple.

Chapter Fifteen

THE TIE

April 19, 1945

W E WERE IN the kitchen having breakfast. Daddy had already gone to work on the farm; he left the house so early that we never saw him until the afternoon. Mum was slicing soldiers for my boiled egg—fingers of buttered toast without the crusts—when she suddenly dropped the knife and dashed across the room to turn up the sound on the wireless. She *shushed* us angrily so we all stopped talking and then we heard the solemn voice of Richard Dimbleby.

"British troops have entered the German concentration camp of Bergen-Belsen. Inside the camp the horrified soldiers found piles of dead and rotting corpses and thousands of sick and starving prisoners kept in severely overcrowded and dirty compounds ..."

Charlotte reached over and cracked the top of my egg. She removed its head with a teaspoon and showed me how to dip my soldier in the yolk. We sat silently, eating our breakfast and watching our mother's face, with Richard Dimbleby's solemn voice in the background. Mum looked pale, with her hand to her mouth and her eyes filling with tears. We were all very frightened. When Daddy came home in the afternoon there was a terrible fight. We heard her shouting at him outside the scullery by the washing machine where he had to take off his work clothes. When he'd had a bath and came downstairs he looked puzzled and didn't seem to hear us when we talked to him. He went to the piano and started playing—bits and pieces from many different tunes, all jumbled up.

Eleven days later when the news came of Hitler's suicide he would not believe it. "It's propaganda," he said, "designed to demoralize the German troops."

But Mum was exultant. "It's over!" she told us. "Germany has surrendered and the war's over! This is what we've been waiting for!"

It was April with tulips and daffodils blooming in our garden, and the lilac and cherry trees covered with buds, almost ready to blossom. We went out between rain showers to our Magic Circle where Charlotte led us and gave us each a turn in making up a Victory Dance. Birdie's was best. We teased Jimmy that his looked like a demented elephant, and we called him Jumbo which is what our mother called him when she was in a good mood, though Daddy sometimes called him Jiminy Cricket—who was an insect friend of Pinocchio—especially when they were doing batting and bowling practice.

On the 8th of May the war really *was* over when the Germans surrendered under the leadership of Hitler's successor, Admiral Doenitz. Everything would change for the better now, Mum said. Our neighbours put up banners and bunting outside their houses and there was clanging and whistling on our street as next door's children marched up and down banging dustbin lids like cymbals and singing *Rule Britannia!*

VICTORY IN EUROPE!—Birdie read the banners easily with Dik Dik standing beside her, proud of her youngest student. Jim had long since mastered reading and was leafing his way through Enid Blyton's *Secret Seven* books. But there were no banners at our house, not even streamers. Our mother wouldn't allow it. And we weren't allowed to march and sing, even though Dad wanted us to join in with the band next door and celebrate peace, convinced as he was that Hitler's battle for world freedom from the Mammon system of financial control would now continue in another guise, without the slaughter of brave young men.

When Uncle Jack came home we were all invited to the Woodlands to welcome him. Granny was happier than we'd ever seen her, and Grandpa shook hands with our father. It seemed as though everybody had forgotten their grievances now that we were no longer at war. But Uncle Jack turned his back on Daddy and wouldn't speak to him.

"Oh come on, Jack, let bygones be bygones," Cynthia said. "It's good to have you home safe."

"It's good to be alive, Sis," he said. "Thanks to my fellow men. We must all cover each other's backs in war."

Granny hovered close to him, her hands darting out every now and then to smooth the lapels of his double-breasted demob jacket which was pin-striped and ill-fitting with wide shoulders. He wore mismatched flannel trousers with flared bottoms and a pair of two-toned shoes like an American gangster.

"We'll have to get you properly outfitted, Jack," Granny said. "You've grown, my boy. None of your clothes are going to fit."

"What, Ma? You don't like my demob suit?" He struck a provocative pose, one hand on his hip and the other dangling a lighted cigarette.

"You look like a London spiv," Ruby said.

"Good enough for my men, good enough for me," he said.

A week later Uncle Jack came to our house with a package. Daddy was at work, completing his final week on the farm, so Cynthia invited her brother in and sat with him in the lounge.

"What d'you have there?" she asked, peering curiously.

"Go ahead. Open it," he said, handing her the package.

She tore at the paper excitedly, thinking that he'd brought her a present from Italy, or perhaps from Paris, another beret, another chance.

"It's a tie," she said, staring with a puzzled look at the khaki material. It looked drab even as she held it up to the light, which revealed some brownish stains.

"What is this, some kind of joke?"

"It's for your husband, Sis. Close as he'll get to the war. I had it made from a German uniform."

She dropped the thing in disgust. "How did you get your hands on it?"

"How d'you think? Shot the kraut before he had a chance to shoot me, then I took his jacket."

She never told Daddy about the tie. She hid it in the air-raid shelter which served as a store-room again, now that the war was over. Birdie still wouldn't go near it, though Jim and Charlotte sometimes played there. And as I grew into a solitary child, with my siblings away at boarding school, I would sometimes go down to the shelter and sit there, trying to imagine what I had missed.

Chapter Sixteen

LOST SOULS

May 8, 1945

OUR BABIES ARRIVED on VE Day, two of them, could you believe it? There were no twins on my side of the family, and none on the Wilkins side that Reg knew of, but there they were, two little babies. Cliodhna came first, racing ahead as she would continue to do throughout her life, and Desmond followed, the sleepy one, lagging behind. It was a joy for me to name my daughter for my lost sister.

There's nothing like caring for new life to bring you into the moment, and into a concern for the future at the same time. "Do you think we'll ever get off the Estates?" I asked Reg. He didn't answer right away, for he was watching me nurse the babies, one on each breast, and his gaze was so intent I thought if I'd had a third titty he'd be on it himself.

"I'm going to get us an 'ouse, Mary," he said.

I couldn't think how he'd do it, but I believed him. I had learned that my Reg was a determined man who gets what he wants, even if he was to wait a few years.

I walked through the village every day with my babies in the double pram I had on loan from Vancy's daughter who'd had her own twins who were now in school. And I found that I received the attention I'd been lacking all my life.

"Are you the mum?" the ladies would ask as they cooed over my little ones, then they'd smile at me as though I'd performed a miracle.

Well I had, hadn't I? It was the best thing in my life and my only grief was that I could not share it with my own mam, and with Cynthia and her own dear children, though they'd be changed by now. It had been two years I'd not seen them.

I wheeled Clio and Des around the Estates in the summer evenings when Clio was screaming her head off. The motion of the pram would calm her and when her sobs subsided she would stick her thumb in her mouth and gaze up at me. Ah, but sure she was the spitting image of Brendan. As the cold weather came on that autumn and through the winter I took them to Meg's caravan for a change of scenery. It was cramped in our own quarters and I was wondering how we'd fare when they started to walk. Cliodhna would be first of course; boys take their time.

I would sit at Meg's table, rocking the pram with my foot, and I would think back to when I'd lived there with no thought but to escape the Walkley Estates, and Reg as well. How foolish I'd been, not recognizing the riches I'd had in my palm all along. I missed Meg, and I pictured the homecoming we'd give her when her time was served. Bringing my little babies to her caravan seemed a way of comforting all those lost souls she had sent on their way before they'd even had a chance at life. She was paying the price, but I had to do my part too, for I had turned a blind eye and was as guilty as her.

Chapter Seventeen

WE STOPPED ASKING

THE LETTER ARRIVED on a sunny day in July. Cynthia ripped it open when she saw the French stamp with its grape-coloured Romanesque head wreathed with laurel leaves. But the writing was not Mireille's. She jumped to the back page and saw Monsieur Plasse's sloping signature. She didn't understand. She ran upstairs to her bedroom to read the letter in private, so she was sitting at her dressing table with a Berlitz pocket dictionary in her hand when she learned of Mireille's death. She went over and over the words, rifling through the pages of her dictionary until there was no longer any possibility of doubt. But still she read the same words again and again, desperate to know what had happened to her darling Mireille. It made no sense. There *must* have been a mistake.

Monsieur Plasse said that his daughter had been away from the house a great deal during the early years of the occupation and that she had refused to answer their questions, saying simply that she was at work and very much occupied. "We suspected," he wrote, "and we worried of course, but we stopped asking." On the tenth of January 1943 she had not come home and they'd learned two days later that she'd been arrested by the Gestapo. On the 24th of January they were informed that Mireille had been sent in a convoy of 230 French women —communists and resistance workers—to a camp at Auschwitz-Birkenau in Poland. She had survived there almost until the end, and then she had died, he didn't know on which day or where exactly, because she had apparently been on a death march from Auschwitz toward Wodzislaw Slaski, 35 miles away. It had been January and bitter weather as the Soviet army advanced on occupied Poland.

"I am sorry, dear Cynthia, that we have not been able to tell you anything before now, but we also have been in the dark, and only now do we receive news of our dear Mireille. They say she was very weak and thin and could not support the march. She was only one of 15,000 prisoners who died on the way. My wife and I are proud to inform you that Mireille was an important member of the Paris Resistance and that she did not break under torture before she was sent away from France. She had carried messages and helped to hide Jewish families. We are not Jewish and we are not Communists, but our family is certainly anti-fascist. I know you will honour her memory and your friendship with her. She always spoke of you with strong affection and kept a photograph of you on her escritoire."

Cynthia's first thought, when her mind began to work again, was that she could never return to Paris, because it would break her heart. For her, Mireille *was* Paris. Then shame flooded in on her, the shame of her ridiculous marriage, of her alliance with a fascist. How foolish she had been to think that her friendship with Mireille could continue even if she had survived, because Cynthia had travelled too far along this road without even knowing where she was going.

She felt as though her life was ruined, that she had abandoned her true calling when she'd left Paris. And she hated her father for the loyalty he had demanded, she hated Christopher, she hated her children —all the encumbrances—and most of all she hated her own stupidity. Was this what life was for, to realize oneself a fool? And then she saw Mireille's face, wan and thin, with her burning eyes, unafraid, and she broke down and sobbed until she had exhausted herself.

Chapter Eighteen

DINNER AT PRUNIER'S

Autumn 1945

CYNTHIA'S FIRST MEETING with Thomas St. Barbe Baker was in the hamlet of River, near Petworth in Sussex. Christopher and Baker had been scouting the countryside since Baker's release on 21st April. He'd been one of the last to be released from Peveril Camp. They had travelled in a sporty Aston Martin recently purchased by Christopher, picking up hitch-hikers along the way and talking enthusiastically about their plans. With the help of a Petworth estate agent they had located a large property and had already gathered a group of like-minded enthusiasts, many of them Peveril detainees like themselves. George Unsworth had pledged a fifty percent interest as a financial backer, while others spoke of contributions in kind, so the balance of financial responsibility would fall on Christopher's broad shoulders.

Cynthia left Vera in charge and travelled down south with her husband in the Aston Martin to meet up with Baker in Petworth. With petrol rationing still in effect Christopher had to avail himself of the black market. Fortunately he was not short of cash. There was a change in him since the war had ended, Cynthia noticed, a lightness to his step as he loaded their suitcases into the boot of the car. He stopped in the driveway and looked down at his new shoes, purchased at Kendal Milne's in Manchester. He turned and smiled at Cynthia as he took his place in the driver's seat, and she smiled back. She had tied a red silk scarf over her hair to keep it in place in the open sports car, and as they pulled out of the driveway, past the tall pampas grass, she tossed back her head to receive the promise of a gentle October sun.

Baker's face was smooth with cleanly chiselled features, his egg-like appearance broken only by a neat brown moustache. When Cynthia shook his hand she noticed that his fingers were gnarled and the knuckles enlarged, which perhaps explained the weakness of his grip. His eyes were pale and somehow lifeless, but in a vigilant, snakelike way. It was her husband's behaviour that surprised her; he was fawning like a schoolboy. She remembered this later, too late, for in the moment she was caught up in their plans for Kingdom House.

The Petworth property was extensive with a beautiful, though neglected old house set on five acres of rich agricultural land. Gabled roofs flanked a central entranceway which the estate agent claimed was Jacobean. The rose garden, so far as Cynthia could tell, needed only a good pruning to bring it back to life. They explored the interior, walking across bare boards and looking up into oak-beamed ceilings while the agent gave a running commentary which Cynthia found annoying, so she went off on her own and found the upstairs room that had immediately captivated her interest when she had seen from outside its latticed window framed by the tangled vines of a flaming red and gold Virginia creeper, just like the one that covered the south wall of her father's house.

This will be our bedroom, she thought, as she perched in the dormer window looking out onto the rose garden and an expanse of fields beyond. For her children she chose the two smaller rooms across the landing with views of an apple orchard. She furnished and decorated each room in her mind, papering the walls in floral patterns, painting the skirting boards cream to tone in with the background of the paper.

They returned to the agent's office in the village and, after conferring by telephone with Unsworth, made an offer on the property, then they drove up to London where Christopher had booked a room at the Park Lane Hotel. Baker had made his own arrangements which seemed not to include his wife because when Cynthia asked after her he was evasive. She couldn't understand how her husband could carry on such an involved and yet impersonal relationship with this man. Christopher seemed to lack curiosity about the normal concerns of everyday life. All his thoughts were abstractions. But what did it matter? You always have to put up with something, as Dorothy Blackwell was fond of saying. In some deep, hungry part of herself she loved Christopher fervently, and surely that was enough.

They were to dine at Prunier's in Piccadilly where they would meet up with Baker and Unsworth, but Cynthia was late in dressing because she had lain down for a nap upon their arrival at the Park Lane. She had wanted Christopher to lie with her and had done her utmost to persuade him, but he'd said quite simply: "I'm not tired, Darling," and had crossed into the sitting room of their suite to read the newspaper.

She had lost her confidence since their encounter in the nursery at Dinglewood. Perhaps she had responded too passionately for him. She'd sensed something afterwards, disgust almost, as though it was too intimate for him, too close and fetid. She'd watched him on the tennis court and the cricket pitch — he was in his element there — and he approached their lovemaking with a similar enjoyment, as though it was a sport, to be engaged in quickly and enthusiastically, like scoring a goal in football. Just as she thought she had him he'd be gone again, back to that distant place from which she was excluded. She had asked Nancy Brooke about Nanny Darlington, remembering what Chris had said in the nursery that day.

"Did something happen to her? Christopher said she was a rather unhappy woman."

"She lost her fiancé in the Great War, dear, and she couldn't seem to get over it, always weeping and ... well, quite unsuitable for the children. We had to send her away."

"Come on, Cynthia. They'll be waiting for us." Christopher stood by the door, hat in hand, overcoat on his arm, glancing at his watch.

"Get my coat, will you?" she called as she pressed the studs of her diamond earrings through her earlobes and quickly applied lipstick from a brand-new tube. As they rode down in the hotel lift she checked her reflection in the long mirror. "We make a handsome couple," she whispered to Christopher, squeezing his arm.

The hotel doorman hailed a taxi and they drove through the streets of London, all lit up now that the blackout was over, and filled with people bustling here and there. It seemed to Cynthia like a fairyland with everything bright and glittering after a long darkness.

Baker was waiting for them in the foyer of Prunier's and he led them to a large table where a group of strangers was seated. Cynthia was introduced first to George Unsworth, a solemn man of about fifty with a grey goatee and a thick head of dark hair. Next was an eager young fellow called Arthur Kern, of Austrian background he said, though he lived now in Kidderminster. "I will be Captain Baker's custodian at Kingdom House," he said, and he introduced his sister Judith, and another sister—rather pretty, Cynthia thought—called Marjorie. There was a Miss Alma Lincoln, apparently unrelated to anyone present, and it was she who patted the vacant seat beside her and smiled invitingly at Cynthia.

Why are we women clumped together? she wondered. She was accustomed to dinner parties where men and women were evenly distributed to ensure lively conversation. But the gathering turned out to be more like a business meeting than a dinner party. Christopher sat on the far side of the table between Baker and Unsworth, and was so involved in conversation that he hardly noticed the menu in front of him and had to be reminded to order.

Prunier's specialty was fish and Cynthia had ordered a shrimp cocktail followed by grilled salmon with new potatoes and asparagus. Rationing was still in effect for public caterers, but the more expensive London establishments seemed to find their way around it with various exemptions. Prunier's clientele was from the privileged class and favoured the best of foods such as Scottish salmon and imported caviar, and there were plenty of fresh vegetables available from the local allotments which had sprung up all over the city during the war.

"A toast to Kingdom House, headquarters of our Legion of Christian Reformers," Baker declared, raising his water glass. "With our agricultural expert"—he gave a forced laugh as he gestured with a flourish towards Christopher—"we will become a self-sustaining community. Arthur here has a strong arm and can operate the farm machinery, while our beautiful young ladies ..."—here he indicated the three

Misses sitting opposite, and perhaps included Cynthia, she wasn't sure — "can do the planting under your supervision, Christopher. And of course, the ladies will take care of the produce when the harvest comes."

Baker let out a burbling chuckle which made Cynthia wonder if there might be some sexual allusion behind his words. She felt almost naked when Baker's eyes met hers, and immediately averted her gaze. She wished Mrs. Baker was present. She would have liked to meet her. She'd heard their son was some kind of prodigy.

"As to the finances ..." Baker said, with an apologetic shrug.

"Brooke and I will take care of that," Unsworth said in a flat nasal voice.

"We must draft a statement of principles for the Legion ..." Christopher said. But just then Judith and Marjorie, with their friend Alma, addressed Cynthia in force and she was unable to follow the thread of the men's conversation, except for snippets heard in between the young women's shrill voices and explosive giggles. Cynthia's face began to ache with smiling. Why had Christopher brought her here? What was her role in it all?

"... end of the reign of Mammon ..." she heard Baker say, "... instrument used to bring the destruction foretold ..."

"My brother and I have been in France," Judith said in response to Cynthia's account of her time in Paris.

"... 'And out of his mouth goeth a sharp sword, that with it he should smite the nations,' ..." she heard Christopher quote from Revelations. She knew it by heart because he'd quoted it many times since his release. He's so convinced, she thought. And all these people. He must be right. If only I could trust him.

"I love your earrings. Are they real diamonds?" Marjorie was leaning into her with an engaging grin and a wink.

"What's the blue stone in the middle," Alma asked, reaching with her index finger to touch it.

"It's a sapphire," Cynthia said, silently judging the girl for her ignorance. They're common girls, she thought, just plain common girls. How can I be expected to live with such people?

"Will Sir Oswald be speaking again?" she asked, her voice bold and forthright like Mosley himself as she remembered him from their meeting at Southport's Floral Hall. She had addressed the whole group, projecting her voice across the table at the men. Christopher looked puzzled, and the others simply stared at her. It was the name of Mosley that had captured their attention, not Cynthia's voice.

"We have our own enterprise now, Cynthia," Christopher said kindly. "British Union is finished."

"Oh. I'm sorry, I didn't know." Every eye was on her. She felt utterly foolish. She had hoped to capture their attention and respect, but their faces looked somehow pitying. Of *course* they were finished with Mosley! How could she have been so stupid? It was all about Hitler now, but how could she talk about *him*? She blushed and busied herself, dabbing at her mouth with a napkin. "Oh dear," she said when she saw that she had stained it with her new red lipstick, and she folded her napkin to hide the stain, but Alma, seated on her right, was watching intently with round blue-shadowed eyes.

Cynthia would happily have drowned rather than continue sitting at that table. She excused herself and hurried with short, heel-clicking steps to the Ladies' Room. It was a luxurious affair with wall to wall mirrors but, instead of admiring herself as she would normally have done, she attacked herself mercilessly in the empty echoing room.

"Why did you have to open your mouth? You don't know the first thing about his life."

She burst into tears and wept, wrapping her arms across her chest, rocking back and forth. Afterwards she splashed her face with cold water and applied fresh lipstick. Now she wished she had not fled— how could she bear the embarrassment of returning to that table? They would all stare at her, but she would keep her eyes down and act quite normally with a smile on her face. She need not have worried for no-one noticed her return, not even the young ladies who were also weeping, but with mirth as they shared some joke or other.

Cynthia huddled into her corner in the taxi, trying to contain her rage. Christopher seemed not to have noticed anything amiss as he chattered on, his spirits buoyed by the evening. She held on until the door of their hotel suite closed behind them and then she let fly.

"I've never been so humiliated in all my life!" she shouted, throwing her gloves down on the bed with an angry snap. "Why didn't you stand up for me?"

"What are you talking about?" Christopher stood in the hallway, his coat halfway off, dangling from one arm.

"You sit me down at a tableful of strangers, you push me off in a corner with those common girls, you ignore me all evening and then, when I try to enter into the conversation, you humiliate me with your dismissive remarks!"

"I don't understand, Cynthia, I ..."

"We have our own enterprise now ... British Union is finished ..." she said, aping him.

"I was only trying to explain ..."

"I won't stand for it, Christopher! I don't want any more to do with your damned Legion of Reformers. I want to go home to my children."

She flounced across the room to the wardrobe and started pulling clothes off hangers, throwing them into her open suitcase. "And I noticed that you paid the bill for everyone—all those hangers on!"

Christopher threw down his coat and walked across the room. He took her by the shoulders and tried to hold her, but she shrugged him off violently and spun around, her eyes afire with fury. Then quite suddenly she slapped his face, her nails raking a fine trail of red lines across his cheek as he flinched sideways, his eyes flickering and his hands clenched at his sides. There was a moment of shocked silence, then Cynthia burst into tears for the second time that night, her face held in her hands as she said in a thick voice: "You shouldn't have brought me here. I don't care about your damned politics. I just want to go home to my family. Let me lead my own life and you do what you want. I don't care!"

Christopher touched his cheek gingerly and looked at his fingers for traces of blood, but there were none. He put his arm hesitantly on Cynthia's shoulder and drew her to him, her body pliant now with the release of her tears.

"I need you on my side, Cynthia," he said.

"But they're common people," she said, sulky and childish now.

"They're my friends, loyal people who befriended me in my time of need."

Cynthia clicked her tongue dismissively. "What about *our* friends? We never see them anymore. The Cartwrights, the Andertons, the Cheshire Set ..."

"You know they disapprove of me."

"But if only you'd try, Chris. All this trouble could be forgotten if you'd only ..."

"What? Give up my principles? All my plans for a new life? Why won't you trust me?"

"I want to. You know I do. I came to London with you in good faith to meet these people, but they're not like us, they're not our sort of people."

"Look, Darling, you're upset. Can we call a truce and get some sleep?"

She looked at him, her deep-set eyes softening. He watched her mouth, the curve of her lips, the mystery of her.

"We'll pack up and go home tomorrow," he said. He reached out and looped a stray curl behind her ear, caressing her lobe, running a finger gently down her jawline. She tilted her head to one side with a quizzical expression, as though she was still battling something she didn't understand. But when he kissed her she fell back onto the bed and allowed herself to be undressed.

Chapter Nineteen

DEEP POCKETS

B UT ON THE way home she started another argument, and it became so heated that Christopher had to pull over onto the grass verge. Cynthia immediately jumped out of the car and slammed the door.

"Please, Cynthia," he called out. "I've told you again and again, close the door gently."

But she was already strutting down the road in her high heels, the tails of her red scarf flapping in the wind. He sat a while, the motor idling, then drove slowly until he caught up and crept alongside, begging her to get in. She opened the door of the still moving car and jumped in, as though she didn't care if she hurt herself or laddered her nylon stockings. She was still furious, but she wanted to get home. She'd had a sudden feeling that something was very wrong there.

They found the house in turmoil with blood trailing from the dining room, dripped across the hall carpet and up the stairs. Cynthia started shouting for Vera and ran to the kitchen where she found her and Birdie at the scullery sink which was piled high with dirty dishes, and the whole kitchen stinking of burnt porridge.

"Birdie had a temper tantrum at breakfast and threw 'er dish across the room and broke the window, didn't ya, ya naughty monkey?" Vera said, wagging a finger at the child.

"I don't like the burnt bits," Birdie said and ran into Christopher's arms as he entered the kitchen.

"Charlotte cut 'erself trying to pick up the glass before Katie could get 'urt," Vera said in a rush. "But then the little one fell and cut 'er leg anyway. I think she might need a stitch or two."

"Where is she?" Cynthia demanded.

"Upstairs in the bathroom with Charlotte."

Still in her coat Cynthia ran upstairs, so Vera turned on Christopher. "I would have cleaned up the blood right away. But not 'alf an hour ago there were two reporters at the door. I told them you wouldn't be 'ome for several days, and I sent them away."

And that is what saved her.

When Cynthia returned from Dr. Pearson's clinic with Katie in her arms, her leg stitched and bandaged, Christopher told her what had happened in their absence and her fury subsided. She could not have borne to come home to reporters camped out on her doorstep again. If only they would all leave her and Christopher alone she might be able to follow him and believe in him. She could read their thoughts —her mother, the Cartwrights, the reporters, even the help—their low opinion of him. If nobody took him seriously how could she be expected to? But she must, or else how was he ever going to get better?

The year drew to a dismal close with people still reeling from the destruction wrought by the bombing. Despite the initial triumph of winning the war, Britons everywhere had to deal with flooded coal mines, lack of housing and transportation, and shortages of every kind of necessity. The shock of the atomic bombs unleashed on Japan in August had seemed vague by comparison; Japan was far away, beyond the imagination of most.

As the Christmas holidays approached the Brookes received very few invitations to the usual house parties and dinners, and the ones that did come Cynthia often turned down at the last minute.

"I don't feel like going, Chris," she said as they stood in the hallway, dressed and ready to leave for Eric and Adèle's party. "Come on, let's take off our coats and stay home."

"But you said you wanted to mix with the old crowd, Cynthia."

She took the hat from his hand and threw it across the hall, laughing at her luck as it landed on the banister post.

"I don't like leaving the children alone with Vera," she whispered, helping him out of his coat and hanging it on the corner rack. "Look what happened while we were away in London. Mary Byrne was a much better housekeeper."

"Couldn't we get her back? She might still be living in the area. We could place ..."

"No! What's done is done. I wouldn't want to let Vera down now."

But they did go to the Woodlands on Christmas Eve. Cynthia couldn't slip out of that one so easily. It was a big celebration, the first peacetime Christmas in six years and all her family assembled, even Ruby with her American GI to whom she was now officially engaged. They would marry in the New Year and sail to America on their honeymoon.

Mrs. Fern opened the door to them and greeted Cynthia, but when Christopher wished her a merry Christmas she turned away and disappeared into the cloakroom with the children to remove their coats and outdoor shoes. Just then brother Richard came striding through the hallway.

"Oh, hello Cyn." He kissed her cheek. "Where are the brats?"

When Christopher offered his hand, Richard did a quick about-turn.

"Must go. On a mission for Pa, down to the wine cellar."

Cynthia took Christopher's arm and squeezed it. "Never mind," she said. "He's only a boy." It was herself she was trying to reassure for she was cut to the quick, but Christopher seemed untouchable, growing taller and taller, his head disappearing into the clouds. Then he surprised her.

"Are you going to ignore me too, Ruby?" he asked as she crossed the hall with a handsome man on her arm.

"Of course not, Chris," Ruby said and embraced him warmly. Still holding onto his hands she looked up at him with that bold and insistent gaze of hers, more reassuring than a smile. "I want you to meet Austin," she said decisively. "Chris is my favourite brother-in-law, Ozzie. He plays the piano like a dream."

"Your *only* brother-in-law," Cynthia corrected.

"Oh, he'd be my favourite no matter how many I had," Ruby said, laughing.

Austin, who was not only handsome but equalled Christopher in height, gave him a firm handshake. "Pleased to meet you, Christopher," he said with a deep twang. "I've heard plenty about you, and let me tell ya, Bud, you'd be welcome in the States. We're a nation full o' mavericks."

Christopher's bemused smile broadened as the couple continued.

"C'mon Ozzie, let's get Chris to play some jitterbug for us."

"Yeah babe! Now you're talkin'," Austin said, taking her in his arms and striking a swing pose. "Got a piano?"

"In the drawing room," Ruby said, moving her body in rhythm with him. "We'll roll up the carpet."

"Sure thing. Hey Chris, ya know that number, *Minnie's in the Money?*"

Christopher was laughing now, enjoying their banter. "Sing it and I'll improvise," he said, following them eagerly to the drawing room.

As they moved into that new post-war year of 1946, and the long slow recovery of the country, Cynthia tried to weave a cocoon around their little family, to make a secure place where they might recover from the consequences of the war, but it was too tight, and it began to suffocate them. The rows became more frequent and more obscure. Cynthia picked on inconsequential things—the cufflinks Christopher wore, his choice of tie, the way he chewed his food. He didn't retaliate, but simply withdrew from her, further and further.

He was away from home a good deal now, travelling with Thom Baker. The purchase of the Petworth property had been completed and its name—Kingdom House—proudly engraved on a brass plaque by the front gate. Christopher had transferred a sum of money into a bank account in the name of the Legion of Christian Reformers, for the purchase of furniture and fittings, for a lawnmower, a tractor, a large greenhouse to start seedlings for the kitchen garden. The signatories of the bank account were himself and Baker. Their plans were moving apace. He had deep pockets and a worthy cause.

Even though James Brooke had banished his son from the business, old Mr. Brooke, who had founded Brooke's Hats, had provided for his grandson in his will, so Cynthia had no cause for financial concern, though she sometimes wondered if a return to the family business might have helped Christopher more than this new venture with Kingdom House. On the other hand, as Austin had recognized, he was a maverick. Perhaps she had, without knowing it, chosen a brilliant and original kind of husband. Was it luck, choosing a man? Was it instinct or intelligence? She stood at her bedroom window holding in her hands the black beret that Mireille had given her, remembering Mireille's hands on it, arranging it for her, standing back to admire her.

"Now you look like a proper French girl," she'd said and she'd laughed, her shoulders shaking slightly.

How elegant and French Cynthia had felt, but she had polluted Mireille's gift with that badge. She'd paid no attention to the significance of the letters—BUF—it had been the badge she'd wanted, to sew on her beret, and those three letters had almost ruined her life. But Christopher had put all that behind him, thank goodness. Surely now he might gather a following with his new venture, something to make him feel important and bring him back to himself. All her thoughts were speculative. Without the guidance of someone impartial to talk to she didn't really know what to think.

When Christopher was home he sat in his study making sketches for the kitchen garden at Petworth. He seemed oblivious to the deteriorating domestic situation at Meadowside, and continued a cheerful though impersonal banter with his children. He began to write letters again, to clerics and politicians. Clement Atlee had replaced Churchill as Prime Minister in the postwar election of July 1945. Christopher wrote long letters to him, signing off: "In the love of God and of England," to which he received formal notices of acknowledgement:

Mr. Atlee has asked me to thank you for your letter of the 8th inst. You will understand that owing to the pressure of work the Prime Minister cannot reply personally ...

Mealtimes were fraught and usually ended in strained silence as their cutlery scraped across the Royal Doulton plates.

"Come on, Birdie, eat up," Cynthia said.

"I don't want it," the child would say, squirming in her chair, blinking obsessively.

"Stop your nonsense. And don't roll your eyes at me," Cynthia said, until all the children became constrained in her presence, and began to move away from her as Christopher had. Even the dog cowered when she came into the room. Jimmy's asthma attacks became more frequent so that he had to stay in bed and have Miss Dixon up to his room to instruct him.

She blamed Christopher, but had to admit secretly that she was herself to blame. She hated what the marriage had brought out in her and she didn't understand it, because she remembered herself as a girl in France, the joy and mirth that had been in her then. She hated Churchill for interning her husband, she hated what the war had done to them all, and she couldn't forgive her brother Jack for his grisly gift that remained hidden in the air-raid shelter. She felt trapped with no way out and it made her vicious. She couldn't live with herself the way that she was mistreating her children.

Then, in the spring of 1946, she hatched a plan, and sought her father's help to execute it.

"Christopher?" she called as she came in from the garden with the first daffodils, drops of spring rain still clinging to their trumpets and petals. "I've been talking to Father."

He looked up, a fountain pen poised in his right hand, the blue ink still wet on a page covered with his sloped handwriting.

"We think it might be a good idea to send the children away to school."

"Away? But we have Miss Dixon."

"That's not the point, Christopher. Haven't you noticed the sores on Birdie's mouth? Every time there are words between us the child starts rolling her eyes and ..."

"Why should we send our little girl away?"

"It would be for her own good. And Charlotte would be with her. I'm thinking of Westonbirt. Jenny Anderton's daughter goes there. It's a very good school, down south in Buckinghamshire."

"If you want them out of the house, Cynthia, there's Cheadle Hulme School. I could drive them."

"But you're hardly here, Chris. All these promises and then you're gone for days on end. Besides, we've both had the advantage of a public school education, and you know what a difference it makes—rubbing shoulders with the right sort of people."

"Birdie's too young. She's only seven."

"Charlotte will look after her. Now that she's eleven she can go into the college, and they'll take Birdie in the junior school. I've looked into it."

"Evidently. Why didn't you consult me?"

"Because you've always got your head in those papers. And we can't seem to exchange two words without arguing."

"What about Jimmy?"

"They can take him at Lawrence House prep school in St. Annes."

"I'd always thought he would go to my old school."

"Well, perhaps we'll send him to Malvern later, but for now Lawrence House is closer. It'll be better for all of them, Darling. They can start in September."

"It seems the decision is made." Christopher shrugged and resumed his writing.

"Shall we drive down to Westonbirt and take a look?" Cynthia asked. "The Andertons say it's beautiful. There's an arboretum full of rhododendrons. They'll be blooming soon. And we could drive on to Petworth, make a tour of it. We are going to move, aren't we? I've been thinking about decorations for the bedrooms. I'll pick up some wallpaper samples and paint chips ..."

"Cynthia, the rooms are already decorated. The young ladies have been hard at work."

"What young ladies?"

"Kern's sisters, Judith and Marjorie, and their friend Alma."

"Oh, you're on first name terms, are you?"

"Of course. We're a community."

"And what else are you up to with 'the young ladies?'"

"Cynthia, I've never been unfaithful to you."

"And I hope you never will." She twisted her wedding ring round and around on her finger. "I couldn't bear that, Chris. I'd never be able to forgive you."

There is an awkward silence, broken by Cynthia's anxious words. "When will we be moving in? You have to give me some warning, there's so much to ..."

His hand went up, silencing her. "Please be patient, Cynthia. We can't hurry this. I want everything to be in place for you; for you and the children to be properly provided for. You must trust me instead of taking everything into your own hands."

Chapter Twenty

THE PENNY DROPPED

August 1946

WE WERE SITTING ON our caravan steps after supper enjoying the last rays of sun when I broached the subject.

"I've been thinking about going back to work."

"What about Clio and Des?" Reg asked.

"I can start weaning them. They're already fourteen months old. I'll do it gradually and get them down to one feeding at night."

"But who'll look after them?"

"Vancy says she'll do it for five bob a week. She's already got her grandchildren to care for, so it won't be much extra."

"Will Mrs. Plumley take you back?"

"No, she's got another girl."

I went inside to refill the teapot and Reg followed me in and sat at the table while I attended to the kettle.

"I was thinking of applying at A.V. Roe They're assembling those prefab homes now, and they pay a good wage."

I spoke softly so as not to wake Clio. Des was a sound sleeper and never troubled us in the night, but once Clio woke there was no getting her down again without a stroll around the Estates.

"No 'arm in trying," Reg said, fumbling in his pocket for tobacco. I could tell he was not enthusiastic about my idea. He walked over to the door and opened it half way, leaning against the doorjamb as he lit up. I had trained him not to smoke inside our caravan; it was too small, and the twins breathing in all that smoke.

"Is something wrong, Mister?"

That was my pet name for him, and sometimes he teased me, calling me Mrs. Wilkins. We were still more like children playing house than a serious married couple.

"Nah."

He wouldn't look at me, just stood there, blowing smoke out the door into the darkening sky. I pulled up my cardigan collar and huddled into it for there was a wind blowing up like it does before rain.

"I want to do my bit, you see, if we're ever to get ourselves a house. Perhaps we'll have one of those fancy prefabs, and I'll be the one helping to assemble it," I said, laughing.

"And aren't I good enough to provide for my family?"

"What d'you mean? We're a team. We both have to work."

"You're supposed to look after our children, not pay someone else to do it."

"Five shillings a week is nothing, Reg. It's our chance to get ahead."

"That's not the point, love," he said, pitching his cigarette butt out into the grass. The rain was beginning to fall now and I shivered.

"Close that door."

"Alright, alright. You'll be wanting to wear my trousers next."

"Oh, go on with you. Where I come from we all pitch in."

"Well it's different 'ere. We're not on a farm, and we're not in Ireland. In this country the man provides for 'is family, and the wife stops at 'ome with the children and keeps the 'ouse in order."

"But first there has to be a house to keep in order."

I should have kept my mouth shut, for it was going nowhere and I could see Reg was getting riled. It took a lot to get that man going, but when he did, watch out!

"I don't feel right about it," he said, pacing up and down in our tiny caravan.

"*Shh,* you'll wake the babies."

"The war's over," he said in an exaggerated whisper, standing with his hands on the table, leaning across, his face in mine. "Everything's supposed to be back to normal, Mary."

That's when the penny dropped. It was his being unfit for service that was at the bottom of this, and he'd never let on, always cheerful and cocky, no hint of the shame he felt at not being a proper man and going to war.

"It's alright, Reg, I'll not cross you on this one," I said, and I let it drop for the moment. I had a plan to boost his pride a little before I tried again, and if he still resisted I would argue for my right. But until he got over his false shame I would be wasting my breath and causing discord between us. He was no different from the Master really, except that he hadn't been starved and driven off his head.

A FOSTER HOME IN STOCKPORT

The problems of victory are more agreeable than those of defeat,
but they are no less difficult.
—WINSTON CHURCHILL

October 1946

"HE SAID WHEN the war ended we'd get married," Vera said, sobbing, "and he'd take me and Sandra to America."

"Can't you write to him?" Cynthia said.

"I don't know where he is." Vera took the lace-edged handkerchief Cynthia offered, covering it with mascara as she dabbed at her eyes. "I only had a couple of letters from the Front, then they stopped. He could be dead for all I know, just like Sandra's dad." She burst into renewed sobs.

Vera had confided in Cynthia about Derek, her childhood sweetheart, who had seduced her before he went off to war, and had been killed almost immediately at Dunkirk, leaving her pregnant. When the Americans had entered the war she'd met any number of GIs on leave in England, but the one who'd fallen for her was Marvin. He was from Texas with a lovely twangy accent, she'd said, and he had proposed to her and promised faithfully to make a home for her and Sandra when the war was over.

"Have you seen Sandra?"

"Last month, on my day off. She's in a foster home in Stockport."

"How about bringing her here, to my house?"

Vera looked up in astonishment. "You mean …?"

"With the children away at school … it's awfully quiet, don't you think?"

"But what would Mr. Brooke say?"

"He might not even notice. He's down in Petworth more than he's here. But I'll ask him."

"Would you? Ooh, if I could get my little girl back, you have no idea what a difference it would make."

"It would be good for Katie to have someone to play with. She misses Birdie. I saw her standing by the fence yesterday talking to the little girl next door, then the child's mother came and whisked her away. 'I've told you before, *not* to play with those children,' she said."

Cynthia's tone was bitter. She had no secrets from this house-keeper because Vera's shame was equal to her own—a child out of wed-lock—what could be worse? It was a blessing for her that Vera's GI hadn't come.

Even though Vera was slovenly and slapdash Cynthia enjoyed her company. She could be herself with Vera because the girl accepted everything she said without question. Let Christopher run off to Petworth and play at being a farmer, I'm in charge in this house, she thought. The irony of his more frequent absence since the children had been packed off to boarding school had not yet struck her because she always half-expected his return. It was an old habit developed during his years of internment—listening for the telephone, ready for the click of the front door, or their bedroom door opening, surprising her in the night.

They drove to Stockport, Katie in the backseat complaining of car sickness, and Vera up front, nervous and excited in equal measure. It was a wet, end of October day, with Bonfire Night approaching and children on the street wheeling their home-made Guy Fawkes effigies on makeshift wagons, shouting: "Penny for the Guy!"

"They look like war victims," Vera said, "with their floppy limbs lolling about, and those ugly faces. Oh well, they'll soon burn."

The streets had been devastated by the bombing. Cynthia was glad at least of her own house, undamaged apart from the clipped chimney.

She heard on the BBC news every day about the housing crisis. Men had come home from the war to find piles of rubble where their houses used to be, and their wives and children camping out with more fortunate family members, sometimes only a few streets over.

That summer people had been setting up home in disused service camps up and down the country, living in appalling conditions, without running water or toilets, just to have a jerry-built roof over their heads. Concrete prefab houses were in production now — Cynthia had heard them rumbling on great big lorries down Woodford Road towards the Didsbury Estates where they were to be set up in dismal rows like caravans.

Many people were simply squatting on vacant properties, which was one reason Christopher's group had so quickly taken up residence at Kingdom House, and of course, he'd had to go down to Petworth to organize them — moving on to the next thing, never looking back, never reflecting. He's like a blank sheet despite all the useless letters he writes, Cynthia thought, her hands clenched on the steering wheel.

He and Arthur Kern had hired some local boys to help with their agricultural project. The girls had proved unwilling to work on the land, and Baker was not much in evidence at Kingdom House as yet, due to family responsibilities, he said, and neither was Unsworth whose contribution was in any case largely financial, so the burden fell on Christopher and Kern to establish an infrastructure for Kingdom House which was to be an international centre, drawing people from all over the globe.

First they must grow the food to feed the faithful, Christopher had said. Acres of land had been churned up by the tractor, and massive amounts of seed sown, but it had been an unusually dry summer and because they'd not had time to install an irrigation system much of the seed failed to germinate. When harvest time came the results were disappointing to say the least, but they expected more success in the next season. As Christopher explained all this to Cynthia she had said nothing, but she'd thought, you fool, I could have told you, why don't you stick to what you know? You're a hatter, not a farmer.

"Here we are! Yew Street! Turn right," Vera said excitedly. "That's it, 'alf way up on the left, there it is, the one with the green door."

She began to primp in front of a tiny mirror she'd pulled out of her handbag, applying fresh lipstick and tugging at her curls.

"I knew it was somewhere nearby. Off the Didsbury Road, didn't I say so? Never mind that wrong turn, I got confused you see, I'm used to the bus. Never 'ad a car of me own. Katie, you're going to meet my Sandra now. I phoned ahead so Mrs. Jenkins will be expecting us."

Sandra was ready, sitting in her coat on the parlour sofa, with a small carryall at her feet, and a ragged teddy clutched to her chest. Cynthia and Katie waited in the hall while Vera took Sandra in her arms and hugged her.

"Come on, lovie, you're going to live with Mummy now."

Mrs. Jenkins sniffed and wiped her hands on her apron. "She's 'ad her breakfast. Not much of an eater, are you Sandra?" The child looked up at her foster mother with a pathetic smile. "Threw her toast on my clean floor, didn't you, my little monkey?"

Sandra began to cry soundlessly, her pinched white face crumpling, her hands clenched and shaking. Vera pulled the child to her bosom, but she wriggled free and clung to Mrs. Jenkins.

"There, there," the foster mother said. "You're better off with your own mother, Sandra. And look, who's this then?" She pointed at Katie, almost five years old, standing in the doorway staring at Sandra. "'Appen she's a playmate for you, Sandra."

They put the children in the back seat together for the journey home and Katie immediately reached out to touch Sandra's hair, which was white blond with tight curls clinging close to her head. Katie pulled on a curl which extended then catapulted back onto Sandra's head, and she began to cry so hard that Cynthia had to pull over while Vera got out and took Sandra into the front, on her knee.

The children shared the nursery, but Sandra cried incessantly, particularly at bedtime. "I want Jenkie," she would wail until Vera slapped her and said: "I don't want to hear any more about that. You're with me now. I'm your Mummy."

When Christopher was home he barely noticed Sandra, as Cynthia had predicted. He was still making plans to move the family down to Petworth, but when he and Cynthia discussed it their conversation was devoid of real intent. They found themselves paying lip service to their dream of a new future.

There was a feeling of disappointment all over Britain like a steady drizzle dampening people's spirits. During the war, terrible though it had been, the expectation of victory had buoyed them, and there had been a feeling of exhilaration after each air-raid, to have survived yet another brush with death. People had begun to feel almost immortal. But when victory came, after the celebrations, the homecomings, and the tremendous relief, there was a let-down; things did not return to normal as they had expected.

Nothing was to be the same ever again. There were shortages of everything from petrol to clothing. Staples such as sugar, tea, butter, cheese, milk and cooking fat continued to be rationed after the war, and each person received only one egg a fortnight on their ration card. But the shocker came when bread, which had been available throughout the war, was rationed for the first time during that long dry summer of 1946. There was a general outcry but by the end of the year people had become accustomed to standing in queues for hours just for a loaf.

Cynthia had thought Vera was lying when she came back so dreadfully late from her shopping trips, claiming to have been on her feet all day. She's probably sneaking off with one of her men, she thought, drinking in a pub, leaving me in charge of her child. But when she went out shopping herself, to her mother's grocer in Poynton Village, dragging Katie along with her, cranky as the child so often was nowadays, they were gone three hours and came home with a packet of biscuits, four shrivelled apples, and a tin of corned beef.

"I told you so, but you wouldn't believe me, would you?" Vera said. "Like I say, you wait there for hours, moving at a snail's pace, and often as not there's nothing left by the time you get to the top of the queue."

Help was supposed to be coming from America, but it would be another year and a half before the US Secretary of State, George Marshall, came up with a plan for the reconstruction of Europe and then it was the vanquished who were to be occupied and aided, not the victors.

Chapter Twenty-Two

KNICK-KNACK PADDY-WHACK

M RS. FERN LET us in. Her left hand was dusted with flour and there was a smudge of it on her chin.

"Excuse me, Mrs. Brooke, but I'm in the middle of pastry-making," she said, wiping her forehead with the back of her wrist.

Mum led me by the hand into the drawing room where Granny Blackwell sat in the bay window working on a jigsaw puzzle. It was a garden scene with a tangle of flowers snaking up either side of a paved pathway.

"Why didn't you leave the child with your housekeeper?" Granny asked, turning to us with a piece of the puzzle in her hand.

"Vera needs some time alone with her little girl. Sandra's living with us now. We took her out of foster care."

"You're a beggar for punishment."

"Vera wasn't so lucky with her GI as Ruby."

"Speaking of Ruby ... this came in the morning post."

Granny held up a thin blue envelope with Auntie Ruby's bold writing in blue ink across the face of it. The envelope had been slit open with Grandpa's paper knife so as not to lose any of the words with a tear.

"Austin has found them a bungalow in Los Angeles. We're sending money for Ruby to arrange the furniture and fittings and they'll move in just in time for the birth. She's going to need help, Cynthia. Will you go?"

"Mother! That's impossible."

"Just for a month or two, dear, to help her with the baby."

"I have my own family to look after."

"But with the children away at school, and Vera living in ... In any case you'd be back in time for the Easter holidays. Your father has agreed to pay for the voyage to New York, and you can fly to Los Angeles from there."

"It's absolutely out of the question. I have a husband and household to take care of."

"He's more or less moved out, hasn't he?"

"No, he has not!" she said indignantly. "He's away on business, that's all."

"Get that child away from the fireplace." A bunch of firelighter spills tumbled from my hands onto the hearth as Mum grabbed me. "*Now* look what she's done," Granny said.

"Why don't *you* go?"

"I can't leave your father, not after his heart attack."

"That was two years ago."

"Don't disappoint me, Cynthia."

"Sit there and don't you dare move," Mum said, plunking me down on the sofa.

"Bring her over here. She can help me with the puzzle."

Granny piled some cushions on a chair and lifted me up facing the window where sunlight streamed into my eyes.

"You can't expect me to drop everything and run off to America just because Ruby's having a baby."

"I should have thought you'd welcome the opportunity to get away."

"What d'you mean?"

"From his religious mania. The man is clearly off his head, Cynthia, and if you don't ..."

"How dare you speak about my husband like that!"

"I am your mother, and I can speak to you as I wish," Granny said sharply.

"And I'm a mother too. What about *my* children? I'm not going to abandon them just because ..."

My arm swung out and—*swoosh*—all the pieces of the puzzle went flying across the room, landing with plops like rain on the parquet floor, then my chair began to rock violently and tipped backwards taking me with it. The last thing I saw was Mum running forward with her arms outstretched as my head hit the floor with a crack, then everything went dark, even the sun.

When Cynthia arrived home she parked her car in the driveway and carried me inside.

"Vera?"

The house was silent. She carried me into the sitting room and laid me on the sofa. I had woken in the car but still felt drowsy. Although my head was not cut, Mum was afraid of a concussion and had stopped at Archer Pearson's surgery, but he'd been out on a call.

"Stay awake, Katie, stay awake. Sing for Mummy. 'Knick-knack Paddy-whack, give a dog a bone, this old man came rolling home...'"

She ran out to the hall and called Vera again. There was a thin wailing from upstairs and she took the stairs two at a time and found Sandra standing in the corridor, the old teddy clutched to her chest.

"Where's Mummy?" Cynthia asked, stooping down to grip the child's shoulders. "Where is she?"

Sandra whimpered and snivelled. Her nose and mouth were encrusted with dried snot.

"Vera! Where are you?"

Cynthia hurried to the end of the corridor and found Vera's bedroom door slightly ajar. She pushed it open and saw Vera lying on the bed, a bottle of gin almost empty on the bedside table, and a pool of vomit on her pillow. She went to the corner washstand and soaked a hand towel in cold water. There was no response when she bathed Vera's face with the towel, nothing but the continued whimpering of Sandra who was now standing in the doorway watching, her eyes huge and watery.

"Go downstairs and find Katie," Cynthia said. "Go on Sandra! She's in the sitting room. Talk to her. Keep her awake."

Just then Vera stirred. When she saw Cynthia she moaned and

struggled to sit up. Cynthia thought she might vomit again so she reached under the bed for the chamber pot, but it was full of bloody urine. Vera tried to speak in a slurred drawl, making no sense.

"For goodness sake, Vera, pull yourself together." Cynthia removed the soiled pillow, beginning to feel queasy herself, then she propped Vera up with another pillow, and a grubby chenille dressing gown rolled up to support her neck.

"Sorry, Cynthia," she said, "Sorry, sorry ..."

"Oh, be quiet," Cynthia said impatiently as she went again to the washstand and filled the tooth mug with cold water.

"Didn't used to drink ... Derek was killed ... 's when it started. Just a nip at night. Can't sleep without it."

"Here, drink this. You're going to have one hell of a headache in the morning. That bottle of gin was almost full."

"I'll pay for it."

"You'll do nothing of the sort. But you'll have to behave better than this, Vera."

"'S the nightmares, Cynthia, terrible nightmares. Derek was me one and only." She sobbed. "Don't throw us out. Pleease don't ..."

"I'm not going to send you away. There's Sandra to think of."

A sly smile slid over Vera's face. Cynthia was a mother herself, wasn't she? She'd never turn them out.

"Now get up and wash your face. Sandra's frightened out of her wits. And Katie's had a bad fall. I'm going downstairs to see to her."

Chapter Twenty-Three

HOW WILL YOU KNOW?

A S MY MOTHER grew older I travelled with her sometimes to Paris. On one occasion as we sat in the Jardin des Tuileries where she had conducted her English classes as a girl, I asked her about my father. There was a long silence as I watched the emotions working her face, and I apologized, because I felt that in asking I had caused her an insupportable pain.

"How will you know if I don't tell you?" she replied vehemently, and she began to speak through clenched teeth, the muscles in her jaws flexing between words. Afterwards, in my hotel room, I wrote it all down, hurrying to record the information before it escaped me. What she had said was shocking to me, and I knew that I would banish it from my mind and be surprised later by finding it in my notebook like a dream recorded and forgotten. But she never told me enough to satisfy my curiosity.

Auntie Alice, on the other hand, was quite willing to talk about my father. "He was such a dear brother," she said. "Never a cruel word. And he always invited me along on his outings even though I was four years younger and a girl. He wouldn't mind now, dear, so I'll show you the letter he sent me towards the end, after it all went wrong."

She got down on her hands and knees, searching in a cupboard amidst a jumble of books and papers, her comfortable backside broadly displayed. She came up with the letter and a few photos, and continued her rummaging while I read:

My dear Alice. It was kind of you to send me the £6 cheque. Thank you so much. I shall be able to keep myself looking all right for necessary clothes ...

He referred her to a book he'd written—*Aryan Testament*—and he quoted Hitler and offered spiritual advice if she should want it. He signed off: "Your loving brother, Chris," and finished with a small swastika penned in heavy blue ink with an explanation of the symbol on the back of the page.

"Ah, here's one of his books," Alice said, leaning back on her heels. "You know that he published several little books and newsletters after the war? Recording his travels and so on. Perhaps you'd like to have this one?"

And so I acquired a slim volume published by The Kingdom Press, a memoir entitled *The Bishop said Amen*, and years later found myself collaborating with my dead father, using his own words to describe the time we had shared in Walton Gaol.

As Auntie Alice went to close the cupboard something fell out. "Well, look at that," she exclaimed. "Chris always loved the panto." It was a Cinderella program from the Variety Theatre in Southport. I flipped through the pages which showed blurry photos of the cast. On the back was an inscription—*In memory of happy times at Mrs. Beasley's, with affection, your favourite Principal Boy, January 1948.*

"Here's another," Auntie said, puffing with the effort of bending and straightening. "I really must get all these old papers sorted out and into a proper chest of drawers. Look, *Bless the Bride!*—a big hit in its day. I believe he took Cynthia to see it. There was a song, very popular at the time, he was always humming it—'This is my lovely day.'" She sang in a clear voice, like a girl.

He grew in importance for us children with the length of his absence, achieving over time a kind of immortality. Some see him as a figure of fun, a man to be ridiculed or pitied—even despised for his mistaken direction. But I am not so sure. In writing about him I seek to understand who he was and what befell him in that strange time and in its aftermath. He was to betray us over and over, though unwittingly.

Chapter Twenty-Four

SOMEWHERE BETWEEN A SALUTE AND A CARESS

Christmas 1946

"**L**ISTEN TO THIS, Cynthia. Sounds like your 'usband's group."
Vera leaned over the kitchen table in her flowered apron, her
face close to the newspaper, eyes narrowed because she needed glasses. She'd read in the *News of the World* about a national health
service that would provide free eye-glasses, but it had yet to pass
through parliament.

"Pastor's Shattering Attack On Hitler Cult: The Sunday afternoon
peace of River village was shattered today when Pastor Victor Walker,
of the Four Square Gospel Church, delivered an ear-splitting challenge
to the disciples of the Legion of Christian Reformers at Kingdom House,
a 17th century mansion in the hamlet of River, consisting of 8 cottages
and a public house, four miles from ..."

"Give me that!" She snatched the paper. "I won't have this gutter
press in my house."

"Isn't that where you went on holiday with him?"

"None of your business, Vera. We have work to do. The children are
home, remember? You get the breakfast ready while I lay the table."

She hurried down the corridor and into the dining room where she
stood behind the closed door, her breath shallow, hands shaking. She
wanted to read the article to see if there was any mention of Christopher,
but she was afraid, then the door was flung open suddenly, pushing
her against the wall.

"Sorry, Mummy, I didn't see you there."

It was Charlotte, with Birdie close behind, glued to her sister since their first term together at boarding school.

"When's Daddy coming home?" Birdie asked.

"Soon, Darling. He's in London on business," she said, hiding the newspaper behind her back. Birdie stared with her big blue eyes but said nothing. She had become a quiet child since leaving home, with a new air of caution about her. "Where's your brother?"

Charlotte shrugged and Birdie looked out of the window at the garden which was covered with thick snow. What was to prove one of the harshest winters ever experienced in Britain had already begun, with snow in great drifts, and storms lashing the coast.

"Go up and get him, Charlotte."

"But he's asleep."

"Well, wake him. Vera's making boiled eggs and toast for breakfast. Tell him we're going to open the last jar of Mary Byrne's blackberry jam. That should stir him."

Charlotte sidled out of the room, and Birdie moved with her like a shadow. As they reached the top of the stairs they heard chattering from the nursery—it was Katie and Sandra, bickering over their toys. Even though Sandra was almost a year older Katie had begun to bully the child as soon as she'd come to live with them. One of the first things she'd done was to daub Sandra's blonde curls with mud from the gulley beside the greenhouse. Sandra had laughed, a tiny tinkling sound, enjoying the attention, but Vera had whisked her up to the bathroom and scolded her with a rough washing of her muddy hair.

"It's the wrong colour," Katie had protested when Cynthia reprimanded her. "I was painting it brown."

"You're starting to whine just like Sandra," Cynthia had said. "Now get into bed."

"But it's not bedtime."

"You're a very bad girl. I'm ashamed of you."

Katie had turned her face to the wall and refused to look at her mother. But she had taken it out on Sandra and continued to bully her, but more cautiously.

"You run in and shake him, and I'll shout from the doorway," Charlotte whispered.

"But I'm frightened. What if he bites me?"

"He won't. He's fast asleep. You just have to wake him up."

"How?"

"Shake him hard. Go on."

Birdie steeled herself and crept into the cold bedroom. Jimmy at age ten was more asthmatic than ever, so there was no carpet on the floor of his room because carpets, Archer Pearson had said, collected dust and were particularly bad for asthmatics. The same was true of feather pillows, so Jimmy slept on a hard rubber pillow with the window open to toughen him up. Birdie was close to the bed now, and she looked back at Charlotte who was in the doorway ready to shout. She nodded at Birdie who burst into a fit of giggles.

"Rise and shine, Jimmy!" Charlotte shouted. "Time for breakfast!" She too started to giggle and gestured frantically to Birdie who reached out and banged her brother on the head with a bunched-up fist.

"Oooow!" he screeched and curled into a foetal position, moaning gently.

"We're having Mary Moo's blackberry jam," Charlotte shouted.

Birdie felt sorry now and reached forward to stroke Jimmy's head.

"Come on, wake up," she whispered.

"I don't want to, I'm tired," he mumbled. Since starting boarding school he had retreated into an early adolescent sulkiness, taking refuge in sleep for as long as he was allowed.

"Come *on*, Jim," Charlotte said, entering the room. "We'll get into trouble with Mum if you don't come down." She sat on the bed and shook his exposed shoulder.

"What time is it?" he asked petulantly.

"Breakfast time," Birdie said. "And sure Darlin's, it's a grand day for a walk in the fields," she said in her best Mary Byrne accent, which made them all collapse with laughter.

"Aren't you happy to be home?" Charlotte asked.

Jim rolled over and rubbed his eyes sleepily. "Mmmm, sort of."

"What's it like at boys' school?" Birdie asked.

"I hate it!" Jim said.

"But we don't have to go back till after Christmas, so let's make the best of it," Charlotte said.

"Yes, show a leg," Birdie said brightly.

"What?"

Birdie giggled. "That's what Matron says every morning to wake us up."

"Where's Daddy?" Jim asked.

"He's downstairs waiting for you," Charlotte said quickly, ignoring the look Birdie gave her.

Christopher Brooke arrived home after the children were already in bed, and received a restrained welcome from Cynthia. Vera was with her in the sitting room, but she soon made herself scarce.

"What's all this about?" Cynthia asked, pulling the newspaper out from under the sofa, waving it at him.

He took the paper and glanced at the article, then he laughed and tossed it aside. "Those reporters blow everything out of proportion. I had a most interesting discussion with Pastor Walker myself ..."

"Then why doesn't it mention you?"

"I was in the house ..."

"With one of your girl disciples, I suppose."

"I was in my study, arranging some important documents and when I came out later in the afternoon I found Arthur and the Pastor drinking tea. I explained to him about our own gospel and our mission to ..."

"Don't start on that again, I'm sick of it!"

She waited for him to speak, but he rose and crossed the room silently, to the piano where he sat and began to play the slow movement of the *Pathetique Sonata*.

"Why were you gone so long?" she asked, twisting her wedding ring.

"I had to go up to London on banking business," he replied without interrupting his playing.

"Where did you stay?"

"The Park Lane, in our old suite."

She walked across the room and stood behind him, her hands resting on his shoulders.

"Did you miss me?"

She leaned down and brushed her cheek against his, but he kept on playing.

Next morning Christopher was at the breakfast table with the children in time to sample the last of the blackberry jam.

"Only two days to go till Christmas," Jimmy said, his voice still boyish though he'd lost much of his childishness in a shocking term at boarding school. The first time he'd been summoned to the headmaster's study he'd not been afraid, even though Carstairs had warned him—"Pad your trousers, Brooke—with handkerchiefs, newspaper, anything—it hurts like billy-o!"

The caning had taken his breath away and made him cry out. Worse than the pain of his smarting bottom was the shame and humiliation he'd felt when the headmaster said—"Pull up your trousers, boy. And let that be a lesson to you. I don't want to set eyes on your miserable backside ever again."

When he'd emerged into the hallway fumbling for his handkerchief, Carstairs had been waiting.

"Bare bottom? He caned you bare bottom!" The boy collapsed into a fit of giggles.

Later, on the playground, the boys had circled him chanting: "Bare bottom, bare bottom, bare bottom Brooke!"

At first Jimmy had laughed along with them, feeling somewhat of a hero, but eventually he'd broken down and sobbed: "Stop it! Stop it! I want to go home!"

Now that he was home for the hols he'd tried to forget about all that, but the feeling persisted, like a cloud hovering over him. He had a secret that couldn't be shared and that made him feel ashamed.

"Can we go tobogganing, Daddy?" Charlotte asked.

"Can't wait to open my stocking," Jimmy said.

"Will Father Christmas bring me a dolly?" Sandra said. Vera *shushed* her and looked down into her lap, her mouth trembling.

"Don't worry, Sandra," Cynthia said. "I talked to Father Christmas on the telephone and told him what you want. He'll be coming down our chimney tomorrow night, but only after you're asleep—all of you."

She smiled at Christopher and he waved at her from his end of the table, a strange gesture somewhere between a salute and a caress. They had lain all night in each other's arms, Christopher so tired that he'd fallen asleep before he could return to his own bed. They had decided to have Christmas at Meadowside because neither Dick Blackwell nor James Brooke was well. Both men had weak hearts and had been ordered to avoid the stress of small children running around.

"It will be a quiet Christmas," Dorothy had said, and Cynthia had understood that they were still not wanted at the Woodlands. She was being punished for marrying the wrong man, and for refusing to go to America to dance attendance on Ruby during her confinement.

"Come on, Charlotte, we'll get the toboggan down from the shelf in the garage," Christopher said.

"But there's only one and it's too small for the four of us," Jim said.

"Five," Vera said sharply, "Don't forget my Sandra."

"You can use the tin trays from the kitchen," Cynthia said. "Now go on, out of here, the lot of you. Vera and I have mince pies to make."

On Christmas Eve Cynthia and Christopher stayed up late stuffing the children's stockings, then they crept upstairs and laid a lumpy, bulging stocking at the end of each bed. She felt almost normal that night lying in bed listening to Christopher's steady breathing. The house smelled of freshly baked mince pies, and a glass of milk stood half drunk on the coffee table by the fireplace downstairs with a plateful of crumbs to convince the children. Birdie's snowman stood silently on the front lawn with his carrot nose, and coal lumps for eyes. The children's footprints circled him, and their handprints patterned his body.

Cynthia felt safe; held close by the house, and by the snow enclosing them in the long winter night. She was relieved that they would stay home tomorrow and that there would be no need for apologies or explanations, nothing at all to worry about. It's just Christopher and me and our children, she thought, and she wished it could always be like that, then there would be no more fighting, no more long absences, nothing to answer for to her ever-inquisitive mother—the humiliation of not knowing where he was or what he was doing—just to live in the moment as her children did. She couldn't believe how she had ever considered moving into Kingdom House with Baker and those dreadful women with their cheap perfume and common manners. She lay awake until the early hours luxuriating in her fragile oasis and then she slipped into a deep sleep.

Our whole house was woken by Sandra's screaming. She had found her voice and it was piercing. Mum was first into our nursery where she found a scarlet-faced Sandra drumming her heels on the floor.

"What on earth is going on in here? Katie, what did you do to her?"

"Nothing." I was sitting up in bed clutching the big brown-eyed doll that had been in the top of Sandra's stocking. All of Sandra's gifts were scattered on my bed.

"You little thief!"

"I'm not!" I protested. "This is how Sandra's hair should be—brown," I said, pulling at the doll's hair. Mum slapped me and I screamed and threw the doll across the room where it hit the wall and cracked its porcelain face.

"What is it, Mummy?" Charlotte was at the door, with Birdie at her side, and Jimmy too, peering from behind them.

"Get back to bed, it's too early," Mum said.

She pulled back the curtain. It was dark outside, with just a glimmer of grey light on the horizon behind the farm where our father had laboured. Vera appeared in the doorway, rubbing her eyes, still bleary with sleep, and with the smell of something strange on her breath.

"Look after your child," Mum said.

"What've you done to her?"

"You should teach her to stand up for herself. She's a ..."

She stopped as Daddy appeared behind Vera, still tying the cord of his dressing gown.

"What the Dickens? ...." He pushed Vera aside, stepped forward into the nursery, and picked me up. "What's happened in here, Cynthia?"

"Vera, go downstairs and make some tea."

As soon as she was gone, taking Sandra with her, Mum turned to him and said in a barely controlled voice, "I can't do all this on my own. It's too much. You have to help me."

"But what is it you want?"

"I was alone with your children all through the war ..."

"You had the housekeeper."

"It's not the same. I need *you* here, their father."

"Why are you crying, Katie?"

I stopped at the sound of my name, clinging to my father and staring accusingly at my mother.

"She's an impossible child. As my mother says, spawn of the devil!"

It was out of her mouth before she knew it. She stood there, aghast at her own words, but Daddy's face was calm as ever, though there was a shadow over it, the faintest shadow as he continued to gaze at Mum in the dawning light.

"I'm sorry. I didn't mean ... I don't know what came over me. Oh Darling!"

She reached out for him and for me, but I turned away sharply, twisting in my father's arms, and Mum ran from the room. We heard her throw herself on the bed next door and then there was the sound of her crying, which frightened me more than anything. It felt like the world was coming to an end. What had I done?

With the morning light everything returned to normal and we opened our stockings, though Mum had wanted to put me to bed for the day as punishment, but Vera said not to worry, Sandra must learn to forgive, and she stuffed all Sandra's toys back inside her stocking and put an Elastoplast bandage over the dolly's face and we played hospital, settling her on the sofa with a blanket tucked around her neck.

But there was a damper on our spirits despite our father's jovial attempts at cheering us up and Vera crashing around in the kitchen. I refused to eat my turkey, then gorged myself on the Christmas pudding and brandy sauce, and vomited all over my new dress. It was an exhausting day but we moved through it, everyone cautious as though something might explode if we moved too quickly.

"I've seen happier Christmases, but we're in no position to complain," I heard Vera telling Sandra. "At least we have a roof over our heads, and I've got you, lovie." Sandra squirmed as though she might pee, Vera was hugging her so hard. "I feel sorry for Cynthia," I heard her mutter. "It was bad enough when her 'usband was away, but worse now he's home."

Chapter Twenty-Five

A DICKY HEART

O N BOXING DAY they left Vera and Sandra at the house and went over to have tea at Dinglewood. Mrs. Ward opened the door with her usual smile and a deferential nod, saying: "Go forward, please."

Granny Brooke was sitting alone, fragile as an eggshell, Cynthia thought, but as she rose to greet them, kissing each of the children first, and then her son, Cynthia observed something else about her mother-in-law. She's unbreakable, she thought, in the way that an egg can withstand a sustained and even pressure however great that pressure may be. But she is a shell, a very thin translucent shell, Cynthia thought, preserving her own world within, so different from my own mother.

"Where's Father?" Christopher asked.

"He's having a day in bed," Nancy said.

"Can we go up and see him?" Jimmy asked.

"Better not," Cynthia said. "Is it his heart?" she asked in a whisper. "My father has the same trouble," she said when Nancy nodded.

Afternoon tea was announced and Mrs. Ward ushered them into the dining room where the children ran around the table looking for their places. Nancy always put name tags between the ears of china rabbits in a variety of colours.

"I've got the red bunny!" Katie said, squealing.

"And I've got the green one, next to Granny," Jim said, holding up his name tag and plunking himself down in the tapestry-covered chair.

The table was loaded with plates of buttered malt loaf, scones studded with fat raisins, bowls of home-made quince jelly, Birdie's favourite Battenberg cake, and thinly iced Christmas cake with a layer of jam and marzipan.

"Eat slowly, children," Cynthia said as Jimmy and Katie chewed with bulging cheeks, already reaching for more, as though they were half starved.

Charlotte picked at the offerings on her plate. Teasing at school had made her self-conscious about her baby fat.

"Won't Father come down for tea?" Christopher asked.

"It would be too much for him today," Nancy said, smiling with that slight nodding of her head that only emphasized her fragility.

"I'd like to go up and see him."

"Well, I don't know, dear, he ..."

"I may be going away for a while."

"Where to? Petworth again?" Cynthia asked.

"Further afield. It's vital that the wider world understands what has happened in Europe before we forget the horrors of war."

"Christopher, the children," Nancy said.

"These rabbits have big ears like pigs," Birdie said, waving her rabbit over the Battenberg cake.

"I must travel, you see, it's part of my work, to reach out with the gospel in order to draw people ..."

"Christopher, please," Cynthia said, her jaw tight and trembling.

"I'll be mother," Nancy said, as she picked up the big silver teapot and began to pour. "Lemon or milk, dear? Sugar? Two lumps or one?"

"I think I *will* go up and see him," Christopher said, pushing his chair back.

"If you insist, dear. But Christopher, don't bother him with ... business details."

"No, Mother, I won't."

"Knock first. He may be snoozing," she called after him.

When Christopher opened the door of his parents' bedroom he saw James Brooke lying prostrate. His eyes were closed and there was a bluish tinge to his complexion.

"Father?" He had already taken a few hesitant steps towards the bed before James Brooke opened his eyes and turned to face his son. "Hello Father. I wanted to wish you a happy Christmas, even though it's already Boxing Day."

"I have a dicky heart today," he said, his voice a low growl.

"Yes. Mother said. I hope I'm not disturbing you."

James Brooke focused his watery eyes on Christopher. He looked long and hard at him, and then his moustache twitched and he patted the counterpane.

"Sit down, my boy. Sit, sit. I was remembering my voyage on the Lusitania. May 1915. Hmmm, almost thirty-one years ago. Hard to believe, isn't it? We were so close to home—half way along the southern coast of Ireland when the torpedoes hit."

"Yes Father." He's heard this before, numerous times.

"There were plenty of lifeboats but most of them overturned while lowering—crewmen lost their grip on the ropes, you see, and passengers went tumbling into the water." He dabbed his rheumy eyes with a large white handkerchief clutched in one fist. "I had my lifejacket on, that's what saved me. Someone picked me up, thought I was a goner. I came to on the dock, laid out with the dead. Hell of a scare to wake up that way, Christopher."

Christopher nodded. He wondered if his father had been tippling again in the privacy of his bedroom. That's what he did, got drunk and relived the sinking of the Lusitania. As a manufacturer he'd been exempt from fighting in the First World War, but *this* was his war, a battle for survival at sea.

"It was the sinking of our ship that turned public opinion against Germany and forced the Americans to enter into the Great War. It did them no good, torpedoing us. We got them in the end."

"And how did Churchill get the Americans involved this time?" Christopher asked, forgetting his mother's warning. "By allowing our great cities to be bombed to smithereens—London, Coventry, Birmingham, Manchester ..."

"And where were you?"

"Father, you know my stand. I survived the war in my own way, but it's not over for me. That's why I came up to see you, to say good-bye, because I'll be going away for a while on my own business."

The old man stared him down, his gingery moustache clumped over his upper lip, making it difficult to read his expression.

"Is there anything I can get for you?" Christopher asked.

Brooke blew his nose noisily, trumpeting like an old mammoth. "You've been a disappointment to me, Christopher … my only son."

He flinched, for the words had reached their mark in a rare unguarded moment. "My life is not over. If you live long enough you'll see, Father, I will prove myself, in the name of the Lord, and in the name of our Führer."

"Get out of here!" Brooke growled, and he turned his face away.

Christopher stood a moment, hands clenched, then turned on his heel and left the room silently, almost tripping on the thick pile of the carpet.

Chapter Twenty-Six

BRENDAN, OH BRENDAN

January 1947

IT WAS JUST as well that I was not to start work yet for soon after Christmas I had a terrible blow. The letter came on a Friday, written in Da's careful hand. I thought it might be news of Deirdre for I was still waiting for her to come to England. But it was Brendan, my big brother Brendan had been killed. There was no details of how or where or why, but I'd seen the passion in his eyes and I knew he had sacrificed himself for the freedom of Ireland, and that it was a waste of his dear life, for Ireland would never be free of the English.

I understood that after living in England and feeling the tenacity of those people. How else did they win the war? And look who they chose to lead them through it—Mr. Churchill who was as stubborn a fighter as you would find anywhere, though it was all in his head and he did not have to put his life on the line. Now if he was leading the Irish revolutionaries we'd stand a chance. The British tossed him aside after the war because he'd served his purpose. They're ruthless like that behind all their smiles and politeness.

And here now was my darling Brendan gone to the cemetery, and Seán home safe. Wouldn't you think it would be the other way around?

I had thought to boost my Reg that winter, but it was he looked after me, for I was down on the floor with my grief. And Vancy did end up looking after my children, but she did it for nothing, out of the goodness of her heart.

Chapter Twenty-Seven

THE TALENT OF INVISIBILITY

THE LETTER CAME in the third week of January, just before my fifth birthday. I hoped Daddy would be home for my big day and that he would bring me a horse. Charlotte, Jimmy, and Birdie had gone back to boarding school and I was left at home with only Sandra to play with. We were in the grip of a deep freeze with huge snowdrifts. We couldn't see the farm behind our house; the field was completely white with big puffs of snow still falling. Vera had done a half-hearted shovelling of our driveway, so the postman managed to make his way to the front door, and that's how we found out.

"Nothing but bills," Mum said, riffling through the envelopes. She opened the hall desk where my father kept his papers neatly stacked in wooden compartments behind the leather covered writing surface, and she tossed the bills in for him to deal with when he came home. He was gone again, but was rarely away more than two weeks at a time.

"Oh, here's something," she said, holding up a plain white envelope with a handwritten address in writing she didn't recognize.

She picked up a paper knife and slit the envelope open. I'll never forget her face as she read that letter. A look of fury came over her, and she began to tremble, then tears spilled down her cheeks. It is a terrifying thing to see your mother cry, for what can be done when the person who governs your life loses control? What had happened? What would we do? I reached up to pat her hand, but she pushed me away and ran

into the sitting room. I stood at the door and watched as she lit a cigarette and sat there trembling and breathing smoke like a dragon.

She read the letter again, more slowly and carefully this time, then
she scrunched it up and threw it into the fire, where it flared and turned
into a brown curl that collapsed into ashes. I could hear Vera's voice
floating down the corridor as she sang along with Doris Day ... 'With a
song in my heart, I behold your adorable face ...' Mum must have heard
it too because she jumped up suddenly and marched towards the kitch-
en. I flattened myself against the wall, feeling a rush of air as she passed,
then I followed her down the corridor and listened.

"Now look what he's done. He's gone to bloody South Africa!"

"What?" Vera looked up from her ironing.

"Can you believe it? This is the last straw."

"What're you talking about?"

"My husband was too much of a coward to tell me himself. He got
Baker to write a letter and post it just before they left. Look, here's the
envelope. It's postmarked January 23rd."

"That was only yesterday. Fast delivery," Vera said.

Mum was silent, her face white and pinched. Sandra was playing
under the kitchen table, and she saw me pressed against the wall, so I
put my finger to my lips, warning her to keep quiet.

"But why would he go to South Africa? It's a long way in the
middle of winter."

"To preach his damned gospel, what else?"

"Is he coming back?"

"I don't know. I'm always the last one to know his whereabouts."

She began to cry again, her face hidden in her hands, her shoulders
shaking, and I began to cry too. I didn't know if I was crying for my
mother's unhappiness or for fear of not seeing my father again. I just
knew I had to be quiet about it.

"Never mind," Vera said, setting the iron down and placing her
hand on Cynthia's shoulder, patting it nervously. "We'll manage, the
two of us, till he comes home. Would you like a nip of gin?"

"I want a cup of tea."

They passed by without seeing me and went into the scullery.

"That's what he was doing all this time away in London, getting his travel papers in order—his passport and vaccinations. How could he have been so cruel as to keep it from me?"

"Well, you're not the only one who's been let down," Vera said. "Look at me with my little bastard ..."

She meant Sandra. I glanced over to see if she'd heard, but she was in her own world, muttering to herself under the table.

"... and that American bastard, disappeared off the face of the earth."

"It's quite different," Cynthia said dismissively. "Christopher is my husband of thirteen years. He's going to miss our anniversary, *and* Katie's birthday. It's so unfair. He never thinks of us, only of that bloody Baker and their ridiculous ... "

"Well, you chose him," Vera said, but quickly regretted her words and backtracked. "I'm sorry, Cynthia. I didn't mean ... It was impertinent of me."

She didn't wait for the tea but swept past me once again. That's when I realized that I was invisible. I knew in that moment that it was my talent and my power to make myself so, and I thanked the fairies for it and resolved to use it well. Adding silence to my invisibility I would go forth to conquer the world, armed with my advantages, spying, and harbouring my knowledge for a better day.

The next few days were very gloomy. Granny Brooke telephoned to say that Grandpa was poorly and wouldn't get out of bed. I heard Mum crying again as she talked to Granny in a low voice.

"... off in Africa ... emptied our bank account ... what can I do?"

I heard her blowing her nose and thanking Granny, over and over. After she put the receiver down she powdered her nose and applied fresh lipstick, then she put on her fur coat and snow boots, took me by the hand and led me into the kitchen.

"Look after Katie," she said to Vera. "I'm driving over to Dinglewood. I won't be long."

I crept under the table with Sandra and we made a fortress out of building blocks to protect ourselves from the grownups.

Chapter Twenty-Eight

THE LION'S SHARE

O N THE 7TH of February while his son was in South Africa James
Brooke succumbed to a massive heart attack.

"Daddy has left on his final voyage," Nancy told Cynthia
as they sat together in the morning room at Dinglewood. She was
veiled, and attired entirely in black with a beaded cap covering her
head. Her dress was a floor length taffeta and she wore thin, elbow-
length gloves, a jet necklace and earrings, and on her feet were high-
buttoned boots, polished vigorously by the gardener to a shiny black.
She seemed to Cynthia more shell-like than ever; she hardly dared to
touch her, but when she did she was surprised anew by Nancy's resili-
ence. This was a woman raised on death and loss, followed by years
of strict discipline and long walks.

Cynthia went upstairs to pay her respects to Grandpa Brooke. He
lay in state on his four-poster bed in the cold, cold room. She felt a
moment of panic as she stood stranded on the thick carpet, alone with
the corpse of a man she had hardly known. She should move forward
and kiss him, but she could not. She prayed fervently that she would
not survive her own husband.

Nobody knew how to contact Christopher. They delayed the funeral as long as possible and, as a last resort, Cynthia drove down to
Petworth to inquire about his return, using all of her valuable petrol

ration, but no-one answered the door of Kingdom House. They've all gone, she thought, every last one of them, run off to South Africa with my husband; then she sensed something, a feeling of being watched and, when she looked up at the bedroom window she had dreamed of as hers and Christopher's, saw the face of Judith Kern. The girl disappeared instantly so that if it hadn't been for that split second of eye contact Cynthia would have doubted that she had seen her at all.

She picked up a stone from the border of a snow-covered flower bed and threw it at the upstairs window. The glass shattered with a satisfying crash, but still no-one came, so she turned and plodded down the icy pathway in her boots, got into her car, and drove to Westonbirt to pick up her daughters and take them home for their grandfather's funeral.

Jimmy arrived by train on the morning of the funeral, immensely relieved to be away from school where he was taunted by the boys in ever more unspeakable ways, and was caned regularly by the masters as he retreated into a stubborn delinquency. They trudged through the snow to Woodford Church, the children taking their lead from Cynthia who was heavy and silent, less so with grief for her father-in-law's death than with the helpless anger and humiliation she felt in Christopher's absence. She had tried to imagine what he might be doing but her fantasies led her into such dreadful scenarios that she had to close her mind and "get on with it" as her mother had counselled her.

"You see, Cynthia, you should have gone to America to help Ruby when we asked you to; then *he* would have been shackled with his children and you'd have been well out of it."

Cynthia half believed her, awash as she was with indecision and regret, but under it all lay a passion that would not die no matter how hard it was battered. It was she who became brutalized by her own affections, she who being brutalized became a brute herself. For the most part it came out in subtle ways and had no immediate repercussions, because children will continue to love a parent through all kinds of abuse. It was in her treatment of Percy, now old and infirm, that she betrayed herself, kicking him when he'd had an accident on the carpet, rubbing his nose in it, slapping his poor old head until her fingers hurt.

The church was crowded with mourners. Nancy sat at the front, supported by Alice and Maurice on either side of her, and by Cynthia and her three children in the pew behind them. Katie, too young to attend a funeral, had been left at home with Vera and Sandra. Alice wept through the eulogy, but the rest of the mourners were silent and composed, especially Nancy Brooke who seemed as absent as her son, even at the graveside as the coffin was lowered through the soft earth that lay beneath its snowy cover.

"There's my place beside him," she told Alice as the hole was filled. "Daddy will be waiting for me."

The funeral tea at Dinglewood was a buffet affair in the dining room with Nancy presiding as usual over the teapot. The children pounced on the funeral foods, though Cynthia cautioned them to take only one sample from each plate because of rationing, and goods unable to move on the snowbound roads.

Nancy put on a brave face and everyone remarked about how courageous she was, but Cynthia knew that she was in fact not there at all, and she wished for that talent in herself, to rise above it all and leave her body like a wraith. But her roots were entrenched, her grip tenacious. Disappearance was beyond her capabilities.

The next news of her husband came through the printed word. Cynthia was sitting alone at the dining room table drinking a second cup of tea after breakfast when she spotted an article, no more than a paragraph, on the back page of the *Daily Express*. **Mr. Brooke barred**, the headline read. Cynthia's stomach lurched as she put her teacup down, rattling in its saucer:

> Mr. Christopher Brooke, a former hat manufacturer, who said he wanted to build a memorial institute to Hitler in South Africa, has been banned from returning there, the South African Department of Interior announced yesterday. Wearing a swastika badge in his buttonhole Mr. Brooke said at London airport last night: "I know nothing about having been refused permission to return to South Africa. I was received there with open arms."

She searched the newspaper for other mention of him, but there was nothing. She walked through the snow to the village newsagent to buy the *Mail*, the *Mirror*, *News of the World*, but found nothing more in their pages. He came home two days later and when she told him about the death of his father he stood silent in the front hall as though he hadn't heard her.

"Christopher? Are you alright?"

"I've had a difficult journey."

"We had to bury him without you. Why didn't you tell me where you were going?"

"It was thought best to inform you in a letter with a minimum of detail. Our trip was top secret, you see. We didn't want any trouble."

"We? Baker again? But I'm your wife." She took him in her arms and clung to him, inhaling his fresh clean smell of soap and shaving cream. "Oh, Chris, I don't want to argue. You're home now. Come on, let's get you unpacked. Is this all you have?" she asked, looking down at his battered carryall.

"I left my suitcase at Petworth."

"You went there first?"

"Judith told me you caused a disturbance at the house."

"Nonsense," she said. "I drove down there to try and get some information about you, that's all. We were desperate to get you home for your father's funeral. Don't you understand what we've been through here?"

"You'll have to excuse me, Cynthia. I have a lot on my mind."

He picked up the carryall and walked into his study.

It was a substantial inheritance. Though James Brooke had been tempted to disinherit his son, or at least to place the money in trust until such time as Christopher regained his wits, he'd procrastinated too long. Christopher inherited the lion's share while Alice got the girl's share, though she was good-natured about it. She adored her brother and knew that he needed the money more than her, because he was in essence without a job, and quite unemployable, while she was well provided for by Maurice, who was in publishing.

Most of the inheritance was tied up on the stock exchange, of which Christopher disapproved. As soon as probate was complete he sold the shares, but then he faced the problem of what to do with the proceeds, since he also disapproved of banking, or the Mammon system as he and Baker called it. They discussed the matter and Baker came up with a solution.

A safe was purchased and installed at Kingdom House with a security code known only to the two of them, and a large amount of cash was placed inside. It was agreed that the remaining sum would be divided between them and placed in separate bank accounts, in Baker's case for use at his own discretion towards the welfare of his family and the upkeep of Kingdom House, while Christopher's account would provide for his own family and for personal needs. The money secured in the safe would represent capital to be used perhaps in the purchase of another property as the need arose, and for all business matters connected with the spreading of their Gospel.

As coincidence would have it, Baker had heard through a family member of a property for sale with extensive acreage on Jersey in the Channel Islands. Since their farming efforts in Sussex had failed, Baker proposed that they keep Kingdom House as a foothold in England, continue with the upkeep, preparing for the day of enlightenment, while moving further afield, towards Europe, to fresh and more fertile pastures. Quoting Christ's parable of the talents, he persuaded Christopher that their safe should not be used for hoarding but should serve only as temporary storage. "This timely inheritance of tainted gold can be cleansed in the service of the Lord," he said.

It was only much later that Christopher understood (though he tried to deny it), how his friend had misinterpreted the parable.

Looking back on her life from the extremity of old age, Cynthia was to remember 1947 as a year of hell, and Meadowside as her house of torture. It had been a vicious winter in every way. March had brought a renewed onset of snow and blizzards continuing into April, accompanied by achingly cold temperatures. She realized it had been her last chance to pull him back. She would spend many evenings alone, huddled in a blanket like a war veteran, lost in the bitter-sweet act of remembrance, replaying the scenes in her mind, wondering what she might have done to salvage their marriage. She was to travel so far from the original memory of her first husband that she would no longer know if Christopher had existed or if she had invented him. Until, towards the end of her life, my mother told me that there was a ghost in her room; that it would enter through her dreams and wake her, trying to tell her something.

"Who's there?" she would ask. "Who's there? Is it you, Christopher?"

Over and over she would tell me. "I know someone is there. He's trying to tell me something."

Chapter Twenty-Nine

A BRIEFCASE FULL OF CASH

May 1947

ONCE THE WEATHER broke Christopher proposed a trip to Jersey to look at the property in question. This time he told Cynthia of his plans to travel, though it was only for a few days.

"Take me with you," she said. "I'd love a holiday."

"This is a reconnaissance trip, Cynthia. Better to wait until the property is purchased and the house up and running, then we can all go over in the summer."

"Oh, please, Chris! We could stay in a hotel on the front and go out for dinner and dancing."

"Thom Baker and I have business to attend to."

She recoiled like a spring at the mention of Baker. But she was determined not to fight Christopher. They'd been getting along well since his return from South Africa; largely because she had learned to censor herself. When she lashed out he retreated and that is what hurt her more than anything—his refusal to engage with her—so she bit her tongue and turned herself into the cliché of womanhood that she saw all around her, in magazines and on billboards—the happy postwar housewife, the helpmeet and supporter. It was easy for her to follow this recipe; it was the one she had chosen in obeying her father.

She tried to keep away from her parents' house now, because her mother's influence unsettled her efforts to maintain peace with Christopher. She was marking time, watching for signs of a return to his former self. She remembered his grinning face as he'd emerged from the sea at Rhosneigr, shaking himself like a dog, splashing her, and laughing, laughing, then kissing her so sweetly that she didn't even feel the coldness of his skin.

Everyone was recovering slowly from the damage — rebuilding, recharging, taking stock. What if you had lost a limb? You learned to live without it.

The boat trip to Jersey would have taken more than ten hours so, at Baker's insistence, they flew from Southampton and landed within the hour at a tiny airport in the parish of Saint Peter. It was May 9th, exactly two years since the liberation of the Channel Islands. Christopher carried a briefcase full of cash for the purchase of the Rue de Manoire property. Baker joked that they would have to watch out for pickpockets. "They'd never take your briefcase," he told Christopher. "They'd think it full of boring old business papers." He feinted a quick theft from Christopher's pocket but found only a handkerchief, and burst into gales of laughter.

The property turned out to be spacious and in good repair, with an extensive acreage. When Christopher bent to scoop the earth, it felt rich and moist in his hands.

"This house was used by German officers during the occupation," said Mr. Coutanche, the estate agent, in his peculiar accent which sounded to Christopher's ear similar to the South Africans he had so recently encountered.

"That's a good omen for us," Baker whispered in Christopher's ear. "Perhaps the Führer himself was here to inspect a house that is destined to be dedicated to his Gospel."

"We're well rid of those bastards," Coutanche said. "We've had trouble trying to sell this place in the past couple of years, so you're looking at a bargain."

They shook hands on it, bid the agent farewell, and spent the evening in La Hougue Inn, celebrating their purchase with a pub meal, followed by various attempts to engage the locals in conversation. But they learned that, after five years of occupation by German soldiers, there was an even stronger hatred of Hitler and his Nazis on Jersey than there was in England.

"Perhaps we've made too hasty a decision," Christopher said.

"Not at all," Baker said. "It was a good price, and look at it this way, Christopher, we are men who seek a challenge. The stronger the resistance the sweeter the surrender."

His laughter had a bawdy ring to it, a trait to which Christopher had accustomed himself and now rather enjoyed. It helped him to expand after the constriction of his domestic situation. He was puzzling over how to set up the place. He had thought it would be easy to engage a local family to run it and start the planting until he could get over again, but when he approached a ruddy-faced fellow at the bar the man laughed in his face.

"You'll never get anyone to go near that place!" he said, slamming down his pint.

"I'll tell you what," Baker said, as though reading Christopher's mind. "I'll move my wife and son over here. The local yokels will forget their prejudices once we establish a respectable family presence in the house."

"Splendid idea!" Christopher said, grinning. "And I'll bring Cynthia and the children over for the summer holidays."

"Your little firecracker, eh?"

"My wife," Christopher said.

"Yes indeed, your wife," Baker said, chuckling. "Well, we're on our way, my friend. Kingdom House, the beginning of our world outreach to South Africa, and now Le Manoire ... what next?"

"We spoke of Australia ..."

"That's a trip for you, Christopher. Sooner the better. I have a feeling they'll be more receptive than the South Africans. Funny bunch they were, eh?"

Chapter Thirty

THE NISSEN HUT

MEG WAS RELEASED from Strangeways in time for the twins' second birthday. It was May 1947 and a good time for her getting out because the worst of the weather was over. We'd had the wettest spring on record with floods all over the country coming after the big freeze-up of winter. The River Thames broke its banks, and valleys turned into lakes. The Shrewsbury bakers, the BBC told us, were lobbing loaves from boats into upstairs windows, and the River Trent in Nottingham rising a foot an hour.

I said to Reg, if we get through this without killing each other, Mister, we'll be set for life, for we were cooped up in our tiny caravan like rabbits, with Clio and Des running up and down on their fat little legs, and me still grieving the loss of my darling Brendan. The worst part was not being home to share the grief with my family. I had the feeling that Brendan's death would hit me anew as soon as I stepped back on Irish soil, and that it could not become a reality for me until that moment.

But I could not afford to go anywhere. I was without money of my own, dependent on Reg for every penny. There'd been no more talk of me going back to work and to tell you the truth I didn't push for it because there was nowhere I'd rather be than with my children, at least until they started school. But Reg had taken my wishes to heart for he came home one evening and said to me: "'Ow about a Nissen Hut?"

"A what?" I asked.

"You know, a Nissen Hut, like they used in the war. It's just another kind of prefab, like the ones you was wanting to build."

"But a hut is not a house."

"Wait till you see this one, Mary. I spotted it today on an empty lot in Stockport, and I thought to myself that's it, I'll buy it and fix it up nice for my family."

"But weren't they for housing the soldiers? Great big places like barracks?"

"They come in all sizes. This one's about twice the size of our caravan. I'll build shelves and a kitchen counter, and a cupboard to 'ang our clothes in. You'll see, it'll be grand."

"Where will we put it?"

"Right 'ere next to our caravan, and you can use this old thing for your sister when she comes."

I had received a letter from Deirdre finally. It had taken long enough for her to find her way to England, but she had arrived in the midst of our terrible winter and had found herself a job at the Royal Liverpool Hospital.

"I lied my way in, Máire," she wrote. "Told them I'd worked at the Cavan General, but I never told them it was only cleaning, so they took me on as a Nursing Assistant."

I knew our Deirdre would be all right, for she was a quick learner and could charm the tail off a horse's arse with her beautiful smile. She'd left her children with Siobhan and Caitlin, she wrote. Mam couldn't manage them—the eldest one wild as a banshee without a father's guidance. Reg was the only one could control Cliodhna, but Desmond was his Mammy's boy, like little Jimmy with Cynthia, both of whom I thought of with great regularity, though I'd seen neither hide nor hair of the Brooke family since our encounter in the Tudor Cinema.

Strange when you think that they lived less than a mile up the road. But they were people who led a different life from us. I thought Cynthia might come calling to see Meg again, or looking for Reg to fix something for her, but I suppose the Master was her handyman now, though he never struck me as the handy type, more of a thinker. And a piano player—that's what he would use his hands for.

I had not been too excited about the Nissen Hut, but I could see that Reg was mighty pleased with the idea, so I smiled and went along with it. He said it was very affordable and he'd got a deal on it because his friend George worked on the lot.

"George'll get it over 'ere on a flatbed next week," he said. "Then I can start work on the interior. Got a deal on some lumber too."

I told him I'd call him Mr. Gotadeal if he didn't shut up and stop grinning about his good fortune.

I had the caravan all nice for Meg with flowers on the table, a packet of tea, a bag of sugar, pint of milk, loaf of bread and some biscuits to start her off. I took the twins over to Vancy and asked her to mind them while I went to fetch Meg. I was at the Strangeways gate waiting for her at ten o'clock that morning, and she walked over to me, slow and dignified, then gave me the hug of the century she was that glad to be a free woman.

"But it weren't so bad, Mary," she said once she had let me go and stood there with her hands on my shoulders, looking at me as though she couldn't get enough of it. "I've got a lot of friends now on the inside. I'll be all right if ever I should end up in there again."

"But surely you're not going to continue with ... the same line of work?"

"Somebody 'as to do it," she said. And the way she stuck her chin out proudly I realized that money was the least of it as far as Meg was concerned.

"You must have been a model prisoner to get out so soon."

"Oh yes, lovie, and more than that—they need people like me on the inside," she said, tipping her head back at the dirty stone building. She leaned in and whispered: "I've been practising my profession in there."

I gasped, and Meg laughed so hard she broke into a coughing fit. When she recovered she whispered to me again: "Some members of the female staff were very grateful to me—well, that were one thing, but then, the Superintendent—a married man—brought 'is lady friend to see me—said I'd be out six months early if I obliged. So, naturally ..."

The bus came along just then and we jumped on it and ran upstairs to the top deck laughing all the way. It was a blessing to have Meg back and it made me realize how much I'd missed her, and how greatly my life had changed in her absence. My babies took to her right away and were always running over to her caravan. Word must have spread about her release for soon there was a steady stream of girls at her door, and as it turned out my own sister became one of her clients.

Deirdre arrived at the beginning of June, a month after the twins' birthday, for she had five days off from her nursing. It was a marvellous thing to see my Deedee again, and as I held her and looked into her eyes I remembered our childhood and the last time I'd been home inside the circle of stones with her.

"It's been three years, Máire," she exclaimed. "And look at you, a Mammy at last."

When she saw Cliodhna the blood drained from her face.

"She's the image of our Brendan," she said, and we both wept for the loss of him, and she wept again for her husband Eamon. "We've lost two good men from our family, Máire, and countless more besides across the country, all for nothing. The Six Counties will never be free from British rule."

Clio and Des called her Auntie Dee because they couldn't manage Deirdre. They followed her around like puppies, forgetting about Meg for a while. Even though Reg was still fixing up our Nissen Hut we managed to camp out in there so that Deirdre could have the caravan to herself. 'Twas as we sat over a cup of tea that she told me about her predicament.

"I'm three months gone, Máire," she said. "What will I do? I can't have another child now. It would ruin my plans."

"Who is it?"

"No-one you know."

"Won't he marry you?"

"He's already married and he doesn't want anything to do with it. He's a surgeon at the hospital and he has too much to lose, he says. He gave me some money, Máire, enough to get rid of it. But I don't know anyone. Can you help me?"

A confusion of emotions rose up in me. I didn't know whether to laugh or cry or to make a run for it, for there I was, angry and upset and frightened all at once with the stupidity of it. My poor sister cursed with her beauty, falling for one of the toffs as soon as she arrived in England. I wanted to take him by the throat and bash his head against the wall, but it was Deirdre I lashed out at.

"You damned eejit! What d'you think you're doing coming to England to be just one more Bog Irish slut? That's how they think of us here, Deirdre. They think they can use us and toss us aside."

"*You've* done all right for yourself," she said. "Look at you, married and with a home and two babies."

I grabbed hold of her arm and pulled her over to the mirror hanging above our sink. "Take a look," I said. "Take a look at the difference, will you. I've been protected by my plainness. I'm no prize and neither is Reg, but we're better off that way. And I'll wager we love each other more than you and your surgeon."

She pulled away from me and began pacing up and down the caravan. But I went after her and spun her around to face me. "Don't you know enough to protect yourself?"

"That would be against the Papal Edict."

"Well, what d'you think abortion is?"

"Don't use that word!" she whispered.

"You can't have it both ways."

She began to cry then and of course my heart melted. I took her in my arms and stroked her beautiful black hair. She was like a raven, all sleek and shining. I felt the magic in her and I knew I had to help her because she was my sister and we were cast out of Ireland together.

"I have a friend can help you," I said.

The way she looked at me then was worth more than all my angry words. And the fear I felt for my own safety now that I was a mother with my own babies to protect—well, that slipped away when I remembered the proud thrust of Meg's chin.

I didn't tell Reg. It wasn't the first thing I'd kept from him neither. And don't ask me why—it was an instinct I had, not to bother him with it. I used one of Cynthia's white lies, and I understood her the better for it. "Deirdre's not feeling well," I said. "I'm going to take her over some dinner." Reg had already fixed up a gas stove for us in the Hut, though the kitchen was a makeshift affair as yet and we made an adventure of it, camping out indoors.

Meg wouldn't take all of the money Deirdre offered. "Special price for you, lovie. Mary's my girl," she said with a mighty sniff.

So Deirdre gave me the rest and insisted I use it for the Hut. "It'll be grand when it's done," she said. "Get some flowers and plant them out front."

That night, with Deirdre settled and recovering, relieved of her burden, I lay awake thinking of what Meg had said—"Mary's my girl." I knew she'd not had a daughter, only her Leonard. He had survived the war, but he'd lost a leg and had been badly wounded in other ways and was still in a veterans' hospital being treated for something they called "battle fatigue," so he'd not been able to visit her in prison. Of course, the first thing she wanted when she came out was to see him, and she travelled all the way down to Southampton to the Royal Victoria Hospital in Netley. It was a dreadful place, she told me, worse than Strangeways, but it had a ghostly beauty when the mist was rolling in off the water.

"I walked up that long pathway with poplar trees on either side," she told me. "And I began to feel frightened long before I got into the building."

Meg is not a woman to be afraid, nor does she have the gift. It is her son has it with his six toes on the left foot, though I should say *had* it, for it was his left he'd lost.

"One of the nurses led me down a long corridor," Meg said. "It were wide enough to drive a tractor through—and she took me into a ward filled with men lying about on their beds, and some of them propped up in bath chairs. It were deathly quiet in there, none of them stirred when we entered. She took me across to a man sitting in 'is bath chair staring out the window into the mist. 'E 'ad his left leg cut off above the knee, and there was an artificial leg lyin' on the floor and a pair of crutches at 'is side.

"'E turned to me and I saw then that it was my Leonard. I couldn't believe it, Mary, 'e were a shadow of 'imself. I leaned down and I said:

'Lennie, it's Mum, don't you know me?' His mouth twitched and 'e began to cry with big gusting sobs and snot running down his nose like when 'e were a nipper. He turned away then, 'is face flushing up just like when 'e were a little lad and 'e'd get so angry. I bent down and took 'im in me arms as best I could, but 'e wouldn't be 'eld. His body were stiff as a board. 'I'll leave you alone for a while,' the nurse said. 'I'll be at the nursing station if you need me.' 'Oh Lennie, my own boy, you've come 'ome safe,' I said. 'I'd be better off dead,' 'e said, and that's when I realized that 'e 'adn't come home. This wasn't my son who'd left for Europe full of vim and vigour. This was a broken man."

Meg had put in a petition for her son to be transferred to a veterans' hospital closer to home. They told her that his name would be added to a waiting list, but not to hold her breath. They had their hands full with all the requests. Next day Meg travelled all the way back to Bramhall and buckled down to work as though nothing had happened. She was a tough woman, but underneath it I knew she was suffering, so I tried to be tender with her, as a daughter would be.

I lay there listening to Reg's snoring, and to our little children breathing in their cot, and I realized what a family I had made for myself in England, with a husband and two babies, and now my sister joining me from Ireland. And if Meg considered me her daughter then I would consider her my mother sure enough.

I turned over and made myself into a spoon for my husband's sleeping body. We created a deal of warmth between us that way. I felt the knobby bones of his spine pressing into my bosom and his tail bone hard against my secret place. I reached up and stroked the back of his neck with my finger. There was a downy hollow there that I loved to touch—a tender place that makes you want to care for someone. In our loving it was always Reg's touch that got me going. You'd never have known from looking at him what magic he had in his malformed body. It was a mystery to me where it came from, and if it hadn't been for the back row of the Tudor Cinema I'd never have known such pleasure. But I worried sometimes that my body was divorced from my head, for it was still the Master who lived there, and who governed my thoughts and fantasies. How can you be making love with one man while thinking of another? Isn't that a betrayal, bringing a third person into the bed with you?

Perhaps I was worrying for nothing. It could be that Reg brought Rita Hayworth or Betty Grable into our bed without my knowledge. Nevertheless, my fantasy-life was a matter I never discussed with Reg, along with Deirdre's abortion and a few other small secrets. I had within me a desire to confess everything, but I did not trust it and thought it perhaps an indulgence. It must be the Catholic in me, I thought, the need to confess, but I had lapsed since coming to England and had no wish to return to the Church and confess my pathetic little sins when there had been such crimes committed in the world.

With the end of the war the news had come about those camps where the Germans had put the Jews and Gypsies and other types of undesirables—to their way of thinking. The pictures were terrible. I didn't want to look at them for they could haunt you and make you feel afraid forever. I did not want to stop trusting people. I preferred to look at the beauty around me, and the goodness of people like Meg and Vancy and Reg, who seemed all related to the Travellers and Tinkers of my homeland. I had not told Mam and Da that I lived on a caravan estate, and Deirdre had not commented when she came to us for help, preoccupied as she was with her own condition. At any rate, things look different in another country, but you soon catch on. What you don't notice is how you yourself are changing, how you begin to think differently no matter how hard you try to be loyal.

Just as I was drifting off to sleep it came to me with a jolt that something bad was going to happen to Deirdre. I'd seen it in her hand as we'd sat drinking our tea, but then I'd been diverted by her news so it only struck me now. There were two more children in her hand, and a patch of criss-crossed lines that I couldn't make out; all I knew was there was going to be trouble.

Chapter Thirty-One

ON DECK

August 1947

CHRISTOPHER BROOKE SETS off from Tilbury dock in mid-August.
"Daddy, please don't go," Jimmy says. "Hols aren't over yet, and I want you to coach me in soccer. I'm trying out for the team next term."

"Remember to kick the ball with your instep, Jiminy Cricket," Christopher says. "And conserve your strength. Don't run around the field like a chicken."

Jimmy giggles. But Charlotte is sobbing, clinging to her father. "*Please* don't go, Daddy," she says. "Something terrible might happen."

"Nonsense, Darling. I have my ticket. There's no going back now."

He walks up the gangplank, turns once to wave at the children, and immediately switches his attention to finding his cabin, which is on the upper level of the *R.M.S. Orcades*. He is to share with a fellow passenger who turns out to be a sallow, dull-eyed man who discourages conversation and spends a great deal of time sleeping. Christopher rises early and strolls on deck looking for passengers to engage in conversation. He has in mind a rehearsal for his Australian mission and declares his Witness accordingly, meeting for the most part with averted eyes.

"This is a momentous time," he says, "as we face the impending crash of Mammon civilization, the end of Jewish influence on global finance, and the task of preparation for the New World which, by God's Grace, will arise from the ashes."

He sets up his routine of a light breakfast, free of stimulants such as tea and coffee, followed by two hours of composition, recording the tenets of the Gospel according to the Legion of Christian Reformers, to be published in their monthly newsletter, the *Kingdom Herald*.

The *Orcades* docks briefly in Colombo, Ceylon, where Christopher learns that he is only a few days ahead of Ernest Bevin, the British Foreign Secretary. He admires Bevin, a former trade-union leader and a member of the Labour party, who has famously remarked at war's end: "The world of Jewry is now at war with the Gentile world." Christopher leaves a letter for Bevin in care of the Embassy, congratulating him on his handling of the Middle East situation, which is quickly moving towards the implementation of a partition plan and the establishment of a Jewish state.

He recalls his conversations with Leo Kaufmann in the potato fields and wonders what Leo is doing now. Has he returned to Berlin, or has he settled in England? Though he does not consider himself anti-Jewish, Christopher believes that the Jews, even the decent fellows like Leo, will be better off when they have their own nation. He believes in collectivity, in the grouping of like-minded people. He is reassured by his own membership in the Legion of Christian Reformers, with their plan focussed on a better future. He can play only a small part, limited by his individuality, but he is sustained by it, by his Mission to spread the Gospel.

When Christopher discovers an exercise room in the bowels of the *Orcades*, he adds to his daily routine ninety minutes of weight lifting and treadmill walking, to maintain his muscle power. He is a man in his prime, 37 years old.

After dinner at the Captain's table on the eve of their arrival in Perth, Christopher goes up on deck to watch the night sky—a mass of thickly clustered stars pressed into the darkness. He senses a presence beside him and turns to see a woman in a green dress.

"Good evening," Christopher says. "Weren't we at the same ...?"

"The Captain's table. Such a bore."

"On the contrary ..."

"Oh, don't tell me ..." Her laughter puts him on guard.

"You're here with your husband?"

She shrugs, her bare shoulders gleaming in the starlight. "I'm here."

"Allow me to ..." he stretches out his hand.

"Christopher Brooke," she says, drawling.

"How did you...?"

"I make it my business to know ... everything."

"And your name?"

"You could probably guess."

It is Christopher's turn to laugh, though uncomfortably. Her eyes are too green, her mouth too wide and soft, entirely without tension, her lips cushioning her words as they escape from the quick cave of that mouth.

"I'm sorry. Should I know you?"

"Oh indeed you should," she says with feeling, reaching out a small white hand to touch his lapel. She lets the pearly painted nail of her index finger scrape down the material of his dinner jacket until her hand has dropped to waist height and hovers there. He grips her hand suddenly and shakes it vigorously. The woman's delicate body quivers like an arrow hitting the bullseye as she throws back her head and laughs.

"Ah, such strength."

"Excuse me, I didn't mean to ..."

"You men love to impress us, don't you?"

"Have I impressed you?" Christopher asks.

She smiles up at him. "It was effortless, even before you shook me to the core."

Christopher opens his mouth to speak, but no words come, and again the woman speaks, the flow of her words like thick honey oozing from her plushy mouth.

"Look at the ocean, thousands of feet dropping beneath us, to the depths where no light penetrates, and where no-one has ever been. Do you dream of the ocean, Christopher?"

She has turned away from him and is leaning over the railing, her shoulder touching his right arm, her hip lightly brushing his thigh.

"No, I don't ..."

"Seventy percent of the earth's surface awash, absorbing our sins.

And here we stand on this fragile little boat, bobbing above it. We can do anything we want. We're floating in a most precarious situation in the middle of nowhere."

"On the contrary, we'll be arriving in Perth at precisely ..."

She turns and reaches up to place her small hand over his mouth, and then she does an outrageous thing. She slips her index finger between his lips, and he sucks on it, savouring the pear drop taste of her nail varnish. It is so instinctive that he shocks himself. His whole body is hard and erect against her and he wants to take her, to hoist her dress and unbutton himself and thrust into her light-filled body.

But he turns and excuses himself. He walks slowly, steadily towards his cabin where he takes a cold shower and lies stiffly on his bed until sleep overtakes him. He dreams of Cynthia, as he had in prison. He feels that he belongs to her in some deep and unbreakable way, and that it would be sacrilegious to betray her with his body.

The *Orcades*, after a short stop in Perth, continues its voyage, steaming across the Great Australian Bight to Adelaide, round the coast to Melbourne and, finally, to Sydney. Christopher has been gone from England a total of twelve weeks and when he returns in mid-November Cynthia is waiting for him.

She has taken the train to London, booked a suite at the Park Lane, and has purchased tickets for a new musical at the Adelphi theatre. *Bless the Bride* is a current hit, its songs played on the wireless almost daily during Christopher's absence. There's one song in particular that she loves and she sings it to herself as she unpacks in the hotel room.

"This is my lovely day, this is the day I shall remember the day I'm dying ..."

She is almost dizzy with excitement, like a bride herself. This will be a fresh start, she thinks. He's coming home to me!

She is waiting for him at Tilbury dock and begins to wave frantically as she spots him walking slowly down the gangplank with people behind him jostling to get past. When he looks up it seems for a moment that he does not recognize her, then a smile spreads on his face and he waves back and continues down the gangplank, stumbling on the wooden rungs. As he steps onto the dock she flies into his arms and clings to him so tightly that he begins to laugh.

"What's the matter?" he asks, pulling back and smiling down at her.

"It's been torture, Chris."

"That's strong language."

"I mean it. I've missed you so much."

He doesn't know how to respond. His only intimate encounter over the past three months has been with the green-eyed woman and her disturbing poetry. He had glimpsed her several times afterwards and avoided her, but one evening he'd seen her again at the Captain's table and raised his hand in greeting. She'd looked right through him as though he didn't exist.

He holds Cynthia's hand during the show and afterwards hails a taxi and takes her to the Pheasantry Club for a late supper. They are ushered into a private room and sit facing each other across a starched linen cloth set with gleaming cutlery. Cynthia plays with her napkin, folding and pleating it nervously. She feels almost shy now that the show is over. The music had caused such a rush of emotion in her—she realizes she has come to associate the songs with her longing for Christopher, but now that he's here she doesn't know what to say. He will think her silly and romantic if she speaks her feelings openly. This is ridiculous, she tells herself, we have four children and he feels like a stranger. She asks his opinion of the show.

"It was pleasant. But to tell you the truth, Darling, I was watching you more than the singers." She looks up at him in surprise, and blushes. He reaches across the table and takes her hand. "I've missed you. How are the children?"

"Jimmy ran away from school. He was terribly upset about something. He wouldn't tell me. My brother Richard came over and talked to him."

"I hope you sent him back right away. It's like falling off a bicycle, you must remount immediately before you lose your nerve."

"I had to keep him home for a while. He had a very serious asthma attack. But he did go back, Richard took him. I think he was upset that he wasn't chosen for the football team."

"Ah," Christopher nods.

When the food comes Cynthia hardly touches hers. She gazes at Christopher until he begins to laugh self-consciously.

"What's the matter?" he asks. "Why d'you keep staring at me?"

"I love you so much."

"I love you too, Cynthia. You're my wife."

"You'll never leave me, will you?"

"Of course not. We've made our vows, for better or worse, in sickness and in health ..." He smiles, leaving it unfinished, and reaches again for her hand across the linen tablecloth.

Later, in their hotel room, Cynthia lies in bed watching light patterns on the ceiling as traffic speeds by on the wet streets. She fingers the lace ruffle of her new nightgown, bought two weeks ago at Kendal Milne's and saved for tonight. It's my fault, she thinks, for expecting too much of him. Things will be better when he settles down. He's only just arrived after all. When we get home ... when we get used to each other again ... when the children come home for the holidays ...

Chapter Thirty-Two

BURNT TOAST

ONCE BACK ON home turf Christopher is in a hurry to get his writings to press. He travels to the Manchester office of Kingdom Press where he duplicates his *Letter from Sydney* as a thirty-two-page booklet, in lieu of the Herald newsletter which has failed to appear during his absence. For the first time in his life he finds himself short of money. He is now maintaining three properties—Meadowside, Kingdom House, and Rue de Manoire—and the Press office—as well as footing the bill for travel expenses for himself and Baker.

He had thought that Baker would have taken charge of the newsletter. No matter. He manages to purchase enough petrol on the black market to fill the tank of his Aston Martin, considering it an essential investment if he is to distribute his booklet. "Strike while the iron is hot," his father had always said—only one of many such clichés which seem to govern Christopher's thinking increasingly these days. In fact Britain has become a cliché-driven nation, he thinks, as he fills his briefcase with copies of the *Letter,* still smelling of fresh ink. He remembers how the prison guards had huddled around the wireless in Walton Gaol listening to Churchill:

> Let us therefore brace ourselves to our duties, and so bear ourselves that, if the British Empire and its Commonwealth last for a thousand years, men will still say this was their finest hour.

And at Peveril Camp, after the German defeat at El Alamein:

> ... this is not the end. It is not even the beginning of the end.
> But it is, perhaps, the end of the beginning.

The man must have been in his cups to have broadcast such rhetoric to a people in the throes of devastation during an unnecessary war. And now his revered sayings are so oft-repeated that they're engendering a new generation of non-thinking Britons who idolize the man as their saviour. The victors always write history and thus control our thinking, Christopher muses. All the more reason to hurry with the dissemination of his message to Britain. He will hand-sell the newsletter at the modest price of one shilling.

When he arrives at Petworth, Christopher finds the driveway knotted with weeds and the garden a tangle of brown stalks collapsing on themselves. As he walks around to the back of the house he sees that his agricultural plots are completely overgrown. He returns to the front and opens the unlatched door to an entry hall in disarray, with muddy footprints on the carpet and thick dust on the furniture. A vase of dead roses stands in dank water on the window ledge, its funeral home aroma fighting with a smell of burnt toast. The sitting room door is closed; he almost knocks but then he thinks, no, this is *my* house. He turns the brass knob, opens the door, and sees a woman sitting with her back to him. When she turns he recognizes her. It is Judith Kern.

"Where's Arthur?" he inquires.

"Oh, good morning to you too!" she exclaims, jumping up. "We were just saying we haven't seen you for a while."

Christopher hears laughter from the next room, light and girlish, then a male voice, with a Cockney accent.

"Give it 'ere, Margie. Come on, you burned it again, you don't know how to cook."

"You have guests?"

"Well yes," Judith says matter-of-factly. "The girls have their young men here."

"And your brother? And Mr. Unsworth?"

She shrugs. "Off philandering, like you. Where've you been?"

Christopher is opening his mouth to reply when Marjorie and Alma burst into the room with two lads in pursuit. Marjorie is waving a piece of blackened toast in the air, shouting: "Catch me if you can!" But she stops, her mouth agape, when she sees Christopher.

"Mr. Brooke!" Alma exclaims. "We thought you'd emigrated."

The young men stare at him. The taller one flips the hair out of his eyes and hooks his arm protectively around Alma's waist. Christopher steps forward, his hand outstretched, but neither take it.

"That's the only future for us," the Cockney lad says, snatching the burnt toast from Marjorie. There's a scuffle and more giggling before he resumes. "I'm going to Canada, and I'm taking Margie and the baby wiv me. I've 'ad enough of this damned country."

"Jumping ship, are you?" Christopher says. "Why not stay and work with us towards a united ..."

"We're going, Mr. Brooke," Marjorie says. "We've decided. Britain is finished."

"Come on, I'm 'ungry. Back in the kitchen where you belong," the boy says, smacking Marjorie's shapely bottom.

"We have to talk to you about the running of the house," Alma says.

"Yes," Judith says. "There are bills overdue—property taxes, electricity, gas, telephone, not to mention the expenses on the livestock. We've had to sell the cow, and the goats. I think there are a few sheep still in the field, aren't there, Alma? We couldn't catch them."

Alma shrugs and leans against her tall suitor who tries to pull her in the direction of the kitchen, but she resists and he throws up his hands and leaves the room.

"I left a sum of money with Captain Baker," Christopher says.

"Oh, he's gone to Jersey for a looooong holiday," Alma says. "Last we heard he was running a boarding house."

"After all that talk he didn't want anything to do with the baby," Judith says.

"What baby?" Christopher asks.

"Margie's little Baker baby," Judith replies. "Where were *you*, Mr. Brooke while my poor little sister was being taken advantage of? You led us to believe we would be a community here at Petworth, with every-one sharing ...″

"We're three girls all alone here, Mr. Brooke," Alma says.

Christopher turns and starts walking towards the hall.

"And he emptied the safe before he went if that's where you're going," Judith calls after him.

Christopher stops short, but maintains a calm exterior. "What about Mr. Unsworth?"

"We haven't seen him for months, have we Judith?" Alma says.

Renewed laughter is heard from the kitchen as Christopher sinks into the sofa and opens his briefcase. He feels unable to process this information. The sinking feeling in his gut takes all his attention. Later —I will think about it later, he tells himself as he fans a display of the *Letter from Sydney* booklets on the table in front of him.

"I thought you might sell these on the streets of London," he says. "Only a bob."

"What d'you think we are, street-walkers?" Alma asks. "And who's Sydney when he's at home?"

Christopher clears his throat and speaks with some difficulty. "I must remind you young ladies that you are here at the invitation of the Legion of Christian Reformers. Kingdom House is not meant as a ... a youth hostel. It is the headquarters of ...″

"No! More like a nursery," Judith exclaims. "Thom told Margie you were going to fill the place with children. Well, you can't have our baby girl. Margie's taking her to Canada."

"Thom thinks girls are useless anyway. He wanted a boy," Alma says. "And while we're at it let me tell you, Mr. Brooke, we were better off at the Women's Land Army Hostel before we ever met you and got taken on as slave labour in this dump!"

Christopher raises his hands to his ears and shakes his head slight-ly. "I'll be moving on now," he says, leaving a pile of booklets on the coffee table, securing the rest in his briefcase. "Perhaps your young men can help with the distribution of ...″

"We told you, they're *emigrating*," Alma shouts.

"Of course. I really must be going."

"What shall I tell my brother?" Judith asks. "To telephone your house about the bills?"

"No," Christopher says quickly. "Tell him I'll contact him, by telephone or … better still, by letter here at Kingdom House. When do you expect him?"

Judith shrugs. "Couldn't say. Perhaps next week?"

Christopher closes the door quietly behind him and walks down the cracked pathway. He places his briefcase on the passenger seat of his car, then walks around and lowers himself into the driver's seat. With his long legs somewhat cramped in the Aston Martin he begins the drive northwest across England towards his home. But he can't return there. Cynthia has thrown him out. He doesn't know exactly where he is going, and he is without funds.

THREE

A man who has been the undisputed favourite of his mother keeps for life the feeling of a conqueror.

—SIGMUND FREUD

The line between good and evil does not separate nation from nation or class from class, it runs straight through the heart of every human being.

—ALEKSANDR SOLZHENITSYN

Chapter One

THE ONLY BOY

N ANCY BROOKE HAS never understood finances. Since her husband's death she's had to learn how to write a cheque. She has placed her financial affairs in the hands of the National Westminster Bank in whom she has confidence. Each quarter a man with a briefcase visits her, a Mr. Trimble, and talks at length about money matters. She smiles politely and pays no attention to what he is saying. It is not within her realm. She is grateful that there are men who spend their days taking care of such matters but she has no wish to know about it.

She offers the neatly dressed, well-groomed gentleman a glass of sweet sherry and joins him, taking tiny sips from her own glass. She remembers when the craze for cocktail cigarettes came in and all the women began smoking at dinner parties. She would take one of her favourite pink, gold-tipped Russian Sobranies, dip it in crème de menthe and suck on the tip. She had no interest in smoking, it was simply a game she played, dissembling, always dissembling. It was required of one.

Nancy is surprised when Mrs. Ward ushers Christopher into the drawing room. She notices that he looks rather pale and has an air of the traveller about him since his return from Australia, as though he cannot settle, having been in motion so long. His petition for financial help takes her by renewed surprise.

"But what about your inheritance, dear?"

He explains at length, something about investments, money tied up, a temporary loan. Of course she must help him. He is her son. And he has never asked before. If James were alive he would surely make the same decision. Nancy glides across the room to her writing desk where she settles herself for the ceremonial task of writing a cheque. This important act of signing away money disturbs the flock of butterflies that reside in her tummy, their wings brightly coloured like her pink Sobranies. Her fingers tremble slightly as she grips the fountain pen and watches the blue ink flow into the wetness of her signature.

"One hundred pounds, to be returned within six months, with interest."

They are Christopher's words, dictated to her, the scribe. This is the language of men—abstract, numerical, dense with hidden meaning. She does not know what "interest" means, what the concept behind it is— something, she thinks vaguely, to do with ... Shylock, the merchant of Venice, the cutting of flesh? The butterflies cluster below her corset. She supposes that word gives importance to the matter—a matter of "interest" to all concerned. An engagement.

She records the transaction carefully in the ledger supplied to her by Mr. Trimble, and with a flourish she lays down her pen, neatly capped, turns to Christopher, and hands him the little piece of paper. For a moment she has felt important, though out of her depth, and now she returns to her familiar role, giving Christopher a motherly smile.

Cynthia has told no-one, hoping that he'll return to her when he's come to his senses. She's been through his wardrobe and chest of drawers and found that he's taken very little with him, which reassures her. At first she'd felt proud of herself for being decisive, being in charge of the situation for a change, asking him to leave instead of losing control and ending up crying. She'd felt certain of his return in the first few days, but now she's not so sure. Doubt is creeping in and she's beginning to regret the drastic step she's taken. Only a temporary separation, she tells herself, but she has no way of contacting him. She feels helpless again, just as she did when he'd gone off without her, travelling all over the world.

His homecoming from Australia, so eagerly anticipated, had proved a sad disappointment as they'd quickly settled into the old patterns of behaviour. She'd done her utmost since his release to draw him back into the family. She'd resisted her parents' censure, feigned enthusiasm for his messianic ideas, forgiven his long absences, hoping against hope to nurse him back to health by accepting his mistaken passions.

But when his absence had outweighed his presence, when she'd been left without financial resources, and when his homecomings had fallen so far from her expectations, Cynthia had become accustomed to managing without him. Hadn't she already survived his three years of internment? That was the thin end of the wedge, and now during this watershed year of 1947 it has been driven in to the hilt. She has perhaps become hardened in her suffering, taking on the appearance of an independent modern woman coping with it all, but in her heart she yearns to step into the past and to move forward in that way. She has only to play the waiting game, as she has always done.

"Home again in the rain," Birdie sings as the children bustle into the hallway, shaking themselves like dogs.

"If it keeps on raining we won't have snow for Christmas," Jimmy says.

Cynthia has driven down to Westonbirt to bring the girls home for the school holidays, and they have collected Jim at the train station in Stockport.

"Where's Daddy?" Charlotte asks, glancing across the hall for the familiar sight of his hat hanging on the rack in the corner, with his coat on the peg below it.

"We'll talk about that later," Cynthia replies. "Now come along and take your bags upstairs, but don't go into the nursery. Katie has German measles."

"I want to see her," Birdie says.

"You can't. She's still infectious."

Sandra appears in the corridor leading to the kitchen, her head on one side and one leg twisted around the other. There is a hesitant smile on her face, like a plea.

"They're still here," Charlotte says, not quite a question.

"Of course. Vera and Sandra live with us. Say hello to her."

"Hello Sandra," the girls chorus, and Jimmy goes over and kisses her on the cheek. The little girl squirms as a strangled sound escapes her throat. Then he pinches her arm and she gives a sharp little cry.

"Welcome home, girls and boys!" Vera says cheerily, coming up behind Sandra, pushing her forward.

"Don't use the plural," Jimmy says. "I'm the only boy."

"Don't you get clever with me," Vera says and turns to Cynthia. "Katie's been a very naughty girl, hasn't she Sandra? She's been out of bed, hopping around, spreading her germs."

"Oh, that child," Cynthia says, clicking her tongue with annoyance.

Later, as they gather in the sitting room, Charlotte asks again about her father.

"He's … gone away," Cynthia says evasively. "But I expect he'll be back."

"When?"

"I don't know any more than you do," she says. "We'll have to wait and see."

She's knitting a long red scarf, the wooden needles clacking against each other, her fingers flying as she wraps the wool back and forth, knit one, purl one—moss stitch.

"Are we having Christmas at home?" Jimmy asks.

"Granny and Grandpa Blackwell have invited us to the Woodlands."

"Daddy too?"

"Oh, will you be quiet! Now I've lost count of my stitches."

Chapter Two

RETRACING THE STEPS

CHRISTOPHER DOESN'T KNOW where he is going as he revs up his car and leaves Dinglewood, the childhood home that is filled with memories for both him and Alice. They picked bluebells in the woods with Nanny Darlington, and chased each other through the maze shrieking and laughing. He drives as though on automatic pilot, in a pleasant haze of nostalgia, west towards Warrington and Liverpool, unconsciously retracing the steps of his first journey into internment.

He is brought into the moment by a screaming siren, and when he glances in the rear-view mirror he sees the flashing lights of a police car bearing down rapidly. His first instinct is to accelerate, but instead he pulls over and waits with the window rolled down as a baby-faced officer approaches. Christopher hands over his licence and waits while the pudgy young man peruses the licence.

"And where are we off to in such a hurry, Mr. Brooke?"

"I was … distracted. Didn't realize I was over the speed limit. My mistake."

"Oh ho ho." His fleshy lips pucker. "A pricey mistake, Mr. Brooke. I'm afraid I'll 'ave to ask you to wait 'ere while I write up a ticket."

He walks back to his police car with the licence clutched in his hand. Christopher waits for what seems an interminable period until the boy returns, like a teenager at a masquerade ball in that uniform, Christopher thinks. He takes back his licence and the flimsy paper with its triple layer of carbon copies, more like the receipt for a purchase at Kendal Milne's than a speeding ticket. He stuffs it in the glove compartment and, without another word, starts up the car and pulls away, keeping his eye on the speedometer. The police car tails him to the next traffic circle where Christopher, unable to face the dense warren of Liverpool's city streets, takes the exit north onto the Southport road, shaking the police car but with the uncomfortable feeling, as he passes through Skelmersdale and Ormskirk, that he's been had.

Only when he arrives in Southport, slowing the car to a town crawl, does his mood change. He drives down Lord Street and loops round Park Road and onto the Promenade where he opens his window and breathes in the sea air, as a long-absent feeling of joy bubbles up in his throat. He drives past Marine Lake and the Floral Hall where he'd heard Mosley speak before the war. Cynthia had been with him, and he'd felt so proud to have her at his side in Mosley's presence—his very own Cynthia.

He drives on past the Zoo and Pleasureland, humming to himself a ditty that has stuck in his brain, one of Cynthia's favourites— "This is my lovely day, this is the day I will remember the day I'm dying." Rather morbid lyrics, he thinks, as he drives down the coastal road until he realizes suddenly that he's heading out of town. He does a quick U turn and drives back to the centre, looking for a hotel for the night. He is so very tired.

Next morning he makes inquiries about a boarding house and is directed to Mrs. Beasley's establishment at #10 York Terrace. It's a three-storey Victorian house with several rooms on each floor. He is shown to a room at the top with a view of a church steeple, and the Irish Sea just visible in the distance. He turns from the window to see Mrs. Beasley's teenage daughter still hovering in the doorway. She is a buxom girl with red cheeks and a sulky mouth.

"Towels on your bed, tea at five thirty sharp, breakfast at seven thirty," she says. "Will there be anything else?"

"No, thank you," he says, bemused by the girl's curtness, so like Cynthia's when she'd told him to leave, holding herself rigid, as though she might collapse if she gave an inch. Her arms had been tightly crossed below her bosom, thrusting it upwards, but she would not meet his eyes, and he, so weary of their repeated arguments, had been unable to summon even the mildest protest.

He sits on the bed and surveys his room. It is an attic with a low sloping ceiling so that he has to stoop, which he learns after a couple of hard knocks to his head. Temporary, only temporary, he tells himself.

He spends the day walking around Southport and is delighted to run into his old friend Cliff Byrd.

"Heil Hitler!" he says enthusiastically, greeting Byrd with the familiar salute, forgetting that it was "Hail Mosley" they used to say.

"How's the piano playing?" Cliff asks, huddling into his coat against the chill November wind.

"No time for that now," Christopher says. "Besides I'm temporarily without a piano."

"I always admired your piano talents. One of the best in my humble opinion." Byrd is about to take his leave, but he hesitates a moment and turns to Christopher. "I shall always remember that concert when you played the *Moonlight Sonata* with all of us sitting in the Grand Stand at Ascot Camp and a full moon rising over the Race Course."

They part on good terms, but whenever he sees Cliff in the ensuing months, the man raises his collar and hurries away.

As Christopher enters Mrs. Beasley's dining room and sits down for the customary Lancashire High Tea, he is met with five pairs of staring eyes. He introduces himself and is immediately befriended by a middle-aged man with a florid complexion and a bulbous nose.

"Henry Braithwaite," the man offers enthusiastically and proceeds to introduce everyone at the table. They are a troupe, it seems, in town for the Christmas pantomime.

"Cinderella this year," Braithwaite says. "I'm one of the ugly sisters, can't you tell? And that there is my sister, Clorinda" — he indicates with a flourish of his meaty hand— "Otherwise known as Dennis."

Dennis is an effeminate-looking fellow with a disturbingly direct gaze, Christopher notes, as the man rises, bows, walks around the table and stands beside him, presenting his hand at a foppish angle, clearly waiting for Christopher to kiss it. Christopher offers his own hand as though to shake Dennis's.

"Ooh Griselda, 'e doesn't want me," Dennis says, sobbing in a falsetto voice.

"Come on, Mr. Brooke, don't be a cad. Give the girl a kiss," Braithwaite says.

Christopher has never questioned the British tradition of cross-dressing, having grown up with the annual Christmas pantomime, especially the favourite Cinderella, and has simply accepted the bawdy, deep-throated clowning of Cinders' Ugly Sisters, but now that he is confronted with the men behind the façade, he feels dreadfully uncomfortable. He reaches for the teapot and, with great concentration, pours himself a cup, then busies himself with the milk jug and sugar bowl as Dennis pouts and minces back to his seat.

"We're opening at the Variety Theatre this weekend," Braithwaite says. "I can get you a complimentary ticket if you like. Mrs. Beasley's coming, aren't you, love?"

"Wouldn't miss it," she says, plunking a plate of steak and kidney pudding in front of Christopher. "Mushy peas and tatties on the table."

Cinderella looks under her lashes at Christopher, catches his eye, and winks. He sees his opportunity and launches into his Message.

The next day Christopher rises early and after a greasy breakfast of fried eggs and fried bread, which he takes alone, for it is early and the troupe has not yet woken, he walks to the centre of town and visits the Lord Street Labour Exchange. First, he peruses the bulletin board which shows very little in the way of employment, so he waits his turn to speak with the counsellor, a pert young woman with a mass of curly red hair and a way of tossing her head that sets her curls atremble. She wears green fingerless gloves and a woollen scarf because the day is just beginning and the tiny radiator is barely lukewarm. As the man ahead of him shuffles out Christopher presents himself, rubbing his hands together to warm them.

"Bad time of year for a job," the girl says.

"It's rather urgent. I'll take anything that pays."

"There's nothing at present, I'm afraid. Not till after Christmas." She pushes a piece of paper across the counter and hands him a pen. "Fill this out and I'll register your application. My advice is come back in mid-January."

"But that's more than a month away."

The young woman hugs herself, rubbing her arms for warmth, her shoulders almost up to her ears so that her shrug is lost on Christopher.

"Do you think there'd be more opportunity in Liverpool?"

"Market there's flooded with Irish Micks, en't it?"

She turns away to fill a kettle at the sink in the corner and plugs it in, then she begins to rinse out the teapot which is still clogged with yesterday's tea-leaves.

Christopher fills out his application, places it on the counter, and leaves. He spends the morning walking briskly around town, re-marking to himself upon how easily accessible everything is by foot in Southport. He will look into the sale of his car in the New Year, but for now he needs it.

Chapter Three

DOUBLE-CROSS

H E ARRIVED ON Christmas Eve and Vera opened the door to him. "Ooh, just in time to play Father Christmas," she said. "Forgot your keys?"

Christopher ignored her remark, not wanting her to know that he no longer had keys to his house. He hung his coat and hat in the hall and was about to pick up his shopping bags when the children, like dogs sensing an intruder (now that old Percy was dead and buried behind the coal shed), came surging out of the sitting room.

"Dad! I knew you'd come," Jimmy said, while Birdie and Charlotte hugged him tightly, Birdie singing: "Jingle bells, jingle bells, jingle all the way ..."

"Steady there, steady," he said, laughing.

"Can we go carol singing, Daddy?" Charlotte asked.

"Remember last year's tobogganing?" Jimmy said.

"But it's a green Christmas this year," Charlotte said.

Christopher's eye was caught by Katie, sitting half way up the stairs, hunched in her pyjamas. The child put a finger to her lips. She had seen Cynthia standing in the sitting room doorway.

"Welcome home, Darling," Cynthia said, smiling radiantly as she walked over to embrace him. "What am I going to tell Mother? She's expecting us tomorrow."

"Never mind that now," Christopher said, smiling back at her. "I've brought presents."

His words set up a clamour, the children jumping up and down, tugging at him and delving into the shopping bags. Cynthia reached up the stairs and swung Katie down—"You naughty girl, out of bed again," she said lightly, and somehow they all got to the sitting room, moving slowly in a throbbing mass, and collapsed onto the sofa.

"Pleeeeease, Daddy," Jim said, "let me open my present now."

"No, no," Christopher said, "we must put all the presents under the tree for the morning."

"Let them, Chris. They've missed you so much," Cynthia said.

But it was herself she was thinking of, her own misery and uncertainty. She was so relieved she hardly dared to think beyond the moment. Look at him, she thought, his old self, and it all flashed through her mind unbidden, all that had passed since that fateful summer day when the Detective Inspector had rounded the corner of their back garden. How had he known? Why had he not come to the front door?

If she'd been able to live it over again she would have been waiting for the intruder, she would have called to him as he tried to sneak in by the side gate. She would have made him come to her, and she would have told him her husband was not at home. There would have been time to hide him, to arrange for an escape with the three children to America. They'd been there before, sailing to New York. It was a familiar place. Everything would have been different.

"A cricket bat!" Jimmy said, gasping.

"Made from the finest willow," Christopher said.

"That's what the Head uses for caning," Jimmy said.

"A cricket bat?" Birdie asked.

"No, stupid, a willow cane," Jimmy said, beginning to wheeze. "Look! It's signed by the Brylcreem Boy himself. How did you do it, Dad? How did you get his autograph?" He began to wheeze heavily, running his fingers over Denis Compton's signature, then he hugged the bat and sniffed at the fresh willow.

"Calm down, Jumbo," Cynthia said. "You know you mustn't ..."

Her words were lost in a flurry of exclamations as the girls opened their gifts—a big doll for Katie with a mass of curly brown hair and long-lashed blue eyes that opened and closed; a kitchen set for Birdie with a little stove and kettle, a tea-set, an ironing board and a toy flat-iron; and a dress for Charlotte in pink chiffon with matching shoes.

"Chris, you've spent a fortune!" Cynthia exclaimed.

"But nothing for Sandra," Katie said, sticking her tongue out at the child standing in the doorway.

Christopher picked up a box of Black Magic chocolates from under the tree and walked over to the door.

"But Chris, those are for ..." Cynthia began.

"Never mind," he said. "They're for Sandra now."

The girl looked up at him, disbelieving, then she snatched the box and ran.

Once the children were in bed and Vera had gone up to her room, they found themselves alone amidst the debris of paper bags and Christmas paper, sitting a few feet apart on the sofa.

"Where are you staying?"

"Southport, in a boarding house."

"Oh, Christopher," she said.

"It's all I can afford for now."

"Have you gone through all that money?" The silence that followed confirmed her fears. "What are we going to do? I was relying on you to transfer a sum into our bank account. There are bills to be paid, you know."

"I'm going to get work in the New Year."

"You'll have to sell one of those properties. I don't know why you ever bought that place in the Channel Islands. It's so far away, and you never go there. Sell it."

"I can't. Thom Baker and his family are living there."

"Is that where all your money's gone, into Baker's pocket?" Cynthia's eyes narrowed. "You bloody fool! You let him double-cross you."

"He's been a good friend to me, Cynthia. Don't slander him."

"I will if it's warranted. You have no judgement about people, Chris."

"Thom is an unusual fellow, I'll grant you that. And he's not always ... trustworthy." He leans forward and takes Cynthia's hands in his. "But he saved me in my darkest hour, Cynthia. I can never forget that."

She stared at him intently, at a loss for words, but he could see that her mind was working, gnawing on the matter. "You'll have to sell the Petworth house."

"I can't do that. It's our headquarters for the Legion. In any case I'm not the sole owner."

"But the Legion has come to nothing. How many followers do you have? Just those empty-headed girls, and Baker who's made off with your money."

"I asked you not to talk about Thom in that way."

"I'm sorry, but we have to do something. We have a family to support and the children's school bills to pay."

"I won't sell Kingdom House," he said. "I have contacts in Australia with good people who may come here and take up residence at our centre."

"Can't you see, Chris? It's like a business venture that's failed."

"This is not a business venture, Cynthia. On the contrary, our message is a warning *against* the machinations of international finance. You've misunderstood me because you never listen to what I say."

"You can talk till you're blue in the face, Darling, but ..." Her voice became soft, conciliatory. "The fact is that Baker has been a very bad influence on you, and now he's swindled you out of everything we have."

"Always spouting your mother's words."

"I am not! She knows nothing about this. Give me credit at least for keeping our troubles to myself. I told her that you're in Petworth entertaining a large group of Legion members from abroad—a white lie for your benefit."

"Not such a lie. Once I get myself settled that could indeed be the case."

"Settled where? You belong here, Chris, with our family."

"It was you who asked me to leave, Cynthia."

"Yes, but ... it's not what I want."

"What *do* you want?"

Cynthia stared deeply into his eyes, and was about to speak, but she turned away and fixed her gaze on the glow of the fireplace.

"It seems I am unable to please you. You always want something more, no matter what I do. I may have better success living alone for a while."

"All right, go then!" She was on her feet in a second.

"May I sleep down here for the night?"

"As you please." She was already at the door, but she turned, her voice thick with emotion. "It's Christmas Eve for God's sake."

"Yes, and I came home for it, for the children."

"Presents for them and nothing for me!"

She slammed the door, and he heard her footsteps on the stairs, nimble and hurried, then directly overhead in their bedroom, then silence.

The children woke early and tiptoed downstairs. When they entered the sitting room to look under the tree for more presents they found their father asleep on the sofa. Birdie and Katie ran at him and landed on top of his sleeping form, bouncing and squealing until he woke laughing and hugged them to his chest, one in each arm.

"Now then, let me get up," he said finally.

"Why are you sleeping here, Dad?" Jimmy asked.

"It's very comfortable on the sofa," he replied.

"Were you snoring again?" Birdie asked.

"Oh, perhaps I was. Yes, that must be it."

Charlotte stood at a distance from the others, staring solemnly. She seemed weighted with more knowledge than her siblings, something which had taken her voice away.

Vera came down with Sandra, and they all trooped into the kitchen to make tea and toast while Christopher dressed. He was straightening his necktie as Cynthia entered the room. Her eyes were puffy and red, but he could find no words to comfort her. It seemed to him that they had been over and over it so many times, and he was tired of being in the wrong and unable to please her. He remembered that feeling at Latchmere where he had tried so hard to be reasonable and cooperative, but none of his explanations had satisfied them. In the end he'd felt like an animal being taunted in the cruellest way. It had destroyed his self-confidence and it was only at Peveril that he'd regained it in the company of good men. He must hold to that memory now and not let Cynthia hen-peck him.

"Are you going to your mother's?" she asked, playing nervously with the cord of her dressing gown.

"Mother's in London with Alice and Maurice."

There was an awkward silence in which neither of them knew what to say.

"I did bring you a present," he said. "It's under the tree."

She clicked her tongue in annoyance. "Wasting our money. There's nothing I need, except ..."

He raised his eyebrows, waiting for her to complete the sentence. Then the moment passed.

"I'd like to take Charlotte and Jim with me," he said.

"What!"

"Just for the holidays. I'll bring them back in time for the winter term."

"Jimmy can't go, not with his asthma. Archer Pearson would never allow it."

"But I could look after him."

"In a boarding house in Southport? Don't be ridiculous. If he has the slightest excitement he'll get an attack, then it'll turn to bronchitis. I won't allow it!"

"Charlotte's hale enough."

"She won't want to go. Ask her. See for yourself." There was something driving her, something hard and cruel that she had no command over. She felt herself digging deeper and deeper, sinking in. She opened the door and called: "Charlotte!"

The girl came hurrying from the kitchen and almost collided with Cynthia in the hall.

"What is it, Mummy?" she asked anxiously. She was thirteen years old, teetering between two worlds.

Christopher joined them in the hall, carrying his overnight bag.

"D'you want to go with your father?"

Charlotte stood with her feet together and her arms at her sides, her head slightly lowered. It was a position of defence she had learned at Westonbirt. "Where?" she asked.

"D'you want to go and live with your father?"

Charlotte bit her lip, her eyes shifting back and forth.

"Just for the holidays, Charlotte," Christopher said, smiling at her. "I could come and pick you up tomorrow."

"But you live here with us ..." she said.

"Not any longer," Cynthia said. "He's going to live in Southport."

The child's brow furrowed and her whole body stiffened until she was almost trembling.

"Well, yes or no?" Cynthia said sharply. "Do you want to go with him or stay with me?"

Charlotte seemed about to cry, but she didn't. She won her struggle, and she said in a very quiet voice, "I'll stay here with you, Mum."

Christopher barely reacted. Just the hint of a shadow passed across his face as Cynthia placed an arm around Charlotte's shoulders. She watched him put on his hat and coat, scarf and driving gloves, while Charlotte stared determinedly at the carpet. He stooped to give the girl a kiss before he left and she flung her arms around his neck and gave a single sob, then held her breath until he was gone. He hadn't tried to kiss Cynthia; he knew that she would have turned her face away.

As the door closed Sandra came running into the hall. "Toast's ready. Mummy says come."

They had taken to eating their breakfast at the kitchen table. Vera said it made more sense than carrying everything to the dining room or passing it through the hatch and picking it up on the other side.

"Too many rooms in this house," she said. "I've never lived in such a big house."

"Where's Daddy?" Jim asked. "Isn't he coming to breakfast?"

"*Shhh*," Charlotte whispered. "He's gone away."

"Where to?" A breathy whisper.

"Tell you later."

Birdie and Katie were chewing on their toast, Katie swinging her legs and kicking at the table leg.

"Stop that!" Cynthia said. "I've told you before."

"You're on edge," Vera said. "Has 'e gone again?"

"Oh, he'll come crawling back," Cynthia replied.

The news was out. Once the children knew, Cynthia had to tell her parents, and she had to tell Nancy Brooke, who took it in stride with the usual tremor in her otherwise steady bearing. All her concern was for Cynthia and the children.

"You must come to tea on Sunday," she said. "Before the children go back to school."

So they did, and they found their place names as usual lodged between the bunnies' ears, and they filled their plates with cake and sticky bread, but it wasn't the same. Nothing was the same once they knew.

"He might have gone to Kingdom House," Jimmy said. "Or South Africa, or Jersey?"

"He's in Southport!" Charlotte said as they knelt on the hardwood floor in the upstairs library, rifling through the books.

"He'll come back."

"No, he won't. It's different this time."

"How d'you know?"

"I just do."

Cynthia sat downstairs talking quietly with Nancy while Birdie helped Katie with a horse puzzle on the tray table, placing the tail, the hooves, the arched neck and mane in their proper places, and finally the body and the long face.

"I'm going to ask my parents to help me," Cynthia said.

"By all means, dear, but you must let me make my contribution. I helped Christopher with a cheque before Christmas, and now I must help you. It will be my first cheque of the New Year," she said jovially as she made her way to the writing desk.

Cynthia sat twisting her wedding ring round and round on her finger as Nancy carefully penned a cheque and recorded it in Mr. Trimble's ledger. When she was handed the cheque, Cynthia looked at the loopy writing, so meticulously executed in Nancy's familiar hand, and she began to cry silently, her head bent in shame.

"Oh, my dear, don't distress yourself," Nancy said, leaning forward to pat Cynthia's hand. "There, there. We must wait and see what will happen. If you run out of funds again you must come to me. I'll speak to Mr. Trimble and see what he suggests."

"Granny, can I borrow these?"

It was Jimmy with an armful of books about railway engines, and Charlotte behind him with *Black Beauty*, which she was to read for the fifth time.

Chapter Four

DOLLY MIXTURES
AND PEAR DROPS

C YNTHIA'S CHRISTMAS PRESENT from her husband was a recording
of Lizbeth Webb singing "This is my lovely day." She didn't listen
to it. She put it at the bottom of a pile of records in the sitting room
and tried to forget about it. This very particular gift was unsettling to
her because it meant that there was something at work in Christopher
of which she was unaware—a perception and thoughtfulness that didn't
show in his outward comportment, but had suddenly sprung at her,
taking her by surprise and making her feel that she had been unneces-
sarily harsh with him. She didn't know what to call her feeling, not quite
guilt, but more a sense of foolishness, as though she had misunderstood
everything.

She was confused by the constant nagging in her mind. Why
couldn't he give her what she really needed, that indefinable thing that
even she could not name? Just to *be* there with her, to be present instead
of miles away, lost in his fantasies; to talk to her about real things like
Mary Byrne had done, or even poor Vera who at least was cheerful.

On New Year's Eve Vera stepped out with a man she'd met, a war
veteran who had been injured in his shoulder but was well enough
recovered to lead her in the jitterbug which she had learned from a
succession of GIs. They'd been going out together over the past months
to dance halls and pubs—usually to the Nag's Head in Poynton—and
Cynthia was glad for Vera, and grateful on this particular evening for
a little time to herself.

Once the children were settled she sat at the hall desk and began to make a budget. There were bills and bank statements spread all over the desk and as she organized them into piles and began to add them up she realized that she could no longer afford to keep Vera. Dick Blackwell had agreed to pay the children's school bills and had pressed an additional five-pound note into her hand with a wink, but it became clear to her now that she would not only have to cut back on her expenses, she would have to find a job. When she told Vera that she and Sandra would have to look for another place, Vera dug her heels in.

"I'm not leaving," she said. "You can't do this to me."

"I'm sorry, Vera, but I can't afford your wages."

'I'll take a cut. 'alf me wages. 'ow about that?"

Cynthia shook her head. "You don't understand. I'm destitute."

"I'll stay on for nothing. I'll 'elp you. We can go into business together. I'll make cakes and you can drive them around and sell them door to door."

"With rationing? One egg a week? Don't be silly. And what about petrol?"

"There's always the black market. I know someone in Poynton who ..."

"Vera, please don't make this more difficult for me than it already is."

"But I need a home for Sandra."

"You can stay till you find something, but ..."

"Oh, thank you!" She grasped Cynthia's hands. "That's all I wanted to hear. You're my best friend."

"You must promise me you'll start looking next week. I can't afford any extras. Two more mouths to feed ..."

"You make us sound like ducks."

Vera got drunk that night, rip-roaring drunk, and she told Cynthia a few of what she called "home truths." It was the last straw. Cynthia threw her out. Vera's veteran came to fetch her in a taxi.

"First your 'usband, now me and Sandra. You'll be all alone and let's see 'ow you like that!"

When Cynthia went up to clear Vera's room she found boxes and boxes of empty bottles under the bed—gin, sherry, cheap wine—and more in the wardrobe stashed behind the evening dresses. Under the sink in the corner was a bag stuffed full of bloody brown sanitary napkins.

"Good riddance!" she said aloud, but there was no-one to hear. The children had gone back to boarding school and Katie, after her sixth birthday in early January, had started school in Bramhall at Miss Amy Barrowdale's Elementary Academy. It was so quiet in the house, so deathly quiet.

She went downstairs to the sitting room and moved towards the gramophone like a sleepwalker. She pulled the record from underneath the pile, slipped it out of its sleeve and placed it on the turntable. She wound up the player and set the turntable going, lifted the heavy, curved arm and set the needle on the outer edge of the record. There was a crackling sound, then the music began to play. Cynthia stood there sobbing as Lizbeth Webb sang, but she listened, yes she did, right to the end, then she slipped the record back into its sleeve and took it upstairs and put it in the wardrobe in Vera's room, at the back where the bottles had been, stuffed in with the stiff-netted ball gowns of her youth, so that she would not be tempted again.

She drove Katie to and from school, always arriving early in the afternoon to wait outside Miss Amy's, afraid that Christopher might turn up there and try to take the child. The school was on Patch Lane, a narrow street with a few small houses darkened by overhanging ash trees. One afternoon in late January with the sky already darkening and the street lamps not yet lit, so that she thought at first she was mistaken—but no, the short plump figure was unmistakable—she saw Mary Byrne wheeling a double pram with a little boy in it and another child at her side, a girl, holding her gloved hand. She was afraid that Katie might see her too and cry out, but if she did see she failed to recognize her. After all she'd been a baby when Mary walked out. It had all gone so fast.

Mary was chatting with the little girl and they were laughing. Cynthia supposed they were her new charges, a local family, but there was something about the three of them, something that made her realize with a shock that these were Mary's own children, that she was a mother now, and perhaps a wife. She hung back in the bushes with Katie until they had passed, then felt a stab of regret that she had not spoken up.

She would have given anything to return to France and find Mireille still living there, to don her black beret and walk by the Seine with her darling friend, to sit in the Café de la Paix in the Place de l'Opéra and eat ice cream with crème de cassis. Even to see Roger again.

The following week she started a part-time job in the newsagents in Poynton, selling newspapers and cigarettes to wounded men, and little bags of dolly mixtures and pear drops to the children. They let her leave early so that she could drive to Bramhall and pick Katie up from school. When Mr. Peplow paid her at the end of her first week she flushed with the same pride she'd felt in her brief office job in Manchester.

She didn't tell her parents. She knew there was no danger of being discovered because her father never went to Poynton, and her mother did all her local shopping over the telephone and had it delivered. She'd have to stop when the school holidays started, but it was something for now, something to help her survive and avoid the loneliness of her house, to stop her thinking about Christopher, though he was always there in the back of her mind eating away at her with his absence. If she had known where he lived in Southport she would have been in danger of driving over there, using up all her petrol ration. But what would she say to him? She would only find herself tumbling down that well of hopelessness again, waiting for the crash. It was foolish romanticism. She'd have to give it up and buckle down to this new way of life.

Chapter Five

BILLY BOY

"**H**ERE'S YOUR TICKET," Henry Braithwaite says, and plunks down a tattered envelope on Christopher's plate. "Two o'clock sharp for the Saturday matinée. You can bring Mrs. Beasley along in that sports car of yours. Eh lovie?" He winks at the landlady as she makes the rounds with her large brown teapot. "Would you like a ride in his fancy-pants car?"

"I'm afraid it's been sold," Christopher says. The Aston Martin had gone for a shockingly low sum, but the matter had been urgent, with only one prospective buyer, and two weeks' back rent to pay.

"Oh, then you must be flush," Braithwaite says quickly, his watery eyes rolling. "But our Cinders here was planning a Sunday afternoon drive with you, weren't you, ducks?"

"I'd as soon take a stroll," the girl says, reddening.

"Give us the marmalade, Clorinda," Braithwaite says with an exaggerated pout across the table.

"Ooh, get it yourself, you ugly bitch," Dennis says, clearly miffed about something.

Braithwaite exercises his boarding house reach and spreads a thick layer on his toast. "Care for some marmalade, Mr. Brooke?"

"Thank you, no, I've eaten my share of toast." Christopher laughs uncomfortably and gulps down his tea. "I must be going. I have work to do."

"Oh, a working man, are you?" Braithwaite feigns mock surprise.

"A writer. The writing life requires strict discipline."

"Discipline!" Dennis exclaims in a high-pitched yelp. "We know about discipline, don't we, Henry?"

"Enough of that, lad," Braithwaite says.

"I also play the piano. If you should need accompaniment at your rehearsals ..." Christopher indicates the old upright in the corner of Mrs. Beasley's dining room.

"Hear that, Cinders?" Dennis says with a screech. "He plays the piano! How about some private coaching after hours?"

"Mind you, you mustn't get Billy Boy jealous," Braithwaite says.

"He plays Buttons, my young man in the pantomime," Cinderella says, indicating a sullen young man sitting to her left. He has fine, mouse-coloured hair flopping over his forehead, and is deeply engaged with his teacup.

"I'll take you up on that," a young woman says, pushing back her chair and walking round the table. "Iris Headley." She shakes Christopher's hand. "Otherwise known as Prince Charming."

She has long shapely legs with the slimmest ankles Christopher has ever seen, and her dark hair swings onto her shoulders as she moves, a sheath over a perfectly shaped head. Her femininity is of a quality different from Cinderella's, Christopher thinks, and then he realizes what it is that attracts him. She resembles Cynthia, the refined and yet pithy nature of her.

"I have a solo in the second act and I've never felt that I have it quite right. Would you ...?"

"Indeed," Christopher says.

Iris nods. "I'll fetch the music."

"I'll accompany you," Christopher says, rising from his chair.

"Yes, that's what I'm after. Wait here," Iris says matter-of-factly.

He stands awkwardly, fumbling with his napkin, then folds it carefully and strides across to the piano which is missing several of its ivories and is horribly out of tune. They all stare at him as he launches into "This is my lovely day," playing by ear.

"He's an ivory tickler all right," Dennis says, fluttering his fingers in the air.

"And Iris is a man-eater," Braithwaite says, exploding into a gravelly laugh.

Christopher laughs alongside Mrs. Beasley in the balcony of the Variety Theatre, but he wishes he had Jimmy and Charlotte beside him. When Miss Headley suggests a drink after the show, he replies: "I'm not thirsty," as he had said to Eric Cartwright at the Midland Hotel in Manchester, but this time he adds: "And I don't indulge in alcohol."

"You can have a packet of peanuts then," Iris says.

"But you can buy *us* a drink," Dennis says. "You didn't really think it was a free ticket, did you?"

They are a large troupe, and heavy drinkers all, so Christopher has gone through an alarming amount of his car money by the time the pantomime players move on to the Preston Playhouse. But he has been able to engage at least one of their number with his urgent message, so he considers the beer money well-spent, in addition to the crème de menthe and cherry brandy favoured by the ladies. He has a convert, and a young one at that—a future leader perhaps. Billy Boy, whose brother had been killed early in the war, was bitter with regret for his own failure to join up.

"I was too young, you see, they wouldn't have me."

Christopher has impressed upon Billy that it was not his fault and has reassured him with insights into the futility of war.

"Keep in touch, Billy," he'd said, pressing a copy of *Letter from Sydney* into the boy's hands as he'd left with the troupe in mid-January.

But Christopher still hasn't succeeded in finding a job, and Mrs. Beasley's weekly rates are eating away at his savings, so he sets out on foot to find cheaper accommodations, which means that he will have to be responsible for cooking his own meals. He moves at the end of January, on a bitter blustery day. His room on Albany Road has no sea view unless he leans out of the window dangerously far, but he hears the waves pounding the shore from his bed at night, and it is only a short walk to the Promenade. When summer comes, he thinks, I will walk to the end of the pier and stand above the sea. He feels a surge of freedom just imagining it; then he remembers the woman in the green dress on the deck of the *Orcades*, her plushy mouth, her provocative words—"Look at the ocean, thousands of feet dropping beneath us, to the depths where no light penetrates, and where no-one has ever been." The memory unsettles him unaccountably. "Seventy percent of the earth's surface awash, absorbing our sins." What did she mean?

His room is sparsely though adequately furnished. There's a kettle and a frying pan, and a set of cutlery and dishes quite sufficient for one. "This will be my office," he says aloud as he takes his briefcase and spreads its contents on the wooden table. He sits and arranges his papers, takes up a pen, and begins his letters. He writes to George Unsworth, addressing the envelope to Kingdom House; and to Arthur Kern at the same address. He writes to Thom Baker at Rue de Manoire, an enthusiastic letter with news of his latest convert. There's a number of people he'd met in Australia, and to all of them he gives news of his new home in Southport—a fertile area for the message, he writes—urging them to contact him by letter as soon as possible so that they might resume their vital and collaborative work. Finally, he pens a short note to each of the three women in his life—Alice, Nancy, and Cynthia—informing them of his whereabouts.

He takes his ration book and goes out to buy a few supplies—a twist of tea, half a pound of sugar, a loaf of bread, four ounces of margarine, a small piece of cheddar, a tin of corned beef, and an egg. He marvels at how many details there are to remember; things he's never noticed before because others have taken care of them. He buys a can of Vim and a dishcloth, a box of Persil to wash his clothes, a bottle of dishwashing soap, salt, a jar of Horlicks, a pint of milk. He spends too much money on what he fears may not be essentials, and finds himself without a shopping bag, carrying it all in his arms, then the milk leaks down his trouser leg just as he turns onto Albany road.

Once inside the house and secure in his room he begins to whistle the Beethoven piano duet that he and Alice played as children. He stocks the shelf above the electric hotplate with his purchases. There's no refrigerator, so he places the milk bottle and the margarine on the window sill to keep cool. He expects to be in different circumstances by summertime, perhaps even back in his own home with Cynthia and the children, but he cannot let himself think of that just now.

When everything is arranged to his satisfaction he decides to go out again, realizing from his restlessness that this new room feels much like a prison cell. But I'm free, he tells himself, those days are over. He spots Cliff Byrd across the street on Albert Road and calls to him, but Byrd hurries on, seeming not to have heard him. Perhaps Latchmere affected his hearing, Christopher thinks, as it had temporarily affected his own sight, rendering him blind for two days.

He recalls his evenings in the pub with the pantomime troupe, the warmth and camaraderie of it and he wants more than anything to re-create that, to be amidst the noise and bustle of people in a closed space, so he hastens to the Fox and Goose on Lord Street and joins the lunchtime crowd jostling at the bar. Christopher orders a Stone's ginger beer and a Scotch egg. He stands at the bar sipping his drink and tries to engage people in conversation, but everyone seems intent on getting their lunch and gulping it down before returning to work. A young fellow in a cloth cap is bobbing up and down trying to get the bartender's attention.

"What will you have?" Christopher asks. "A pint of bitter?"

He orders the pint, pays for it and passes the foaming mug. "Cheers, mate," the lad says, tipping his cap to Christopher who launches into a speech similar to the one that had so engaged Billy Boy. But this fellow is already hurrying away, and Christopher sees that there's a girl wait-ing for him at a table in the corner. He watches them as they share the beer, and he feels more alone than ever despite the press of bodies around him. Someone nudges him just as he's lifting the Scotch egg to his mouth and it slips from his fingers and rolls onto the floor where it is crushed into the carpet.

In the evening the house on Albany Road comes to life like a war-ren with scurrying sounds in the walls and footsteps on the stairs out-side Christopher's door. Someone turns on a wireless and he hears the low rumble of a BBC commentator. He'd like to have a wireless himself, but he'll have to manage without it for the moment. He misses his piano too and Cynthia's record collection of popular songs which they would listen to in the evenings, but he has a recital of classical music in his head, the music that kept him sane in his cell at Walton Gaol in those first weeks.

There's a sudden scuttering across the ceiling and he looks up and realizes that it's only a woman's quick steps he hears, crossing the floor in high heels. She sounds like a ballroom dancer. He wonders if he might venture upstairs and knock on her door and introduce himself but decides to wait for a chance encounter on the stairs. A smell of frying onions creeps teasingly under the door as he busies himself with the preparation of a corned beef sandwich accompanied by a pot of tea. Afterwards he reads from the Bible and is comforted by his own recitation of the Lord's Prayer. He considers taking a trip to Jersey but first he must gather a following here in Southport. He stands in front of the mottled mirror above the sink to practice one of his speeches, studying his own facial expressions and gestures, repeating certain phrases until they are exactly right.

"... clear beyond all doubt that the Hell of Mammon which mankind has endured for thousands of years ..."—modulating his voice for dramatic effect—"... to inevitable destruction with its unrepentant followers ..."—working towards a climax of conviction—"... that the Kingdom of God on Earth will rise triumphantly and ..."

"Shut up, you bloody lunatic!" shouts a muffled voice through the wall.

Christopher is unable to summon a suitable retort. He moves cautiously to the table where he takes a fresh pad of paper and sits a moment, his pen poised:

I sit in my office. The desk feels smooth beneath my fingers. The light of a streetlamp shines into this room where the smell of cheap paint seeps through the walls. There are scurrying sounds in these walls, which are stained with dampness. Under the small sounds, drowning them out, is the pounding of the ocean. This room is twice the size of my largest cell, more comfortable than my camp accommodation. But without the camaraderie of my fellow men I am unbearably lonely.

That night he has a strange dream. There is a woman standing with her back to him by a kitchen sink. In the background a gramophone plays a familiar tune. There is a knife on the counter. He picks it up and plunges it into the woman. She cries out and spins around, but before he can identify her she turns into a snake, twisting and writhing in pain. He tries to move, but he is paralyzed, and then the serpent spits at him, a poisonous fluid spurting from its mouth.

As Christopher wakes to find his pyjamas wet and sticky, he realizes that the woman in his dream was of course Cynthia and a rogue wave of emotion breaks over him. He lies there gasping and realizes that she will always belong to him, and he to her. But it is too soon to approach her after the rejection of Christmas. He has felt but not understood her anger. He must be patient and work to prove himself, to her and to Baker, by gathering a following in Southport.

Chapter Six

UNDERWATER

Spring 1948

WHEN MY SIBLINGS were away at boarding school Mum took me for swimming lessons on Saturday afternoons. She would hover at the poolside, blocking the sun that filtered through the high windows of the indoor pool at the Buxton Hotel. It was almost spring and she was as determined that I should learn to swim before the summer holidays as she had been that I should read. Swimming seemed to me a magical thing, quite unlike the struggle of learning to read. The instructor wore a white cap and a navy-blue bathing suit with white piping, and she had a whistle dangling from her neck for emergencies. She supported me with her hand under my stomach as I floated precariously, trying not to get water up my nose.

"Kick your feet, Katie ... one two three, one two three ... relax your knees and ankles." Her voice echoed past the quivering diving board and into the high green ceiling.

I kicked and wobbled, filling up with fear as I watched Mum's legs out of the corner of my eye, her nylons and high-heeled shoes, the slit in the back of her tweed skirt. Even when she was out of sight I could hear the click of her heels as she followed us on our slow progress through the water.

As we approached the deep end the instructor let go of me and I panicked, flailing with my arms, inhaling water as I went down. It was silent under the water, and everything trembled. My hands and arms were liquid with wavy contours, and I felt like a mermaid with my eyes open and my hair streaming out from my fishy head. What could I discover here in my magic realm as the silence of the water enclosed me? Babies are natural swimmers. How had I become a non-swimmer? Was I going to drown? I felt quite calm until strong hands lifted me to the surface of the pool and floated me to the shallow end, gulping and spluttering, with water streaming from my nose.

"There's nothing to be afraid of, Katie. You can do it," the rubber-capped instructor said. "But perhaps that's enough for now. Same time next week."

No, no, I want to go under again, to sink into the silent watery world, to swim with my slow limbs in the green quietness. That was it. I was an *underwater* swimmer searching for something there, something that did not exist outside the water. It was the air and the light of the world above that confounded me, and where I began to drown.

Chapter Seven

THE DARK WET HEART

I T WAS IN the early part of the summer that Leonard came home to
the Walkley Estates. The twins had just turned three and they were
all agog at his artificial leg. Des came running to get me and tugged
at my skirt. He wasn't one for talking, he was backward in that department, and Clio talked more than enough for both of them. He took my
hand and dragged me across to Meg's place, and there was Leonard
sitting on the front step in the sunshine—I recognized him from his
photograph in Meg's caravan.

"What ya lookin' at?" he asked gruffly, glaring at me as though I
were an intruder.

"Well, good morning to you too," I said. "And welcome home to
the Walkley Estates."

I was having none of his chip-on-the-shoulder nonsense this sunny
day. He'd recovered well enough from his physical injuries with help
from the doctors, but now he had to do the rest himself. He put his head
down and continued with the strapping on of his leg, with Clio at his
side, patting the leg and grinning.

"Want one, want a leg," she said, tapping at it with her fist like a
woodpecker.

"We'll get you some stilts," Leonard said. "That's the closest you'll
get to artificial legs. Come on then, 'elp me up, take me for a walk."

I could see that he wanted to be alone with my children, so I wiped

Dessie's nose and told them both to be good and sent them off across the fields with Len. Meg came out of her caravan and we stood and watched our little group setting off. It was marvellous to see how the children helped him when they came to the stile. They had him up and over in no time. If I had gone with them it would have been a humiliation for him. I suppose he thought himself not a man without his leg. His sweetheart from before the war had gone off and married a GI and moved to America, Meg said. Wars make people move around, just like me moving to England, and my sister too. Deirdre never would have left Ireland if Eamon hadn't got himself killed. And now what's happened to her, I wondered, for I'd had no news and I worried about her all alone in Liverpool, which was bigger even than Dublin, I'd heard.

Meg and I sat in the sun for a while, taking advantage of the rare bit of warmth. England is like Ireland in that way, always covered in fast-moving clouds that tease you with their movements, giving quick glimpses of the sun before they plunge you into the shade again. Meg was unusually quiet that day, puffing on her cigarette, flicking the ashes into the grass. I could see how the years had ravaged her face. It was full of lines and wrinkles, with a dullness to her eyes that had not been there before. It was prison had changed her. For all her brave talk of friends on the inside Meg had been broken by that place. We'll never hear what really happened in there, I thought, for it must be an unspeakable horror to be locked up with criminals, deprived of your life for months on end, subject to the will of others like a child but without a child's freedom to roam as my children were doing now with Lennie, getting the best of him.

"He's a bugger to live with," Meg said, stubbing out her cigarette in a sardine can set beside her on the step. "I'm doing me best for 'im, but it's not easy." There was a sad expression crossed her face then. "You should have known our Lennie before the war, Mary. He's not the same lad now."

I thought of Mr. Brooke and wondered what he'd been like before the war—not that he'd fought, but he had been wounded in his own way. I remembered my evenings in front of the fire with Cynthia, and I wished I'd had the boldness to ask her more questions about the

Master, for he was a curious man who nagged at me for the unsolved puzzle that he was.

"Have you 'eard him screaming in the night?" Meg asked, bringing me out of my reverie.

"No, not a thing."

"Well you know how small my caravan is. He wakes me up every night, and when I go to 'im and try to calm 'im he starts flailing his arms around. Clipped me a good 'un last night. Look."

She turned the other side of her face to me and there was a big bruise on her cheek bone under her left eye.

"You want a nice piece of beefsteak to lay on that."

"Good luck with the rationing. Only meat I've seen lately is a grisly piece of mutton, old as the 'ills, too tough even for a stew."

I fetched a cold cloth and held it to her poor face. I had a bad feeling about Meg, about what would happen to her, and then I thought you're being foolish, Mary Byrne, worrying all the time about Meg and Deirdre, and Reg with his hacking cough, and Mam and Da growing old in Ireland, and I determined to get myself out of the rut of the Walkley Estates, and go on the train to Liverpool and see for myself how my sister was doing.

I left the twins with Meg and she was glad of their presence for they had in only two weeks become fast friends with Lennie. Cliodhna liked to polish his leg every morning with a dustcloth while Desmond stroked his hand and gave him little kisses all the way up his arm. He wouldn't allow the rest of us to touch him, not even his mother. But he was getting used to that leg and with the children's encouragement he'd learned to walk so well that you'd hardly know the difference until he rolled up his trousers to take the twins paddling in the stream that ran behind the Estates. I'd pack them a picnic and off they'd go, Clio chattering like Birdie used to, while Lennie and Des studied the ground before them.

Reg was working on a building site in Stockport, operating the cement mixer. With all the bombing there was years of work still to do on reconstruction. It was a regular boom, Reg said, and good enough for the likes of him. We'd grown accustomed to each other and rarely had our spats now. When you live with someone day in day out you start to take them for granted. Some days I felt I'd hardly seen him, even though I'd sat across the table from the man at breakfast, lunch and supper.

But I did not truly see him for he was too familiar—which is not to say that I didn't sense his feelings. If Reg had something on his mind I could feel it before he entered the room. And he did have a lot on his mind and some nights he couldn't sleep because of it. "What's wrong?" I would ask him. "Come on now, Darlin', tell me what's eating at you." And then he would come out with it—the horrors he'd seen on Home Guard duty, searching through the rubble for bodies after the bombings.

"Sometimes we'd end up with a whole lot of body parts and we'd 'ave to somehow form the bodies for burial so that the relatives could believe that their loved ones were more or less intact for that purpose, once they were dressed like. But it were a difficult task, Mary, with so many pieces missing. As one of the mortuary attendants said: 'A proper jigsaw puzzle.' And if you was too lavish with one, then another would have too many pieces missing. I'm sorry to burden you with it, love, but I can't get those pictures out of me mind."

Sure enough after that telling it was my burden too, but with the sharing of it his pain lessened and then he would be able to sleep. When I remember Reg now he is curled around me in our bed, where we lay together like two bright stars in the darkness. That is where our real life existed, the dark wet heart of it, with a beat so strong that it blocked out everything—the children, the day's work, our humble surroundings, and even the horrors of war. That is how I got through my days, by remembering that I would be lying with him at night like a queen in my realm, receiving the worship of a man who became his true self in such moments and who I had almost missed in my pursuit of something better.

I took the early train to Lime Street Station and from there I found my way to the Royal Liverpool Hospital for that is where I expected to find my sister. It is a grand building and I felt quite lost there, but I walked up to the Reception desk and asked for Deirdre. The girl had to inspect her nails first and it was only after chewing off a hangnail that she saw fit to look into the directory of names.

"Nurse Brennan," she said. "Obstetrics." Next she consulted a big chart on the wall and turned to me with an apologetic smile. "Bad luck. This is her day off."

"She lives at number 49 Mount Vernon Street, near the Sacred Heart Catholic Church. Can you direct me there?"

"We're not supposed to give out staff addresses."

"I'm not asking for her address. I already have it. It's the directions I need."

She sighed. "You'd better go up and ask on the Obstetrics ward. Walk to the end of the lobby, take the west wing lift to the fourth floor, turn left and follow the signs."

At the Obstetrics reception a friendly girl gave me a smile and asked if she could help me. I repeated my request and she said: "You're Deirdre's sister? But you don't look a scrap like her."

"Deirdre got all the good looks in the family," I lied, not mentioning my other beautiful sisters and our three handsome brothers, our Brendan, dead nearly a year and a half from a gunshot wound to his neck. She brought out a notepad from her desk under the counter and drew me a map of the area, far more than I needed to know, but at least she remembered to mark down Mount Vernon and the Sacred Heart, so I was soon on my way, praying that Deirdre would be home.

It was not a long walk, which was just as well because it was beginning to rain and I had no brolly with me. It was one of those light summer rains, just enough to refresh the grass and set everything sparkling, and somewhere for sure a rainbow, though I could not see it.

I found number 49 and walked briskly up the path, which was covered with those crunchy white pebbles you find on graves, and that were all over the front where the garden should have been. When I rang the bell a curtain drew back in the bay window where a woman stared out at me then pulled the curtain again quick as a whip. I stood there a long while and no-one answered so I rang the bell again and after another minute or two a child opened the door, a girl of seven or eight years, her hair in plaits tied up with red bows.

"Me mam says go away we don't want any."

"Any what?"

"Anything."

"But I'm looking for my sister, Deirdre Brennan."

The child stared at me, her tongue examining what might have been new teeth in her head, or perhaps a gap where one had been.

"Is there a lady lives here with black hair and blue eyes, and an accent like mine?"

She nodded and turned away. "Mam," she shouted. "She wants Mrs. Brennan."

"Upstairs, turn right, second door on your left," a voice shouted.

I closed the front door behind me and pushed past the child who was blocking my way. The stairs had those brass runners that hold the carpet in place but the stairs were narrow and the carpet threadbare and slippery, so that I almost lost my balance at the top, but I righted myself and followed her directions to the second door, where I knocked and heard footsteps on the other side. When Deirdre opened the door I burst into tears and grabbed hold of her.

"Why can't we live together? We're family," I said when I had recovered my voice.

"It's my job, Máire. They're training me as a nurse."

She looked awfully pale, and tired around her eyes, but there was a sparkle to her in spite of it. We sat at her table by the window which looked onto the white pebbles and Deirdre put on the kettle and gave the pot a pinch of tea leaves. I could see that she hadn't much in her cupboard.

"Have you news from home?" I asked.

"A letter from Siobhan. The children are doing fine. They're in school."

"What about Mam and Da?"

"Patrick is running the farm single-handed now, because Da has lumbago and he can't get out of his bed some mornings."

"That's why I haven't heard from him. Oh, Deirdre, we should be at home to help them. Poor Mam, he'll be giving her a hard time if he's in pain."

"She can stand up for herself."

I heard the hardness in her voice. She and Mam had been at logger-heads since Deedee turned thirteen. That was when the devil entered her, Mam said. She'd always been a wild one, but then she became a rebel and all. It's her should've joined the IRA with Brendan. She had to get married, pregnant at sixteen and Eamon only seventeen himself.

"This is my day off," she said for she was still in her dressing gown.

"That's what they told me at the hospital."

"You were there! Isn't it a grand place?"

"Is that where you found your surgeon?"

"I broke it off with him, Máire, right after the termination. I wasn't having any more of that." She sounded bitter though it had been more than a year since her visit to Meg. She spooned sugar into her tea and stirred thoughtfully, a little smile spreading on her face. "I have a lovely man now."

"Married?"

"Divorced."

"Well, that's an improvement."

"He's going to look after me."

"I hope so. He's lucky to have you." In the silence that followed I could sense a hesitation in her, which was unusual for Deirdre who had always been ready to spill the beans.

She clutched at her stomach. "I'm not feeling well, Máire."

"What is it? Something you ate?"

She shook her head. "I wanted to get my training done first. I'll have my certificate in September, but if they find out before then ..."

Her voice trailed off and I had a flash of my old feeling that something bad was going to happen to my sister.

"Deirdre, you're not ...?"

"I am."

"How long?"

"Four months."

"Too late for ..."

"I wouldn't do that again," she said fiercely. "I've made my confession and I've been absolved, Máire. I go every day to the Sacred Heart and pray for this baby. I won't have any more dealings with baby killers."

I didn't like to hear her speak of Meg in that way, because I knew what my friend had suffered for helping the likes of Deirdre, but I said nothing for after all she was my sister and I loved her dearly and would love her little one too and help in every way I could.

"Is he Irish?"

"A little bit."

"And is it a little bit you're expecting? Is he or isn't he?"

"Not really, but he's all for home rule. And he's a great talker."

"I can imagine for myself the bit of him that's Irish."

"It's a healthy bit."

We laughed then, and I threw my arms around her again and almost knocked over her tea cup.

"When's the baby due?" I asked.

"End of November. D'you think I can hang on at the hospital till the end of September, Máire? If they put me out before I get my certificate I'll have to start all over again."

"Don't ask me. It's different with twins. I was big as a house at five months."

She gasped and put her hand to her mouth, staring at me with those deep blue eyes which had turned almost purple with the upset she was feeling, so I had to comfort her as best I could.

"If you wear loose clothing and keep your strength up you'll be alright, Deirdre. As I remember you didn't show until the last minute with the others."

"But this one might be bigger, with a different father, you see. He's taller than Eamon. I've been trying not to eat too much, but ..."

"You dirty eejit!" I jumped up off my chair I was that mad with her. "You mustn't starve the baby. It's a crime. You might as well abort it as starve it!"

Her face went pale, and I thought with a shock how I'd become the big sister by virtue of my place here in England and my status as a married woman, and so I resolved to be gentler with her.

"Come on, Darlin'," I said. "Get yourself washed and dressed. I'm taking you out for lunch."

"Oh, Máire, I'm that hungry," she said, almost drooling at the mention of a lunch, and I wondered what she'd been feeding on for there was nothing but an empty packet of digestive biscuits in the cupboard where I got a better look while she was dressing.

"Will we go to the hospital cafeteria?" she asked, bright as a button now that we were on a mission.

"Isn't there somewhere else?" I asked. "After all it's your day off, isn't it?"

"There's a nice pub ten minutes away that does meals. That's where I met him. I was there with one of the student nurses and he came over to talk to us."

"Will we see him there?"

"He's away just now—on business."

"What sort of business?"

"Travelling salesman."

"And what does he sell?"

"Oh ... books ... little travel books and the like."

She wasn't forthcoming so I let it drop. The poor girl could hardly walk for hunger, hanging onto my arm all the way.

"Remember the tale of Diarmuid O'Donnell?" I asked as she laid into her fish and chips.

"Shoved his dinner plate in the drawer when a neighbour came knocking," Deirdre said, spluttering and covering her mouth.

"'What's that nice aroma I smell?' says the visitor."

"'Not a scrap of food in the house,' says Diarmuid."

"That's right, and himself on tenterhooks for the neighbour to leave."

"And your man spinning out his visit, then watching Diarmuid through the window pull the drawer open and set to at his plate like a dog at his dinner," Deirdre said, laughing.

Though I'd dredged up the old family joke to entertain us I could see now that it was in bad taste to make fun of a person's hunger. We'd never gone hungry on our farm despite the size of our family, and here was my dear sister starving in England, the land of plenty as we had supposed, all alone without the support of a man. What sort of fella gets a girl pregnant and then goes away on business leaving her with an empty cupboard? I thought then of the Master and his wife and how he'd been away so long but through no fault of his own.

"I want you to take me to the grocery and we'll stock up for you."

"Oh, Máire, you can't afford it."

"Don't argue with me," I said. "Reg is working. We can help you. And when you stop work here in Liverpool you come and live with us on the Estates."

"But ..." She looked at me with her wounded eyes and I could see in them all her hopes for the future.

"If you've nothing better by then, that is. Families should be together."

And so I finished my day in Liverpool and took the train back to Cheadle Hulme, standing all the way for in those days the trains and buses were always crowded, due to the petrol rationing. There was a queue a mile long at the bus shelter so I walked home from the station, deciding along the way to renew my discussion with Reg about finding a job for myself, for it was clear to me that I must help Deirdre and send her a little money each month. Besides, I was ready for a new adventure.

Chapter Eight

AT THE WOODLANDS

IN AUGUST MUM took us to St Annes for our summer holidays—a week crowded together in a rented room. The Lancashire coast was a Mecca for British holiday-makers in those days. But why did she suddenly choose to take us there? We knew no-one in St Annes, and we usually went to Grandpa Blackwell's summer house in North Wales.

Lytham St Annes looks directly south, across the mouth of the inlet, to Southport, so it may have been a comfort for her to feel that he was nearby; perhaps a feeling of flirtation, a game of chance continuing into the day after our nightly excursions to the bingo parlour. When someone still inhabits the world there is always a faint hope that one day ... maybe ... you might glimpse him on the street, see him running for the bus ... the shock in her breast each time she saw a tall man, wearing a brown fedora, disappearing around a corner. We spent our days on the beach swimming and building sandcastles. My eyes were bloodshot from the salty sea.

"Keep your head above water where I can see you, Katie," Mum would insist, but I couldn't stop diving. It had become a compulsion.

One night we drove to Blackpool to see the illuminations and watched holiday-makers walking along the front *oohing* and *ahhing* at dirty postcards of weak little men clasped to the bosoms of big women with breasts ballooning out of their skimpy swimsuits. Charlotte was already fourteen and disappearing into the adult world; Jimmy too at thirteen, though chubby and awkward and still wheezing, seemed beyond my reach. Birdie had turned ten and didn't want to play our games anymore.

Whenever I asked about Daddy they all turned away as though they hadn't heard me, so I asked louder and Charlotte *shushed* me, then I would see her whispering with Jimmy. Six was a lonely summer, squinting into the sun and the sparkle of the waves, watching the magic disappear as the clouds came over, while Mum sat on the beach gazing down the coast, her eyes visored with her hand. It was the summer of shirtwaist dresses with belts and full skirts and ruffled bibs.

Our mother was very beautiful. She and Charlotte were often taken for sisters, not only because Charlotte shared her dark beauty, but because she was heavy with responsibility, carrying some secret knowledge that gave her the weight of adulthood. I knew there was lots she could tell me, but she wouldn't. She did, however, look after me better than my mother did. Charlotte cared for me, and so I suppose did Cynthia, but *her* care took the form of worry which became a burden for us all.

There was a man on the beach that summer who stood out from the crowd in his straw boater, striped jacket and white trousers. He walked by each morning and tipped his hat to our mother and on the third day he stopped to converse with her. We watched them from our vantage point in the sea, and Jimmy ran up the beach to intercept, but the man had gone by the time he arrived.

"It's all right, Jim," she said. "He was just talking about the weather."

But after that he was always buzzing around her. We called him "The Wasp" because of his jacket which had yellow and black stripes, and we worried about our mother, but we needn't have because she didn't take him seriously. She never took men seriously. She belittled them and made jokes of them. And there were many over the years because she was beautiful, though strangely unavailable.

She took us to the cinema two or three times a week during the school holidays and we would sit together in a row chewing toffee, absorbed by the flickering screen, struggling to escape by tunnelling underground with the prisoners of war. Thudding feet jolted our bodies as men vaulted over a wooden horse in the prison exercise yard, and we would hold our breath, cowering in the tunnel beneath it, waiting for the Germans to discover us. The tension of those life or death situations united us as we left the cinema like sleepwalkers, reliving the plot, digging deeper under the earth, down a long tunnel to safety or sudden death with a bullet in the back, arms flung out, clinging to an electric fence; or else the long panic of smothering as the tunnel caved in.

The summer passed and in September there was the usual flurry of preparations before sending my siblings back to boarding school. Their school trunks were packed with neatly labelled pyjamas, underwear, socks, and the requisite tunics, ties, blouses and gym knickers. I hated it when they were gone, leaving me alone with my mother. I think she hated it too. The house was so quiet, but as it turned out things were to be different that year.

I was enrolled at Cheadle Hulme School which had a bigger playground and more children than Miss Amy's, and it was on Guy Fawkes' Day, November 5th, that Kay Chatterton caught fire and began to haunt me. One of the boys had been throwing burning sticks in the darkness and Kay Chatterton had caught fire because she was wearing a frilly nylon dress. She'd run in circles, waving her thin arms and screaming until someone had thrown a blanket over her. They'd rolled her up and carried her away to a car which already had its engine revving, and when Kay came back to school near the end of term she was transformed.

I stared at her pale puckered skin, her scarred mouth and soft pleading eyes. She was like someone back from the dead, and I had to keep a distance from her, uneasy with the initial we shared—the three flaming sticks of a K flying into the night, falling on the bonfire where the Guy was burning. My mother said that I was not to stare at her, even though she looked like a war victim, like Hoddy-Doddy who stumbled around Poynton village like an idiot. He'd been driven mad by shell shock in the First World War and had gone back for more in the second and had been burned up in one of the planes they manufactured at A.V. Roe down the road from our house.

I was often in the car with my mother, driving back and forth to school, or from our house to Granny's, waiting for Mum while she dashed into the shops. She wouldn't let me out of her sight. She was afraid that someone would kidnap me, she said. I must on no account leave the school playground or get into a car with anyone I didn't know. Who could the phantom kidnapper be but my father, a strange man, made stranger by his absence? Absenteeism, I had learned, was punishable because Mum often kept me home from school. My father was permanently absent which gave him an air of mystery. I dreamed of diving to the ocean floor to find him. I knew that once I got past the darkness I would discover a place flooded with light, like the Blackpool illuminations, and that it would be alive with fishy creatures, and my father would be there waiting to take me in his arms.

We moved to the Woodlands in November, just after Kay Chatterton's accident, because Granny was having an operation for women's troubles and Mum had to look after Grandpa who was also unwell. There were people in and out of the house all day—nurses, the doctor, my aunts and uncles. During her long recovery Granny required complete quiet, so I kept out of her way; I was the devil's spawn—living evidence of Granny's lack of control over my mother.

It was in Granny Blackwell's house that I launched my career as a spy, utilizing my skills of invisibility and silence discovered earlier at Meadowside, and honed during long evenings shivering on the stairs at the Woodlands, listening to the cadence of adult voices coming from the drawing room. It was in the middle of one of those winter nights that Grandpa had his second heart attack. There was a rustling of dressing gowns, slippers slapping the floor, a clamour of frightened whispers. The night was suddenly charged with an atmosphere of towering anxiety as though the house would burst from it and scatter all over the garden, down to the woods where generations of family dogs were buried, and over to the deserted stables where the uncles had kept their horses until they'd married and left home.

I heard Doctor Pearson's clodhopper boots on the stairs, taking them three at a time. The Woodlands had two flights, divided by a landing where one of Granny's statues stood on a pedestal beckoning to its companion in the downstairs hall. In summer a bowl of roses sat next to that statue, shedding fragrant red petals on the window-sill. When I heard the doctor's booming voice, lower than usual, from Grandpa's bedroom, I ran down the corridor in my brother's cast-off pyjamas and hid in the box room which had been the maid's bedroom before the war when Granny'd had live-in help. I was safe in there, squeezed in amidst the stored remnants of Grandpa's travels to Egypt and India, to Africa and South America—anywhere that railways were being built and fuel injectors required for steam engines. The curtains smelled musty as I huddled against the window frame, waiting for the threat of death to pass.

When the crisis was over I came out of hiding more secretive and vigilant than ever in the perilous territory of that house, now made more dangerous by the addition of an electric chair lift. It operated on a pulley to transport Grandpa up and down the stairwell because he could no longer manage the stairs. He needed help getting in and out of the chair, which had a bar across the front to stop him falling out, and there was a gate on the upstairs landing where my mother stood panting after running upstairs to let him out.

There was so much that could go wrong, so many accidents that could happen, so much to worry about, and the house had to be deathly quiet during Grandpa's recovery, so I escaped into the garden and played in the woods amongst the gravestones commemorating Peko, Teddy, Mitzi, Chang and Rex, while my mother ran up and downstairs twenty times a day bringing Grandpa beef tea to build him up and Senna pods to keep his bowels open. She also delivered messages from Granny. And newspapers to entertain him. That is how I heard the news about my father.

Chapter Nine

THE GHOST AT THE WINDOW

November 1948

WELL, I FINALLY got my job at the A.V. Roe Aerodrome. Reg had
to agree, didn't he? After all, it was my own dear sister was
needing help. Des and Clio were already four years old and
running Lennie's life for him, so they had their own private baby-sitter,
and since he was living on a veteran's pension he refused my money
and I reckoned it was a point of pride for him so I backed off and kept
my mouth shut and vowed to give the extra to my sister.

First day out they gave me a set of overalls and put me on the assembly line for the Avro 707. It was a great hulk of a thing shaped like
a triangle with a long pilot's cabin pointing out front. Lord knows why
they were still building bombers with the war over. Reg said Britain
had to be ready for anything, and who might think to attack us next
—Russia?

"You'll have to tie up your hair, Mrs. Wilkins," the supervisor told
me. She had a face like a hungry rat and a nose to match it. I could see
from the start that she didn't like me. Had some ideas about "the shifty
people from the Estates" and a few opinions about "the bloody Irish"
too, so I was doubly damned. Might as well have been a Tinker and
the brown bunny that my Da teased me for.

But the girls on my team made up for it. They were a grand bunch
and one especially who became my best friend. Harriet worked alongside me. She'd heard the supervisor snipping at me and she made a face

and said not to worry about that old crotchet and handed me one of her own scarves to tie up my hair. It was a bright red banner with polka dots, cheerful as Harriet herself who was a lively girl and always ready for some fun. Mavis was the quiet one. We had regular tea breaks and a nice lunch room looking over the runway, and Mavis would sit at our table with her chin in her hand, gazing at us with her dreamy blue eyes. She didn't say much but I had the impression she was taking it all in and savouring our company.

My only complaint, aside from the watchful eye of the rat-faced crotchet, was the noise and exhaust fumes as they tested the aircraft. But you get used to everything, and it was a blessing at the end of the day to walk away from the factory and turn onto Woodford Road where I could hear the birds sing and their rustling of leaves in the hedgerows.

The next time I went to visit Deirdre it was with a bundle of pound notes in my handbag, and I was proud to be able to buy her a nice roomy dress for her final weeks. I was that mad with her when she told me she'd been binding her stomach and breasts to hide her condition until she'd received her nursing certificate.

"Well you have it now," I said. "So you can come home with me and have your baby there."

But she was determined to stay in Liverpool even though she was no longer working and had only her baby to think of. It's a wonder that little soul saw the light of day, but she did, born two weeks early in the middle of November. The Catholic Services took care of my sister and put her into the Royal where she was looked after by nurses who knew her.

"Come home to us, Deirdre," I said as I sat at her bedside with that scrap of a baby in my arms. Barely six pounds she was. "You can take the old caravan for yourself, and we can have our dinners together like a family."

"I want my little girl to have a chance to know her father."

"Well, where is he?"

"He came to see us yesterday."

I knew she was lying from the way she avoided my eyes, my darling Deedee who never had cause to utter a false word to me until now.

"We've decided to call her Fiona."

"That's a grand Celtic name," I said, trying to sound cheerful, but I could see the sadness in my sister's eyes, and I cursed the man who'd taken advantage of her and failed to live up to his responsibilities. I was lucky indeed to have my Reg, as solid a man as you could wish for. And I thought to myself that perhaps Deirdre's beauty was a curse, for sugar will draw flies, but a plain loaf of bread will attract a hungry man.

I soon forgot the reason for starting my career at A.V. Roe for it had many benefits aside from the money. Often as not I would walk part-way home with the girls. Mavis lived alone with her widowed mother who had lost her two sons in the war.

"I'm desperate to get away," she said. "But I can't leave Mum after all she's been through."

"C'mon, Mave, come dancing with me and Trev on Saturday," Harriet said. "He's got a friend who's looking for a girl. Not much to look at, but he's a grand dancer."

"I can't leave Mum all alone on a Saturday night," she said. "I'm all she's got left."

Harriet lived on Chester Road, past Cynthia's house on the way to Poynton. I asked if she knew the Brookes, and she rolled her eyes and said: "Who doesn't?"

I didn't let on that I'd worked for them. I didn't want to contaminate myself with their reputation now that I'd made my way in England as a respectable married woman, and a mother. But I longed to see Cynthia again. I still missed our late-night conversations and the feeling of closeness we'd had during the war, at least until the Master came home. I knew in my heart of hearts there was no going back, but one day when we got out early I walked with Harriet half way down Chester Road.

"I need to stretch my legs," I said. "And the twins are safe with Lennie."

As we passed #132 with its name—*Meadowside*—written on the gatepost by the pampas grass and the old monkey-puzzle tree that Birdie had wanted so badly to climb, I glanced out of the corner of my eye, half afraid that I might see someone at the scullery window. But

there was no car in the driveway, and besides, the house had a neglected look about it and the garden where I'd replanted the roses and
azaleas all overgrown now with weeds. We walked on and I parted
company with Harriet when she turned off on the road to Poynton,
then I turned back and ventured through the gateway of #132.

The crunching of my feet on the gravel alarmed me for I thought
that any minute someone would come to the front door, so I sneaked
down the side lane by the garage and into the back garden. There was
the greenhouse, a tangle of old tomato vines, brown and shrivelled,
though they'd clearly borne fruit for they were tall and had fought to
get out of that glasshouse before they died. I walked through the vegetable garden to the fence at the back, bordering on the field where we'd
had our summer picnics, and I looked over my shoulder to the back of
the house, thinking that I might see her at one of the windows. That's
when I had the shock of my life, for it wasn't Cynthia I saw but an old
woman with long white hair, standing at the window of Jimmy's room.
Her chin was resting like a child's on the windowsill, and I knew it at
once for the legless woman Charlotte had seen. Then the face was
gone. So there it is, I said aloud, the house is deserted and the ghosts
have taken it for their own. I wondered where had the Master gone,
and Cynthia and the children.

I hurried away as though someone were chasing me, and with a
panicky feeling in the pit of my stomach which made me think that
something terrible was going to happen. I remembered the fear I'd felt
in that house, the dreams I'd had, and Cynthia's sadness with the cigarette smoke curling around her in the evenings. I thought how foolish
I'd been, landing in the first job I'd tried for, entering that doomed
house and letting the fear of the place overcome me with no protection
against it. I was mighty glad when I reached the Walkley Estates, a
place full of life and noise, and found my little Clio chattering away at
Lennie and Des.

Chapter Ten

A WIDER AUDIENCE

C HRISTOPHER HAS BEEN living on Albany Road for nine months and in that time his savings have dwindled to almost nothing despite his efforts at joining the work force. He has worked as a day labourer on various construction sites during the summer of 1948 but, though physically fit, he is not manually skilled, his physique being more attuned to sports than labour, besides which, he's been fired from several jobs because of his proselytizing, which has drawn violent reactions, forcing Christopher to defend himself. Though his training as a boxer has proved useful he has nevertheless suffered a black eye and bruised ribs. Working men, he's discovered, have no sense of decorum. Unable to speak their minds, they resort to fisticuffs.

"What are you, a blooming storm trooper?" a lout had screeched at him last month, shaking his fist as Christopher walked down Lord Street in breeches and black leather boots. He keeps his hair closely cropped, though he notices that many of the young men of Southport are beginning to sport longer hair.

He remembers the old days of dress-up with Alice, and how their mother would take them into Manchester to be photographed, him in his sailor suit and Alice in a fairy costume with a frilly skirt and a wand in her hand. He remembers the masquerade parties at the Cartwright's, the Cinderella dances in Manchester, and the dance halls he frequented, dressed to the nines in white tie and tails, with his shoes shined, and always a willing partner in his arms.

He's been dancing again, with that girl he met and took for a prostitute. There had been two girls, one of them strikingly beautiful, seated at a table in the corner of the pub. What were they doing there? The women he knew did not frequent such places without a male chaperone. His need had been so great. It was a matter of health, and he'd thought that with a professional woman it would not count as infidelity, but when he'd tried to pay her she'd thrown the money back at him, a little spitfire like Cynthia. To make amends he had invited her to the Grafton Rooms and she had proved an excellent dance partner. They hadn't talked much, it had all been physical, like a long spell he'd been under, something about her arousing in him a vague memory of the girl who had worked in his house and with whom he had conversed in the kitchen one morning.

The familiar world is slipping away. He feels like a man alone on a raft drifting out to sea with nothing to anchor him. He has tried to return to farming but there is little work of that sort around Southport. He thinks of travelling to Jersey to work on the land there, but Baker has not replied to any of his letters. He has received a terse note from Cynthia telling him to come to his senses, nothing more. He takes comfort in the knowledge that she is informed of his whereabouts and could at any moment knock on his door should she come to *her* senses. Alice has written a loving and sisterly letter, counselling him to take good care of himself and to visit her in London whenever he can. And from his mother comes a hand painted card of an African violet, the envelope containing pressed rose petals from her garden with a message of undying love.

George Unsworth has written with distressing news about the Petworth property. Kingdom House has been raided by a local vigilante group and subsequently closed down by the police, though Unsworth fails to reveal for what reason. The young ladies, he says, had vacated before the incident occurred, and consequently he has sold the property. It turns out that he in fact had a fifty-one percent ownership and therefore did not require Christopher's permission for the sale, which was a hurried affair, he writes, the house going for a price much below its true value due to the neglected appearance of the place, for which he clearly holds Christopher responsible. "To wit, there will be no funds forthcoming," Unsworth writes, "all proceeds having gone to cover the outstanding bills and expenses etcetera pertaining to the property."

The idea comes to him in the night. He sits bolt upright, wide awake, staring into the darkness. He gets up and switches on the overhead light with its dim bulb and peers at his diary to check the date. He suspects that he is beginning to need eye-glasses, but that is out of the question for now. His vision will have to wait. With the grey morning light he takes his brolly and strides down to the railway station to purchase an advance ticket. He will take advantage of the long trip to London and visit Alice while he is there, staying overnight before the big day. He will write to advise her of his arrival.

On November 10ᵗʰ Christopher packs a small bag, including copies of his *Letter from Sydney*, several *Kingdom Herald* newsletters, *Aryan Testament*, and a more recent book — *The Bishop Said Amen* — documenting his 18b detainment experiences — which he plans on giving to Alice. He sets out on his journey to London, changing trains in Liverpool.

"Christopher!" Alice exclaims as she opens her door. "What a lovely surprise your letter was." An expression of concern crosses her face. She hasn't seen him for a while and ... "Of course you must stay the night, Darling. Stay as long as you want." Something about him is changed; she can't put her finger on it. Perhaps his clothes are a little worn. But their embrace is strong and reassuring, reminding Alice of a lifetime of affection for each other.

"What brings you to London, Chris? You wrote about reaching a wider audience. Do you have a speaking engagement?"

"You'll see Alice, everything will come clear in time."

"Oh don't be a tease! Are you coming to live in London? You could always stay with us while you're looking for a place."

His niece and nephew come running into the front room and the little girl drapes herself on him, her soft arm around his neck, while the four-year-old boy brings his train set to show Uncle Chris. He feels a pang of longing for his own children, and immediately thinks of the other one coming. If he had planned it better he could have stopped in Liverpool to see the girl. He regrets the whole incident now and his prolonging of it beyond that first encounter—the dancing, the weekly visits, her seductive body after his long deprivation, never thinking that she would not protect herself.

He has betrayed Cynthia in a way that he finds unforgivable in himself; this is what has prevented him from going to see her and the children. He can't face any more lies, and he can't face her anger and the pain she would surely suffer were she to find out. She had told him once, and he'd never forgotten it, that she could not bear an infidelity, that she would never be able to forgive it. Perhaps the girl will return to Ireland when her baby is born. That would be best, he persuades himself.

"Chris, you're miles away! Come on, Darling. Come to the table—we have fish pie for supper," Alice says cheerfully.

Just then Maurice arrives home from work. She must have known his exact time of arrival, Christopher thinks. They live a calm, well regulated life, as he once did himself. Maurice is stiff and formal in his greeting, wary of Christopher since his detainment. All the more reason to keep things under cover until tomorrow, Christopher thinks, then he'll hit the newsstands with a splash, he feels sure of it.

November 11th is, as usual, a grey and drizzly day but Christopher does not take his brolly. He wears his wide-brimmed fedora instead. He has his briefcase to carry, filled with books and pamphlets, and he wants at least one hand free. Perhaps he will place the briefcase at his feet when the time comes, the better to gesture effectively. He doesn't feel nervous because he's an experienced public speaker and he speaks not for himself but for a larger cause. He is simply a mouthpiece and for this reason he feels neither afraid nor rejected by the crowd's response when they turn on him so viciously. They're not ready to hear the truth, he thinks. They're still wounded by the war, trying to hold onto the lie that all their suffering was worthwhile, still revering old Churchill even though they've kicked him out of office.

He goes quietly when the Inspector arrests him, realizing now that he must revert to the individual approach and save his message for the inevitable interrogation at police headquarters. He is locked in a cell for the night, but first they allow him one telephone call. He dials Alice's number from the call box in the corridor and tells her that he won't be staying the night in Finchley after all.

"Unexpected business, Sis. You'll hear about it in due course."

At 7 a.m. a guard comes with a tepid cup of tea. He waits, confident of an interrogation and an opportunity to deliver his message. Finally at 11 a.m. he is led into a small examination room where a doctor gives him a physical, and they bring him another cup of tea. After more than an hour a man enters, a psychiatrist it turns out, and asks him a series of questions.

Christopher is eager to answer at length, but the man is not interested. He wants simple answers—yes or no—the date, the time, family history—nothing of the incident for which he has been arrested—"disturbing the peace," as they call it. He is released on the second day and given a copy of the doctor's affidavit which declares him to be "of sound mind." There will be a court case, the Inspector says, and quite probably a hefty fine to pay. He will be informed of his court date in due course.

"I welcome it," Christopher says. "It will be an opportunity to give my testament as an Aryan and an Englishman."

He realizes now that though his plan may appear to have backfired it has in fact led him to the wider audience he sought—that of the Court which purports to uphold justice, a fact he will remind them of when his day comes.

He travels to Alice's house to collect his overnight bag, and she greets him as usual with a warm embrace, but her face is troubled.

"Chris, how could you do such a thing? It's all over the newspapers." He feels a flush of success and asks to see them. "Take them with you," Alice says, handing over the *Daily Mail* and the *Express*. "And promise me you won't do anything foolish like this again. Mother is so upset. She's been on the telephone to me several times, and Cynthia too."

But Christopher is not listening. He is eagerly reading the newspaper account of his interruption of the two-minute silence at the Whitehall Cenotaph.

"I can't repeat Cynthia's words. They were quite insulting." Alice turns away, trying to hide her tears, but a sob escapes her, and he looks up from the newspaper.

"I'd like to help you, Alice. There's so much I could tell you for your greater happiness if only you'd ask. But I suspect that your husband is anti-Hitler and anti-German. I know Cynthia is, and all her family." He delves into his briefcase and slips a copy of *The Bishop Said Amen* onto the table.

"Here, I've made you some sandwiches." She thrusts a package into his hands, wrapped in brown paper and tied with a shred of string. "I'm afraid you'll have to go now before Maurice comes home from work." Alice kisses his cheek. "Take care of yourself, dearest. You look so weary. Go home and rest."

After he is gone she sits down and weeps, soaking a handkerchief embroidered by her mother. When Maurice arrives home, newspaper in hand, Alice's eyes are puffy and the children have returned from the neighbour's house clamouring for their supper. Later that night Alice faces her husband across the kitchen table. "He's poles apart from us, Maurice," she says. "I don't know what to think."

"I don't want him in our house again, upsetting you. It's gone too far this time."

"But I've known him in a different time, dear. It's the war, you see, he was different before the war."

"We were all different before the war, Alice. I know you want to take your brother seriously, but really, he's travelled beyond the realm of normal judgement."

As the train approaches Liverpool Christopher thinks of stopping off at Mount Vernon Street, but he feels a strong urge to reach Southport, and the closer he comes to his destination the more excited he feels. It is almost sexual, so he should have recognized the feeling, but it is only after leaving the station and walking to Albany Road that he realizes, it is an old habit, anticipating that Cynthia will be there to greet him. It was my night in prison, he thinks, reminding me of Walton Gaol, the early days, longing for her and for my freedom, the two desires inextricable. As he enters his cold, empty room, emotion overtakes him and he sits down at the table and weeps.

Chapter Eleven

THE THING WE HAD IN COMMON

I WAS CROUCHED behind one of the statues in the downstairs hall with my ear straining towards the drawing room door. Granny's voice was getting louder and more agitated. "You must stop taking him the newspaper," she said.

"But he likes to read it. He asks for it every morning," Mum said.

"It was after reading that dreadful article about your husband that he had his attack."

"Oh, Mother, don't be ridiculous."

"Don't you 'Oh Mother' me. It was too much of a coincidence. His behaviour brings shame on our whole family." I wondered what it was that my shameful father had done. "You should divorce him."

There was a long silence, then Mum said: "Not yet."

Granny's laughter sounded like a bird crowing. "Surely you don't expect to take him back? Your marriage is beyond repair."

"I have four children, Mother."

"And how are you supposed to manage them alone? You should go after him for support, get a divorce settlement. If your father and I weren't helping you where do you suppose you'd be?"

"Somewhere else!" Mum shouted, and the door flew open only inches from my hiding place. She rushed out and slammed it behind her and dashed upstairs without seeing me.

It's no accident that I chose to be a spy. Growing up in the aftermath of the war, with bomb sites everywhere and shocked people pretending to be normal, I was bound by circumstance. My choice was also a reaction to being called a liar. Children are frequently accused of lying, because they see things as they are and must learn to dissemble and tell the white lies that keep the world afloat and the naked Emperor in power. But I was not prepared to do that so I hid my knowledge well and paid the price with a peculiar kind of isolation, for intimacy does not flourish in an atmosphere of secrecy.

I found the newspaper article under my mother's pillow and I was glad then that I had worked so hard at Miss Amy's, learning to read:

"Heil Hitler" Fan

Christopher James Brooke, 38, of Southport, who was alleged to have shouted "Heil Hitler" during a two-minute silence at the Whitehall Cenotaph on Sunday November 11th, was remanded in custody for a mental and physical report. Mr. J. Averill, government prosecutor said: "The chimes of Big Ben had just completed 11, and while everybody was silent, Brooke, surrounded by people, shouted during that extremely solemn moment. He said: 'This is the day of judgement. I speak the truth. English children must be saved. Trust God and eternal Christ. Heil Hitler!' He then raised his arm in the Nazi salute." When the crowd became hostile Brooke was held by two police officers. Inspector Ratcliffe told the court that while he was taking Brooke to the waiting police car people shouted: "Cut his throat!" "String him up!" Inspector Ratcliffe said he was convinced that if Brooke had not been arrested he would have been manhandled and perhaps seriously injured. Brooke, a tall well-built man with close-cropped hair, gave evidence and took the oath in the normal way.

I put the cutting back under her pillow and smoothed the pillow case, already adept at covering my tracks. But even though I was rarely found out or questioned about my spying activities I felt my mother's suspicions, which only strengthened in me a fidelity to my absent father who was so connected to the war and to all those films about flying aces and spies dropped into France, the country of my mother's dreams. I would never tell. I knew how to keep a secret, even when I didn't entirely understand its content. The only one left at home while my siblings escaped to boarding school, I became the family's repository of unexpressed emotions.

We moved back to our house in time for the Christmas holidays, and with Birdie and Charlotte at home I felt more cheerful, though there was still the daily task of waking Jimmy which we all dreaded. He picked on me and Birdie and teased us unmercifully. He must have learned it at boarding school because he wasn't like that before. When it was my turn to wake him I would ride away on my bicycle, pedalling as fast as I could down the laneway beside the Avro runway and through the churchyard onto Wilmslow Road until I could feel Mum's rising anger, which made me turn and cycle home. Jimmy was usually up by then, sitting at the kitchen table in his pyjamas eating cornflakes, his hair tousled, his eyes still bleary with sleep, the right one drooping from the damage of a forceps birth. I was always punished for missing my turn, but it was the lesser of two evils.

Auntie Ruby came home from America in the New Year. Her GI had turned out to be a bad lot, Mum said, so Ruby came to stay with us because her two-year-old son was too much for Granny Blackwell. Cynthia managed to get along better with Ruby after her prodigal return with suitcases full of American goods and her own sob story. They would sit up late at night commiserating about their husbands.

"Never mind, Sis," Ruby said in her new American accent, "Christopher's had a breakdown, that's all. Religious mania. It happened to lotsa guys during the war. You should've seen some of the soldiers and airmen I had to deal with in the ambulance service, screaming about God and their Moms. Nothing visibly wrong with them, but they kicked up a worse stink than the boys with their arms and legs blown off."

I had to share a room with my American cousin. He was pampered and whiny and had to have his own way or else he would scream and drum his heels on the floor, even worse than Sandra had been.

Mum said I must make allowances for him because he was in a foreign country and missed his father. I missed my father too. It was the thing we had in common. But I was seven years old and didn't want a two-year-old trailing after me. I wanted to be alone in the world, without encumbrances, especially not an American cousin. My trial didn't last long. Grandpa bought Ruby a house of her own in Wilmslow and in the spring holidays, just after Easter, she and her son moved out of our house.

Chapter Twelve

THIRTY SHILLINGS A WEEK

May 1949

WHEN THE NEXT newspaper article appeared Cynthia started divorce proceedings. Even before the shock had sunk in she was on the phone to Archer Pearson who offered to come over with a bottle of tranquillizers. "No," she said, "I must do this with my wits about me."

She made an appointment over the telephone with Archer's brother and drove into Manchester next day to his office. Ronald Pearson counselled her to go for the jugular.

"But he has no money," Cynthia said.

"Brooke's Hatters?" Ronald said. "Of course he has money. There's a family fortune there."

"It's all gone to his Aryan Union and the Legion of Christian Reformers."

"Are you sure? He must have something stashed away for security."

"No, Ronald. The man is a fool. I married a fool." Her eyes filled with tears as she struggled to control herself.

Ronald coughed and cleared his throat. "Hmm ... uh ... How does he live?"

"He's getting a weekly allowance from his mother."

"I see." Ronald steepled his fingers and tipped them to his furrowed brow for a moment's silence. "Well, Cynthia, family friends and all that, I should warn you that divorce is a pretty pricey business."

"Don't worry, I can pay my bills," she said proudly.

"Of course, of course," he said, picking up a fountain pen and uncapping it nervously. "Now then, I'm afraid I'm going to have to ask you a few, um ... uncomfortable questions." He coughed into his hand. "A clear case of, um"—he swallowed, his neck jutting forward—"adultery."

She flushed and handed him the newspaper cutting.

Cynthia had been scouring the newspapers since the Cenotaph scandal six months earlier, seeking the shorter articles on the back pages where Christopher had often been featured. In the early days it had seemed possible that he might come, or that she might go to Southport, to Albany Road, and find him there. But she'd been preoccupied with the children, with her parents, the upkeep of the house. Too much time had passed, and now she was glad that she hadn't made a fool of herself. What if she'd walked in on them, lying together in bed? She could have killed him.

She despised the press. They got everything wrong. The article said that he'd spent three years in detention under Defence Regulation 18B for preaching that Hitler was right. Rubbish! It was only *after* his detention that the Hitler nonsense had started. It was Baker's fault. How she hated that man! The article read:

> Brooke was director of a Lancashire hat company for 13 years and was reported to have spent 40,000 pounds since 1945 establishing his Aryan Union. Today he lives in Southport and draws only 5 pounds a week, he says, from the Union. On May 1st the Southport magistrate ordered him to pay thirty shillings a week to Deirdre Brennan for the support of his illegitimate daughter. Brooke told the court he had been in touch with his organisation and was instructed to accept Mrs. Brennan, a young Irish widow, as one of his wives. The Aryan Union would accept financial responsibility, he said.

Cynthia went straight from Ronald Pearson's office to the Woodlands. "I need to speak to Father alone," she said firmly.

"Very well, dear," Dorothy said—surprisingly compliant. "But don't upset him. He's had a bad night."

Dick Blackwell was sitting in his armchair by the fire, his face hidden as usual behind a newspaper.

"Father?"

He lowered the paper and peered over his spectacles. She bent to kiss his forehead. It was slightly damp and there was an unhealthy hue to his skin.

"How are you, Daddy?"

"Holding up."

"I need to talk to you about this business with Christopher. Mother told you?"

Blackwell nodded.

"I'm divorcing him."

He nodded again. At times he could be a man of infuriatingly few words.

"Ronald Pearson's taking on the case."

Her father kept on nodding his head. He probably knew what was coming. How she hated having to ask.

"Ronald's going to try and break this Aryan Union and salvage some money to put in Trust for my children. He says that's the only way. We can't get our hands on it otherwise."

She paused a moment to see if he would say anything, but his face was impassive, his lower lip pushed out, giving him a distinct resemblance to Churchill, Cynthia realized with a shock. The thought of the damnable Churchill emboldened her. Bloody men with their bloody rules and regulations, with their wars and disregard for human life, with their money and control and betrayals.

"Father, I need your help," she said decisively. She was perched on a footstool in front of his chair, forcing her to look up at him. "Ronald Pearson needs an advance for the divorce."

"Have you forgotten that I'm already paying your children's school bills?"

"No, I haven't forgotten. And you know I'm grateful. But now I'm asking for help with my divorce. Once I'm clear of Christopher I can get a job, I can ..."

"I'll give you a weekly allowance, Cynthia. And you tell Pearson to address his account to me, here at the Woodlands."

"Thank you, Father." Cynthia bowed her head, surprised by his response and by her sudden tears. She had been ready for an argument.

Blackwell reached into his waistcoat pocket and pulled out a white five-pound note. "Here's the first instalment," he said, waving the note at her.

She hesitated before reaching for it. There was something humiliating about her father's gesture, as though he were deliberately taunting her. She didn't know whether to thank him or to turn her back on him and walk out, but of course she smiled and thanked him because he was her father and she loved him, and because she had no choice but to stifle her pride along with all her other stifled feelings, hardened into the bitter gall of anger that held her together. She had to control herself with Dick Blackwell because he had just established himself, once again, as her lifeline.

Nancy Brooke had decided to move from Dinglewood to a smaller and more manageable house. With the help of an estate agent she had found and purchased The Haven, a house at the end of a cul-de-sac on the edge of Bramhall village, with space enough in the drawing room for her grand piano; and with an elegantly terraced garden where she planned to ramble away many an afternoon. She had to sell a great deal of her furniture and fittings and took with her only the choicest items, of which there were many, even after the cull.

Mrs. Ward, already well past retirement age, took the opportunity of the move to fold up her apron and retire to Grimsby to live with her maiden sister. She had been with the Brookes for more than thirty years, ever since her young husband had been killed in the First World War.

Nancy hired a new housekeeper, a Miss Thorpe who was in her mid-forties, had an excellent reference, and seemed in every way admirably suited for the job, though Nancy had never before had to interview anyone for a staff position. That was something her husband had taken care of exclusively.

During the week of the move, in late September, Cynthia helped with the packing and sorting, working alongside Alice who had come up from London, leaving her children in the care of Maurice. The three women manoeuvred around each other and, with the help of a team of movers, finally got everything packed up.

"Christopher has offered to come to the new house and help me with the unpacking," Nancy said, to no-one in particular. "He'll be staying for a few days, until I'm settled."

Cynthia felt herself blanching, as though he had walked into the room suddenly, taking her by surprise. "In that case ..." she said.

"I understand, dear." Nancy patted Cynthia's hand. "I'll manage perfectly well with Alice and Christopher. Don't you worry about me."

She opened her handbag, a dainty beaded affair, took out a number of freshly minted bills from a zippered side pocket and pressed them discreetly into Cynthia's palm.

"Oh no, Granny, I ..."

"Please, dear ... after all you've done for me."

It was a month later, on a damp November morning, when all the world seemed muted and stricken, that Cynthia drove Katie to school and stopped in Bramhall village to buy a can of paraffin at the hardware shop. She was exhausted with battling her irrational hopes. She had felt sure that he would come to the house, at least to see Katie, when he was so close by, helping his mother with the move. Or had the Irish woman been with him, with *her* child?

She couldn't ask Nancy, it would have been too embarrassing for them both. Besides, Cynthia didn't want to know, for then her hopes might be dashed. She had uncontrollable fantasies of slashing at the woman with a kitchen knife, screaming abuse at her as Christopher stood silently by. One night she woke breathless and sweating from a nightmare in which she was beating the woman to death, knowing it, but unable to stop; and she had lain with her heart racing, her muscles taut and strained.

When she got home she gathered Christopher's papers, his Fascist books, even some of his piano music because there was too much of it, too much of everything cluttering the house. It was *her* house now, awarded in the divorce to house her children. She had her *decree nisi* and in six weeks it would be absolute. She had to claim the property and stop him from haunting her.

She went into the back garden with her wheelbarrow full of books and papers and trundled it down the path to the compost pile behind the hedge. She poured paraffin on the twigs and twists of newspaper she had carefully arranged and lit a match to get the fire going. Even so her bonfire smouldered and smoked reluctantly, stinging her eyes, permeating her hair and clothing with its acrid smell.

"Damnation! I can't even do this," she said, but there was no-one to witness her frustration, only the distant cows in the farmer's field.

She remembered a picnic she'd had in that field with Mary Byrne and the children, waiting for the war to end, waiting for Chris to come home. She thought of him working on the farm, coming home in his sweat-soaked clothing, his body warm and tanned, filling her senses. She couldn't believe how everything had passed so quickly and brought her to this desolate place. She would have given the life of one of her children to turn back the clock and try again. Yes, she would, because she had never asked for those children, never thought of herself alone with them. It was him she had wanted.

The fire took off suddenly in a flare of orange and yellow flame, consuming its own smoke now that the twigs had dried out. The rabbit skin glue that held the older book covers together crackled as they released their thin fabrics to the blaze. Cynthia began to throw Christopher's papers into the flames, watching them curl and change colour and crumble into dark ash. How he'd sat on our veranda day after day, she thought, writing down his deranged ideas, while I looked after his children and ran his house. She hurried to keep up, throwing his books into the eye of the bonfire, blinding it and feeding its insatiable mouth. For a split second she saw herself flying into the flames to be consumed along with all the evidence of the past, and she almost welcomed it, that flash of insanity. She left the smouldering circle of glowing ash and went into her kitchen and drank glass after glass of cold water.

Chapter Thirteen

BESET FROM ALL SIDES

November 1950

C HRISTOPHER SITS AT the table in his room on Albany Road. He goes out less and less now. He can run his enterprise from here, strategically placed on the west coast of England, between Wales, Ireland, and Scotland, with the mass of Europe to the south-east and Germany embedded in the centre—the promised land—just as the Jews have their promised land in Palestine, he thinks. Everyone must have an imagined landscape to house his soul.

He recalls the trip he made to Germany in 1938 when everyone had been full of hope for an Anglo-Germanic alliance. Not a German speaker himself, he had travelled as an observer, gathering documentary information on the culture and well-being of the German people, rather as he had operated during his South African and Australian research trips, noting points of universality, focussing on the common good.

He remembers visiting Dresden, and how beautiful the city had been, nestled in a valley with the river Elbe snaking through it, bordered by baroque and rococo buildings, giving Dresden the name "jewel box." He cannot conceive of the destruction wrought by the British fire-bombing; the brutality of it; people melted in their shelters.

He mustn't let his mind wander to those dark places. He's writing an article about Aryan Union. He'll have it typed up, and copies run off for street distribution and mail-out. He stays in touch with Baker, Unsworth and Kern despite their truancy. It's all up to him now. He must keep the faith. It's only a matter of time.

Across the table lies his journal which documents another life, the life he avoids dwelling on because he is helpless to affect it. He wonders what has happened to the Dresden china he brought home for Cynthia. She had turned it over in wonder, examining the delicate hand-painted leaves and flowers encrusted on the lid of the bowl before she'd placed it in the china cabinet for safekeeping. He would like to visit the house to see if it's still there in its place despite his absence, and to collect his books and papers. He will need his notes, written in a time of inspiration, intended for inclusion in a major work. He sees himself now principally as a writer. His oratory has fallen flat because Britons are not ready for his message, but the written word endures, and he is a patient man. His words will live on, surely, long after he is dead.

During this year he has been beset from all sides. When Deirdre had taken him to court for child support and the press had got hold of it, his hopes for reconciliation with Cynthia had been dashed. Soon after that a man had come to his door and served him with a petition for divorce. He'd had no defence. Guilty as accused, milord, a man faithful through fourteen years of marriage, and then one fatal mistake, crossing the floor of a pub and introducing himself, thinking that for once in his life he could indulge in casual lust and get away with it.

How do other men manage their lives? he wonders. What would Henry Braithwaite and his ugly sister Clorinda have to say about it? He misses the company of those down-to-earth people and wishes he could return to Mrs. Beasley's boarding house. But you can't go back; you have to keep on and forge a new path. And so he returns to his article on Aryan Union because *there* he is secure. *There* is a perfect order to his thoughts *There* is a rationality and logic that he can't find in the chaos of his personal relations.

Even his own mother now stands in silent judgement upon him. She has taken Cynthia's side. Though she says nothing he feels her censure. Alice is the only one who is a true Christian, but even she will not understand his message. He picks up his pen and resumes writing, but in the back of his mind his children clamour for him and Cynthia stands with arms crossed, her eyes smoldering.

Chapter Fourteen

QUITE UNSUITABLE

C YNTHIA'S DIVORCE BECAME absolute in January, just as Britain entered a new decade, the 1950s. There was a feeling of hope, the
recovery from war finally taking hold. Cynthia invested herself in
this optimism, living daily over top of her unresolved grief, determined
to put it all behind her and stop dwelling on the past with its false hopes.
But though she had no expectation of reconciliation with Christopher
there was still a wild, uncontrollable part of her that half-expected to
see him every time she climbed the stairs and entered her bedroom.

Dick Blackwell suffered a fatal heart attack in mid-January. Cynthia
was at his bedside when he died. The previous afternoon Archer Pearson had paid a house call and said that the patient must be kept warm
and quiet, but shortly after the doctor left Jack and Richard had arrived to speak to their father about the Engineering Works, and there
had been yet another argument with the boys' voices raised in what
Dorothy described as "out and out bullying."

"How dare you speak to your father like that?"

"Look, Ma," said Jack reasonably, "We simply want Father to sign
over the Works to us. We're the ones running it now. Pa doesn't even ..."

"Be quiet! Can't you see you've made him ill. Help me get him
upstairs to bed."

Dick Blackwell had made his final ascent in the electric chairlift, his heart fluttering like a bird trying to escape and everything heavy around him—his limbs, his head, his belly like lead. Dorothy had telephoned Cynthia and she'd driven over immediately, dropping Katie off at a school friend's house. She had spooned brandy into her father's mouth and smoothed his brow.

"You must get better, Daddy," she'd said, but Blackwell could see the fear in her eyes. When the pains began they circled his heart and stabbed at it, taking his breath away. He felt himself collapsing onto his knees, though he was in fact lying in his bed with a hot water bottle under his feet. Towards morning Cynthia saw his eyes cloud over, losing their rich brown colour, and she bent her head and sobbed uncontrollably.

Dorothy Blackwell had to be sedated for the funeral. Archer Pearson came to the house and gave her an injection and some oral medication so that she could get through it. The 1950s was a time when pills were regularly prescribed, especially to women—for depression, insomnia, suppression of appetite. Cynthia took Dexedrine to help her function for there was a deep exhaustion in her body, dragging her down and holding her under until she managed to stagger her way to the kitchen and down her pep pill with a morning cup of tea.

It was like magic. She felt for a while that she had regained control of her life, but then she became nervous and jittery and, worst of all, she couldn't sleep. She would lie in bed unable to banish Christopher from her mind. She would see him in the arms of that Irish woman, and a shameful desire would take hold of her until she was in its grip, unable to enjoy her own body without their presence, the two of them jeering at her. It was a sickness that made her despise herself and dread the nights. Each time she would resolve never to do it again, but the pleasure was too great.

Nancy Brooke came to the funeral dressed in mourning with a black beaded veil hanging from a pillbox hat perched on her delicate arrangement of waves. She said little, but her undemanding presence was a comfort to Cynthia compared with her own mother's raw need.

Nancy was nicely settled in her new house. She had placed the grand piano in a corner of the drawing room which gave onto a veranda, which in turn led to a terrace of flagstones veined with woolly thyme. She loved to walk there and inhale the scent released by her footfalls as she descended three stone steps to the garden proper with its tree-shaded lawn bordered by shrubs and perennials. Mr. Muffet was all she could have wished for in a gardener. If only she could have said the same of her housekeeper, but Miss Thorpe had turned out to be quite unsuitable. Her cooking was at times inedible, and on the few occasions when Nancy had ventured into the kitchen she'd found it in complete disarray. The woman was working out a month's notice. She had begged to stay on, saying that she had nowhere to go. Only later did she admit to being unwell, and Nancy had by then already placed an advertisement in *The Lady* and had received six replies. She'd interviewed three of them and had made her decision. There was no going back.

It was a Saturday, exactly one month after Dick Blackwell's funeral, when Cynthia and Katie drew up at The Haven at eleven o'clock as planned. Nancy opened the door to them herself and explained that the housekeeper was upstairs packing her belongings. She was to leave the next day. "I'll be without help until Monday morning," she said.

"Katie and I could stay with you tomorrow night," Cynthia offered.

"Oh no, dear, I expect I'll manage."

She had invited them for lunch in Manchester, at Kendal Milne's. It was to be an outing, with perhaps a little shopping—something to lift Cynthia's spirits after all that she'd been through. It was a long day. The traffic was bad and Katie had to sit in the back where she got carsick, so they had to stop at the side of the road while the child vomited, her face chalky and damp. When they returned to Nancy Brooke's house it was exactly four o'clock.

"Will you come in for a cup of tea?"

"Thank you, Granny, but we have to get back. I'll see you to the door with your parcels. Get in the front, Katie, and don't move till I come back."

They walked up the pathway and Nancy opened the door with her own keys, not wanting to disturb Miss Thorpe in her packing. As soon as the door opened Cynthia smelled it.

"What's that?" She sniffed and made a face. "There must be a gas leak."

Nancy seemed confused. "I don't know, dear. Where would that be coming from?"

"Wait here, Granny. I'll check."

As she opened the kitchen door she immediately clamped her hand over her mouth. She knew then what she would find as she wrapped her scarf around nose and mouth and turned the corner into the scullery. The first thing she saw was the woman's legs, splayed apart on the floor, as though removed from her body. She didn't want to enter that galley, she didn't want to look at the bloated face, but she had to turn the gas off and see if she was still alive.

After she'd opened the back door and all the windows, letting the cold January air rush through the house, she dialled 999 and asked for the police.

"There's been a suicide," she said. "At ninety-three Mayfield Road. Yes, yes, dead, quite cold."

She found Nancy Brooke standing in the middle of the drawing room, still in her coat and hat, holding onto her parcels. Cynthia made her sit down, and then she told her. Nancy sat rigid with just the hint of a smile quivering on her face.

"You must come home with me, Granny, at least for tonight, until the house is aired out."

"No, dear, I have a lot to do before the new housekeeper comes. She'll be here first thing Monday morning and I must have her room ready with the new curtains hung."

Cynthia drove Katie into Bramhall, to her school friend's house again, and was back in time to see Miss Thorpe's body being transferred into the police van. She stayed with Nancy that night and slept in the room next to Nancy's. The house was icy cold with all the windows open, but by morning the smell of gas was barely discernible, and Cynthia had slept peacefully, strangely comforted in that house of death by the presence of her mother-in-law, the woman who had given birth to Christopher and named him.

They could find no-one to take Miss Thorpe's belongings. There

was no next-of-kin, and her one reference turned out to be fraudulent
—someone she'd met in a pub apparently, and who had agreed to do
her a good turn—so Cynthia packed up her things and took them to the
Salvation Army in Cheadle Hulme. The post mortem revealed that
she'd had a cancer. "Eminently treatable," the forensic specialist said.

Chapter Fifteen

SQUINTING INTO THE SUN

February 1950

I'D BEEN AT A.V. Roe a year and a half already, and had been promoted along with Harriet and Mavis to work on the Vulcan cold war bomber, when I received one of my sister's rare letters.

I was disappointed that Deirdre had not been to visit us. I hadn't seen little Fiona since she was newborn and I was anxious to see what sort of a child she was, so the photograph that came in her letter was very welcome, though the baby's face was hidden by a sun bonnet so I couldn't get much sense of her. She would have been fifteen months old by then.

Deirdre was holding her, and she looked mighty pleased with herself with a fancy man at her side. He had a moustache and curly fair hair, all in all a handsome devil and I wondered if he was the father of the child. But when I read the letter it said that Michael was her new sweetheart and never a better man. I reckoned he must have been a brave man to take on a woman with four children, though three of them were in Ireland, but one day surely she'd have to go back and take responsibility for them—either that or send for them.

Michael did not look like the prosperous type. She'd met him at the hospital, she said, when he'd come to Emergency with pain from an old war injury. She was back nursing and the landlady on Mount Vernon Street was looking after Fiona. Everybody was looking for work in those days, especially the women who'd had a bonanza during the war with the men away and their jobs going begging. It was a mixed blessing when the survivors came home and claimed those jobs.

We had decided not to have any more children. Our family was perfect as it was, and we had found a way to avoid it without going against the Catholic Church which would have made me feel uneasy, though I'm not as devout as Deirdre and would have availed myself of Meg's services if our efforts had failed. But Meg was thinking of retiring. She was almost fifty, and just wanted to look after her Lennie who had become a happier man, partly due to the love he received from my children, I like to think.

Deirdre thanked me in her letter for the help I'd given her in the early days before she'd managed to get maintenance from the baby's father.

"He's kept it up," she wrote. "Thirty shillings a week, which is a wonder, for he was never a man of his word. But with a court order he has to pay."

Though you can't squeeze blood from a stone, I thought to myself, so he must have the money. The whole affair had been a blessing in disguise for me, because it had got me my job at A.V. Roe and now I was keeping it no matter what. Once he had a working wife Reg found that it wasn't so bad, and he didn't mind the extra money.

She'd kept the best news for the end.

"I have something important to tell you," she wrote. "Me and Michael are going to be married. Not right away. We'll have a long engagement. I'll take him home to meet Mam and Da so he can ask them properly for my hand. And I'll bring my children to England if they want to come."

There were tears in my eyes as I read it. We Irish will be populating England before they know it, I thought. I propped the photograph on the windowsill above the kitchen sink so that I could look at it every time I washed the dishes. I looked and looked at the little one but I couldn't really see her for that hat. She seemed to be squinting into the sun. I must go over to Liverpool for a visit, I thought, but there never seemed to be time what with my job and the children, and only the weekends to spend with my family.

Chapter Sixteen

BLIND MAN'S BUFF

March 1950

WITH THE COMING of spring Christopher Brooke is assaulted by a fit of nostalgia. The season affects him as never before. He has learned from his mother that Katie is still at home with Cynthia, though she will be going away to boarding school in September to join Birdie and Charlotte. She is taking piano lessons, Nancy says, and shows some promise. That is his pretext, to see the child, to play the piano for her.

When Cynthia opens the door Christopher watches something too fleeting to identify cross her face before it turns to stone. She stands there, holding the door like a servant.

"What d'you want?" she asks.

He wants to take her in his arms, to remove his gloves and smooth her hair with his naked hands. He wants to claim her.

"I came to see Katie," he says, hoping the child is at school. But she's been kept home with a cold, Cynthia says, and leaves him waiting in the hall while she goes upstairs. He hears her voice, low and urgent, from the room above. They come downstairs together, Katie holding onto her mother's hand. Cynthia will not look at him, so neither does the child. Cynthia pushes the sitting room door open and sends Katie in.

"You can go in now," she tells him, and as he passes by he feels her shrink away from him. He is still wearing his coat, like a stranger in his own house. Katie seems to have disappeared, but then he sees her, standing behind a chair in the corner. She is shifty-eyed and has a little smirk on her face. Christopher turns to see Cynthia standing in the doorway, like a prison guard, watching his every move. He turns again to the child. He is caught between them, desperate to change the situation.

"Would you like me to play the piano for you?" he asks Katie.

"Yes please," she whispers.

He walks over to the French doors and looks out onto the red-tiled veranda, remembering the summer afternoons when he'd sat there writing, and the children would be playing—Birdie on the swing squealing as Charlotte pushed her higher and higher, and Jimmy pestering him for a bowling lesson. There are acres of green fields stretching behind his house with barns shimmering in the distance and cows lumbering their way down to the pond to drink, gaunt haunches swaying ...

"Well come on, what are you waiting for?"—Cynthia's impatient voice. He has remembered her differently. He sees then that it is raining, a steady drizzle, and the field is bleak and empty. He removes his damp coat and places it carefully on the carpet, then he sits at the baby grand with his back to the French doors and plays without hesitation, *Liebestraum*. How he has missed his piano but did not know until this minute. He is safe, home once more inside Franz Liszt's "Dream of Love," but all too soon the music ends. It is his last attempt. When she shows him to the door his ability to imagine a future ceases. He has always thought that she would come back to him eventually.

Christopher rises from the chair and walks the three steps to his bed, pulls his suitcase out from under it, and packs his clothes as though he were going on a journey. How else to prepare? A handkerchief, socks, underwear, a worn shirt, a navy-blue pullover, grey flannels, that is all. He is wearing his black trousers—a bit loose on him with the meagre rations—and an open-necked shirt with his old sports jacket, and the brown shoes that need repair. They will not get it now, he thinks. Perhaps from someone else. Once he is in motion he keeps on, one gesture flowing from the last as he dons his raincoat, glances in the clouded mirror over the sink and smooths his hair, noting that it is in need of a cut.

He takes a last look around this room, sweeps the crumbs from the table with his hands and throws them into the sink. He picks up his suitcase and opens the door. He does not look back. He lets the door close behind him with the familiar click, the key inside. They will have to break it down, he thinks with a spark of satisfaction.

He sees a couple of fellows across the road as he steps out and feels the wind fill his lungs with a shock, reminding him that he has not been outside for a while, how many days he cannot remember. In prison there was enforced daily exercise. Now he suits himself. He crosses the road to walk along the front. He has a feeling that he is being followed, but when he looks round there's no-one there. Waves crash over the break-water, anointing him with spume. There's no-one in sight. He keeps his head down and walks stoically out of Southport.

He walks and walks, remarking nothing beyond his bodily sensations—the wind in his face, slapping and stinging his cheeks, the involuntary narrowing of his eyes against the onslaught. He has a sensation of crossing the water, returning to the Isle of Man. But no, he is free. He is at the edge of the bluffs on the Great Orme looking over to the Irish Sea where he sees the Mersey ferry steaming towards Dublin. He looks down at the water churning around broken rocks, sharp and craggy, their blackness flecked with foam, and a nonsensical rhyme tugs at him—"Three Blind Mice, Three Blind Mice, See How They Run ..."

"I'll be the blind boy," he says aloud. It's his birthday party and Mother is tying a handkerchief over his eyes. She spins him around and he staggers in a game of Blind Man's Buff, arms outstretched, feeling for somebody, something to steady himself. But there's no-one, and he has a suitcase in his hand, which he places carefully on the carpet, on the deck, on the edge of the cliff. He reaches out again with both arms, feeling the emptiness of the air all around him, and now he is flying, wind in his ears, a *whooshing* which ceases as he enters the silence of the water.

A young woman was out walking with her four-year-old daughter. They lived in the nearby town of Crosby, north of Liverpool, and would walk across the sand-dunes and down to the beach almost every day. The countryside around Crosby was flat and sandy, and in some places very marshy so that deep ditches had been dug to drain the fields. A broad stretch of sand-dunes extended along the northern half of the coast.

The woman looked back and saw her little girl crouched, prodding at something with a stick.

"C'mon, love, what ya doin'?" she shouted.

The child looked up but didn't move. Whatever it was, she was intrigued. The mother smiled to herself, sprinting back up the beach to fetch her little beachcomber. Shells crunched under her feet and her shoes left damp imprints in the sand that dried slowly in her wake. She was almost there, reaching out her hand to the child when she saw what it was she was poking at. There was no smell. The waves kept washing over it, refreshing it, but it was clearly a putrefied body. There were the arms, the legs, a bloated torso, and where the head should have been there were jagged edges of spongy whiteness, more like seaweed than flesh.

"C'mon, darlin'. C'mon, take Mummy's 'and." She heard the tightness in her own voice as though from far away and she tried to control herself, not to frighten the child. "We 'ave to go and get help, Sweetheart. Somebody's drowned."

The girl looked up, her brow furrowed.

"Drowned? What's that?"

The mother felt panic rising in her now, a desire to run away before the grisly sight imprinted itself on her.

"Come *on!*" she insisted, and grasped her child's hand firmly.

As they walked down the beach the little girl kept twisting around to look back, all the way until they were over the edge of the sand-dunes, descending to the town of Crosby.

When Cynthia saw a policeman at her door a shock of fear went through her.

"Mrs. Cynthia Brooke?"

"Yes, what is it? What's happened?"

"I'm afraid I have bad news."

How many times had she imagined women opening their doors to such news—a war telegram, your husband killed, your father, your brother. But the war was over, wasn't it? Not the children, please God, not her babies. Thoughts raced through her mind as she stalled for time, not wanting to know, not wanting to be involved in whatever it was.

"There's been an accident. Mr. Christopher Brooke, we believe."

She covered her mouth.

"We need you to come to the coroner's office to identify the body."

She stared at him, her eyes widening as they filled with fear. "The body? You mean he's dead? Christopher is dead?"

"As I say, we need you to verify the identity, Mrs. Brooke."

She knew him by a large mole on his chest, still intact. She had teased him about the mole that lived in his heart and only came up for air in the night when no-one was looking.

"But I see you," she'd said, laughing. "I see you, Chris."

There were no tears on that first day. She kept herself cold and hard. There was Nancy to deal with, and Alice, and the pathologist's report, and the police investigation. But when she told her children she was humiliated by her tears, because she saw that it touched neither Birdie nor Katie. They were more upset and confused by their mother's grief than by the death of their father.

"Why are you crying, Mummy?" Katie asked. "I thought you hated him."

Only Charlotte and Jim wept, because they had known him in a better time.

Chapter Seventeen

A CIRCLE OF FIRE

April/May 1950

S HE HAD TO go to Albany Road to clear the room of his belongings. A grim-faced landlady let her in.

"There'll be two month's rent to pay," she said in a broad Lancashire accent. "And the price of a new lock. Me 'usband 'ad to jimmy the lock."

"Yes, I'll see to it," Cynthia said. "Now could you leave me alone, please?"

The landlady sniffed and left the room with the door ajar. Cynthia heard her slow steps plodding downstairs and when she was sure that she was gone she pushed the door closed, then she sat on Christopher's bed and wept. His familiar smell permeated the entire room—the sheets, the curtains, the air. She lay down and held his pillow against her body until she feared her heart would break with the pain of it. She wanted to scream with the anger that rose in her, welling up like blood bubbling from a fatal wound, but she muffled her face in the filthy bed cover, sobbing till her throat was raw and the bed cover sodden.

When she had recovered herself she looked around the room and was overcome with a sense of shame that the father of her children should have lived in such a place. The walls were grimy with old fingerprints, the mantle thick with dust, the table stained with overlapping circles from a succession of tea mugs. She rose and took a breath. The room was stifling on this warm spring day, but she didn't want to open the window and let him escape. She had to hold onto him, all that was left of him.

She noticed through the grimy window pane a slipknot of men staring up at the house from across the road. She felt menaced by their gaze. She turned away and walked to the sink. It was ringed with dirt and grease and there was a wad of hair plugging the drain. She was thirsty, so thirsty. She steeled herself and cleared the sink, handling what must have been Christopher's hair, dropping day by day as he had combed it in front of this fly-blown mirror. She washed out a clouded glass with the sliver of soap that remained and filled it with cold water from the tap and drank it down, drank him down, irrigating herself with the memory of him.

There was very little to clear up. The chest of drawers was nearly empty. A few pairs of underwear, some balled socks with holes in the heels, a shirt, a pullover. On the back of the door hung the familiar cloth laundry bag he'd had since his schooldays, sewn by Nancy Brooke. She wanted to keep it all, every scrap of it, to harbour it and tend it as she had failed to tend him. But he had not allowed it. In his madness he had moved so far from her, so very far away from all of them.

On the mantel she found a photo lying on its back in the dust, slipped she supposed from a propped position. It was their little family standing in the back garden—Cynthia and Christopher, Katie a few months old in her arms, Charlotte, Jimmy and Birdie arranged according to height. No-one was smiling. Tears sprang anew but she controlled herself. She had to get through this.

She moved to the table and saw through the window the men lurking around her car. What on earth are they doing? she wondered. What can they possibly want with him now? She hammered on the glass and shook her fist at them. They looked up at her for a moment, then huddled together with their heads down in conversation. One of them stared up at her again with an expression she couldn't quite read, then he raised his collar, thrust his hands into his pockets, and the three of them walked away up Albany Road.

There were piles of books and papers and pamphlets—all the Kingdom Press nonsense, his grandiose ideas. Cynthia looked around but there was no waste paper basket and nowhere to throw them. She would have to take everything with her and dispose of it later. She sat down, exhausted, in the one chair at the table where she supposed he had spent most of his time.

There was his fountain pen. She picked it up and opened it. The nib was dry, though stained with the deep blue Parker Quink he'd liked. She would give it to Jim as a memento of his father. She reached across the table to a notebook lying at the far edge, opened it and saw line after line written in his sloping hand. She began to read, skimming over the familiar material:

> I had a sheltered upbringing—childhood in the nursery—sister Alice—Nanny Darlington ... her fiancé killed in the First World War ... life governed by wars ... Nanny's bed ... my childish body ... always take care of my body ... take pride in being ... upright man ... ballroom dancer ... well- shined shoes ... light on my toes ... cricket, tennis, boxing ... appropriate gear ... there were always servants ...

She flipped through the pages hoping to find something—there must be something.

> My countrymen, as we survey the world position of our island home today we cannot fail to feel the bitterest regrets that we did not, in the years of peace and affluence, have leaders to keep our country free from the death-dealing grip of ... matters not that I was unjustly imprisoned for warning you of the evils ... crippling problems of war aftermath ... cannot kill patriotism ... determination of true men to serve God and ...

She slammed the journal shut and looked up to see her cloudy reflection in the window as a weak sun began to penetrate the grime. Just like the note the police had shown her. It had been handed in anonymously after his body was found. The man had made a statement saying that after he'd read in the newspaper about the discovery of the corpse on

Crosby beach he'd put two and two together and fished the note out of his jacket pocket where he'd shoved it that day on the ferry crossing.

"Man tried to engage me in conversation in the ferry cafeteria," his statement said. "Bit of a nutter, raving about God and Hitler. He insisted I take his message, said something about deliverance. I thought it was a religious tract and I forgot about it."

It had been a suicide note, ending with the words: "Through the sacrifice of the Aryan martyr the world victory is assured. Heil Hitler." It was like some ridiculous game he was playing, Cynthia thought, to shield himself from reality. She opened the journal again at what must have been his final entries, dated April 1950.

> Always lived in my head … a fantasist who thought my dreams were reality … another war looming … listened raptly to Mosley … his words made sense … a boxer like me, and a fencer … his wife named Cynthia the same as my own darling wife …

Cynthia turned the page, almost afraid now of what she might find, because it was too late, too late to be doing this.

> It is a wild blustery day, clouds scudding across the sky. There is a great noise around me and a clamour in my head. A pool of sunlight soaks my hand, resting on the table in front of me. I have nothing more to say. I have written and spoken so many words into the void. I have made my decision and now I take stock. My hand is alternately warmed and cooled by this flickering sunlight. In Britain nothing stays still, the sky a constant presence, opening up then bearing down, changeable. So we must endure. But I have reached my limit and I cannot go on. The light illuminates my wedding band, a circle of fire around my finger. I will not remove it come what may. It is part of me, welded onto my flesh. She is always with me, filling my mind as I wake, her dark shadow falling across the day, dogging my steps, watching me silently. I cannot live without her, God knows I've tried. I cannot live …

The words were swimming, Cynthia could no longer read. Her heart beat in her throat with the terrible knowledge of his enduring love, and of all the time wasted in anger and resentment. It's too late now, it's too late, she thought, the finality of death beginning to dawn on her.

After a while she began to gather everything onto the bed, where she bundled it inside the tangle of sheets and bedcovers, making a swag sack that she hoisted over her shoulder and carried downstairs, out onto the street, and slung it into the boot of her car. But in her pocket was a slip of paper. As she had transferred Christopher's journal and papers to the bed it had fallen; she'd seen his writing on it and had picked it up and read eagerly—

> When we sleep we dream about each other.
> I see you smiling down at me,
> and when we wake our toes are curled with pleasure.

Chapter Eighteen

A GRAVESITE
IN HER OWN GARDEN

IN SEPTEMBER 1950 Cynthia found herself living alone for the first time in her life. With Katie away for her first term at boarding school, all the children were gone, and Dorothy Blackwell had moved from the Woodlands to a small house in Wilmslow, close to Ruby. There seemed no reason to get up in the morning, but Cynthia forced herself. She got up, dressed, made tea and drank it. One morning she put salt in her cup instead of sugar and was half-way through drinking it before she realized.

For so many years she had held out hope for a reunion with Christopher that now, nearly six months after his death, she was still unable to squelch that hope. It rose in her unbidden, like spring run-off bubbling up through a drain. It was her shame, her humiliation, the hope she held, burning like a black candle. She was inflamed with it, consumed by it—she couldn't call it love—Katie had been right—she did hate him, for his betrayal, for his bloody politics, and his damned Irish woman, but most of all for his final unforgivable act which had left her helpless with anger, so angry that she felt she would die from it.

The fury in her seemed endless. Some days she scoured the house from top to bottom, dusting and hoovering, polishing and rearranging furniture in an attempt to exhaust herself so that she could sleep. She had grown thin in the months since his death and now that the children

424

were away she rarely cooked a meal, but nibbled on biscuits with her tea, and on bread and cheese and apples like a mouse.

In early November when Guy Fawkes' bonfires were crackling all over the neighbourhood and children were bobbing for big red apples and grinning with mouths and teeth blackened by treacle toffee, Cynthia loaded up the wheel barrow with the remains of Christopher's belongings and lit a fire in the back garden. She picked a different spot this time, on the back lawn. She piled kindling and scrunched newspaper inside the ring of grass that grew differently from all the rest, and where her children had banded against her in a tight circle. It was a curse and she would burn it away along with Christopher's lunacy.

"Don't throw the baby out with the bathwater"—Dorothy's voice echoed in her head as she tossed his notebooks into the fire. She was hell-bent on destruction. She could have burned the entire house and stood out on the road and exulted in the flames. She threw his books and papers and journals into the fire, the remains of his clothing from that Southport hovel, everything she had harboured, even the blue cashmere pullover she had given him one Christmas and which he had worn with such pride, the blue of his eyes intensified by it. There was a foul smell as the wool burned; she had to wrap a scarf around her mouth and nose to stop from inhaling it.

She burned his letters—all those letters that Mary Byrne had seen her snatch from the postman with such delight. She would have thrown his tennis and cricketing trophies on the fire too and watched them melt in the intense heat, but they had already been sold because she needed every penny she could lay her hands on. She took pleasure in watching the flames leap, in rekindling the fire as it burned down, kicking the scorched remains from the edges of the circle into the heart of the fire.

She was out there so long that she lost track of time, and when she went into the house finally and dragged herself upstairs to bed, she sensed the glow of the fire at her bedroom window, for it was a moonless night, cold and clear with a star-encrusted sky, and the intermittent explosion of fireworks lighting up the sky, reminding her of the wartime bombing.

In the morning mist lay heavy on the ground and across the fields behind the house. As Cynthia leaned from her bedroom window she could barely see her own hand stretched out before her, but as the morning progressed the fog lifted and she saw that there was nothing left, not a scrap of evidence, only warm ashes inside a charred circle. But if she had hoped to cauterize the wound of Christopher Brooke, she had failed, for he continued to live in her and haunt her until she felt she had become a mad woman. She was afraid to go out, afraid of what would come out of her mouth, afraid of the force that resided in her awaiting its opportunity.

But the school holidays were approaching and she had to pull herself together, so she bought cans of paint in pink, cream, and pistachio, threw down drop sheets and rolled the paint on in great swaths of ice-cream colour with some vague unplanned desire to please her children. When they came home, exclaiming over the newly painted kitchen, she hugged and kissed them and laughed as though everything was alright.

The ground was covered with snow so they did not see the burnt circle beneath it. And in spring grass grew over and obliterated the damage, though a discoloured hardness remained under the new shoots, like scar tissue. Cynthia would go outside and stand over it in the darkness until it became like a gravesite in her own garden, invested with longing.

Chapter Nineteen

THE CUTTING

January 1951

THERE WAS A chest of drawers in my mother's bedroom. It was honey-coloured with swirling patterns that matched the wardrobe and the dressing-table with the big round mirror that reflected Mum's tray of red lipsticks and her silver-backed hairbrush. The chest had four long drawers. The bottom two were deep and smelled of wood and a musty sweetness, and in one of them were fillings for the Christmas stockings that Mum started collecting soon after the summer holidays, picking up bargains when she could afford them.

As a child I'd had to stay in bed for days on end with measles, scarlet fever, chicken pox — one illness after another picked up at school — and I'd been bored so I'd looked, and after that I'd kept on looking. I learned to express surprise on Christmas morning, exclaiming over the toys and knick-knacks that our mother had carefully accumulated. The other deep drawer was for gifts that nobody wanted, like Auntie Alice's lavender-scented pillow, a set of lime-green plastic egg cups, and Granny Brooke's purple bath crystals in a fat round jar with a pink ribbon.

I shared the room with my mother, sleeping in what had been my father's twin bed, but in the holidays I moved into the old nursery with Birdie, which is where I was sleeping when the stomach pains started just before my second term at boarding school.

"Could be appendicitis," Doctor Pearson said, prodding my stomach.

"Better wait and see." So it was decided that I should be kept home under observation, and Mum moved me back into her bedroom—"To keep a close eye on you, Katie," she said.

One day at the end of January, just after my uneventful ninth birthday, I sat in bed watching the pale winter sunlight glimmer through the curtains. They were patterned with big red roses and green leaves, and everything seemed to shimmer like the underwater of the Buxton baths. I had strict instructions not to get out of bed, but Mum was downstairs talking to Doctor Pearson who had just examined me yet again—I could hear their voices from the sitting room below—so it was safe to tiptoe from my bed to the chest.

I heard laughter from the next-door children who were playing tag, chasing each other around the garden. I hated having to stay in the house, missing everything. I shut my eyes and remembered the game we'd played on my eighth birthday, everyone in a circle and Birdie carrying things on a tray, telling us to feel them with our hands and guess without peeking. My favourite had been the peeled grapes—dead man's eyes, Birdie had teased.

Behind my own closed eyes it was Guy Fawkes again and Kay Chatterton had caught fire. Over and over she burned, running in chicken circles, scarring my mind with her foolishness. Why did her mother let her wear a frilly nylon dress to a bonfire party?

I gripped the handles of the second drawer. It slid open and I smelled my mother's perfumed silk petticoat and her thin woollen twin-set with mother-of-pearl buttons. My hands caressed the softness of her garments and crept up to the shallow top drawer, my heart beating faster as I whispered: "Open Sesame." It slid open, surprising me every time, for I half expected it to be locked, but yes, there was the envelope glowing amidst a jumble of odds and ends—old birthday cards and letters, single earrings, scarves and handkerchiefs—all the things she had no place for but didn't want to throw out with the bathwater. A sharp rectangle of newspaper slipped out of the envelope. As I held it between my fingers a rotten fishy smell filled my nostrils and I saw him washed up on the beach below the sand-dunes. I felt the grass stinging my legs, cutting them with salty lashes, Daddy's head cut off, dashed on the rocks, and I knew that I would have to spend the rest of my life diving under the ocean to search for it.

Mum didn't know that I knew; about the decapitation, as the cutting said.

"No, you can't see him, he's gone," she had said. "We'll never see him again."

But she had seen him, she'd identified his body. When I'd found the cutting I'd understood. But for me he was still alive. He'd been in our house, talking to me, playing our piano, his fingers on the very keys that I still played.

I'd heard them downstairs in the front hall.

"I came to see Katie."

"You can't take her."

"I only want to see her … a few minutes … please?"

The bedroom door flew open. "Katie, your father's here to see you."

When we went downstairs he was standing in the hall in a long raincoat with big shoulders. He looked different from the daddy I remembered, something coarse and uncared for about him.

"Hello, Katie."

"Hello." My voice had shrunk to a fairy voice. I didn't know what to say. I was under a spell.

"You're not at school today?"

"She's got a sore throat."

"Shall I play the piano for you? Would you like that?"

He walked over to the piano and sat down, his hands poised over the keys a moment as though he was thinking of what to play, and then he began. I heard the sad music from a great distance, slow and gentle like nothing else in my life. I wanted it to go on forever.

Mum was perched on the arm of the sofa with her lips tightly clenched, and I could tell that she wasn't listening to the music. She leaned forward and snatched a Turkish Abdullah from the cigarette box and lit it with a snap of her lighter. The cigarette was flat and white with golden threads curling from the tip, sticking to her lips.

"That was *Liebestraum*, Katie. Did you like it? It's by the composer Franz Liszt. Can you play the piano? Do you take lessons?"

"I pay for her lessons," Mum said, sucking on her cigarette, blowing out a plume of dense white smoke.

"Be a good girl and practice every day, then one day perhaps you'll play for me."

He reached for a cigarette and lit it, then there were two swirls of smoke rising in the air, smelling of sadness and tears. I couldn't bear the silence, the awkwardness, the thickness choking my throat. I burst into tears, and there was a rush of air around me, her hand clamped on my left shoulder, then angry voices, the slam of the front door. I could hear Mum crying in the hall. I ran over to the piano and there on the floor was the book he'd left behind. I shoved it in the waistband of my skirt, under my jersey, just as Mum came back into the room. And when she sent me upstairs I hid it where she'd never find it; an old Bible with a burgundy cover, and inside was tiny spidery writing in pencil.

I was well practiced in placing the cutting back in the envelope face down as I'd found it, and I slipped the envelope exactly half-way between the jumble of papers with the tattered stamp sticking out and the green-faced queen staring at me, then I slid the drawer closed and stepped away from the chest. As I turned my face was dazzled with colour from the setting sun that filtered through the curtains. I felt the roses patterning my skin, and I thought I might at that moment have been twinned with Kay Chatterton, all the colour the burnt girl lacked emblazoned on my face.

When I try to imagine my father he is usually on deck looking out to sea, searching for something on an empty horizon; or sometimes he is looking down into the waves, a boy on a cruise ship steaming into the port of Alexandria, Alice at his side, their parents at a safe distance reclining in deckchairs; or he is himself sitting in a striped deckchair, voyaging alone on the Orient Liner *Orcades* from Tilbury to Sydney, a notebook in his lap as he writes and writes, the same words he has repeated to his fellow passengers—fervent, evangelical. Sometimes he is on the Liverpool ferry voyaging for the first time to the Isle of Man with a group of detainees, prisoners of the British Government.

Lately he has been on his final voyage, standing on the deck of the

Mersey ferry, his destination irrelevant this time for he is about to jump. Would he look down at those gigantic wooden paddles churning the waters? Or would his eyes be fixed on the horizon? His father survived near death in the ocean and was resurrected to die years later in his own bed at home, but my father commits himself to the waves from which his own father escaped. He is familiar with the sight of the waves, having stood through so many voyages observing the wake of the vessel. He throws himself easily, leaving everything and everyone, no strings to hold him. His way is clear.

It is Cynthia who must suffer his death, over and over, his body flying through the air, plummeting, tossed in the waves, the water turning red, churning into a froth, merging with the sea and disappearing as his headless body is sucked under and swept with the tremendous pull of the tide, until he arrives finally, a decomposed torso on a sandy beach near Southport, to be discovered by a young woman beachcombing with her child.

Was he really decapitated by the paddles of the Mersey ferry? Or did he jump on a stormy day from the Welsh headland cliffs of the Great Orme, flinging himself like a dark bird into a downward wind, to be dashed on the rocks, his body claimed and carried by the ocean? And does it indeed have to be either/or, a cliff or a paddle steamer, depending upon whether you choose poetry or prose, mythic metaphor or mundane reality?

In either case all is lost and unverifiable. The real question is whether we can bear the telling and re-telling, the splintering of truth and fantasy into the many versions of our lives that we create? We hardly know our own selves, untrustworthy and unpredictable as we often are, determined by so many invisible and unacknowledged forces, not least the power of the cauldron that holds us. A man's behaviour will be seen differently in times of war than in peacetime.

I have read journals, letters, reports declassified after more than sixty years and released to the National Archives and Public Records Office in Kew, a few miles from Latchmere House where my father was incarcerated. I have listened to anecdotes passed down with the family albums. I have sought the testimonies of family members, many of whom are reluctant to disturb the sediment of memory that has settled over that peculiar time. I have read the notes in his Bible; and I have read his slim volumes from The Kingdom Press.

Charlotte thinks our father may have been murdered by those men who gathered outside his flat on Albany Road; or by any of the war-damaged Britons bent on vengeance for what they had suffered, for the sons and daughters they had lost. Like the crowd at the Cenotaph shouting: "Cut his throat! String him up!"

Whether he was murdered or decapitated or drowned, why at eight years old did I not feel that moment of passage in my own body, so linked to the prison of my father's body which I had escaped silently to become a fugitive like him—the one who gave the game away, who shamed my mother and infuriated my grandmother by daring to exist in my own right, the traitor's child?

Chapter Twenty

JUST LIKE BIRDIE

June 1951

W HEN NEXT I saw Deirdre she was married already to her
Michael, and they'd finally found the time to drive over at
the weekend with Fiona. The other children had refused the
move to England, little nationalists the lot of them. Des and Clio were
that excited to meet their cousin for the first time they were clamouring
at the car before it had even stopped in our driveway, if you could call
it that—more of a mudhole it was for it had been raining the whole
month of June, but now the sun had come out and everything was sparkling. My twins had just turned six and would be starting school in the
autumn and they were raring to go, in any direction life could take
them.

Reg had brought home a nice rib eye roast of beef. Since the building boom had dwindled he'd started work at the slaughterhouse, so we
were eating like Henry the Eighth, gnawing on our bones and letting
the juices drizzle down our chins, but I had to heat him a tub of water
every night and lean over it to scrub him down, for I would not sleep
with the smell of a butcher in my bed.

When I saw Fiona, who was already two and a half years old and
a chubby toddler, it was a shock to my system for she looked just like
Birdie. What's this? I asked myself, but I didn't even want to think about
it until I had a chance to discuss it with Deirdre, which wasn't until
after our dinner when Reg took Michael to the pub, and the twins and
Fiona were running around outside in their wellington boots.

"You're happy with him?" I asked.

"Oh yes, Máire. He's a good man."

"He's a good looker."

She blushed, so I knew that everything was all right in that department.

"I know you think I've abandoned my children," she said.

"And how is it that you've become a mind-reader?" I asked. "You're certainly not good at it for those are not my thoughts at all."

"They're better off in Ireland, Máire. It wouldn't suit them to be here. Anyhow, they're growing up. It's Fiona needs me now. And Michael. His work is in Liverpool."

"Sure it's not her father you're waiting for still."

"No," she said, her face clouding over with a painful expression. "He died, Máire."

Something clicked in my mind then, like a piece of the puzzle fitting in, something I knew before I knew it, and perhaps I'd always known it. I had seen the notice in the newspaper more than a year before and it had brought it all back to me, all my predictions. I had never forgotten him, even though I had not seen him since that day in the Tudor Cinema and had barely missed him on his day of humiliation at Mrs. Plumley's café. The notice said his body had been washed up on the beach near Southport. A suicide, it said, estranged husband of Cynthia, father of four, no mention of a fifth.

"Deirdre, you never did tell me the name of Fiona's father."

"His name was Christopher."

There must be a thousand Christophers in England, I thought, my face flushing up as I asked her: "Christopher who?"

"Christopher Brooke."

"That's the man I worked for, Deirdre."

"The one with all the children?"

"A tall handsome man ... well built ... with long fingers and startling blue eyes?"

She nodded as I spoke, bobbing her head up and down with the progress of my description, but I could tell she was as shocked as I was.

"Sure but he never told me he had a family."

"He was a wealthy man, Deirdre. What happened to all his money that you had to beg him for thirty shillings a week in court?"

"Last time I saw him he was raving about Hitler, that he wasn't dead at all, but was going to rise again and lead the world."

"That war did no-one any good."

"But I couldn't resist his smile, Máire. There was something about him."

"Don't I know it, Deirdre."

I'm ashamed to say I felt a pang of jealousy then, for my own dear sister had stolen my dreams and taken the Master for herself. But it passed in a moment, and I comforted myself with the thought that she had acted innocently without knowing who he was. I didn't tell her that I had recognized him in Fiona, but indeed I had. She looked exactly like Birdie who so keenly resembled her father.

Our conversation cast a cloud over the visit and in bed that night Reg asked me what was wrong. But how could I tell him?

"Nothing, my darlin'," I said. "Nothing is wrong."

Another of my white lies, covering a family secret better kept quiet. Though it *was* nothing really, nothing more than my fevered imagination which had led me to lay claim to Christopher Brooke, so how could I tell anyone about that, especially my own dear husband who I loved in a more real way than I could ever have loved Mr. Brooke. When I remembered our early morning conversation in the kitchen I realized how far away he had been in his own world, and no-one could bring him back.

I could tell by Reg's breathing that he was fast asleep and there was I, wide awake with my thoughts. I wondered about Cynthia and how she must have felt when he died. When I'd learned of his death my heart had ached for her and I'd thought again of going to call on her at Meadowside, but the memory of that pinched white face at the upstairs window had stopped me. It was a haunted house and I wanted no more of it. It seemed a place where no-one had a chance, all caught under a strange spell. I remembered the children and their Magic Circle in the grass—how Charlotte had protected them with her magic, which was nothing more than love when you came down to it.

Now that the years have passed and I reflect on it there's only one thing I still can't understand—my outburst that day in the dining room. I could never have believed that I would behave like that. But then you can't predict everything, especially not the strange ways of your own heart.

Chapter Twenty-One

THE FAIRGROUND

T HE MAN WHO was to become our stepfather came to Cynthia's door in the springtime of 1953, during my third year at boarding school. Our mother had by then become accustomed to living alone and seemed to need no-one. This man had been a neighbour during the war years, and his wife, now divorced from him, had been one of the few who had not shunned our family.

He took our mother out for dinners and dancing, and brought her to life again, a foolish girl with butterflies in her stomach, waiting at the door only to find herself tongue-tied upon his arrival. She couldn't believe she had another chance, though still a part of her had to be dragged up from the depths of her secret life with Christopher.

Nancy Brooke and Dorothy Blackwell each gave their blessing and Cynthia married this man and moved to his house. She gave up my father's name, of which she had once been so proud, and took her new husband's name. Charlotte and Jim had already left home, but Birdie and I moved to our stepfather's house and watched our mother resume the kind of life for which she had been groomed—a life of travel and privilege, with expensive clothes, perfume and jewellery.

She spoke sometimes of Mary Byrne, and of her friend Mireille who had been a heroine in the French resistance. I had only a vague memory of Mary Byrne, but I felt I knew her because I'd grown up with Jim mimicking her accent, spinning stories in a thick Irish brogue, about Finn McCool the giant, and Connla of the Fiery Hair. There was something cruel about the way he did it, as though he had some deep grudge against Mary, or perhaps it was just to make us laugh. At any rate Jim had a good ear, for it was Mary's way of talking that I recognized when we met finally.

I was in England to see my family in 1975 and had rented a car to visit the area where I'd grown up. Driving through Bramhall village and past the Walkley Estates I saw that there was a summer fairground in full swing with a hurdy-gurdy playing and a merry-go-round with children riding gaudily-painted wooden horses. I stopped on impulse, parked my car in a muddy field and paid the entry fee. I was drawn first to the merry-go-round where I watched a little boy in a sailor suit clinging onto the silver pole that impaled his horse as it rose and fell in a fake gallop. He was perhaps six years old, his face betraying a mixture of terror and excitement, his little body rigid. He looked as though he might burst into tears, but when the ride ended he screamed for more.

The fairground was full of children running to and fro, some of them with pink clouds of candy floss in their hands. There were screams as the roller coaster soared and swooped, and sparks from the dodgem cars as they collided like great big shoes carrying their reckless drivers across the smooth expanse of the arena. I felt nostalgic for my own childhood, remembering the fairgrounds our mother had taken us to, the bingo hall in Blackpool, the swimming pools, the cinemas.

I wandered past a line of tents and awnings where children played hoopla, throwing horseshoes at big stuffed animals, and boys shot pop guns at a moving row of mickey mouse cut-outs. At the end of the row was a fortune-teller's tent — "Reading Your Future," it said in big red letters. Just as I was passing a woman came out of the tent, and through the flap I glimpsed a shoulder, a shock of peppery hair and, I don't know why, call it impulse or instinct, I doubled back and lifted the flap. There she was, a small woman with a comfortably plump body, something familiar about her even before she spoke. She sat at a table covered with a royal-blue cloth, and in the centre was a crystal ball, beside it a deck of tarot cards. She unwrapped her arms which had been folded under her ample bosom and gestured for me to sit in the chair opposite.

"Your fortune is it," she said, more of a statement than a question, and something echoed in my brain even with those few words.

She didn't recognize me right away. How could she? She'd not seen me since I was a baby, though she sized me up with a quick glance, then took a drink of water from a chipped glass at her elbow. She was in no hurry. She settled herself comfortably, squared her shoulders and took a deep breath. Only then, and slowly, did she reach across the table for my left hand and laid it gently on the table. I was surprised by her touch as she smoothed my palm with her own, as though she were washing it, beginning to read it even before she looked down into it. And then it must have dawned on her, as it dawned on me an instant later as she began to speak.

"Your father is Christopher Brooke," she said, looking at me with the eyes of a lively bird. "He's in your hand. And you are Katie. I saw you in *his* hand before you were born."

She invited me to her home and we drank tea and spoke in low voices so as not to disturb her husband, resting in the next room.

"He has a consumptive lung disease," she said. "He sleeps a lot."

She told me her daughter lived nearby and that she had three grandchildren who were a delight to her. Her son had moved away to his wife's family home in the Lake District. She said she would go and live in her daughter's house when the time came.

"It's too late to return to Ireland now," she said. "There's nothing there for me."

When I asked her about my father she leaned forward intently.

"I have never forgotten him in all these years. He was a fine gentleman who met a bad end due to circumstances that affected us all."

She brought out a photo album and showed me pictures of our childhood taken with a box camera my mother had given her. There we were in the back garden, inside our Magic Circle, staring back at Mary as she snapped us.

"You must write his story," she said. "You must find out what happened to your dad and write it all down. It's in your hand. You can't escape it."

She scribbled an address for me on a scrap of paper. "My niece in Dublin," she said. "Go there and look for her. Fiona takes care of her mam. You will want to meet each other."

And then she asked me about Cynthia.

Chapter Twenty-Two

WHO'S THERE?

S HE LIVED ON for thirty years after our step-father's death, which
was a natural death from heart failure. But Cynthia's heart was
strong and she lived into her nineties, tenaciously rooted on the
earth like the tough plants with which she surrounded herself—ama-
ryllis, snake plant, rhododendron and peony. She might have lived even
longer had Jim not died prematurely. After forty years of chain-smoking
his asthmatic lungs gave out.

She had watched her son grow into Christopher's stance and gestures. She had been haunted by the smell of him as she ironed Jim's
shirts. He was a difficult boy, and continued so as a man, moody and
rebellious, confronting Cynthia with his physical presence. When he
was dying he refused to see her until, at the very end, when he was
comatose, she sat at his bedside in the hospital murmuring: "My darling son, how I have loved you."

"Time heals all," Granny Blackwell had been fond of saying, but
Cynthia's wounded memory of our father was kept fresh—through Jim,
through Charlotte's first-born with his familiar features, and then, breath-
takingly, through Birdie's son, a spitting image to break her heart. She
could never have forgotten Christopher even if she had wanted to.

I sat opposite my mother at her kitchen table. "If I can love him,"
I said, "surely you can own up."

She looked at me with those intense brown eyes and reached her hand across the table to grasp mine. Cynthia had frightened me during much of my life. She was a force of a woman whose energy I could not match as a child. But this time, as her eyes met mine, I recognized in their depths, grown cloudy with age, an unconditional love, and my fear ebbed away, along with the humiliation and shame and my purist ideas about what love is or should be.

She began to speak then, telling me about her youth in France when the future had been a clear path stretching ahead. Her homecoming, her engagement to my father, their marriage, their life together, the war and his internment, the post-war struggle that ended in their separation and his suicide—she remembered it all, and she remembered my brother's bedside in that hospital room with its smell of flowers in dank water. It was the intervening years that escaped her, the life she had led above a bedrock of unresolved grief, trying to pretend that it didn't exist as fresh grief accumulated.

"Who's there?" she asked, gripping my hand painfully. "Who is it? I'm never alone. There's always someone with me, night after night, waking me. I get out of bed and make my way down the corridor to this kitchen. I sit here, drink a cup of tea and take my pills, then I go back to bed and sleep for a while, but I wake again and lie there for hours, a prisoner like him. I don't understand it. Why can't I forget him? When he came home from the camp he was a stranger in our house.

"There were reporters squatting on my doorstep. I remember the crunching of the gravel as they walked up and down the driveway beating their arms, breathing vapour like dragons. I watched them from behind the curtains of my kitchen window. All the doors were bolted. I was a prisoner in my own home, trying to protect you children." Her hand went up. "No, don't stop me. If I don't tell you, how will you know?

"I lost my youth in that war," she said, twisting the ring of her second marriage round and round on a crippled finger. "And when it was over the war between your father and me raged right to the end. He escaped and left me with it. But I can't go on hating him. I must give it up."

She did not weep, there were no tears left for this exhumation finally of the love buried alive within her.

Memory begins to fail. Something to be written in her calendar-book before she forgets. But what day is it? Something else here that she can't read. Who wrote that? Dr. Crowe, yesterday, with his bent nose, like an apothecary with herbs in his beak to ward off the plague. Impudent questions about her bowels! Public property now to be poked and prodded, stared at and talked down to as though she were stupid.

"I'm old, that's all, old and failing," she says aloud in the empty battlefield of her room. But he won't give her any more pills. He won't give her a stronger dose. And her silent children have grown hostile. "I hate you! I hate you!" one of them says. Which one said that? She can't tell them apart.

The crush of white gravel underfoot as she walks down the driveway, each pebble a bone chip burrowing up from the grave, grinding pathways in her mind. One last path, keep to it, no wandering off. The earth is soft under her feet, she must tread gently, gentle as Mireille when she'd held her feet and laughed at their smallness. She looks up and the sky is golden, not a cloud. She remembers the texture of his skin, the smoothness of his long fingers entwined with hers, each one with its own pulse—a pianist's hands—and his sweet smile and soft mouth like Nancy's, with the lucky gap between his front teeth. They're walking along the green lane with pheasants scuttling into the hedge on either side; a measured pace, his hip bone brushing her waist, his arm resting lightly across her shoulders, all of their lives before them. Ah yes, this is what she'd forgotten. She lifts the pen and writes in a wobbly hand, January 13th, 70th Wedding Anniversary. She counts the days on her fingers and thumbs, ten days away. She feels Christopher rise within her, surfacing from the deep pool of memory as her drowning heart breaks the watery surface. She has wept and wept, not knowing why.

"Who is it? Who is there?" she asks. "Is it you, Christopher?"

She asks and asks until one night she sees him, across her room, beckoning, and time collapses. It is as though her whole life has been in parentheses and it slips away as she steps outside the brackets.

EPILOGUE

OUR MOTHER LAY paralyzed as we gathered. She'd had a stroke and we three sisters had decided not to intervene in her death because it was what she had wanted these last five years, since our brother's death. I was the last to arrive, with Birdie's son who so resembles our father. He had picked me up at the airport and we'd driven an hour's journey to the Care Home. As we entered her room it was as though Cynthia rose to meet him, her eyes widening with a sudden intake of breath, audible in the hushed room.

As he approached the bed she was transformed into the girl she had been, in a place far beyond that Senior Care Facility. Then her spirit fell back and we gathered around her bed and witnessed the long struggle to leave her body, that so familiar part of her that I have remembered and can smell yet on the scarves I have kept—ephemeral wisps of fabric I nuzzle into like an animal, savouring the perfume of their softness.

What I have discovered about my father is that he is unknowable, and that despite the huge though shameful stature I gave him in his absence I will never be able to reclaim him. He has effectively escaped. It was our mother who was always there, taken for granted, often hated for her cruelty. But she held us together, banded against her to protect ourselves. I suffered her presence as I suffer his absence.

I have been tempted during the writing of this story to let Mary Byrne take over and have it for herself. She is a born storyteller and could well have written her own story, which is easier than mine and more entertaining. But she has made me her scribe and, with the same love and care she gave me when I was new in the world and quite adrift, she has guided me and affirmed my right to tell.

In this story Mary exists only in relation to my father. After she left our house and delegated the narration to me, her connection to the story became her memory of my father and her fantasies about him. But when he died, even though she discovered herself blood-related to him through Fiona (as am I, and thus related also to Mary), her connection to the Brooke family was essentially severed, so I must leave her with the memory of her daily life at the Walkley Estates of which she made a grand adventure because of who she is, a dear and remarkable woman with a great heart and a rare capacity to love and learn. I have come to love Mary Byrne myself and am uncertain of what that means within the context of my story, but it is a gift that I accept without question.

And what of Deirdre? Did Christopher Brooke ever see the child to whom she gave birth three days after the incident at the Whitehall Cenotaph? Deirdre told Mary that he had been to visit her in the hospital, but perhaps she was comforting herself with "a white lie," trying to ward off a feeling of total abandonment. Or perhaps she was merely trying to save face.

If I were to write a scene in which my father gazed down at his infant daughter in the maternity ward of the Royal Liverpool Hospital that scene would take hold in my imagination and become over time a reality for me, and perhaps a comfort. And if my half-sister were to read this story she might also be gripped by such a scene and try to elicit in herself some memory of the imagined, or perhaps true, event.

By the time I followed up on Mary Byrne's advice more than a decade later there was no-one living at that Dublin address. The house had been demolished and no-one knew of Fiona or Deirdre. But I have discovered them by other means, though it took a further twenty years for me to come to the realization of what Mary had told me—that I could not escape what was scored in my hand.

AFTERWORD

MAD *HATTER* IS my father's story as imagined by me, based on historical and family research. It took more than fifty years to arrive at the place where I could begin my first tentative attempts to write this book. I had to wait actively for the shame-induced fog to clear in order to reveal to myself the simple facts of this deeply emotional story. I had to believe those facts as real and not simply a story I'd grown up with; and then I had to transform them into a story laced with memory and imagination. I had to hone my craft as a writer until I was sufficiently skilled in imagining believably what could not be verified by memory.

This is why *Mad Hatter* is a fiction—not a biography of my father, not a memoir of my own experience of his absence, nor even a tricky creative non-fiction, though elements of those genres do punctuate the story. And this is why, after a lifetime of active waiting, the actual writing took so long—twelve years of exploratory writing and research followed by six years of full-on intentional writing. I had to take hold of my experience, take charge of it and make it part of my identity by creating the memories which have been denied me and which I have hungered for all my life.

Key issues have been: censorship, taboo, shame and humiliation, silence, secrecy; reclamation of emotional memory through various means, the tipping points being sculpture and writing. Once I had reclaimed the memory of unconditional love for my father I had to surrender to an overwhelming and debilitating process of grieving his death. The reclamation and the grieving have been the most painful and the most rewarding, because they have given me back my humanity.

—AMANDA HALE, JANUARY 2019

Acknowledgements

In gratitude to all those who have so generously contributed to this novel as readers, listeners, critics and consultants: Sally Goodwin and Bridget Goudie, Kenneth & Mary Walker, Susan Pérez, Virginia Hiller, Steve Paulsson, Mathona Thomson, Ted Goodden, Amnon Buchbinder, Cornelia Hoogland, Shae Rankin, Bernice Friesen, James Leslie, Kim June Johnson, Wendy Burton, Sylvia Sienikeha, Mary Roche, Rory O'Connor, Steve Rigden, Susan Cohen, Anne Ngan, Ellen Leonard, Angelika Littlefield, Nicole Saltz, and many more—a book is always a collaboration.

Special thanks to Robert Best who came out of the blue to provide me with key information, to Malcolm Ring who opened his house to us, to Julie Simmons for vital information about my father, and for her comment about daddies and prizes. Thanks to Suzanne Bardgett at the Imperial War Museum, to the UK National Archives, Birmingham Archives, Nick Howe at the Stockport Hat Works Museum, and the Guards at Latchmere House. To Marie Staunton, Ann Gwilliam, Peppy & Dave Yates, Thomas & Sue O'Malley. To all the deceased members of my family who populate this story filled with their memories as passed on to me. To Jim for his three posthumous lines of poetry. And to my mother Cynthia, who I now understand and love more deeply since I have walked in her shoes.

Thanks to Guernica Editions: Michael Mirolla for his belief in *Mad Hatter*, David Moratto for the cover design, Anna van Valkenburg for promotional support.

And with deep gratitude to my editor Seán Virgo, who gave me inspiration along the way, and the unstinting support I needed during final edits; and who blessed this story with many insightful touches, the accumulation of which have helped lift it to the surface, and given it life.

The following books have been extremely helpful in researching the historical aspects of *Mad Hatter: Cruel Britannia—a secret history of torture* by Ian Cobain, *In the Highest Degree Odious* by A.W. Brian Simpson, *Fascism: A History* by Roger Eatwell, *Blackshirts and Roses* by John Charnley, *It might have happened to you* by Guy Aldred & John Wynn, *The Hell of Ham Common* by John Warburton & Charlie Watts, *Hurrah for the Blackshirts* by Martin Pugh, *Blackshirt* by Stephen Dorril, *Island of Barbed Wire* by Connery Chappell, *The Secret Purposes* by David Baddiel, *Aftermath* by Rhidian Brooke, *Very Deeply Dyed in Black* by Graham Macklin, *Searching for Memory* by Daniel Schachter, *A Life in Secrets: Vera Atkins and the Missing Agents of WWII* by Sarah Helm, *If This Is A Woman: Inside Ravensbruck: Hitler's Concentration Camp for Women* by Sarah Helm, *Rules of the Game/Beyond the Pale: Memoirs of Sir Oswald Mosley and Family* by Nicholas Mosley, *A Train in Winter* by Caroline Moorehead, *Now the War is Over* by Paul Addison, *Never Again: Britain 1945-51* by Peter Hennessy, *The People's War: Britain 1939-45* by Angus Calder, *That Neutral Island: A Cultural History of Ireland during WWII* by Clair Wills, *Oswald Mosley* by Robert Skidelsky, *Mosley (Life & Times)* by Nigel Jones, *Jim Battersby: British Political Prisoner* by Keith Thompson, *The Bishop Said Amen* by Larratt Battersby, *After the Party* by Cressida Connolly, *Warlight* by Michael Ondaatje, *Dominion* by C.J. Sansom, *The History Thieves* by Ian Cobain, *Empire of Secrets: British Intelligence, the Cold War, and the Twilight of Empire* by Calder Walton.

About the Author

Amanda Hale has published three novels, two collections of linked fictions set in the Cuban town of Baracoa, and two poetry chapbooks. She won the Prism International prize for creative non-fiction for *The Death of Pedro Iván*, and has twice been a finalist for the Relit Fiction award. Her novels and Cuban stories have been translated into Spanish; *Sondeando la sangre* was presented at the 2017 Havana International Book Fair. Hale is the librettist for *Pomegranate*, an opera set in ancient Pompeii, premiered in Toronto in 2019.

www.amandahale.com